I0675374

Einarr's Saga,

The Winter

By Gilbert de Jonestun

Nighthawk Publishing, Suffolk, UK.

© Gilbert de Jonestun 2013, 2015, 2020

All rights reserved. No part of this publication may be reproduced, stored in a retrieval system, or transmitted in any form or by any means, electronic, mechanical, photocopying, recording or otherwise without the prior permission of the publisher.

Gilbert de Jonestun has asserted the moral right to be identified as the author of this work.

British Library Cataloguing in Publication Data
A catalogue record for this book is available from the British Library.

ISBN 1-84280-138-4
Published by

Nighthawk Publishing
Halesworth
Suffolk
United Kingdom

Published for Print On Demand distribution
By Nighthawk Publishing

Table of Contents

Part Three   Ivar's Bargain   127

Part Four   Deception and Confusion   185

Part Five   The Gatherings   249

6

Part One: -

Landfall

One

The logs crackle and glow in the broad hearth, casting out a cone of heat, keeping the bitter cold air at bay in the margins of the stone chamber. The cruel North gale howls around the tower. The heavy tapestries hanging against the walls shiver in its chill, the rush lights gutter and flare. It is an early winter this year of 1564, the first snow deep and crisp.

I miss my dear Margaret this first winter since her death. Such troubled times, with no good prospect in sight. The Queen but a girl, a girl without the wit to rule. Her half brother, James the Bastard, circling in the shadows like the cowardly cur he is, puffed by English gold, driven by hatred and ambition.

Still, I have much to be thankful for.

The food stores and cattle pens are full, more English beef than our people can eat, an unintended tribute from our neighbours across the border, our defences in good repair, my first son Erik a fine warrior and a strong leader. An imposing figure in his steel bonnet, his leather coat covering a breastplate of steel. On land we still hold to the ancient peel, its own harbour within the walls. Where the English built in massive stone, our people used wood and clay. The first defence is a dense hedge of thorn and scrub that traces a wide arc around the broad wetland that is our real defence to landward. The soft wet ground, the pools and quick sands, would slow and swallow armoured man and horse alike before they could even cry out. The causeway is firm, supporting wagons when need be, but in places it is always below water, only inches, but the water hides its route, at high tide it is invisible. For those who come through the brier and swamp, there are our outer ramparts, timber and earth walls with a coating of clay that protects from fire and blends into the wild landscape.

Within those ramparts are buildings of stone and timber beside the dock. At the heart is the tower, beside the Great Hall, the latter mostly built in timber, but the tower of rough stone, my quarters and also the pharos, lighting the position of the dock for our boats.

Our final defence is not the walls and ramparts, but our own boats, a clear way to the sea. There are always boats bobbing in the water, nefs and plump carracks for trade, lean galleys for war.

Our newest ship, just arrived from the Danish yard, copied from English lines, a race built galleon, fast, a good sea keeper. The Black Hawk is more powerful than our other vessels, with fewer compromises. She will carry cargo, but her purpose is to fight, fine Swedish cannon giving her reach. I know that I will never take her to sea for purpose, but just standing on her deck is a great joy. How I would have wished for such a fine vessel to employ in my youth. When I was young we had only carracks pierced for guns. Good enough to deter most galleys, but with little prospect of striking a fatal blow. For those well commanded galleys that came inside our puny guns, our defence was no more than the greater height of our covered decks, the smaller guns and bowmen in the two castles, and the spearmen and bows in the fighting tops. My father always preferred our galleys, fighting he knew well, fighting he did well, but even he recognized that the future was with greater ships. One day the Black Hawk will be seen as a small ship in relation to the greater ships that will follow.

On our northern sailing, the carrack is a fine ship, a generous hold for Russian fur and for the goods we would trade. Well enough armed to hold off a likely attacker, strong enough to take an English ship when opportunity presents. What we lacked was the power to stand against the new war vessels of England, France and Denmark, or the great ships of Spain that carried more wealth in one ship than Elizabeth Tudor paid James the Bastard over three years and more.

When Erik told me of the new English galleons, I knew

we must build our own. When I first saw our own Black Hawk she was beauty and power, everything that our people sought through the generations. A living thing of wood and canvass and rope. I joined Erik for a first cruise to Man, to Douglas Bay, and on to Carrickfergus before turning for home. Such speed and grace with the endurance for deep far waters, such promise! I had thought our carracks large ships as they towered above the war galleys, three sturdy masts adding to their height, above the single stunted mast of the galley. The Black Hawk was an order greater. Her long bowsprit mounted low like a lance questing for a knight. The foremast raked forward, the height to carry two great square sails, to the single sail of a carrack foremast, rising from a low forecastle. From a half deck below the forecastle, the main deck swept up to the stern, stepping up to give the captain a clear view forward past three more masts. The main mast was a mighty tree sprouting from the deck, higher than the foremast and upright, carrying two great square sails. Aft of this giant were two smaller masts, each with the triangular lateen sail, not unlike that carried on the aftermast of the carrack. Two rows of cannon pierced her sides, chasers and light cannon mounted on swivels, are placed at the forecastle and the afterdecks. I canna describe the thrill of racing through the waters on such a craft.

Great though all these gifts, there is a greater gift that I have come to value since the death of my dearest Margaret. We had spent so much time apart through our life together but, on each return, it was as though I had never left. She attended so well to all the matters of our home and lands, matters that never fired in me much great enthusiasm. Her death was a terrible blow to me. For weeks I wanted solitude, to ride out into the hills and forests, or to take a small boat out onto the Firth, but then I began to discover a great gift that filled me with new joy, filling the hollowness left by my dearest Margaret.

My greatest gift was here, spread out before me. James, Erik's first son, a robust boy, almost fourteen, good natured and always a question to ask. William and Gilbert, the youngest of Erik's sons, lively squabbling boys of five. Then my great joy,

Mary, daughter of my second son Robert. A bonnie child of twelve, already a beauty with broad green eyes and thick flaxen hair. So much like my own dear departed Margaret in so many ways, yet so very different.

Where Margaret had been gentle and calm, warm, home loving, my strength and comfort, Mary was a bold child, interested in boyish things, strength and grace together. Already a skilled archer, with more promise than her cousin James at sword play, and he no laggard. Bold to the point of recklessness. She would ride out along the shore to fish the salmon but, on this coast, it was a risky hunt. When the tide turns, even a rider at full gallop canna be sure to reach the safety of the strand. I always made sure that a servant went to watch over her, even though his common role was to carry home the fresh speared catch.

Janet, Eric's wife, had chided me for encouraging Mary, but our family has produced many strong women and we have never considered the chance of birth any barrier to developing an interest, or a talent. I know it is different for the Hepburns and those in the eastern border lands, but that is no reason to weaken our traditions. We Galwegians are a proud people, proud and independent, children of the seas. Janet would poke her long nose into any matter that was not her concern.

Perhaps she thinks I favour Mary above her own children. Perhaps I do, but what matter when I rejoice now in all my grandchildren, for their future will be guided by my sons. If Mary should change her likings as she grows, I would encourage her to follow the new course. Ah, that the gods grant me time to see them grow, go forth, produce the next generation of our family. On nights like this my old wounds ache in remembrance, I feel my years, but soon another Spring will break, the sun warming us, promising renewal and new fortune, as it has from the first in rehearsal for Ragnorock. Strange, I am still the man of my youth, only this poor body is aging.

"Gran Faddi will ye no tell us a tale?", piped up Mary. "Oh yes, yes - will ye no?" chorused her cousins.

"Aye, that I will," I replied, "afore I do, James will you warm a drink for us?"

My maid Annie had already prepared a silver bowl of rich punch, the liquid flashing red as the garnet ring on my right hand in the light of the candles, the bowl reflecting the scene around it. Beside the bowl stood silver mugs. In the fire the irons have heated cherry red. James pulled an iron from the fire and carried it to the bowl with great solemn purpose. He thrust the glowing iron into the liquid, which bubbled furiously, the full spicy aroma spreading across the room. The others crowded around him. Mary dipped a mug into the punch and carried it to me, returning to fill a mug for each of her younger cousins. Gilbert took his eagerly, but William pulled a face when he saw that their mugs were only half filled. Strange how twins could be so alike, that few would know which one was which, yet be so different of character. Both were full of energy and mischief, but Gilbert has a generous nature and the enquiring eagerness of James, his elder brother. William readily takes slights, as his mother's dissatisfaction with the minor irritations of life. When all goes his way, William is cheerful and lively. When he does not get his will, a darkness descends, a shade that his character is slow to shed.

James helped himself to a mug of punch and the children gathered around my chair, sitting on the Turkish carpets that cover much of the floor. I have always disliked the rush covering that is common in other homes. I dislike as much the earth floors that so many households accept. All of our ground floors are dressed stone flags. The Great Hall is covered with a carpet of fresh rushes, no benefit in parading wealth to our neighbours, or risking good carpet to their eating habits. When they dine with us they litter the floor with bones and food scraps, drink slopped carelessly on table and floor.

Kara, my favourite hound, stretched, scratched, then curled up her great body close to the hearth, to dream of the hunt, her feet twitching. Like me she grows older, but she will still bring down a stag.

"What tale will you tell us?" demanded Mary.

I thought for a moment. I looked up at Gale, the great sword above the fireplace, glittering blue in the flickering rush lights and candles, the darker patterns in the blade seeming to flow with life, the life of the smith who created her those many years ago and quenched her in fresh blood. Above Gale, the round shield, emblazoned with the phoenix, the colours as vivid as the day it was completed, below them the rack of dags and my fowling pieces. My meeting chamber is armoury for the relics of our past and the weapons of the present. My manservant Jamie grumbles when he polishes the ancient steel, but he is proud as I of the traditions of our family, a family he has served with loyalty from boyhood, as his fathers afore.

Then it came to me. I realized for the first time what cord was always struck when I saw Mary.

Strange.

Why had I not seen before?

She was Gudhrun made flesh.

I took a swallow of the hot spicy drink and let its warmth flow through me.

"Don't tease Gran Faddi," cried Mary her face turned up expectantly.

"I know", I said, pausing, "I shall tell ye a saga of a time long ago, when our family was still young and charting its course".

I looked at each of them and saw I held their attention. I

noticed James about to ask a question but, then, decide against. I was sure it would not take him long to find something to ask. It pleases me that he has an inquiring mind, thirsting for knowledge.

James is the future. He will be a great strategist. He embraces new things with a deep enthusiasm. Never satisfied until he knows what makes a thing work. Always questioning, always learning. Dearest Mary is the glorious past, courage, passion, strength, will, determination, but so good with people, perhaps another future.

Mary sat, her feet drawn up under her, Gilbert on her right and William on her left, an arm round each of them, ready to grab an ear if necessary. She had a greater authority over them than their mother ever would. They adored her, but they also respected her quick strength.

Then I began, the story flowing through me as though I was listening to it for the first time when my grandfather had told it to me in this same chamber, on long winter nights, so many years ago.

I could feel the place and the time as though I was an invisible witness to events at another uncertain age of troubles, when our people faced great danger, but also a greater opportunity. I could hear the water, smell the mingling of sea and land as though on my own quarter deck, knowing the joy and caution of a new landfall. The joy of successful navigation, the caution for the dangers an unknown shore holds for every ship.

I ken well the burden and reward of bringing a ship to successful landfall on a strange shore. When I was a child I enjoyed this story as a great adventure, so much I could not understand yet. Then, it came my turn to put behind me the things of childhood, to pull on the responsibilities honoured by the generations afore me.

I learned the power of the seas, the weaknesses and strengths of man, the feel of a good ship.

At last I could understand fully the stories that once entertained me. At my grand father's knee I had learned, without realizing it, the great lessons of command and duty. Now I understood how much remains the same down the centuries, where our family came from, how we should go forward.

As I began to tell the saga, I saw also what had passed in my life, the innocent joys of childhood, the challenges of life.

Two

He watched the figure, fifty paces ahead, fading and sharpening as the tendrils of mist rolled across between them. The figure was very still, a statue carved from wood, or stone, could have displayed no less mobility. It seemed that time stood still, only the mist gave fitful movement. Einarr fought to maintain focus on the figure. It was not cold, but the mist condensed on every vertical object, creating a damp, sapping, atmosphere, in which the tedium of waiting became crushing.

His brain screamed to be released from concentration, for variety, for life. Thoughts flickered into his mind, fighting for dominance. He thought of Gudhrun, her luminous green eyes filled his mind, a recurring image, excluding all else. Then, even her spell was broken, a creaking of leather, or rope, or wood, chasing her away, to be replaced by the lone silvered figure, still in exactly the same position, illuminated through the mist by the bright fullness of the moon.

Moisture dripped onto the deck. The watcher's hair was damp, straggling, the few days growth of beard moist. His woollen shirt was warm and dry to his body, but the surfaces of the sleeves were spotted with tiny droplets of moisture, the body of the shirt protected beneath the sleeveless jerkin of wolf fur, the tip of each hair, making up that pelt, ending in a tiny silver droplet of crystal water. The legs of his dark brown leather trousers, below the hem of the jerkin, were streaked by tiny moist tracks where droplets had combined and formed short-lived rivers in miniature, running down towards his short, soft, red leather boots.

Those green consuming eyes again fought for his attention. He had known Gudhrun for all of his life, for sixteen summers, always there like his sisters. For ever he had felt a comfort, a warmth, a completeness in her company, as with no one else. They were always together, knowing each other's thoughts by instinct, or familiarity. A common entity, closer than twins.

When the boys and girls of the community grew older, they separated as they prepared for the life beyond childhood, not Einarr and Gudhrun. Whatever the chores or lessons that separated them, they found time to be together, an odd couple, of odd fathers — some said,   but never in the hearing of those parents. Gudhrun of the flowing golden hair, thick to her impossibly tiny waist, the long legs, the rounded hips, the strong chest, swelling to the fullness of womanhood, the powerful shoulders, but always those large green eyes, pools into which a man could fall and drown. A great beauty but one of which she seemed unaware. A hearty zest for life, a pride in her skill at arms.

Einarr reluctantly shrugged the thoughts back, to concentrate on the figure ahead, still so immobile he must have been carved from the very wood, against which his raised left arm rested, supporting his body as it leaned forward, a hunting dog pointing to the prey. Head slightly to one side listening for some crucial sound, nose seeking the air for the vital scent, eyes focused into the near distance. Every nerve and sinew stretched to the quest, prepared for danger, prepared for success.

Einarr was aware of a gentle regular sound, swishing, faint, but distinct, the gentle caress of the sea breaking languidly on a smooth, gently sloping, sandy beach. He knew they must be within five hundred paces of the shore, perhaps closer. In the light of a summer day, he would have been able to see the sand and gravel below the keel, fish darting through the clear water. In the moist air there was a scent of earth and vegetation, rich and full, that confirmed the closeness of land. There was a luminescence on the patches of flat still sea, lit by the moonbeams that cleaved the thinning walls of ghostly mist.

This was the time of the great herring shoals heading South, a host in annual migration. Shoals so thick with fish, a net would fill almost as it hit the water. Einarr had marvelled at the sight when his uncle Bjorn first took him to fish the herring. It

18

was a night like this, a full moon trying to chase away the banks of mist hovering just above the calm waters, flat as the surface of a summer pond. Clearings in a broken forest of mist. The oily fluorescence marking the passing shoals of herring, reflecting strange muted colours, a counterpart to the pale and eerie lights that oft times flickered across the North sky. On a night like this it was difficult to believe these same waters could be a violent maelstrom of towering, crashing walls of grey green sea, crested, flecked and veined with white, but Einarr had seen this terrifying change for himself many times.

On this voyage they had passed through three worlds, the strong friendly winds speeding them on the first leg of their journey, ragged white clouds chasing across a wide, pale blue sky, a gentle swell of blue green water, a sun still warm in the closing summer. Then, the black violence of a storm as they reached into the Poison Sea. The Frakokk lifted skywards as easily as an empty walnut shell, a dead leaf on the wind, to be dropped back into a trough, jarring the bones of ship and crew, below towering black cliffs of water that threatened to engulf and drown the Frakokk, the elation when she rose, shaking herself dry like a hunting dog. Now, in contrast, as they approached their destination, a mist-shrouded calm through which they drifted silently, lifelessly, dark ghosts. Each world seeming to have no connection with the next.

He almost missed the first signal from the figure in the bow, now clear in a strengthening moonlight that made Frakki an unnecessary relay as he stood by the mast, mid way between the two of them. Einarr had been trying so hard to concentrate on the distant figure, that Frakki had been but a rough form on the edge of his vision. As he now repeated the gestures of the remote figure, Frakki leapt into the conscious vision, much more distinct than the distant figure, the detail of his clothes visible, the moonlight glinting in the gem that gave balance to the dirk by his right hip. Bare headed, his hair hung damply to his shoulders, his beard a wet bushy mass. The woollen shirt beneath the inevitable fur jerkin, the woollen hose tucked into short soft leather boots, warm comfortable sea clothes, a uniform shared with his shipmates. The distant right hand waved, and then dipped to the right three times. Einarr lent on the stock of the steerboard and instructed Gismund to beat three strokes. The instruction was almost superfluous. Old Gisi had been watching the figure with unflagging attention, already prepared for the command, the voice of the beat drum a dull base note that carried through the length of the Frakokk but little further. The Frakokk shivered and pointed as commanded.

The figure waved its right arm again, then dipped the hand forward to point dead ahead. Einarr called for the rowers to pull steadily, easing the steerboard. The noise was deafening after the near total silence. The leather and wood creaked as the long oars dipped into the flat oiled surface of salt water to the dull, insistent, regular beat of Gisi's stroke drum. The faint lapping of water against the planks had given way to more even sound, of water washing past the moving hull as it picked up speed, driven by the strength of eighty men, toughened by their life, strengthened by their labours. Most in their prime, the oldest not yet twenty five summers, five and more the senior of their shipmates.

There were fainter sounds from astern, sometimes a muffled cry of command. Einarr sensed the invisible boats following him. He resisted the urge to look back across his shoulder. Looking back would achieve nothing. It would neither slow, nor speed, the followers. There was no time for diversion. He had to watch that lonely figure ahead, ready to react quickly. At another time they would have waited for the dawn sun to burn through the mist before they attempted to enter a strange river, but this was not the time to delay.

The figure raised its arm again, seizing his attention, then pointing slightly to the right. Einarr leaned gently, but firmly, on the stock of the steerboard, closely watching that arm as it moved to point again to the front, easing the pressure on the steerboard to match it. Gisi was calling the strokes from his position on the small raised quarter deck, the left bank of oars ahead of him and below. The Frakokk flexed and rolled very slightly, as though sliding over some corrugations, a sinuous living creature of grace and power.

Einarr knew they were now in the current from a river that he could not yet see. He thought that he could make out a low darker mass ahead. The figure in the bow would see it more clearly, the mist easing further. From the stern the approaching land looked like a low wall in their path, before it the pale white flash of gently breaking waves. On this coast, the land started as a bank of sand, and gravel, and shells, rising slowly from the surf, marching inland, topped there with coarse spiky grass, ripped by the storms and sculpted by the chilling North wind that drove relentlessly down from the icy wastes, piling water ahead of it, or the bitter East wind blowing unimpeded from the great grass sea that reached forever eastward beyond Golden Kiev.

Einarr knew that they would have to move with care to avoid the sand banks. Like all the rivers along the coastline ahead, this one carried silt from the low flat lands behind the coast and, at the shock of meeting the sea, dropped the silt to mix in mounds with the sandbanks that were shaped as the salt currents swept up and down along the coast. The long bars of sand created invisible barriers across the mouth of the river that could trap even a boat that drew as little water as the Frakokk. The tide was flowing out but had only turned as they had found the river's narrow mouth. Their cautious approach had been in the period of slack water. Had they tried, they could not have made landfall at a better time.

The figure urgently swept its right arm again and Einarr leaned harder against the steerboard, bringing the bow round towards the North. He knew they were about to enter the river and, as the bow came round, he saw clearly, for the first time, the land. It looked at first like a sand bar, but then he could make out the rising mass in the thinning mist and knew it to be the beak of land built by the sea current, forcing the river to change its march East in deference to the power of the sea gods. Never a permanent change. Each winter the sands would move and the sea would force false channels through the beak that had once been a sandbank lying off the estuary, then an island, before forming the beak they navigated this night.

The distant figure relaxed visibly as the tension ebbed with the tide, the landfall successful. The Frakokk was safely into the river, with low banks on either side as she headed upstream. It was a strangely narrow channel. The need for a close lookout in the bow was ended for this voyage, as the reed-grown margins could be seen now to both sides of the boat. The figure moved, its left hand came off the stem head in a lazy fluid movement, the right foot was taken from its perch, half way to the top plank of the hull. The body turned smoothly on the left foot and the figure stepped lightly down to the deck boards, briefly becoming invisible to Einarr. This was a novel feature of the Frakokk, which was an advanced design.

The longship followed an ancient form, an open rowing boat like its descendants that we know so well, the birlinns, the West Highland galleys, that mounted a mast and square sail, from the smallest fishing boat to the mightiest ship of war. Before the Frakokk, the standard was for a small foredeck at the stem, sometimes no more than two planks across the upsweeping bows, a main deck close to the hull bottom, and then a small raised quarter deck at the stern for the steersman, nestled into the upward-curving stern. The Frakokk was a warship, over fifty paces from stem to stern, with the traditional raised stem and stern decks, but also with a new raised deck amidships. This platform served as a fighting deck, only one plank from the top of the sides, giving archers and spearmen the advantage of height over other vessels, an idea Einarr's uncle Bjorn had brought back from his voyages down the southern rivers to the great warm sea, where epic sea battles had been fought for a thousand summers and more. It also provided a protected space below for the less robust supplies, with an awning being rigged between the stem and the central platform in a bad storm, when they would run under the reefed-in great square sail alone.

Ivar Ragnarsson made his way back towards the stern, walking between the two banks of oarsmen who pulled steadily on their long oars, seated on the chests that held their personal items. He stepped up lightly onto the central platform, becoming fully visible again to Einarr, making a brief comment to Frakki as he paced past the mast. Then, stepping lightly down from the platform to the deck between the rowers. As he passed each bench he made a comment to the oarsman, a commendation, a greeting, a joke.

Ivar was unlike those he passed, a man below the average height, lighter built, with black hair, dark brown, almost black, eyes and a darker tint to his skin. He was so different from Einarr Ivarsson, an improbable father, as some whispered cautiously behind his back. Einarr was an exact facsimile of his uncle Bjorn, taller by a head and more than most of his shipmates, a fair skin, hair almost the white of birch bark, with eyes of pale ice water blue. In sixteen summers he had grown and matured, with broad shoulders and strong arms that could beat down the sword of any other. A well matched mate for Gudhrun Pedersdottir.

Ivar reached the steersman. He was clearly in good humour and threw an arm around Einarr in fatherly affection.

"Odin has smiled on our venture. This is a good landfall my son".

Ivar reached for the water skin hanging from a peg on the stern post. He took a long pull of the cold water of home.

" Faddi how far will we travel inland today?" asked Einarr.

"First we must await the others. The river widens shortly into a lake and reed beds. We will meet the others there. Then we sail inland to the site I have marked", replied Ivar.

They both looked astern to the reassuring sight of other similar ships following them into the river, materialising out of the fading mist. First, the carved figurehead, atop the high stem, cleft the white tendrils of mist, like a monster from legend. Straggles of mist drooling from the wooden teeth and jaws. Then the bows took shape, then the low dark midships of each boat, with the steadily rising and falling oars to each side, like the raven's wings, lazy but powerful.

These first arrivals were ships of war, long and slender, with a keel that flexed like a spring to meet the demands of the sea, a long cutting line for speed. Behind would follow broader vessels designed more for trade and fishing, but showing a strong kinship with the ships of war. Both types of boat were of similar beam, about six paces, perhaps a little more for the larger traders, but the larger trading boats were no more than thirty paces in length, against the larger warships, like the Frakokk, of over fifty paces.

Each vessel showed its uniqueness in the detail. Most warships carried fearsome carved heads on high stems that swept up out of the water in strength and purpose, giving them their feared name, *'the dragon ships'*. Stern posts were often carved into complex tails. Some were decorated with lavish carving, picked out with paint, displaying their owner's wealth and power. Other warships were much plainer, workmanlike, having little, but the carved head at the bow, to distinguish them from the humbler trading vessels. A few, from the poorest communities, had little carving, the stemheads finished in token carved heads, more like a bird's head, with the deep rounded bill of a puffin, than a gaping mouthed dragon.

Traders relied on the wind, not on oars, the great square sail dominating the boat, with provision for no more than sixteen oars to each side. Even then, many trading boats did not have the crew to fully man all oars. Those that did often relied on women and children to make up the numbers. On a trading voyage, the entire family would sail together, with animals and fowl.

In contrast, the warship was equipped with up to forty oars on each side and additional warriors to fight as the rowers powered the vessel forward. The warship still carried a great square sail for passage making, but it was more usually stowed, the oars manned. The Frakokk carried additional warriors who could fight from the raised platform as she forged ahead under full power, with the luxury of extra hands to relieve the rowers in turn.

The moonlight had been strong, brighter than a fleeting winter sun where some crews came from. As each boat made the main channel of the river, the whale-fat lanterns were extinguished. These had been hung from a spar in the stern of each boat, low to the water, the steersmen's night eyes shielded from their glare by the upswept stern, so that their glow could be seen through the mist only from a closely following vessel. Once in the river, and in the fading mist, these lights were no longer necessary to hold the fleet together, but could betray them to a hidden watcher ashore.

Soon the sun would rise, burning away any last remnants of mist, the last of the cloak of invisibility. Already, the sky was lightening to the East, the dangerous half light at the dawn spreading across the water. In preparation, the crews mounted their round shields on the rails along the sides of their boats, providing extra protection as they sat at their oars, positioned close to hand when need arose. Muted conversations between rowers broke with the occasional short flutter of laughter. Not all the oars were needed to propel Frakokk inland. Those not manning oars checked their equipment, or broke their fast with food and water. Food was passed around those rowing, to be eaten without interruption of the task of driving the ship forward.

Ivar beckoned Knut Ottarsson from the five figures standing on the centre of the quarterdeck abaft the last oarsmen. These were the crewmen who stood, in reserve from rowing, as guards against any sudden attack, but ready to replace a shipmate when need arose.

"Knut take the masthead watch" instructed Ivar pointing in reinforcement towards the masthead.

Knut was a Jut Lander from Heddeby, where Ivar had made his base, of average height, but broad and strong, a farmer, steady, stolid, with keen eyes and patience. He was fast and light on his feet for a heavy man, strong of arms, making fast work of climbing to the top of the mast, where he would sit in the rope cradle, seeing above the mist to the land beyond the river banks. From sunrise his keen eyes would see the first signs of any danger from the shore and the lowlands beyond.

Already, he could see the brightening band on the Eastern horizon that hinted at the coming day. Looking down, the deck was an indistinct darkness. Astern, he could see the gathering forest of masts poking above the fluffy whiteness of the remaining mist. These twisted trees began to take sharper form, seemed to grow as the mist shrank away. Knut saw the sun was rising, about to burst into what would be a completely clear sky. He would have to be vigilant. It would be a long morning, with the makings of a warm one, marking the last days of a late Summer, on the point of easing into Autumn with its rapidly shortening days. The sun, already lower in the sky as the days shortened, would give them some protection from any watcher ashore as the ships came out of the sun.

He was aware of the birdsong from the shore. He could make out the widening of the river into a reeded lake and marshes, everything taking clearer form, with the mist becoming a series of small shrinking clouds floating above the surface of the water, and in soft ribbons entwined with the reed banks. Every now and then he could see and hear the flurry of a startled water bird scurrying towards the shelter of the reeds, startled by the huge dark shape of the Frakokk, gliding unbidden into its world. The splash of otters playing at the edge of the reed beds.

"Good fishing my friends", thought Knut, as he saw the small heads break surface and, with a twitch of whiskers, a flick of tail, to disappear as quickly. As the first eyes of the fleet, he noted every movement around him, however small.

From the quarterdeck the river suddenly began to widen. It came almost as a surprise after the seemingly interminable curve of narrow river that had been so reluctant to turn inland, preferring to follow Northwards inside the low coastline, close enough to the sea to hear the waves breaking softly on the beach. So typical of this coast were the salt marshes and lakes, formed a short distance inland from the sea.

"Keep to the left bank Einarr and follow it as it curves", ordered Ivar.

Einarr adjusted his weight on the steerboard and the Frakokk obediently edged around, her course in exact parallel to the curve of the reed margin. The final remnants of mist seemed to fade as the banks of the river diverged into a broad lake, the banks remaining visible in the growing light. In places reed beds broke the surface as much of the lake was shallow on the falling tide. A few small islands dotted the broad expanse, each with a halo of reed banks, some with a crown of stunted willows. In places, small groups of trees waded out into the lake, bent low by the wind that swept across the water for much of the year, branches twisted together for mutual support. Across the lake's surface were groups of ducks, busily paddling and submerging their heads to search out food. As the ship approached any group they took little notice, other than to paddle away from the line of approach in an unhurried and unconcerned way. Here and there a single swan, or a stately pair, glided gracefully across the calm water in a majestic morning progress to nowhere in particular. Knut's keen eyes also noted isolated sentinels, blending with the reeds that thronged the banks, herons patiently looking for an early breakfast.

The Frakokk followed round the arc of the southern shore and approached a river, leading inland from the lake. Wider than the entrance from the sea, this river showed little sign of movement, its surface flat, untroubled. In the growing light it could be seen that the number of trees increased as the river snaked inland. From his vantage point atop the mast, Knut could see above the trees that fringed the first few bends, but then the stands of willows merged into the broader mass and variety of trees that formed the start of a forest further inland.

The following boats were now hard forms as the dawn lightened. The fine details stood out for the first time, the colours distinct. Down each side, the ranks of shields added a bold splash of colour. Some were disks of a single colour, some painted with stripes of contrasting colours, some carried designs of boar and eagle, or runic symbols. Yellows and reds and blacks dominated. Those crewmen standing added to the colour. Many wore jerkins or jackets of fur. Those colours were mute, but cloaks in different colours, and dyed woollen shirts, added to the kaleidoscope. A few had already donned their coats of mail, which shone dully in the early sunshine. Here and there a cloak pin, or a sword hilt, caught the probing rays of a rising sun, flashing brightly.

Soon they would know how many boats had maintained the convoy, and in which order. Ivar called the oarsmen to stop, taking in their oars as the Frakokk slowed. Some of the oarsmen placed their oars alongside the furled sail on the racks that held them along the line of the hull and out of the way of those on deck.

At Ivar's signal, Ulf dropped the anchor stone over the bows on its length of rope to act as a mud weight, bringing the boat to a halt in the still water, stem pointing towards the river, which was their highway inland. An ugly giant, Ulf made the stone look like a pebble in his mighty arms, always bare, devoid of hair and corded with muscle. Ulf made the rope fast before it had fully paid out, the line came taught, then slackened, as the Frakokk lost all forward movement, to drift very slowly astern on the sluggish, out-flowing current, for the line to come taught again, the stone anchor holding in the muddy bottom below their keel.

Ivar, not a man for self doubt normally, wondered if all the vessels would be able to assemble together in the space of the lake, and how they would sort out the order in which the fleet would make its way up the river. Questions raised as the falling tide began to expose mud flats. Much of the lake area became mud at low tide, the rest only covered by shallow water. The lake bed changed from year to year. It was now more than a year since he had scouted this coast in a small trading boat, just him and Gisi and six trusted men, dressed as local traders. Then, when they first discovered this inland water, it had seemed a vast space viewed from their small craft, not even a canoe in sight, just the water fowl and a few otters. Now it seemed to be bursting with boats as more and more crowded in from the sea. A seemingly endless stream of vessels, pouring into a shrinking lake. When the tide was full, there would be a depth of water to allow even the largest of their ships to range across the lake, but at low water many would be trapped on the mud, until the tide turned once more.

There should be more than five hundred vessels, of which roughly half were fighting ships like the Frakokk, the remainder of trading vessels. The cargo capacity of the latter was vital to the venture in hand. This was no fast raid. There was no guarantee that needed supplies would be found when they landed. Those trading boats would be returning in company with most of the fighting ships, lightly crewed, after landing men and supplies, to return in the Spring with more men and supplies, or to battle the winter storms if additional supplies were needed by the advance party. If the weather was kind, there would be a regular flow of vessels through the winter, but this could not be counted on. Part of the daring plan created by the extraordinary tactical mind of Ivar, the first landing was in force to establish a winter camp with all the supplies needed until the next Spring.

The first stage of the plan was the establishment of a base camp before the arrival of winter, but this was no small challenge. Rarely before had a raiding party stayed longer than to fight, to load up the booty, before fleeing for home. Only Ivar's father Ragnar had chosen to winter over in these islands, and then to be able to raid rich traders sailing out of the great river to the south. Ivar's brothers, Bjorn and Halfdan, would have preferred the fast attack and withdrawal, avenging their father, enriching their men, but avoiding heavy casualties. Ivar had required all of his skills of leadership to prevail, turning their efforts to an entirely different campaign, one which had taken two summers to plan and prepare for, then this summer to get ready to sail, drawing together all of the boats from across the lands of the People.

29

This marked the unique character of Ivar, the Dark One, the Boneless, respected by many, feared by most. Rumoured to have the cartilage of a shark in place of the skeleton bones of a man. Happy in the company of Peder Pedersson, in communion with the gods.

Peder was expected to have strange and terrible powers, any son of Halla Siguroardottir would have, but Ivar was from a long line of warriors. Some wondered if he took his powers and strange ways from his grandmother, the Alan princess, taken as wife by Einarr Blood Axe. When the sagas were told in the long winters, the Alan were devils living in the great grass sea that stretched for ever to the East, known to bewitch the unwary, to drink the blood of children. Those, who had travelled the great rivers south, to trade with the people there for spices and silks, added to the saga, recounting their memories of a very different people, smaller, dark, with strange customs, rich, brightly coloured clothes, but sharing with the People the belief that today is a good day to die. It all explained why Ivar was so very different from his kin in looks and thoughts.

That difference, and brilliance, formed a broader vision. Before, the People had voyaged in search of trade, to find new farmland, sometimes to raid. Often, raiding was just trade continued through a dispute, or trade at the greatest profit. More frequently they would flee back to their ships, take to the seas, avoiding conflict and losses far from home. In all the generations that stretched into the future, the sea was the refuge, the source of food, of wealth, never the land.

Sometimes a family, with a few friends, would set sail in a trade vessel and chance their luck. If they found good land they might settle and live in peace amongst the natives. If they found good trade they might stay until their boat was fully loaded, to return home in triumph. Some families left, never to be heard of again, others returned months, or years, later. Some took a short voyage of weeks. Those trade vessels were built by a family, with just friends to help, using their own skills and labour, working local materials, the same way that they built their homes ashore.

Wood was used generously, iron sparingly, and rope as needed.

A warship was different, the pride of a community, built from taxes, at the direction of the local Althing, the council of elders. Those taxes sparingly raised, wisely used and frequently in labour and skill. The completed warship was crewed by volunteers for each voyage. Some communities boasted several warships, used each year to raid, or to lie in wait for unsuspecting trading boats.

Where a small fleet was assembled, it might not come home together. When each crew had exhausted the opportunities for trade, or sacked a foreign community, they returned home, even if their comrades in the other boats were not ready to return. In any two years the crews were not the same. It was all very flexible, casual, even down to changing captains with the same ease as changing crews, but it rewarded success, it built on triumph.

Ivar had a different vision built atop the traditions. He was just as much driven by vengeance as Bjorn and Halfdan, but his vengeance was measured and controlled. He wanted nothing less than the complete destruction of all those involved in his father's death, he wanted assured destruction. No half measure, no prospect of failure.

That desire demanded the collection of people and resources, training and preparation, the building of new boats. It called for a communication, a co-ordination, a discipline that the People had never undertaken before. The People of the Northlands were free and equal. In families and communities they worked together, helping each other by agreement. There was no overlord, no formal system of taxation to pay a lavish life for a despot. When the Althing agreed an expense for the community, the community agreed to share the cost, according to each ability to pay that price. All of these plans that Ivar had developed demanded the collection of taxes, the management of a huge enterprise and a new commitment. In this he had been aided by his brothers Bjorn and Halfdan.

It still angered him that the forth brother had chosen not to return from the south to join them. Riki was the youngest of the brothers, vain, wild, hot tempered. He could understand a quick vengeance raid, but the idea of planning and long preparation was alien to his nature. Ivar knew that his presence would have caused argument and trouble, but he still took the absence as disloyalty, an insult to their shared blood. Even the two sons of Ragnar by his first wife Thora had offered to bring men and ships to the great enterprise.

Ivar had created a new kind of empire never seen before. The Varangians, the Russ, the Jut Landers, the Princes of Kiev, all had made commitment to this Great Army. Each had their own motives, but all came to Ivar's call, sharing a vision beyond anything they had done before, a Great Army, an invincible host. The advanced party had to assemble before the Winter because there were not the boats to carry the host as a single fleet. When the reinforcements arrived in the Spring, the vessels would be used yet again to carry two more armies.

Through the coming winter, the People at home would not be idle in the warmth of the Winter Halls. They would be collecting together the materials to be carried across in the Spring, working to repair damaged boats, completing new vessels. Even through the Winter gales, Ivar would send messages to the homelands, receiving back: reports of progress; of new intelligence, and; further supplies. If the Winter was gentle they would increase this traffic, reducing the need for vessels in final reinforcement.

Ivar watched with pride as yet more longships glided into the lake from the sea, dropping their mud weights as they came to rest. His vision was taking form before his eyes. The years of work, of encouraging, cajoling, threatening, forcing, had worked to produce this gathering. By any past standards, this was a mighty army, but it was only one part of the grander plan.

Ivar was pleased to see that his captains had all kept together. He had feared that the storm would scatter the fleet across the Poison Sea, that only a handful would make the planned landfall with him, their numbers too small even to allow the first part, of the first stage, of the grand plan to be completed.

The scale of this undertaking was so great that there had not been enough sailing masters like Gismund Auounason. Old Gisi was reputed to have seen more than fifty summers, many more than fifty. He certainly had the great white beard, a few blackened, broken teeth, the rounded shoulders, lined face and veined skin of an ancient. He claimed to remember Einarr Blood Axe, but no one was really sure if that was true. He was a great teller of stories, ever popular in the Winter Halls.

What was beyond doubt was that he had a huge experience of sailing to far lands, of meeting strange people. He could read the surface of the sea, as others might read a track between villages. He knew the clouds, and the winds, the places of monsters, the lairs of trolls to be avoided. There were few like him. Few who could read the sun wheel to know their course and progress, or the magic straw that could see the North Star, Odin's one eye, through cloud and fog, or the sunstone that could see the sun through the darkest days. Only many years of voyages produced that level of wisdom and there was no time to train the extra navigators to crew all of the new boats. Not enough time, and too many new boats, and still insufficient to carry the Great Army as one fleet.

To ease the problem, Ivar had spread the seasoned navigators through the fleet, so that each group of vessels included a boat with an experienced sailing master. It had not been easy to persuade all the captains to agree on the distribution of skills. It had meant that not all the boats from a community would stay together, and some communities were not easy friends, but the plan had prevailed, the fleet had taken shape to Ivar's design, now the benefits could be seen as the boats collected at their first rendezvous since setting sail.

Three

A s the boats came together, friends called across to each other, boats were rafted together, the crews mingling. It was a carnival mood as they relaxed, grateful for their survival, for reaching the rendezvous without serious damage. Here and there could be seen a fished spar, or some other repair, souvenirs of the three storm-tossed days, when each vessel ran ahead, rarely sighting another vessel, never close enough to hail, not knowing how many of their comrades would reach the rendezvous without loss

Einarr searched for the Gylla, which carried Gudhrun and her father, the ship was not in sight. The captain of the Gylla was young but very successful. Red Osten, with his flaming hair, the ragged scar across the left side of his face, would be a great captain, immortal in the poems told in the Winter Halls. Einarr did not doubt that the Gylla would make the rendezvous, but he began to pace uneasily, impatiently. He did not want to call to Knut, displaying his anxiety, but he envied the big man his view across the growing mass and tangle of vessels. He felt her presence, she must be near. Was this just hope, or the invisible thread that joined them? He saw her in his mind as clearly as if she stood with him, he knew that she would see him.

"My love for ever", she called through time and space. "For ever my love", he replied. They shared warmth together. They knew that they could never be apart.

Collected in the centre of the lake, the vessels and their crews were safe from surprise attack. Several of the longships had lookouts at their mast heads. The last remnants of the mist had long been chased away by a strengthening sun. Each lookout could see some distance beyond the lake shore, across a flat land, with few trees to mar the view. A strangely empty place, not hostile, but not welcoming either. In Winter it would be bleak, as the North wind ripped through the reeds and bent the stunted willows in homage to its strength, the mighty waves angrily tearing at the beaches, a place of great wide skies, of sound and fury.

A seemingly endless stream of new arrivals joined the growing mass of vessels. As the numbers grew, the vessels came together in a broadening artificial island. Soon it was easy to walk across this raft of decks. Ivar sent Tryggvi Swenson to call the senior captains together in a meeting on the Frakokk.

Tryggvi was the youngest member of the Frakokk's crew, a gangly boy on his first voyage, in awe of everyone around him and the sight of so many ships together in one place. He came from a small hamlet, one day's walk from Heddeby, where they fished, and herded cattle. He and his family lived in basic comfort, never hungry, with adequate clothes and shelter, augmented when the boys and men joined a trade venture, or war voyage, bringing home their share of profit. He jumped and scrambled from one ship to the next as he passed Ivar's summons to each selected captain.

As the captains made their way across, only Sighmar the Bald was missing. None of the assembled captains had seen his ship since the storm broke upon them. Ivar stood at the centre of a rough circle of sea chests arranged on the deck, aft of the raised centre section. The fourteen senior captains, still dressed in their sea clothes, sat on the wooden chests. Finni and the missing Sighmar were seasoned leaders, nearing their last voyages, old men who had each seen more than forty summers, but with experience and cunning that still earned great respect. Finni wore much gold and fine clothes from southern voyages, testament to his skill in trade and fighting. Of the assembled captains he was the only one to wear his sword, with its jewelled and decorated hilt, the fine blade in its gold trimmed, red leather sheath, the others choosing to wear only their smaller dirks and daggers.

Finni may have been born in the far North, but he was a true

Rus Viking of Golden Kiev, accustomed to displaying the wealth of his success in fine clothes, jewels, and decorated weapons that were no less deadly than the plainer possessions favoured by his comrades. There was a tradition that warriors carried their swords at all times, but it was all too easy to trip on a sword, or be caught in rigging when ships were rafted together, as today. Mail coats were rarely worn unless battle was to be joined. The padded undercoat was bulky, and heavy when wet, to which the added weight of the mail coat was dangerous at sea and deadly if the owner went overboard. Even those, like Einarr, who wore supple leather below the finest Frankish coats of mail, to give the greatest freedom of movement in battle, avoided the wearing of mail aboard whenever practical.

The other captains were younger than Finni, some of only twenty summers. Age itself was no qualification for command. Einarr had been relieved to see Red Osten climbing across the ships towards the Frakokk. He had felt the growing presence of Gudhrun through the morning, warming his very core, but had not yet seen the Gylla amongst the tangle of vessels.

"The girl is well", said Osten, replying to the unspoken question from Einarr.

As he spoke, his characteristic lopsided grin swept onto his face, the heavily scarred cheek staying frozen. Einarr nodded his acknowledgement, trying to keep a neutral expression on his face, but not succeeding. Einarr had learned to accept the reactions of others to him and to Gudhrun, although it still resulted in a bloody fight with those of his age who thought to try him, finding to their cost the folly of their action.

In his community it was not unusual for someone of his age to take a wife. It was not unusual for a girl of Gudhrun's age to be a warrior. It was not that rare for a young man to take a warrior girl for his wife. What was unusual was for two young people to have such a strong bond, to stand together in a fight, but not live together as man and wife. Ivar had not encouraged their union, neither of them knew why, perhaps Ivar himself did not know, but they both felt that there was some greater darker reason that Ivar understood.

To any observer they were clearly special, different. Two young, beautiful, powerful animals. They shared a closeness from their earliest childhood that few would ever achieve in life with another, a closeness of equals who thought together. In battle they were one person, four arms, two swords, a single invincible machine. Perhaps Ivar saw some tragic vision, or some greater purpose for one of them. Certainly he felt that he had much still to teach Einarr of the world, of people, of battle. Perhaps Ivar saw Gudhrun as a threat to his tutelage of Einarr. It was a partly formed opposition that might have become stronger had Einarr shown any inclination to become a captain, as many would have liked. Einarr had the wisdom to realize that he still had much to learn from Ivar. It was not uncertainty in his own abilities, more a thirst for knowledge to ensure success, a feeling that ahead of him lay something of great importance, of which he was an essential and unique part.

Each community built its ships and chose its captains by their success, and the willingness of others to sail with them. In trade, when whole families sailed together, a boy could have more experience of the sea than many a full grown man. Einarr had shown leadership and skill in a succession of voyages, enough to develop a following of supporters. Each captain knew that he owed his position to the success of his last voyage. This company of captains grouped around Ivar was the most successful, the most experienced, the most respected, often the most feared, in the fleet. In meetings, robust debate was normal, sometimes bitter argument, but today the best captains sat in obedient silence and rapt attention as their acknowledged commander spoke.

Ivar outlined the next stage of their campaign and detailed each captain to fulfil his role. His surprisingly soft and gentle voice carried great authority, his presence dominating the meeting. Few had ever heard Ivar raise his voice in anger, fewer had lived to remark of it. At times, Ivar seemed almost gentle and kind, but always there was a menace, a concealed strength and power that shaded his speech, making him a man to follow, not an easy friend. The power came through his eyes, hypnotic and compelling. Dark eyes that could be as blank and cold as stone, or flash with consuming fire.

The conference concluded in a quiet but confident mood, each captain making his way back to his own vessel. On his return he would gather around him the leaders of his group of ships, to pass his instructions. Ivar had cast his influence widely, chosen his senior captains well.

Once, meetings of war would be boisterous occasions, lasting a day or more, each leader expecting to have his say, and his will, his people expecting no less of him. Those meetings were a year past. All acknowledged that Ivar had a campaign plan that they could understand, but never hope to improve on. Now was the time to follow orders from a man that none would challenge, that none could better.

Meetings quickly concluded, there was bustle and activity amongst the crews. Out of the tangled mass of ships, a new order began to establish. The Frakokk was quanted out from the western edge of the assembled boats. Close together, and in shallow water, it was safer and quicker to use poles to push the ships out from the throng. A line of vessels began to assemble behind Frakokk. As the longships formed up, oars were run out, first to hold position in the line, and then sufficient to power the vessels further inland. In a broad, shallow, lazy river, there was no need to man all oars. The perfection of the hulls glided through the still water with the effortless grace of a swan.

As the selected rowers powered their vessels forward, their comrades readied for the fight they expected. Most now carried sword belts, but the sword was not always the favoured weapon, many preferred the axe, or the war hammer, others preferred not to encumber themselves with a full sword, relying on a shorter dirk, where the axe could not be employed. Each warrior treated his weapons with a fond respect. This was more than respect for a tool on which the user's life would depend. Many weapons were given names in a sign of affection and value. Edges were honed with wetted stone, the blades polished with sand and vinegar until they were perfect and deadly smooth. When the steel was perfect, it was coated with clarified fat. This was a process that filled any spare time and was always employed before a battle.

Every weapon represented wealth. A sword consumed a great quantity of iron and charcoal in its making. Much skill and much time. Some swords were made with the addition of star metal from the skies, all displayed a unique pattern from the blade construction, when the separate pieces, that made up a blade, were forged together to give strength and flexibility, keen edges to cut muscle, and bone, and metal, but flexible to avoid breaking in the jarring clash of combat. The axe was a simpler weapon, some of its attraction its lower cost, affordable to those who could not pay for the sword master's art.

Many warriors were skilled with the bow, some favoured the war hammer. Each warrior owned a circular shield. This was of wood and iron, being painted, often in very bold colours and designs. Not all warriors chose to carry this large shield into battle, a few using much smaller shields strapped to the forearm, those armed with axes often preferring no encumbering shield, however small, as they wielded their axe with both hands around the shaft.

Clothing was varied. It often depended more on the success of earlier voyages. The clothing of the farmer and the fisherman was common as sea clothes, and the poorer, younger warriors would wear these into battle. The richer warriors owned coats of mail, or scale armour, and most wore a helmet. The cost of iron and steel meant that some warriors had only a helmet of boiled leather with an iron band, extending in a simple guard to give some protection to the nose and eyes.

Wealth and experience were displayed in helmets, as in the other equipment of war. The wealthy warriors owned helmets of steel, with guards around the eyes and nose, sometimes extending to cover most of the face and neck, being decorated with crests and feathers, a few topped with a spike, a souvenir from the campaigns beyond Kiev. A few used more complex armour, trophies of the raids to the south and east, but this was an army of volunteers and individuals. Bjorn Bluetooth was famous for the strange armour he had brought back from a great journey on horseback across the endless grass sea. It was made from some kinds of wood and bone, bound together, its companion a strange sword with a gleaming curved blade, an oval guard and a long hilt of finely carved ivory. It matched the uniqueness of his two blue metal teeth, hammered into his jaw to replace those lost in battle.

Warriors were organized in multiples of two. A warrior selected a comrade, perhaps a kinsman, or a friend, and each would defend the other to death, always in close company. Pairs of warriors joined with other pairs, following a leader elected from their group. Boat crews formed from pairs. The captain commanded not of right, or descent, or simple wealth, but by trust and confidence.

Einarr stood on the Frakokk's centre platform with Ivar and his bodyguards. From there they could watch the passing banks and the ships behind, Old Gisi now the steersman. Ivar was plainly dressed. No one would have taken him for leader of this great enterprise.

Clearly he was a warrior, with a helmet that suggested rank. It protected his head above his mouth and clean shaven chin, the broad, rounded guards, curving back up from the end of the nasal to the rim of the helmet, protecting his cheeks, casting deep shadows on his dark eyes, making it hard to read any expression, a curtain of mail sewn into the helmet to hang down over his neck, almost to his shoulders, but there was no adornment of the helmet to suggest wealth, the metal a dull brown, not rust, but some kind of paint, or etching. His arms were bare from the elbows, and the short leather sleeves of a coat, or maybe it was a shirt, protruded from the shorter sleeves of a mail coat. The coat descended to mid thigh and his plain, faded brown, woollen hose reached out from below his mail coat to russet brown leather boots. From knee to ankle the hose was loosely bound by crisscrossed light brown suede leather thongs. A cloak of thin dull grey green material hung loosely across his shoulders, secured by a plain clasp made from a dull metal, a Frankish design, the hilt of a sword protruding from behind his left shoulder, the scabbard hidden by the cloak. A long dirk was just visible, hanging on his right side, from a plain brown leather belt. His hands were clasped together loosely around the shaft of a fighting axe, its blade resting on the deck, the bright sharp edge pointing away from the figure. The whole effect, increased by his below average height, was of a warrior who might have seen better times, of note only because the larger figures close to him were clearly an escort, or bodyguard.

The bodyguards were taller than Ivar, the shortest being half a head taller. They were identically dressed, which was in itself unusual. Each wore a plain conical steel helmet with a straight nasal extending down to provide some protection to nose and eyes. The sun reflected off the polished metal. All the guards were clean shaven. All carried a fighting axe, a circular shield hung behind the left shoulder, and a long broad-bladed dirk hung from their belts, but none of them wore a sword. All wore the berserker's three quarter length chain mail coat, the broad sleeves coming half way down the guards' forearms. Beneath the coat, each wore a padded jacket of a faded yellow brown material. The only individuality being the colour of their hose, some of which were dark blue, but most were shades of brown or grey. All wore narrow leather crisscross bindings on their legs and short leather boots on their feet. None wore a cloak. The plainness of their clothing and equipment, although apparently richer, matched more closely that of their leader, contrasting with the other figure in the group.

Einarr could have been the leader had he not stood to one side of the half circle of bodyguards. He was taller than the tallest of the guards and, in his evident pride, stood full tall. His broad shoulders matched his height, indicating great power. He was now dressed for battle, his sailor's clothes confined to his sea chest.

He still wore the dark brown leather trousers, now tucked into dark brown boots that came half way up to his knees. In place

42

of a woollen shirt he wore a light brown suede shirt with wide sleeves that came almost to the thick studded leather cuffs he wore on his wrists. Over the shirt he wore a chain mail coat that came down almost to his knees, with sleeves to his elbows. The sun glinted off the oiled mail coat, but it flashed from the helmet. It was a rounded shape, closer to the skull than the traditional conical helmet, a raised ridge running along the crest. The rounded guards and nasal protecting eyes and nose ensured his vision was not restricted. A chain mail curtain ran round the helmet and its guards, extending down to his shoulders. The most striking aspect of the helmet was that the steel shell was covered with copper plate, a design inlaid in silver of an eagle, its wings outstretched, leaping from the front of the helmet at his forehead. His sword hung on his left shoulder, sheathed in dark brown, almost black, leather with silver trimming, a bold red stone glowed from the sword hilt in the sunshine. A almost circular shield hung behind his left shoulder over the sword, dressed in a sheet of bronze, an eagle design embossed on it, copying the eagle decoration of the helmet, red stones for the eagle's eyes. From the dark brown leather belt around his waist hung a dirk and a dagger, both in leather sheaths, black hilted and bejewelled. The dirk was more like a short sword, a broad blade, similar to those worn by his father's bodyguards.

Most of Einarr's equipment was a gift from his uncle Bjorn, trophies from a southern voyage beyond the lands of the Rus. Ivar had not been impressed, but it would have been a great insult to refuse his brother's gift to a son whose delight in receipt was obvious.

This display of difference and wealth could mark Einarr as a target in battle, a leader to be destroyed. Ivar in his faded clothes was anonymous, merging into the mass of warriors. Even his bodyguard would merge into the line of battle as they created a protective screen. He would only stand out briefly as a great leader when he leapt onto a shield, a platform held up by his bodyguards, to see across the tangled scrum of warriors, to better gauge the progress of battle. This was a well-practised movement.

His extraordinary supple agility allowed a fast and seemingly single fluid movement, up to survey the battle, and rapidly down again, to be noticed by very few.

At the same time that the group of ships had been forming up behind the Frakokk, two smaller groups of vessels struck out, almost unnoticed, one to the northern shore of the lake and one to the south bank. Each group included warships and trading vessels. As they reached the shores, they grounded. Already the tide was again more than half out and the sun long past its full height. Most of the crews scrambled ashore, leaving behind the horses, that had been part of the cargo, in the charge of a small guard. By the time these parties had landed, the Frakokk was already well into the river, heading inland, her consorts following at regular intervals, a line of swans moving serenely across still waters. Each in quiet purpose. There was no need for speed, each ship idling with the minimum number of oars employed and, on the great sweeping bends, one bank of oars would be inactive as the other bank helped maintain steerage round the bend.

Four

My audience was sitting still in rapt attention. Even James had resisted the urge to ask questions, wrapped in the embrace of the tale. I remembered once sitting, as they sat now, the same fascination, lost in time. I realised that we had all been immersed in the tale. For the evening, all had ceased around the telling.

The logs on the fire crackled and glowed, the rush lights had burned down, some still strong, others guttering. My manservant Jamie had made up the fire, but even this had not distracted me, or my audience. Neither had the boys' mother, hovering in the doorway, made any recognition with me, or with her sons.

I could have continued with the tale, but the children needed their sleep and it was well past the time they should be abed. I confess that seeing Janet hovering there had encouraged me to talk on. I could not resist it as she was afeared to interrupt, but the children deserved their sleep.

I paused, then, "and now is time for ye to be abed", I said.

They sat up as though surprised. James and Mary wanted to hear more of the tale, although the twins had been fighting to keep their eyes open.

I held up my hands. "Whist, tomorrow, if ye have been good, and our guests not arrived, I will tell ye more".

Janet rushed forward to gather up the children before I changed my mind. She always scurries and scuttles. I canna blame it all on the Hepburns. Her cousin James is a fine young man, a natural hill and forest fighter and an able admiral. I should not allow her manner to irritate me, perhaps it is age, impatience, knowing the time ahead is so much shorter than the time past. Perhaps I feel we could have made a better match for Erik.

Maybe I am harsh on her. She has been a good and loyal wife to Erik, she cares well for the bairns, but still her manner angers me and I look for faults that in others would go unnoticed. Perhaps she fears me. Should I be more generous with her? My dearest Margaret had always softened my feelings. When I returned home it was as much and more her household. I eased back as the temporary master knowing that she had made all the decisions, the judge and counsellor to our people during my long absences. She had always seen the strengths and qualities of our women, equally with their weaknesses, when my unpractised eye saw only the flaws. Margaret had always seen qualities in Janet

Give me a ship's company, or a band of soldiers, to a household of women.

My thoughts returned to the story. I looked forward to another evening. The time to tell to my grandchildren the lessons of our past, the promise of our future. I wondered how many generations had shared Einarr's Saga around a winter fire, snug from the chill outside.

I had enjoyed the telling of the story as much as the bairns had enjoyed the listening. This last year they had been my comfort. I had spent little enough time with my own children, or my dearest Margaret. There had always been matters to take me away, matters that filled my time and my mind. Time rushed by before I realized it. I had most enjoyed a ship's deck beneath my feet. Soldiering was a duty. It was bloody, dirty work, sleeping most times in the saddle, or wrapped wet and cold in a cape, on muddy ground, so far from home. At sea it could be more terrifying, but it was always clean, the ship my home, the crew my household, sharing the joys and the hardships. When we returned it was to joy and comfort before the next voyage.

In this last year I had seen what I had missed in my own children. I realized now that they had been almost strangers, on their best behaviour when I was home, pleased by gifts. Margaret had attended to their upbringing, they and I owed so much to her, aided by my father in his closing years. When the boys came to me later, to soldier and to sail, they were developed people. I could only polish skills they had already gained. As we came to know each other it was as adults, in an adult's world. This I knew only from the precious year I had enjoyed with my grandchildren. It was a great joy and comfort amongst my grief. For the first time I began to understand my own father as I had never in his life.

With these thoughts, and a measure of aqua vitae, I felt myself drift away, Kara curled up against my outstretched legs, the fire glowing in the hearth. When I awoke, it was to the din of Jamie clearing the dead embers of the fire, fresh light streaming through the windows. A new day ahead, the first guests to greet perhaps, matters to discus, plans to lay, but beyond that the warming prospect of other evenings with my grandchildren. If I regretted anything, it was that this night would most probably be with guests, guests I had little enough liking for, but necessary to duty and to our family's future.

I suspected that they would be with us some days. The winter chill would make their journey to us slow and painful. There would be little urgency to return, but they could not be missed for long. I would play the generous host. There was a need for friends, even if the enemy's enemies would be some of those friends. This was long the way of the Borders, alliances shifting over time, friendship and treachery never far from each other, even where there was a tie of blood. Those before me had walked this road with care and skill. My duty to our people was to exercise the same skills. Our family had oft times supported our own kings, and chosen them, but we had to recognize the English Kings, at times taking their part. A dangerous road that was also a path to great opportunity.

Part Two -

First Blood

Five

We gather tonight in the chamber that is my sanctuary. My sons still away with their men, there is no attraction in the Great Hall. Instead I instructed Jamie that the table in the turret room be prepared. I invited Janet to join me with the children. I should make an effort to understand her better.

Robert's wife Morag is with us. I have a strong liking for Morag, she reminds me much of my own dearest Margaret. A gentle woman, but a strong woman, a good mother to her children, a support for my son, and more, a natural good humour and a ready laugh. It is she and not Janet who has kept my household for me since the death of my wife.

My quarters are spacious, taking the whole floor at the very top of the tower. The main chamber leads from an anti-chamber, through which runs the stone stairs that continue up to the roof, a stout oak door set in a thick stone wall. To the South West corner of the chamber is the turret room. In summer I love this room with its grand view across the Solway. It is half a floor higher than the chamber, a short flight of broad stone steps leading up to it. A heavy round oak table takes much of the space, enough left over for the sturdy high-backed oak chairs, but little else. Our food is offered by Jamie and Annie from the narrow doorway.

Dining in the turret room is so much more comfortable than the Great Hall, when there are but a few of us to share a meal. The Great Hall seats a very large party on two great tables, a raised table running across their tops, when the room is filled it is joy, noise, bustle. With but a few of us, huddled round one end of the cross table, it is miserable and draughty. In the turret room, the candles in the iron chandelier cast a warm glow, the heavy Belgian tapestries and velvet hangings keeping out the winter chill.

My life has been full of violence. A Border life could be nothing else. I have enjoyed most my times at sea, but I hold duty to our people. More now, I am the judge and arbiter, my sons taking my place in battle, or leading a trade expedition. When my father died, my dear Margaret was the shepherd of our people whilst I was away. Now she is gone, the burden is on me. In time it will pass to Erik, but Janet will make a poor substitute when he is away. Morag would make a much better steward, managing the affairs while the young men are at war or trade.

To eat together with old friends and family is a welcome break from duty. A time for companionship. To have my grand children with me in an evening is the greatest joy. I am reluctant to share them with their mothers, but Janet needs to learn the lessons of our past, the guide to a future, even Morag has much to learn. I know not if my life be short, or if it be long. Time flows an endless stream, wicked fast, a man's time is short and I have cheated the reaper more than my share.

We eat a simple meal. Morag is her usual happy robust self, even Janet joins the talk and laughter. As we work our way through the food the children are eager to finish, to gather by the fire in the chamber. I feel my own impatience rising. Strange that the telling of the tale is as much an entertainment for the teller as for the listeners. I realise that I have thought of little but Einarr's Saga in the quiet moments since we gathered round the fire three nights ago. I had much to do in the time between.

Each morning Mary had asked me when I would tell them more of the Saga. I would in all truth have much preferred to spend the evenings with my grand children, but duty must be done. George Douglas is nay so bad, for a Douglas, but the others from Edinburgh had been dour and mean natured, their clothes ill-patched, their manners to match. I canna abide the town but it is fitting for the people who live there, dirty, mean and twisting, the tall buildings leaning together across narrow streets in conspiracy. The evil harg sweeping in off the Firth, trapping the filth of the town's fires in a yellow, sticky, choking cloak.

At last tonight, a welcome break from duty and intrigue. A

time to relax and enjoy the company of close family.

We had done justice to the food. A civilized meal with spoons, knives, forks and plates of silver, so different from the past nights' guests who tore the meat from the bones with their hands, wiping the grease from their beards with their coat sleeves. Then, we feasted in the Great Hall, though a pigsty might have suited better. Even young William and Gilbert could have taught these noble lords manners.

We moved from the table to the chamber and the great crackling fire. Jamie and Annie are clearing away the remains from the table. The punch bowl stands waiting on the small table near to the great fireplace. Time aplenty for the irons to heat in the fire, after a hearty meal washed down with watered wine.

Janet has brought her embroidery. She sits to one side of the fireplace on a stool, concentrating on her stitches. Maybe I am too hard on her. The Hepburn fortunes wax and wane like the moon, they always have, they always will. James Hepburn is a man of honour, but no courtier. He is happiest on the battlefield, or at sea, preferences I ken well, his refusal to follow the fashions of politics means lean times with the good. He will again be in exile, one of our ships will carry him to safety, that much was agreed. While he is away, his weaker neighbours will try their chance to seize his lands and houses. It had been the same with his father. That made life uncertain for his kin. As a cousin, Janet would have been at greater risk, further from the remaining family power, closer to their enemies and jealous friends.

I was glad those before me had the wisdom to settle as they had. This is the third castle to stand in this place, its dark red sandstone gloomy in the dull days, but alive in the sunlight. I have always enjoyed the sight of it thrusting up from the surrounding low ground, the sun on it as we approached along the Firth. It stands, as its predecessors have, on the higher ground within earthworks and stockade walls, its real strength being the flooded ground beyond the walls, the thorn hedges that surround the marsh, the dock within the outer walls. Strong defences, but always the choice to put to sea if the enemy is stronger, and in times past great armies have marched past. In the lands around Jedburgh, the Hepburns are always vulnerable to a greater host.

Morag sits on the floor with the children, their faces raised expectantly for the story to begin. Where Janet has long narrow features, Morag's rounded face, glows with health and humour. Only two years younger than Janet, Morag looks much younger. Difficult to believe that she has birthed her fourth child only these few months past. She could be sister more than mother to Mary. Janet looks older and worn before her years, yet the two women are easy together. It is rare for Janet to smile, rarer to see her laugh, but, when she does, it is most common in Morag's company. I hope the women will give each other strength when I am gone and the burden of stewardship falls to them.

Now the warm glow of the fire spreads out across the chamber. It has freshly snowed, the wind dropped, the night quiet, before the next storm sweeps down from the ice lands. The light from fire, rush light, and candle, dances in the armour and weapons, glows in the gilt tracings of the richer velvet hangings. We are embraced in the warmth of fire and the satisfaction of food. Even Janet has a relaxed expression, almost, but not entirely, a contented smile.

I relax into the abbots chair. Its bare oak surprisingly comfortable, a masterpiece of carving and woodworking. Its strength and simplicity not out of place amidst the thick Turkish carpets, the French and Belgian wall hangings, but it would have been as much at home on bare stone flags against white-washed, rough plastered walls.

As I begin the story again, the three days between might never have been. There is a familiarity, a continuity. I could have been in that place, at that time, yet I have never trodden the ground.

Once I had sailed down that coast as a young man, most times we would stand off for the coasts of Holland and France, away from the English ships. On that one voyage there had been storm and rain, a piled slate sea, ripped and rippled with white foam, a sky filled with dark grey clouds, scudding close to the wind-whipped water. Our deck heavy angled, the water rushing along the lee rail, token reefed sails stretched, straining before the North wind. The land dimly seen through the curtain of rain as it briefly parted.

Land so flat and low that it might have been a sandbank, freshly risen on a falling tide. Not the hills and forests of our home, but a blasted land, and yet it was not unlike the shores of the Firth with the slow shelving sand that can be so treacherous at low water and on a rising tide, the sinking sands a trap for those crossing them at low water, the tide creeping like an assassin around the unwary to cut them off from shore, fierce currents and undertow to suck down the strongest swimmer.

Six

The sun was sinking quickly in the Western sky. Soon a full moon would brightly light the scene, but mist was starting to form once more, providing the needed cloak. Everything had gone more smoothly than Ivar could have hoped. If any native had seen the fleet, he had not raised an alarm. When the ships reached their next objective they could expect to have surprise on their side. As an exercise in planning and command, with such an independent band of warriors, it was amazing. All the more so when the storm had threatened to disperse the ships, so that it could take days for them to collect. It might yet be days before all arrived, but the majority were safe within the inland water, exactly as planned.

Timing was crucial because the first objective was only a short distance from the lake where they had made their rendezvous. Once, many generations before, it had been at the edge of the sea. The years had seen the crust of coast built up in front, for the lakes and marshes to form. The slow river had cut a wandering path with ever broader curves. This day, the wide bends turned back on themselves, the river threatening to take a short cut, leaving the bow to form a new horseshoe lake. The banks were lined by thickening belts of willow and alder, reed to their base.

Einarr was frustrated by these trees. In places, where the river almost cut through the remaining narrow neck of swampy ground, one of the ships, far down the line, could be briefly seen through the trees. As the mist thickened, the brief sightings became fewer. The river seemed to wind on interminably. Each time Einarr had looked, but it was never the Gylla that could be seen. He was denied his hoped for glimpse of Gudhrun.

While they frustrated Einarr, these trees would screen the ships until they burst out into the next lake, by which their objective lay, and their dark bulk marked the margins of the serpentine river in the murk. To arrive early could lead to discovery, to arrive late risked other dangers as the mist thickened and visibility was less than the length of the Frakokk.

When Ivar had scouted the river the year before, he had burst suddenly upon the objective. In rounding yet another bend in the lazy river, the space and water exploded before his eyes, a vast expanse, after the confining walls of the tree-lined river banks. Then, his cloak was their disguise as peaceful travellers, their small trading boat was no vessel of war. Now, their purpose would be all too obvious to any watcher. A mist that broke up the lines of their vessels would deceive a watcher ashore, but not obscure the target from their own masthead lookouts.

The campaign was truly underway. The preparations had been completed, the action committed. Until the advanced fleet had entered the river it was possible to turn back unseen. Now this group of vessels was well inside the river, turning back would be a very difficult manoeuvre, for some it would be all but impossible, still, Ivar had no intension of turning back. He would move forward whatever the opposition. No one would think of turning back if he did not. No one would dare.

For most, there was a great excitement to be a part of such a bold campaign. The riches promised were strong motivation, the immortality of joining the sagas of heroes was even stronger. For those who fell, Valhalla was assured, for those who survived, the future would be good, better than most could ever have hoped for, a time of honey and milk, the respect of grandchildren.

The mist had formed again into low banks that covered the longships to the tops of their figureheads. The mast tops stood above the mist. At each masthead, a lookout could clearly see his neighbours at the masts ahead and astern but all would be invisible from the river banks. Above the thickening carpet of mist the moon was full and strong, lighting the tops of these clouds of moisture. Occasionally a ship drifted too close to a bank, a frantic thrashing as the oars fought with the reed margin.

After what had seemed an eternity to Einarr, the Frakkok's

lookout signalled the destination in sight. A simple set of signals had been agreed as tugs on a line hanging down the mast. Knut was again at the top of the mast, Frakki holding the bottom end of the line, again the relay. Ivar signed to Old Gisi and the oarsmen to let the Frakkok coast forward. Soon the line of vessels would begin to group together as they advanced cautiously on their objective. Silence was vital, the slightest sound carrying to raise an alarm.

Knut slid silently down the mast to report directly to Ivar. They stood huddled together on the central raised deck beside the mast. Ivar gave Knut the signals for the ships close to them, to be relayed down the line of lookouts. Knut, once more jammed into the rope cradle at the top of the mast, tugged on his line to tell Frakki what message to pass quietly to Ivar, who was standing close to Frakki beside the mast. Ivar signed to Gisi to start the oarsmen and move slowly ahead. There was no stroke drum now, each oarsman watching carefully the back of the man ahead of him. The oars moved easily without noise in the greased ports, the lubricating slime of cod liver reeked but the familiar smell went unnoticed by the crew. The faint sounds close by indicated other ships copying the Frakkok's stealthy movement.

Knut tugged urgently on the line. Ivar signalled for the oarsmen to stop and to bring in their oars. Knut signalled to the lookout on the following masthead and saw the mast move to the left of the Frakkok's line of approach. He could just make out the mast of the next behind his neighbour begin moving in parallel to the left. Eight boats would come to land, roughly in line abreast. The group of eight behind them would form on the left of their lead boat, the masthead lookouts watching as they closed on the first boats. As the oars were pitched, the Frakkok gave a short gentle shudder, followed by a firmer movement as her keel lightly grounded. Almost as she came to a complete stop, armed men were slipping quietly over the side into the shallow water, to wade ashore with great care to avoid the noise of splashing. The lake bed was surprisingly firm, of sand and gravel. As the load was lightened by the crew going ashore, the Frakkok was hauled closer in towards the bank by those who were first ashore. Muffled sounds to either side indicated that other vessels of their group had grounded as planned. The next group would interleave between the sterns of the first, the groups following them rafting into the sterns of the first two groups, their crews coming ashore by climbing across the first boats.

The Frakkok's crew gathered round Ivar and realized, for the first time, what he and Knut had already known, Ivar from reconnaissance a year before, and Knut this night from his perch at the masthead. The low bank, sloping up from the lake bed met huge stone walls that towered menacingly above them. To people from lands where wood was plentiful, the common material for any construction, a stone building was a novelty, but nothing prepared them for the sheer size of this massive structure rising from the barren flatlands at the side of the lake. In the mist, there seemed no end to the walls in either height or length. The surface was rough, many small rounded stones built into a barrier of enormous strength by a material that seemed harder than the stones themselves. Only a few crew members, who had journeyed far to the South, had seen its like before.

Ivar cast along the wall in each direction before he was satisfied that he knew where he stood. Certain now of his position, and with his bodyguard around him, he began to follow the huge wall to his right. Einarr followed with another group of warriors. After no more than seventy paces, Ivar stopped beside a small doorway in the wall. He could see that the door had not moved since his visit a year before. The thick wooden door, with its iron studding and iron straps, stood ajar. There was just space for a man to squeeze carefully through. To open the door fully was to risk the noise of rusty metal grinding and shrieking on rusty metal. The men followed Ivar through the sally port. They could now see just how thick the walls were, the sally port like a tunnel through rock, ending in a second door of thick iron bars. This door was ajar like the outer door.

The party assembled inside the walls, that enclosed a space at least the equal of the massive walls. Visibility was poor in the thickening mist, but the outlines of buildings wavered in obscuring moisture. There was the sound of domestic activity, of music and animals, sounds of an active village, not yet asleep.

All the Frakkok's crew were within the walls, formed into two groups, one around Ivar and the other around Einarr. Crews from the other ships were gathering around their captains, five hundred men, but occupying so little of the enclosed land that they made no impact on the space.

Seven

From his reconnaissance a year before, Ivar knew that the ancient fortress was used to enclose a village, but was also guard fort against invaders. In the ancient times of the Romans it had protected two neighbouring villages and the route inland. The villages had long since vanished back into the soil, the once broad Roman road, with its ditches to either side, its verges cleared of vegetation, was now a rutted lane, the trees and brush encroaching from both sides. It was marked out from Saxon tracks only in the arrow-straight line it carved across the landscape.

What Ivar could not be sure of was the size of the population now within the walls, or how many of them were warriors. From seeing the fortress in daylight, he knew it contained a large area of land, the walls built many generations before, by another people. Once Roman soldiers had patrolled these walls and rested in their protection. Within their stone embrace had nestled warehouses holding supplies, landed there for the Legions. Two villages had farmed the land to feed themselves and the Roman garrison. The road, then newly built, had been a busy thoroughfare of Empire, carrying troops and supplies from the depot within the fort and the ships that docked beside it, deep into a still hostile land. The fort and villages abandoned, the original buildings within the mighty walls had decayed, to be replaced by simpler Saxon buildings.

Ivar and Gisi had observed from a distance, their disguises would not stand close scrutiny, they dared not enter the fortress. They noted the people coming and going across the narrow wooden bridge that joined the fort to dry ground and the road inland. It seemed nothing more than a small village nestled within those massive walls. There was no sign of soldiers, or lookouts, no sentries at the ramparts. From their vantage point they could not see into the fort, but they could see two of the enormous walls, the gate towers in one.

Through the day there were few movements. Cattle were driven out to pasture at first light and brought back within the walls before nightfall. A small party of mounted warriors rode across the bridge at late morning, stayed but a short time, before riding out, to return inland. Through the day individuals, men and women, came and went, gatherers of firewood, reed cutters, farmers. In the late afternoon a small ox-drawn wagon rumbled across the bridge, completely filling the width of the rickety structure. There was no sign of any further military activity.

Ivar was frustrated. He and Gisi had found a hiding place, in a thicket of stunted trees, from where they could watch the bridge and two walls of the huge fort. They could go no closer without risk of discovery, the land before the bridge having been cleared of trees, reed and all other vegetation. They could not see the other two walls that completed the enormous square enclosure, but they knew that the lake lapped close to them for much of the day, leaving a narrow irregular fringe of mud and sand at low water. The lack of ridge, or hill, or even a suitable tree to climb, prevented them from seeing over the high stone walls. The only signs of life were those few comings and goings across the bridge, and the smoke of fires, from somewhere within the walls. During the day, the massive main doors, facing the bridge, were left open and unattended, to be closed at last light each evening.

Ivar and Gisi maintained their vigil for four days. They observed that the six mounted warriors arrived in the late morning every second day, stayed briefly, then returned the way they had come. That suggested that the warriors originated from somewhere that was a day's ride from the fort, although they could not know how many villages the warriors passed through, so their base might be much less than a day's ride directly and they could not be certain that the same warriors visited each time. Beyond that, they had learned little. From the meagre traffic across the bridge there seemed to be few people living and working within the walls, but the enclosed space was vast, generous enough to hold a town.

On the second day they had observed a woman and some children on top of one of the towers of the gatehouse, but of lookouts there was no sign. The only other intelligence they gained was that those few people who left during the day, including their cattle, returned before dark, when the massive wooden doors were firmly closed behind them. The wooden bridge was fixed and showed signs of age and neglect. Ivar realized that the great stone fort stood on an artificial island, created by cutting a broad channel, across which the bridge now spanned. The banks had been cut sheer and faced with stone but this facing had collapsed in places for want of maintenance.

By the end of the forth day, Ivar knew that they must take some risks to learn more.

Eight

Their shipmates had moored at the edge of the reeds in the evening before the first day to allow them to slip ashore in the falling light, taking up their watch in the thicket that they had noticed when they sailed into the lake. When they burst into the lake, they could not at first see the fort. In front of them was a low island with a small wood growing from its sandy soil, hiding the fort from them, but also hiding them from the fort. The stone walls only came into sight as they sailed around the island

Having dropped the scouts, the boat had then left to follow the river inland. They had agreed that they would return for Ivar and Gisi before dawn on the fifth day. That gave time for the boat crew to gather intelligence further up the river, but with reduced risk that they would raise any suspicions.

Just before dusk on the forth day it had started to rain hard, the light fading quickly. As the rain petered out, there were breaks in the cloud, providing some moonlight. Even in the rough shelter they had fashioned, both men were soaked to the skin. It was miserable and cold but they were accustomed to hardship and discomfort.

Leaving Gisi at their watch point, Ivar had cautiously walked along the track towards the bridge. Seeing no sign of any movement, or sentry, he carefully walked across the bridge, which was more solidly built than it had seemed from their hiding place. The decking was still wet from the rain and his leather boots made no sound but gripped poorly. At the end of the bridge, there was a paved area leading to the main gate. To the left of the bridge the water lapped close to the base of the wall. To the right a paved path led away into the darkness. The gates were closed, their substantial timbers reinforced with heavy iron bands and studs. The gates were much wider than the bridge merited and more than the height of four men. The filtered moonlight was not strong enough to penetrate the shadow above, but the gateway seemed to be topped by a curving arch, between two enormous square towers.

Ivar crept along the wall to the right. The paved path was broad, wider than the bridge, stretching from the base of the thick stone wall to a quay. In places, the wall that buttressed the quay was crumbling into the dark water of the lake. It was now full tide and the water reached to within a pace of the top of the quay wall. By the time that Ivar had crept along the path for half the length of the wall from the gate, he found the quay heading was crumbling badly. In places there was only enough space to walk at the foot of the fort's outer wall. This was disappointing because the quay, from the bridge to that point, provided little space to bring longships in to land their crews, and the high wall with its massive gate towers provided any defender with domination of the quay below. A handful of determined defenders could beat off an attacking host with ease.

He now had to move with care to avoid falling into the lake. In places more of the original stone quay survived, but never the full original width. As it had crumbled away, it had created a treacherous rocky margin that could take the bottom out of an unsuspecting boat. At the corner of the wall with the next, Ivar had to scramble with great care around the tower, in places wading through the water and having difficulty in keeping his balance on the uneven stone below the surface.

Once round the corner of the wall, Ivar found a narrow fringe of natural bank, following along the foot of the wall. Here there had been no stone embankment, or any that once skirted the wall had long since disappeared. The grassy bank was reasonably level, never less than two paces wide and, at one point, the bank reached out from the wall for four, perhaps five, paces. He gingerly edged towards the bank. The light was poor, but enough to see that the bank had been worn away, undermined by the water, leaving a shelving beach. Very carefully, he edged out into the water which quickly reached his waist. Feeling with his foot, he found that the ground beneath him continued to shelve at the same rate. It felt firm like sand, rather than a gluey mud. This would make an ideal place to run longships ashore, although the narrow fringe around the walls offered little space to assemble a large group of warriors and there was still the important matter of gaining entry into the fort without heavy casualties. He carefully waded back to the dry land, his sodden clothes uncomfortable and surprisingly cold, as though they were already freezing.

Having regained the dry ground, Ivar continued along the great wall. He had counted out seventy paces as he built up a plan of the fortress in his mind. That was when he found the small door that was mysteriously left part open. From the rust on the hinges it showed no sign of having moved in recent memory, perhaps not for generations. In his seaman's clothes, he could easily step through the doorway, but a warrior would have to be careful with the greater bulk of mail coat and equipment. He was now in a narrow tunnel formed through the massive stone wall. At its end, he saw the inner iron gate, also partly open, but he could go no further, seeing a group of people around a fire feasting. He watched them from the shadows through the bars of the iron gate. They seemed to be men of the village, not soldiers. It was a small group, perhaps the men of one family. What they could have been celebrating he could only guess, perhaps a marriage, or a religious festival. Why they would choose to eat outside, after the earlier rain, he could only guess. The fire was both a help and a hindrance to him. In the firelight he could make out some buildings that looked like barns or halls. Dark timber structures in a familiar shape, like the buildings in Heddeby. He could also see cattle pens in a large grassy field that faded into the darkness but, with the fitful moonlight no match for the glare of the feasting fire, he could not see beyond the first buildings that were lit directly by the fire.

Unable to sneak into the enclosed area, Ivar watched for a time from the deep shadow of the doorway, before slipping away, when the group around the fire showed no inclination to move to the buildings. Back outside the encircling walls, he decided to examine the remaining length of wall and the forth wall. This proved to be difficult. The bank was now a narrow and uneven fringe, tight to the foot of the wall. In places he had to press close to the rough stone of the wall to avoid sliding into the lake's waters. By the time he reached the third corner, the moonlight, mostly hidden by thickening cloud, was sufficient only to see an unbroken wall stretching towards the fourth corner, the water lapping directly against the stone, only short slivers of bank remaining against the base of the wall.

There would have been little to gain by working further along the wall. Importantly, Ivar could see that the fort was a large space enclosed by four massive walls that were reinforced by towers along their lengths, culminating in the main entrance with its imposing twin towers and equally massive gates. However long the walls and towers had stood, they were as robust as that day long past when the fort had been completed. Without attention they would stand as long again and perhaps more.

Ivar decided to retrace his path to the bridge. This proved difficult in places. Three times he lost his footing and had to scramble back up the bank, wet and muddy. By the time he again reached the wooden bridge the moon was only occasionally breaking through thickening cloud. A cold curtain of drizzle began to fall. It was a miserable night and he had no warming fire to look forward to. He searched about carefully to make sure there was no sentry, before creeping stealthily back across the bridge. To the time when he regained their hiding place, the only sign of people had been the group gathered around the fire inside the fort.

He would have wished to know more about the fort, but their observation in the days before, and his nocturnal expedition, had provided enough intelligence to consider an attack. He now knew the size of the enclosing walls from pacing along two full sides, and he could estimate the heights of the walls and the towers that flanked the main entrance to the compound. The soft grassy bank along the back wall of the fort, and the small sally port that pierced that wall, provided the place to make a first landing and gain an entry to the fort. Unless sentries were mounted on the wall, it would be a perfect landing, with any sounds blanketed by the broad stone structure. That made it possible to risk bringing later boats directly in along the quay beside the great gate towers, ready to enter through the main gates once the first party had opened them. Should the boats be seen at the quay, it could only distract the inhabitants of the fort from the real danger presented by those coming through the open and unguarded sally port.

The weakness of the reconnaissance was that Ivar still did not know how many people might be inside the fort when he was able to launch an attack. The very small numbers, apparently there now, could be reinforced by a considerable host. The space contained by the stone walls could have provided the area to build a town, or at least a very large village.

Just before dawn, Lodin brought the Hildr back to their rendezvous on the lake shore. As they made their way back towards the sea, Lodin reported on what they had found during their journey upriver.

Nine

The Hildr had been chosen for this voyage because it was unadorned, typical of the multitude of small vessels used for trade and fishing on both sides of the sea. There was nothing to distinguish it from similar boats, seen frequently along these coasts and in the rivers. The small crew were clearly not a raiding party, their clothes simple and typical of seamen engaged on a commercial voyage. They carried no weapons except the dirks and daggers carried by most people, several of the crew carried the seaxes popular amongst the Saxons and some Northlanders. The seax was a large knife with a single curved edge, with an antler or wood hilt, that hung from the belt across the front of the body, the hilt to the owner's right. These knives had decorated blades and were held in decorated sheaths, as much a sign of the freeman and the hunter as a weapon. The bales on the deck before the mast contained food and goods that could be traded, concealing weapons and coats of mail.

Lodin and his comrades sailed on up the river, after dropping Ivar and Gisi for their surveillance of the fort. The waterway was still very broad as it curved and twisted its way inland. Lodin was surprised by the lack of people. They passed some reed cutters, and a boy fishing from a small hide boat. These river folk showed only fleeting interest as the Hildr passed them, no more than a brief glance, the raising of a hand in greeting, to be returned in similar fashion by Lodin and his crew. Beyond the reeds and willows he could see smoke from isolated dwellings, but no sign of any village.

Their knowledge of the inland areas and the people was sparse. They knew that there were several large towns much further inland, but they had expected a greater population closer to the coast. There was little sign of farming. Lodin suspected that the flat lands along the river were too wet and marshy. Further back, hidden behind the fringe of forest and marsh there would be rich meadows, fields and villages.

At several points they came into the bank and one of the crew jumped ashore to search for signs of habitation. All that they found were isolated huts, mostly showing no signs of recent occupation, and in poor condition. In places, streams led into the river but most were choked with weed and banks of reed. There were also many signs of the productive beaver population that had built dams, causing flooding and diverting the flow of many small streams. Some streams were broader and could have been sailed by a boat smaller than the Hildr. Lodin suspected that some would lead to habitation, but he had no means, or time, to see what might lie deeper in the marsh and forest beyond the river's broad banks.

As darkness fell, they found a convenient bank to moor to. Lodin decided that there was too much risk to sail at night with a heavy black overcast of cloud blotting out any light from moon or stars. This made it impossible to see where there might be shallows. Some of the broad bends had a deep channel following closely the inside of the curve, but mud banks extended out from both sides for much of the river. On other banks, the outside bend contained unexpected mud banks, invisible at high water but only just below the surface. Periodically they tested the depth with the long poles used for quanting the Hildr in shallow water. Even at its deepest, the river was usually less than four paces in depth, with a soft muddy bottom and weed. Lodin could not risk the Hildr grounding on mud. It was safer to rest up until first light. They took turns to stand watch but at least each man could sleep and wake refreshed. Lodin knew that if anyone was abroad, it was natural for harmless traders to moor up for the night and explore again for trade in the next day's light.

Ten

L ate in the morning of the second day they came to a riverside village. It was a meagre hamlet, a sparse straggle of wattle and reed huts built on sloping ground, topped by a fringe of trees and scrub, that reached towards the river, boasting a wooden quay in much need of repair. The modest buildings were almost hidden by undergrowth with signs of long neglect, much like those isolated dwellings that they had already encountered on their way upriver. There were a few small boats and canoes tied to the rotting timber piles, with barely space enough for Lodin to bring the Hildr alongside to tie up.

As they drifted gently towards the timber pilings, he greeted an old man who was fishing from the quay. The ancient showed little curiosity, continuing with his solitary, and apparently fruitless, occupation, after directing Lodin to the centre of the village. Leaving his five comrades with the boat, Lodin climbed onto the wooden boards of the quay and began walking up the rising earth track into the village.

As he gained the top of the rise, he was met by an earth embankment, surprised to see it topped by a wooden palisade of recently cut tree trunks. The dull brown grey bark had not been removed from the trunks and only the ends showed bright, fresh-cut timber. From the river this had been hidden by the thin fringe of trees. Behind the trees the ground had been cleared and a shallow trench dug to provide the embankment on which the palisades stood. In front of him was a wooden gateway of two small wood towers, from which hung rough wooden gates that were held open with props. There was no sign of sentries, but he could see the gates were sound, their hinges greased in evidence of daily use. The towers were simple, each no more than a platform on stilts, protected by timber walls and topped by a simple roof of reeds. The rustic appearance of the solid defences suggested either a lack of carpenters, or a degree of haste in the construction.

Through the open gates Lodin could see that the village was far larger than they had first thought, having seen only the straggle of old huts outside the defences. It was neither poor nor wealthy. Except for one, the buildings were all simple round huts, with walls of wattle panels smeared with clay, and topped with steep conical reed roofs, showing signs of recent repair. The exception was a timber hall, little larger than twelve of the simpler buildings combined. It was located in the centre of the group of rustic huts. Between the buildings were dirt tracks. No attempt had been made to pave any of these with timber, gravel or stone. Behind the hall there were signs that new buildings were under construction. Most of the huts had a fenced enclosure for livestock, but the pens were empty. Chickens and geese foraged between the buildings, a sow grubbing in the earth beyond the huts. As he walked past the first huts, he saw a child's face peep from an open doorway, to disappear again into the shadows. Approaching the timber hall, he was met by a second old man who greeted him politely, without either suspicion, or any great cordiality. Having satisfied himself that the stranger was no immediate threat, the old man invited Lodin to follow him to the hall.

As they approached, Lodin saw that the hall was well built and decorated in the Saxon style. Where the huts used materials from the waterside, alder, willow, clay and reed, the hall was built of oak, planks clenched to a substantial frame of smooth oak. They entered through a broad arched doorway to the centre of the building, perhaps half its area, perhaps less, with partitions leading to the two remaining sections. Light streamed in through the open doorway and through a canopied hole in the centre of the roof above the large open fireplace. Standing by the hearth was a handsome woman, introduced deferentially by the old man as Ælfwyn, the village leader. Lodin introduced himself as Leofraed, the persona he used when trading with the Saxons.

Ælfwyn was a jolly rounded woman of perhaps thirty

76

summers, perhaps older, exuding good health and vigour. Clear blue eyes in a smooth rounded face, flaxen hair braided in two plaits, a heavy gold torque sat around her neck, gold torques on her wrists. A high waisted blue skirt, embroidered with red and white flowers, a sleeveless shirt of pale yellow, and a cloak of darker blue, secured by a round gold broach with a dark stone at its centre. Her clothes, and the well-built hall, did not match the simple huts of the village. Lodin knew that the Saxons, as his own people, were an equal society where leaders held their positions by broad support from the community.

Ælfwyn settled into a high-backed chair by the hearth and gestured for Lodin to take the similar chair beside it. As they talked, Lodin in his guise as the trader Leofraed, the anomalies were explained. Unnoticed by Lodin and his comrades, the Hildr had been observed some distance before they reached the village. They had been taken for the traders they pretended to be. Ælfwyn was curious to learn who they were and where they headed, satisfied that they posed no immediate threat. Lodin felt the presence of others close by, probably behind the cowhide walls at each end of the room, large though this room was, three similar rooms would fit into the frame of the building. He was sure that Ælfwyn could call on support should the need arise.

Eleven

This was Ælfwyn's tale. She was the widow of Ealdwulf who had been killed by raiders two summers before. Ealdwulf had taken men from the village to help a neighbouring village against the attackers. He had fallen in the fight, only one of his men surviving to bring warning to their own village, sufficient for the villagers to flee into the marshes with whatever they could easily carry. The attackers had then fallen on Eadwulf's unprotected village and sacked it. The raiders had been fellow Saxons. The kingdom was under threat from the kingdom to the North, and from treacherous earls within the kingdom. The villagers had elected Ælfwyn to lead them, but she had been forced to send most of the men to fight for the kingdom, their duty to their king. The main threat and conflict was from the new Northumbrian king who had murdered his father and seized power.

It was hard for Ælfwyn's village, having already lost warriors. To the King they were warriors, to the village they were men who tilled the fields and herded the cattle, built and repaired the homesteads, crafted the tools of farming, fathers, brothers, husbands, sons. In other times no more than half the trained warriors would serve the king. When they returned to the village, the remaining half would go, should the king still have need of men. In more certain times, the King would await the end of harvest before taking to the fields of battle. That allowed his people to bring in their harvest to keep them through the coming winter and it meant that the King's war bands could live off the harvest stores of those they attacked.

Now, Ælfwyn had been forced to send all her warriors, and some of the untrained men, to make the numbers their village owed to the king's service. This left the village without its trained defence, with few hands to tend the harvest, few to meet the task of replacing buildings destroyed in the raid. It was a village of women, of children, and of a few old men.

Ælfwyn had decided to move the village, which had sat across the main road inland from the coast. The only building to survive the raiders intact, itself a small miracle, was the hall. This was dismantled and moved to the nearby fishing hamlet, a long neglected outpost of the village. Once it had been home for Ælfwyn's people when she was but a young girl. She was surprised to find herself at home in this neglected place, to remember the times of childhood when the village saw no conflict, when food was plentiful. The growing population had spread out onto the higher ground beyond the marshland, a new village sprang up and prospered around the straight road inland, built long ago by Roman soldiers, the old hamlet allowed to wither. Its poor neglected buildings provided temporary shelter until new and better buildings could be thrown up. The villagers were aided by the nature of the ground.

A narrow causeway connected the land, on which the hamlet was constructed, to a track that led to the destroyed village. In parts, the causeway was washed at the low water, twisting between swampy ground and marsh ponds. At high water almost nothing was visible. To a stranger, it was all too easy to lose the causeway and sink into the mire and tangle of reed and willows. On this site a village had stood before the first Saxons and even before the Romans. The ancient earthworks, enclosing most of the land, survived, needing little effort to restore them. Timber was brought from the woods, around the destroyed village, to augment that cleared from the ancient hamlet which nature had been repossessing.

The shortage of hands had made the work slow, as the demands of harvest competed with the need to build adequate shelter for the coming winter. The lack of carpenters and other skilled villagers resulted in a rustic appearance. There was no time and no people to select and saw the timber. It was stood in post holes, still with its bark, much as it had before being cut down and carried to the village for its purpose. Some of the old men could advise and assist, but it was a construction by children and women unused to the work. The thatching was as crude as the timber and wattle walls. The first task was to repair old buildings that could keep out the weather, the mud and clay being roughly smeared on the wattle panels. Later, inner panels could be made and fixed in place, earth being hammered into the space between to keep out the winter winds.

Ælfwyn had insisted that the priority, along with the repair of old buildings, must be the building of the stockade atop the earthworks, knowing that their depleted numbers, and lack of trained warriors, made them vulnerable to any future raid. With a shortage of tools and skilled carpenters, the work had been rough. Mature trees were cut and dragged with great labour across the causeway and stood to form the stockade walls.

Old huts were repaired and the work started on new huts. Without the skilled labour and time, the new buildings took a different pattern. Suitable younger trees were cut to length and stood into a circle to form walls for new huts. Lighter branches and boughs formed a framework for the steeply sloped roof. Then reed thatched the roof of each hut and clay filled the gaps between the timbers and branches that made the walls. The work may have been rough and ready, but it provided the shelter they needed to survive the coming winter.

She had also arranged the villagers to form a co-operative community. There could not be the luxury of hides allocated to families. In Saxon society, the hide was taken as a right of land, sufficient to support a family, with each family looking first to itself and then to its neighbours. To survive this first winter in their new home, all the available buildings had to be shared by the survivors as a single group. Their skills and resources must also be shared. The rebuilt hall was first their storehouse, Ælfwyn and her children living in one of the small huts. Good natured and fair, Ælfwyn had the steel beneath that every leader needed. Through her leadership they had survived the winter. Perhaps more of the older villagers had died than in past winters, but everyone had pulled together in mutual need. Food was in short supply, but no one had gone hungry.

Ælfwyn had begun building a new village, hampered still because most of the younger men were away, fighting for the King. She intended to build a new quay, with new paved roads through the village, but for now they would use the old huts and raise more new homes in the time not spent tending their cattle and crops, which were the wealth and survival of the village. She hoped the men would soon return, that work be speeded before the coming winter.

The last winter had been hard, with little food and poor shelter, the coming winter would be easier, but still a fight. Her eldest son had briefly returned with six of their warriors in the mid summer, only as they travelled close to the village on the king's business. He had left a boy, still a boy to his mother's eyes, but in those short months was a man, a battle leader, hope for the village of a better future. He told his mother that the King had agreed to send half their warriors home, that they would arrive any day. Since then she had heard nothing from him, or any of the other men. She hoped that Lodin had news and was disappointed to find that he did not.

Twelve

odin took a liking to this Saxon woman and her determination to rebuild the world of her people. From the moment when they had first met he had felt great ease, almost a homecoming. He sensed that she felt as he did. Both had lost their partners, Lodin having lost his wife and son to the sea. There was much in common between the people. Generations before, the Angles had come across the sea from Sweden, also from the sandy plains of Jutland and Saxon lands to its South.

Lodin was a Rus Viking, but many of his comrades were of Jutland and those same sandy plains. They had common language, that they could understand each other. Those, like Lodin, who traded on both sides of the sea, soon learned the dialects, becoming fluent and indistinguishable in speech. Many of the Angles had taken the new religion of the Celts, but most still believed in their hearts in the old gods and the old ways. Over many generations, since before the Romans arrived, new families had travelled across the sea to these islands with their kind climate and fertile lands. Some said that once the islands were linked directly to the mainland and the peoples had mingled freely. He knew that Ivar would be most interested by what he had learned from conversation with Ælfwyn. What would interest him strongly was that the fort he was watching was controlled for an earl suspected of collaborating with the Northumbrians, Ivar's enemies.

As he talked with Ælfwyn, food and drink was brought to them by two young women. Where Ælfwyn was a strong and handsome woman, these girls were great beauties. Cyneberg and Hildelith were the twin daughters of Ælfwyn, their older brother Wulfmaer was away fighting and their younger brother Ordric was tending the cattle, so Lodin could only guess what the sons would be like, or what manner of man the dead Ealdwulf had been. He took from Ælfwyn's account that Ealdwulf was a brave warrior. His sons could be no less, although the best qualities of parents did not always pass to their children.

In return for the generous hospitality, Lodin could only present his disguise as a trader who had never travelled so far North before, seeking new opportunities. Ælfwyn was eager for him to fetch his companions from the boat to learn more of them and about the places they normally travelled to in trade. She hoped they would feast this night, a welcome diversion for the whole village.

Lodin had to use all his skills to avoid this. Hafgrim, he knew, would pass for a Saxon, but Thoraldr and Oleif would not stand close examination. Knut and Alfarr would be even more of a liability in sustaining their disguise. He felt strangely uncomfortable. Often he had spied for the People, deception came naturally, but he was becoming increasingly uneasy in continuing his deception of Ælfwyn, increasingly anxious to leave, but reluctant to go. Ælfwyn was showing every sign that she would like him to stay longer, that he and his crew should sleep in the village, rather than sail off into the growing dusk. He knew that, as visitors from afar, the village would hold a feast and all would expect tales of travel and great deeds, details that he and his crew could not sustain.

He had already told her, in deception, that he was travelling to a meeting further North, that he had sailed up the river on a whim. He had been about to turn back to resume his voyage North when they had seen the village. Even so, he was finding difficulty excusing himself from her hospitality.

Lodin was saved by the reappearance of the old man who had brought him to the hall. Hengest was Ælfwyn's advisor and he re-entered the hall in some agitation. There was a dispute between villagers over some grazing and Ælfwyn was needed to resolve the dispute. This gave Lodin the opportunity he so desperately needed to take his leave.

"My Lady Ælfwyn it sorrows me that we can stay no longer, but we must follow the tide and you have business to attend,"

"My Lord Leofraed, it sorrows me that I cannot persuade you to stay here this night. I will release you only on your promise that you will return again and feast with us", said Ælfwyn, warmly embracing him in farewell. " I pray that should you learn of my son's health, and of the men of our village with him, that you or he will find a way of sending news to me without delay."

"My Lady, you have my promise gladly, I look forward to once again meeting with you" 'Leofraed' replied as he moved back from the embrace. They parted at the doorway, he turning towards the river and she turning to join Hengest to go to arbitrate the dispute.

Able to walk back to the quay on his own, Lodin had much to be pleased about. There was a new spring to his step and he felt younger. His meeting with Ælfwyn had provided valuable information for little expenditure of time or effort. He now knew that there was local war between Saxons, something Ivar had suspected, that the warriors might be away from their homes for long periods. He also had a place that he could return to if necessary without raising suspicion.

As he reached the quay, the old man was still fishing. Lodin greeted him, and his comrades on the Hildr, in the Saxon tongue. The old man grunted an acknowledgement and continued with his fishing. Lodin jumped down into the boat, paused, and then took a smaller outer bale from their cargo. There was weight to it but he threw it onto the quay with ease calling to the fisherman,

"Old man take this to the lady Ælfwyn with the thanks and best wishes of Leofraed the Trader".

The old man grunted again as an acknowledgement and began to creak to his feet, turning towards the bale which contained cloth from the Franks and a selection of trade goods, tools for working wood, needles and silk thread, work cloth and combs.

Hafgrim cast off as Thoraldr and Oleif fended their boat away from the quay with their oars. Knut and Alfarr stood ready with their oars on the other side. As they drifted clear, Lodin steered them back towards the sea. He glanced across the widening water to the old man, stooped and struggling to move the bale up the path towards the village. Lodin felt almost a loss, a sadness, at their leaving. Hafgrim shook out the sail to take advantage of the favourable wind, the four oarsmen providing steerage until the sail bellied, driving them Eastwards on the broad sweep of water.

Thirteen

Tonight, Ivar and his band were little wiser than on that earlier reconnaissance. They were inside the walls, but sloping banners of mist hid what lay beyond the first buildings and even parts of the foreground. All that Ivar could do was to form his force into two groups, moving out along the walls to surround the buildings, or whatever lay beyond them. They risked discovery, but any attempt to attack the first buildings could alert a larger force in the unknown expanse beyond. Ælfwyn had told Lodin that the earl Esla led five hundred warriors, but Ivar could not be sure how many of these would be present in the fort. His own surveillance had not suggested that the fort was home to many people, there had been no direct evidence of warriors, but perhaps they had been away fighting, as had Ælfwyn's much smaller band of warriors, to return again, presenting a greater threat.

As Ivar's party crept forward and around the first buildings, Einarr made for the gatehouse. His task was to deal with anyone trying to escape from the fort and to open the gates to his comrades who were still outside the walls. Two boats were to have made their way round to the quay beside the main gate, landing a second party of warriors to reinforce those inside the fort. As they cleared the quay, two more boats would replace them and disgorge their companies.

Until he swung open the gates, Einarr had no way of knowing whether these boats had come alongside to discharge their cargo of reinforcements. That there were no sounds of the boats arriving, or of their crews coming ashore, was good because no alarm had been given, but it was also disconcerting as Einarr would only know who, or what, was outside when he swung the great gates open.

Einarr had found the gates by following the walls round,

there was little moonlight and the mist was now thick in places. His bare left hand ran silently along the rough wall, keeping him an arms length from it. He found the first tower, then its gateway. Where the sally port's gates had seized iron hinges, rusted from long disuse, the main gates were hung from well-greased hinges. The timber bolts swung easily and silently on their pivots and the gates were drawn back with equal ease. As they were pulled open, Einarr came face to face with Red Osten, behind him a mass of warriors. They greeted each other quietly, as warriors filed silently through the open gate to mingle with Einarr's men, fanning out along the wall to join up with the second group that had been working round towards the gate from the other side. There was now a complete, but sparse, ring of warriors surrounding the area enclosed within the walls. This circle began to contract as the men moved in towards the centre, much as beaters flushing out game.

Einarr instructed Red Osten to send a small party to the landward end of the bridge to provide an advanced picket against any Saxon attack. Osten was to retain a larger party inside the gates, ready to swing them closed and bolt them against any determined assault, and to prevent the escape of any Saxons from within the walls. The other warriors with him were to join Einarr's group. As Einarr was completing his instructions to Osten he felt a presence close to him. He looked around and saw a tall warrior, indistinct in the poor light, but he knew it was Gudhrun. He turned and embraced her.

"My love for ever", he breathed in her ear, "For ever my love", she responded softly.

Then he turned back to Osten and she moved to stand by Einarr's left shoulder. A feeling of calm certainty flooded over him. Strange, how much they were one. He understood now the uneasy feeling he had suffered, it was like missing a part of him. That part was Gudhrun, now he was whole again.

Having briefed Osten and seen that the gate was left well

guarded, Einarr turned to follow the contracting circle of warriors, Gudhrun following half a pace to his left and a pace behind, watching to protect his back. If danger threatened, she would turn to her left and they would make a circle with their swords, each protecting the other, close enough to move together, far enough apart to avoid hampering each other's sword strokes.

Suddenly, ahead, to the right, there was shouting, steel on steel, a glow of light. The surprise was gone. The circle of warriors continued to contract and now was small enough to form two rows of closely packed fighters. There was slight confusion for a moment to the left. Part of the unbroken line had reached some kind of animal pen. Some warriors climbed over the fencing, it looked like a cattle pen, but was empty, and the broken rank flowed around the pen to reform on the other side.

Einarr could now see a pool of light ahead, the noise of weapon on weapon to his right was louder. A light breeze was parting the mist, the shapes of the buildings emerged in the moonlight.

He stepped through the advancing line of warriors, Gudhrun close behind him, towards the patch of light. He did not need to look, he knew she was with him, tethered like a shadow. Saxons were spilling out of the lighted doorway ahead of him, their eyes not accustomed to the darkness, their shapes silhouetted by the light behind them from the open door. The noise of battle to Einaar's right seemed much closer, then a warrior advanced towards him, a Saxon, no white cloth on his right arm, framed by the light behind him. He was a smaller man than Einarr and, although he had a strong sword arm, Einarr beat him back and down in less than a dozen quick strokes, striking his head from his body. Gale sung, as Einaar swept the great sword across and down into the Saxon's neck, sighed into the flesh, sending a faint vibration down into Einarr's arm as it cut through the bone and sinew, swishing into the down-stroke as it cut through the remaining flesh and broke free, power still behind the stroke. More Saxons emerged into the pool of light from the doorway of a hall. Einaar kicked the headless body to the right, it collapsed into an untidy heap on the ground, and he advanced into the emerging Saxons, Gudhrun moving close behind him.

There was the noise and confusion of battle. It was difficult to know an enemy in the poor light but Einarr's warriors had the advantage that they could maintain a line behind the groups of warriors taking on the Saxons as they struggled to come out through the lighted doorway. Einarr's comrades were too strong and too numerous. At their head was a whirling circle of sword steel as Einarr and Gudhrun swept through all opposition. It seemed much longer, but it was only moments before Einarr burst into the hall, to see women and children cowering in a far corner.

"Spare them", shouted Einarr, holding out his blood soaked sword as his comrades poured through the doorway behind him.

He saw no purpose in slaughter, but benefit in slaves and information. As his men formed up across the smoky, but well-lit, interior of the hall, they cast giant shadows, against the walls and roof of the hall, that towered above the terrified Saxons. He detailed a dozen warriors to guard the women and children, with instructions not to harm them unless threatened. He knew that Saxon women rarely fought as warriors but, in fright, or in defence of their children, they might be dangerous. A dozen of his comrades would be adequate to control them and prevent them escaping to cause confusion outside.

The mist was thinner, the moonlight stronger, but it took moments for Einarr to regain his night vision as he stepped out of the hall. Fighting like this at night was difficult. He could appreciate the disadvantage the Saxons faced as they came out of their well-lit hall into the blinding darkness to face an unknown number of assailants who had their night vision unimpaired. The white armbands helped to distinguish friend from foe, but it was still hard to know where the fight was heading.

Then there was a crackle, a whooshing sound, as a building to his right burst into flame, bathing the area around in a yellow glow, illuminating small groups of warriors in close combat, the heat of the fire driving away the patchy mist. Ivar had ordered that no Saxon warrior was to survive and the uneven fight was quickly coming to a close, uncommitted warriors watched, spectators to the conflict, offering suggestion and ribald comment to their comrades as they dispatched the last of the Saxons. Einaar became a spectator. Gudhrun leaned against him, a forearm on his shoulder, the other hand holding her bloody sword, its tip resting on the ground. They were splattered with blood and smelled of that mixture of leather, sweat and blood that was a familiar part of any fight.

For the first time, the intruders could see a large portion of the area within the walls. The building continued to burn brightly, driving the mist further away with its heat. The crackling and roar of the flames became louder as the roof collapsed into the heart of the fire with a great crashing sound, showers of sparks flying up and outwards. The burning building was the largest of eight halls, widely spaced to the East of the centre of the enclosed area and some distance from the surrounding stone walls. The pale stone walls were stage to giant dancing shadows of warriors cast upon them by the lively flames that consumed the hall. Einarr noticed small groups of prisoners, but all were women and children. Ivar was keen to avoid unnecessary slaughter, seeing the benefit of Saxon prisoners, but trained warriors would have required more effort to guard than any benefit their capture might have brought from sparing them. There were no old men, it seemed that the fort was home to the young, warriors, their wives, their children, rather than a protected village with the extended families that would be common in that community.

Fourteen

As dawn broke, wood smoke drifted across the walled area, mingling with the remnants of mist, the smell of fresh spilt blood and burnt flesh. Only one building had caught fire, the others being separated far enough to avoid the clouds of sparks that had periodically burst out when another shard of building collapsed into the flames.

All the other buildings were undamaged. In addition to the seven surviving halls, there were a number of smaller simpler buildings with daubed wattle walls, shelters for livestock, storage for food and supplies. The space inside the walls was a large open grassed area. It included a number of animal pens, some containing cattle. It was cattle in one of these pens that had alarmed the Saxons and begun the brief fight outside the halls.

Sullen groups of women and children had been gathered together in one animal pen surrounded by guards. Parties of Ivar's men were collecting bodies, separating those of their comrades from the fallen Saxons. The Norse warriors had suffered few casualties, a dozen dead and near twice more wounded, some by the accidental hands of their comrades. Fighting at night was always full of risk. A small group was busy forcing shut the freshly greased gates of the sally port, as sentries walked the tops of the high walls.

Red Osten had kept the main gates open, a detachment of his people guarding the landward end of the bridge. Outside the main gates, and just inside, he had placed a stronger detachment, posting archers and spearmen to the tops of the gate towers. Having made sure that the main gate was strongly protected, he had sent out scouts, some on horseback, to search along the road that led inland. One welcome discovery had been horses, corralled in one of the pens, providing mounts before their own horses could be brought upriver that morning. As was the custom, the warriors had brought bridles and saddles with them so that they were equipped to ride any horses that fell into their possession.

Ivar's captains had been reporting to him as the light strengthened. Their victory seemed complete and heavily one-sided. Within the fort there had been one hundred warriors. Many of these were not professional warriors but villagers who had received some military training. All had been killed, as had some women and children. There had been sixteen prisoners of the garrison, all Saxon, three being women, the remainder warriors. Ivar intended questioning them later in the day for current information on conditions in the kingdom. In the meantime, they had been kept in the prison that had been built by Esla's men in one of the halls as a cage of iron bars, easily guarded and visible to anyone in the hall.

Of his own people, twenty had been wounded and some of these would die during the day. Only twelve had been killed during the fight to take the fort. Under the confused circumstances of night fighting these were very light casualties. Equally good fortune was surviving buildings in good condition, large quantities of food, fodder and other supplies. Of greater surprise was the discovery of a large quantity of new weapons, stacked in a store house, as though awaiting a small army. These supplies and weapons would be a very valuable reserve through the coming winter, and Ivar was pleased to discover that the fort contained two deep wells, providing drinking water for garrison and livestock. Without further reinforcements and supplies, Ivar could survive a siege for months if attacked in force by the Saxons.

Through the morning, the victors stripped the dead of their clothing and weapons, while the bodies were carried out to waiting boats, to be disposed of at sea as the vessels returned home. This was the most economical method of disposal. Their own dead were buried at the north corner of the fort. A party with buckets damped down the remains of the burning building, ensuring that the neighbouring buildings would not catch light from wind-blown embers. As importantly, it ended the column of smoke which would be visible from some distance away. Ivar was not pleased that a building had been destroyed, because they would need all the shelter they could find, but it was still a very small price for the successful conclusion to an important step in his grand plan.

Towards the middle of the day, one of Red Osten's patrols returned with two wounded Saxons. The patrol had been sent to capture anyone approaching the fort. A party of six warriors, mounted on ponies, fell into their ambush, the patrol that Ivar and Gisi has witnessed making visits to the fort a year before. Four were killed immediately and the two survivors were taken prisoner. From these prisoners it was learned that their party now made a three day journey around the Northern boundary of earl Esla's lands, visiting the larger villages and the fort, and meeting other patrols at each end of their patrol route. This gave Ivar perhaps two days before anyone noticed that they were missing, perhaps longer for the information to reach Esla. Even then, it would not be immediately apparent where they had fallen to some mishap, or what that mishap might be.

Einarr and Gudhrun were walking arm in arm along the quay outside the walls. They found a convenient spot to sit, their backs against the rough stone wall, their helmets on the ground beside them. They still wore their mail, but both had taken off the coifs they had worn beneath their helmets and Gudhrun had shaken out her golden hair, cascading down over her cloak like a shorter cloak of gold. She wore the three quarter length mail coat of a berserker over a soft doeskin leather shirt and dark brown leather trousers, tucked into laced boots that came half way to her knee. Neither of them had worn the bulky padded jackets beneath their mail as was custom when going to battle. In a night fight such as they had just joined, the padded coats impeded movement and were of benefit only in a battle line where the opposing warriors might slash and stab at each other for hours, the jackets absorbing the blunted force of sword and axe through the protective mail.

Apart from Gudhrun's flowing golden hair she looked much like the other warriors, her mail coat concealing her feminine contours. They had both taken off their swords and dirks, but these lay on the ground within easy reach. They enjoyed the close companionship, the warm morning sun, the bustle of boats coming alongside to discharge their cargoes.

Through the day, most of the fleet would come up the river to unload men and supplies at the fort, or on the large island in the centre of the lake where a party of warriors was already cutting down the trees to provide an unobstructed view across the lake from the fort's high walls and towers. Many of the boats would then return home with minimum crew, only a small number of fighting ships and a smaller number of cargo vessels would remain through the winter. A party of craftsmen was already working in the repair of the ancient quays so that more vessels could dock to discharge their cargoes.

Gudhrun and Einaar shared the food and beer they had brought from the captured Saxon supplies. The sun warm on them, but not hot. It could have been a carefree summer only brief seasons ago when they would go off together as children to sit by the seashore to watch the seabirds circle in their search for fish. No longer children, they both felt their relationship changing. For all the past summers they had felt as brother and sister. These past two summers they had become a fighting pair, but now they felt something more, something they could not explain to themselves, much less to each other.

Their peace was broken by the arrival of Tryggvi with a message for Einarr to join his father inside the fort. With some reluctance they stood up, fixing their weapons and following Tryggvi towards the main gate.

As they reached the gateway, they had to pick their way through a growing pile of stores that had already been landed, awaiting removal inside the fort. The high level of activity was more like a commercial port than the collection of an invasion force and its supplies. There was much good-natured shouting and laughter as crews jostled their boats to a free space, or away for the voyage home. There was little evidence of anyone supervising the work, or any order in the landing of supplies, but Einarr knew that everything was following careful planning and expert ship handling.

As they walked through the main gate, they were met by more feverish activity. Carpenters from the crews were constructing the frames of new buildings under the watchful eye of Agmundr Ingimundsson. Aggi had been chosen by Ivar to plan the additional building that would be required when they took the fort. He was a strange thin man, bent back, sparse white hair, a bird-like appearance reinforced by his hooked, beak-like nose and small chin. As a worker of wood he was without equal but, more importantly, he was a born organizer and supervisor of craftsmen. In the previous year he had selected the timber and, through the winter, his carpenters had worked to construct the labelled parts. Some of the early arrivals were boats stacked with Aggi's timber, cut to length and jointed, ready to assemble. In the coming weeks supply vessels would bring more of these pre-fabricated buildings, designed in the Norse style of planks on timber frames. Ivar knew that time might be against them and did not want to send out gangs to cut timber locally, to be used to make frames, or be split as planking.

On following Tryggvi into one of the surviving halls, Einarr found his father and Lodin questioning the Saxons who had been prisoners of their own people. Ivar acknowledged the arrival of his son and Gudhrun, but returned to the questioning, which seemed to be almost cordial. Lodin was asking most of the questions in an easy relaxed conversation, Ivar periodically interjecting with a short question of his own. The prisoners were a further piece of good fortune.

The Lady Gytha and her maids Agatha and Hildithryth had been taken hostage by earl Esla while travelling through his lands. As cousin of King Edmund, the Lady Gytha was a valuable, if dangerous, hostage for Esla, but an even more valuable acquisition for Ivar. The warriors in the group had been taken captive in battle, some recovering from wounds. Four of them were of great interest to Ivar and Lodin.

Wulfmaer was a strong and handsome young warrior taken prisoner by Esla several months before. Little older than Einaar, he was of seventeen or eighteen summers, the flaxen hair and clear blue eyes of his mother Ælfwyn. Even as a prisoner he had the assured manner of a leader. Theodric was older, clearly a professional warrior. Shorter and broader, he was as impassive and immovable as a great rock. Horsa and Hunstan were young, with the look of farmers, little skilled in the arts of the warrior, offered to the service of their king by their village. Hunstan reminded Einarr of Tryggvi, eager but clumsy, a gangly youth, all elbows and knees and feet, and all moving without regard to their neighbours. All four were from the village Lodin had visited the previous summer. With the other prisoners, they had been held in secret by Esla, their fate unknown to their families. None knew why they had been taken prisoner, when others had been killed. Whatever his purpose, Esla had not yet shared it with them.

Wulfmaer had kept his ears and eyes open, gathering unguarded comments from their captors. What he had learned was that Esla was expecting reinforcements from somewhere, but he had not learned who these would be. So far, the main activity had been the arrival of weapons and supplies, brought to the fort by river in small boats, early and late in the day, in obvious secrecy.

For Ivar, the prisoners were a great opportunity. His vengeance was against King Aelle and his Northumbrians, not against all Saxons. By landing his advanced army in the Kingdom of the East Angles, Ivar risked increasing his enemies, a risk acceptable only because there was no other alternative for landing the total force necessary to achieve complete victory over Aelle. Now Ivar might have a solution that would avoid battle with King Edmund. From what Lodin had learned, in his visit to Ælfwyn's village, and what he and Ivar were learning from the prisoners, Edmund had his own enemies within his kingdom and enmity with the Northumbrians and the Mercians, whom some called Southumbrians. Ivar knew little of the Mercians who held middle England, but of the Northumbrians he knew much. Ivar had no quarrel with earl Esla, or any other of the Anglian rebels, but he now knew he shared an enemy, in King Aelle and his Northumbrians, with King Edmund. His difficulty in reaching some agreement with the Angles earlier had been a question of credibility. He knew that the Angles would see him as a Norse invader and a direct threat. To have sent an embassy before the landing could have achieved no more than to prepare the Saxons to resist. Now he might just have a way of opening a dialogue and convincing them that he was not their enemy, but a valuable ally. There was further beneficial change of which he was not yet aware.

Ivar ordered that new clothes, food and weapons be brought for the sixteen prisoners, that they be freed from the cage, in which Esla had kept them, that he might treat them instead as allies and honoured guests. As that was done he drew away to the far end of the hall with Einarr and Lodin, Gudhrun was sent to fetch her father to the meeting, Tryggvi was sent to summon others as Ivar required them. There was much to discuss, new plans to be made, new instructions sent to Black Gædda and Dagfinnr the Bold.

In the original plan, Ivar would have built a strong base around the fort and any close villages, leaving a large enough force to hold this base against determined attack, whilst he took his main force North to meet the Northumbrians, hoping to catch them unawares as battles were normally fought after the harvest was brought in and not immediately at the end of winter. Although this protected his rear from attack, it meant bringing a much larger force and leaving an important part of it to guard the new base.

With the discovery of the prisoners, Ivar now had several very worthy alternatives that would reduce his potential losses on the march North, allow a reduced force to be left at the fort, and allow a faster march on King Aelle. Ivar was already beginning to think about a more permanent situation after he had killed Aelle, and defeated all of his forces.

Ivar had long wanted a settled arrangement with the Angles

that would give him a staging point for voyages further South. He had been hoping that this might come after he defeated the Northumbrians when his power was demonstrated and the Anglian King would be keen to avoid a similar fate, seeing the advantage of ceding a small area of coastal land to Ivar in return for friendship. Now he could see a much more productive arrangement before he marched North, reducing the risks of attack on his flanks and rear by the Angles. Here were considerable opportunities that would need skill and thought to fully develop.

Fifteen

The oarsmen backed water and the Øvind moved smoothly away from the quay. Ivar watched her swing her bows, beginning the journey upriver. The Øvind was one of the smaller longships, some thirty paces in length and broader in the beam, more like the knarr, the trading vessels with a higher freeboard. Her great sail was furled to the spar and secured on the supports along the centre line. She only needed ten oarsmen on this sluggish river. The other ten oars were stowed alongside the sail. All that indicated her status as a warship were the shields footed in the shield rails along both sides. In the Varangian style of shipbuilding, she was heavier than ships built in the southern territories, a deeper draught, heavier timbers, better to cope with ice in winter. Ivar had chosen her for this voyage from those vessels anchored by the island that emerged from the centre of the lake. She was more suitable for carrying the passengers upriver than her larger sisters like the Frakokk.

In her bow was a small deck, today crowded with seven people. The Lady Gytha, attended by her maids Agatha and Hildithryth, talked with Gudhrun. The Lady Gytha's maids were not common servants but companions treated equally. Standing to their left, Einaar and Wulfmaer were watching the banks ahead, Wulfmaer pointing out some of the local features as they continued upriver. Theodric stood slightly back from both groups, as far as the small deck would allow. The men carried their weapons but were dressed in the comfortable clothes of seamen without mail coats or helmets. The Lady Gytha and her maids were dressed in high waisted skirts and decorated shirts, brightly coloured cloaks with hoods, embroidered bands along the edges, a splash of colour. Gudhrun wore trousers of dark brown leather, boots, a soft yellow brown leather shirt, a jerkin of sable pelts drawn in to her narrow waist by a broad leather belt, crossed belts at her hips, from which hung her sword and dirk, her golden hair loose, streaming down towards her waist. She was easily head and shoulders above the Saxon women.

Lodin stood in the stern beside Gisi, who was steersman, both in seaman's clothes but wearing their weapons. The stern deck, and the sail cloth that hung from its forward edge, formed a low cabin that had been reserved for the Lady Gytha and her maids. In the body of the Øvind, the other released Saxons mingled with forty of Ivar's warriors, half of them oarsmen. Ivar had decided that all the Saxons should carry weapons and Lodin had selected the best of those taken from Esla's warriors in the short battle for the fort. Wulfmaer had been given a fine sword by Ivar, forged by the finest swordsmith of the southern Emperor's court, but, fine though this weapon was, the young warrior regretted the loss of his own sword, which had been his father's, taken when he was captured. Also taken in capture had been the shield that had been handed down through his family, an unusual rectangular shield covered with highly decorated bronze.

There was a relaxed atmosphere, the liberated prisoners merging with the crew in easy comradeship, as though they had long campaigned together. With the party standing on the small foredeck, it could have been a royal progress upriver, the banks of oars rising and falling in a leisurely rhythm, the Øvind gliding through the sluggish water. Relaxed though all appeared, they were ever watchful, still sailing through Esla's territory, weapons ready to hand. On the advice of the released Saxons, Ivar had decided to delay the sailing of the Øvind until late afternoon, so that she would pass through the area of Esla's lands, where a ship was most at risk of being observed, in the falling light. The sailing time would enable the Øvind to arrive at her destination during the following afternoon, even if Lodin decided that they must moor up to a bank for the darkest hours..

Lodin recognized some of the landmarks from his earlier journey, but the river had few features to distinguish progress. The banks were tree lined and there was a narrow fringe of reed to both sides. The Øvind sailed along the centre of the river, which was still broad enough for three of her kind to be comfortably rowed in line abreast. At no point did the river run straight, in places, long gentle curves, in others, a series of tight bends as the river turned back sharply on itself like a writhing serpent. There was no sign of other human activity, the birds and animals went about their interests without concern. It could have been a year earlier for Lodin, the only difference being in the relative sizes of the Hildr and the Øvind, and of their companies.

As dusk crept over the river, the breeze against them stiffened. Broken cloud scudded across a moonlit sky. The wind against them only slowed their progress slightly and ensured that the river would see little mist. Lodin decided to moor up for the night as the cloud thickened, hiding the moon. He had only brief experience of the waters and none of the Saxons were sailors, having little appreciation of the position of shallows. This straighter stretch of river was a good place. As the Øvind coasted into the reeds, Lodin sent two men ashore with ropes to tie up to a stand of willows. The mooring ropes were left long to allow for the rise and fall of the tide in this brackish waterway, allowing the Øvind to float free from the bank. Behind the bank was boggy ground and marsh, bounded by a horseshoe lake. Although the swampy ground made it unlikely that anyone would attack them from the shore, Lodin posted guards on the river bank.

The Lady Gytha retired with her maids to the rough shelter in the stern. Einaar and Gudhrun remained on the foredeck, standing close together, oblivious to the light showers of rain that periodically swept by on the wind. Apart from the creak of rope and timber, the brushing of reed against the hull, the smack and gurgle of water washing down the sides of the boat, it was quiet and peaceful, just the occasional brief muttered conversation between those on watch. Lodin sent Guthrum Ericsson forward as lookout in the second half of the night. Einarr and Gudhrun stepped down from the foredeck, to sit together on the main deck, leaning against the centre support for the foredeck. There they could doze until dawn, but be readily awoken should need arise. Along the main deck, those not on watch curled up on the deck boards or propped against a sea chest. Some sat, their backs against the pile of goods stacked around the mast, gifts for Wulfmaer's mother and the village.

The night passed without event. The sun broke onto a clear but cold morning. The fickle breeze had dropped again and blew fitfully from the West, backing sometimes towards the North, before returning to West again. Gudhrun stretched cat-like and rubbed her eyes, before nudging Einarr awake. She smiled at him and brushed her lips against his face. Still the morning greeting of a sister, but arousing new feelings in Einarr. The Øvind was again underway, moving steadily inland. Lodin expected to reach their destination by late afternoon.

As they carried on inland, Lodin ordered Tryggvi aloft to keep special watch from the mast head towards the North. The river banks were higher now and the land behind them firm, heathland dotted with small wooded areas but, in places, the North bank was a narrow fringe, large swamps lying behind the firm bank, before giving way to higher ground five hundred paces and more to the North of the river bank. After only a short time, Tryggvi slid down to the deck to report to Lodin that there were riders approaching the river bank around the next bend.

Lodin positioned archers in the bows and the waist of the ship, while Einarr formed a small party of men to deal with any attack. On rounding the bend, they saw that the horsemen were led by Dagfinnr. This was one of the two groups put ashore as the Frakokk and her consorts headed upriver to attack the fort. Lodin and Einarr had been expecting to meet up with them at some point, but had not been certain exactly where, not having detailed knowledge of the land to the north of the river, or the opposition that Dagfinnr and his men might meet in their reconnaissance.

The Øvind was brought in close to the bank so that Lodin and Einarr could jump ashore. Dagfinnr dismounted to join them, handing his reigns to one of the riders. The horses had been ridden hard, their flanks streaked with sweat. Dagfinnr was an accomplished horseman, a stocky man who walked with a limp, the result of broken bones set badly. He had spent much time in the south and wore a coat of scales, bronze plates on leather, the heavy coat being split at the back for riding, secured against his legs by leather straps.

"My Lord Einarr, I thought we would not make this rendezvous", shouted Dagfinnr as he walked towards them.

"It was an easy ride until this morning. We found a large village just after dawn and it took much time to work around it. It is on a finger of land that points into the marshes, forcing us to go back to find a way to come down to this bank. We have ridden hard since then and feared we would arrive behind you."

As he spoke, Dagfinnr sketched a rough map in the earth with a stick he had picked up. Einarr and Lodin could see how this stretch of firm dry ground was also a narrow curving finger that reached down towards the river, a small stream cutting through the marsh alongside the higher ground, signs of beavers building in the stream. Dagfinnr and his men would have a long ride back around the swamp to find a place inland where they could easily return to the river, to cross with the horses to the southern bank. Dagfinnr made a full report of his ride from the first lake.

Sixteen

They had found great difficulty in bringing the horses across the swampy land from their boats. It had been slow and exhausting, with the ever-present danger of sinking into the soft deep mud and sand. They had to carefully work their way through this dangerous place for more than a thousand paces before the ground became firm. This ground rose rapidly, almost as a low cliff, and roughly followed the river inland, never coming closer to it than a thousand paces and often more than three times that distance, but from the high ground they had been able to watch the ships in the falling light, heading inland for the fort, passing several bends where there was no tree cover between river and riders.

As they rode inland along the edge of the high ground, into the gathering night, the moonlight was strong, the mist rarely rising above the bank. During the first morning, Dagfinnr had sent pairs of riders to the north of their line of travel. These searchers failed to find much sign of habitation, occasionally a disused hut, never a person, sheep, or cattle. They were surprised not to find villages, or at least scattered hamlets. As the trees became more numerous, collecting into forest, there were signs that someone had cleared areas in the past for farming, but new tree growth indicated that it was some years since anyone had tried to farm the land, signs of turbulent years, or of a great sickness.

Dagfinnr was in a quandary. Ivar had instructed him to scout the land along the river to locate any villages, looking for soldiers and fortifications that might threaten them as they took their ships inland. The constraint was that the riders were to reach a stretch of river to meet whichever boat Ivar decided to send inland, indicated by Lodin from the rough map he had prepared after his visit the year before.

Before the discovery of the prisoners in the fort, Ivar had intended to send Einarr and Lodin with a few men in one of the smallest boats. They were to meet in the second half of the morning on the second day and the boat would continue sailing inland. If they missed that rendezvous, they would have to ride back to the north before the firm ground continued round along the line of the river because they did not know the next place to head back to the river to catch up with Lodin. This limited Dagfinnr's actions. In what was now forest, he could not send scouts far to the north and know they would be able to catch up with the main party. This made his view of the land ahead, to the north of the river very narrow and, just a few hundred paces away from the scouted area, might be a camp of warriors. It did not help that the wind was blowing away from them, carrying off any Saxon wood smoke. Black Gædda and his riders should have an easier task, scouting the area to the south of the river.

It was fortunate that Dagfinnr had decided to continue riding through the night. They came upon the village suddenly, warned only by the faint smell of smoke and sounds of cattle. The trees continued close to the boundary of the village and they had not yet reached the track that served the villagers. Dagfinnr sent two of his men forward to take a closer look at the village, while the other riders very cautiously and quietly turned and rode back for some distance, before they turned again to the West. In the strengthening light they found the village track and, almost immediately, the western edge of firm ground.

The two scouts caught up with the main party shortly after, reporting that they had seen only villagers. It seemed to be a large village, perhaps two hundred men, women and children, but very poor, without tilled fields, or good grazing. Beside one of the nearer huts, the watchers could see two leather boats and what looked like stilts, suggesting the villagers lived off the marshes, depending on fish and eel for food. The two scouts did not see any warriors in the village and there was no palisade around the scattered buildings, just a rough fence of wattles. It was unusual for a village not to have earthworks or palisade around it to keep out wild animals and provide defence against any attack. The poverty of the hamlet, together with its isolated location, might be the reason for having no defensive works. It was no real and immediate threat perhaps, but cost the riders time as they worked towards the rendezvous.

Dagfinnr decided to avoid the track, not knowing how frequently it was used, riding as fast as possible through the trees, keeping as close to the line of the river as he could without straying onto the swampy ground. Keeping just inside the line of trees, the horsemen would not be visible, either from the river, or from the track that led inland from the village they had so nearly stumbled into. From their line of march they could not see far into the forest, but they could see out across the marshlands to the river. At several points they could see lakes, that had once been bends in the river, and islands of higher ground were scattered across a reed grown marsh. As they rode he saw the Øvind in the distance and knew they must ride faster. It was relief to see the ship just to the east of them as they rode down the finger of land, marked out on the map for them by Lodin, towards the river.

Einarr was pleased to learn that there were no large groups of Saxon warriors close to the north bank of the river and that Dagfinnr had suffered no losses. He was also glad that the horsemen would have time to scout ahead of them and their destination, and then be ready to be brought across the river to the south bank.

Lodin knew that the Øvind would reach her final destination some time ahead of Dagfinnr's riders, as intended, even though the ship would not now reach that point until just before dusk. Einarr decided that Dagfinnr should aim to arrive at the next rendezvous by the middle of the following day. He called the Øvind back to the bank. He and Lodin jumped back aboard. Dagfinnr followed along the bank until the firm ground led back inland. He waved a salute and the Øvind's crew watched him lead his men inland, disappearing through the trees on the edge of the forest.

Seventeen

The river seemed to wind interminably inland. Rarely was there a straight stretch of river, but it was still broad and the bottom could only be seen through the clear water in a few places close to the banks. The centre of the channel was deep and free of mud banks. Although higher ground to the north was some way back from the river, making a very wide flood plane, the southern bank was backed by a ridge of higher ground that came close to the river in several places. This was an illusion. The high ground was an almost straight line of earthy cliff and it was the river that snaked towards and away from it.

As they rounded the next great bend, they came across two small leather boats, each with a young boy in it. Wulfmaer called to them and they waved back enthusiastically, recognizing him standing at the bow of the Øvind. Now well out of Esla's territory, they were close to the village across the marshes, but the river still had some way to wind before they arrived. The two boys had paddled out towards the longship but their craft and paddles were no match even for an idling longship, their furious paddling at odds with the slow deliberate stroke of the longship's oars. Wulfmaer waved encouragement but the small leather boats continued to fall further astern. Light to carry, easy to manoeuvre in reeds, these simple craft made good fishing platforms, but not efficient boats to travel at any speed.

The leather boats out of sight, the longship continued through three more bends of the river and into a broad straight stretch. A rider galloped along the south bank, calling to the boat. Wulfmaer turned and began to wave. Lodin recognized Hildelith, Wulfmaer's younger sister, riding a grey pony. The higher ground came close to the water's edge and the track followed close to the edge of the bank. Lodin brought the Øvind closer to the southern bank but there was still some distance between the reeded margin and the higher ground where the girl rode her pony. She tried a shouted conversation with her brother but they were still too far apart to convey much more than their happiness, to share the knowledge that they would soon be reunited. With a bold last wave, Hildelith kicked her pony to greater speed and galloped away through the trees beyond the bank, her plaits of flaxen hair bouncing on her shoulders, the red ribbons and her cloak streaming in the wind behind her.

Eighteen

The sun was falling fast in the west, now little more than a thin red streak across the horizon, the wide sky layered to the darkest blue, as they rounded a last bend, to see the riverside village ahead. The rickety wooden quay was crowded with what must have been the entire village, Ælfwyn, Hildelith and Cyneberg at the centre of the front row of the throng. The quay was swaying alarmingly under the unaccustomed weight of so many and as more people thickened the crowd there was a real danger that those in the front would be pushed into the water. Lodin ordered the oars tossed and the Øvind coasted towards the quay. It was nicely timed, the vessel moving so slowly in the final paces that it touched the quay with no more force than a feather falling to the ground. Wulfmaer jumped lightly to the quay, finding just enough room to balance on the edge, embracing his mother and sisters, a boy shouldered his way through to the front, Ordric playfully punched his elder brother's arm.

Hildelith had ridden fast to the village and told her mother of the strange vessel, of Wulfmaer and Theodric in good health and free, but she had not noticed Horsa and Hunstan amongst the crew, or recognised anyone else on this strange vessel that was the largest she had ever seen. Responding to Ælfwyn's request, the villagers had been edging back to clear a space for the travellers to step from the boat to the quay. As Wulfmaer, Theodric, Horsa and Hunstan had come ashore the villagers surrounded them and there was much excited conversation. Wulfmaer had to part the crowd so that the others could come ashore and be introduced.

"Mutti, these are my new friends who have freed me from Esla's prison," said Wulfmaer, holding out his hand to Einarr and Gudhrun, welcoming them to his land. " I was held captive with

113

the Lady Gytha, her maids, and these warriors in the service of the King".

As each stepped ashore, the crowd began to spill from the quay to the track that led to the village. The bubbling of conversation became louder as the crowd milled, everyone shouting questions. Ælfwyn called for quiet,

" Lest we forget our duty to friends and guests, make way to the Hall". Then she noticed Lodin step ashore. "Leofraed, how come you here?" she called above the heads around her. "Gentle Lady," he replied, " I have much to tell you., but my story is the minor tale. May we talk after you have spoken with my lord Einaar and lord Wulfmaer".

The crowd began to make its way towards the Hall. As Lodin had ordered, the Øvind's crew stayed with her, making a strong guard for the vessel. Einarr had also been anxious to avoid overwhelming the villagers with more strange faces. As he walked with Ælfwyn and Wulfmaer at the head of the throng, followed by Gudhrun with Gytha and her maids, the conversation was of the release of Wulfmaer and the other captives, their health and joy to be free, their capture and treatment by Esla. Behind them the conversations were the same. For Horsa and Hunstan, there was rejoicing as they were reunited with their kin. Theodric had found his wife Bebbe, their young son Gadd and his sister Ricola. For the villagers, the returning warriors were miraculously back from the dead.

For Ælfwyn there was joy and confusion. Joy to see her son alive and well, when she had feared him dead, or captive. Confusion at the manner of his arrival. He had said he was with friends, most of those come ashore were Saxons, some she had met before, of the others, she had not met the lady Gytha but knew of the King's cousin and had seen her once at a distance. She still thought 'Leofraed' was a Saxon, but Einaar and Gudhrun were clearly not, even though they spoke her language. Neither was the ship decorated as a Saxon warship and it was unlike any trader's vessel that she had seen before. To the villagers Gudhrun was a curiosity, dressed as a warrior with a great sword at her side, head and shoulders above the tallest Saxon women, and a head above most of the men, she was young, lithe and beautiful, more than a wife to the tall young man, at ease with the Lady Gytha, as she was with Gudhrun.

The knot of people flowed into the Hall and around the tables that had been set up on either side of the hearth. As they sat on the long benches, food and beer was brought and placed before them. The whole village seemed to be crowded into the space with their guests.

Ælfwyn took her seat at the centre of a cross table that spanned the gap between the two long tables at one end of the hall. Unlike the main tables, the cross table had carved, high-backed wooden chairs set behind it in place of benches. Einarr was seated to her right, with Gudhrun to his right, Wulfmaer to his mother's left, with Gytha to his left. Gytha's maids had found places on the long benches.

There was a great bubbling of sound that swelled as the congregation reduced the supply of beer and food with great enthusiasm. Laughter and animated conversations made it difficult to hear what was being said beyond immediate neighbours. Einarr would have preferred greater privacy to discuss Ivar's proposals, but this was a homecoming feast for sons thought lost forever. On the one hand it had made the coming discussions easier because Ælfwyn had been swept along with the joyous excitement of the return, just like her villagers. The mood of celebration was firmly established, goodwill abounded, and Ælfwyn had not asked any searching or difficult questions yet, preferring to hear her son's account of how he had been taken prisoner and held, and of Esla's disloyalty to the King. Einarr and Gudhrun had been accepted into the community by association with the return.

Gudhrun was making a concerted attack on the food before her. Einaar was long accustomed to her ability to eat and drink most others under the table. With meat and bread between the fingers of her left hand, she deftly sliced pieces of each with the razor sharp knife in her right hand and, with equal dexterity, took the morsels from between blade and thumb with her strong white teeth., putting down the knife only to lift up the foaming mug of beer to her lips.

Einarr felt her elbow stab his side.

"Eat my love", she mumbled through a mouthful of food, a smile of enthusiasm on her face, "should I be your taster?".

With that she picked up a chicken leg, took a bite, offering the remains to Einarr. It was only then that Einarr realized that he had been absorbed in trying to pick out the conversation between Ælfwyn and Wulfmaer from the tide of noise that swept the Hall. Food and beer set before him was untouched.

Gytha was in shouted conversation with Lodin and Theodric who were seated on the long table that touched the cross table where she was seated. The long room was amiable chaos. It was lit by the last rays of the dying sun that still found their way through the open doors and through the smoke vent in the timber vaulted roof above them, augmented by rush lights, the fire in the central hearth not yet lit. Enough light to see neighbours but only an outline of those seated opposite. Einarr realized that Hildelith must have ridden hard for this feast to be prepared before they docked. He was aware that Ælfwyn had turned to him and said something that was lost in the noise. They leaned closer together.

"My Lord Einarr, I have heard much from my son this day of his ordeal and of your help in freeing him. How come you to fight Esla and his people?"

"Gentle Lady," Einarr replied, "It seems that your enemy is our enemy. You know we are not Saxon, but we have not come to invade your lands. We pass through on a blood debt. My father Ivar Ragnarsson has sent me to return your son and to seek your help."

He paused. Ælfwyn had not reacted in any way when he admitted he was not Saxon. She was still relaxed, happy, attentive, unsurprised.

"Last summer we sent a party to make a reconnaissance of this river. We learned of your difficulties with your neighbour, but we wanted only to select a place where we could land, rest for the winter, and continue unhindered to our destination in the spring. We have learned from your son more of the troubles in this kingdom and my father sees a way for us to help each other. Now we know that Esla is a friend of our enemy, that both are enemies to your King, to your village. Your own son and men of your village have tasted the hospitality of Esla and learned something of his dealings with the Northumbrians."

Ælfwyn leaned in closer to him, her clear blue eyes looking candidly into his, assessing his true thoughts and offering hers for his appraisal, two dealers deciding on the bargain.

"My Lord Einarr, I know you for Norse, from your ship, from your appearance, from your name. I take you for friends who have returned to me a son feared dead, the dearest gift any could proffer. For the future, who can say what we may mean to each other. For the present you are welcome. Know you that we are honest people, free in the ways of our fathers, loyal to our King, content in our lands. True, we rest uneasy with my lord Esla. The news that Wulfmaer has brought gives us grave concern. That you helped my son, you may help my village. That he and I may accept. That you help our King is for him to accept. Tell me more of your intent".

Einarr explained why his family owed a blood debt to the Northumbrians, of the betrayal of his grandfather, of his death. With pride he described how his father and his uncles had assembled a great host, how they had reached the land of the Angles, how they had taken the fort from Esla's men and found

Wulfmaer and the other prisoners held there. At times Ælfwyn asked a question or made a comment. Einarr felt he could trust this woman but Ivar had put bounds on what information he could share. Until they knew more in deeds, it was dangerous to share too much of the great plan. Ælfwyn wanted to know how many men had arrived, how many more were yet to arrive. She knew that a great force would be needed to defeat the Northumbrians. That force would need food and shelter, she was cautious that this could be at her expense. Einaar decided to tell her how many would be landed before winter. He told her that they had brought provisions, that they wished to trade for more, that ships would continue to bring in supplies and equipment as the weather allowed, and that they intended to march for Northumbria in the spring as the weather improved. This was in contrast to the traditional campaigning season of the Saxons, which followed harvest and into developing winter. For the Saxons, this made sense because it allowed them to raise crops and harvest them for the coming winter and it meant that their armed bands could travel light and take their opponents' harvested crops to feed their advance.

Einarr reassured her that Ivar had no ambitions in the Kingdom of the Angles, wishing safe passage to the North when he was ready to march, how they had intended to treat with the Anglian King, how they would avoid a fight unless pressed. Einarr also told Ælfwyn how Esla threatened both of them. It was certain that Esla was communicating with the Northumbrians and other rebel earls, that he could pass news of Ivar's landing to his conspirators, that Ælfwyn had only the choice of standing with her King, or with those who had slain her husband and taken prisoner her son. Einaar pointed out that by standing with her King, Ælfwyn's people were protected only by Einarr's warriors from an immediate assault by Esla.

"Let us withdraw to a quieter place," Ælfwyn said to Einarr and Wulfmaer, gesturing to Gytha, Theodric, Gudhrun and Lodin to join them.

The feast had now progressed to the point of total chaos and indescribable, happy, noise. The sun had gone down behind the horizon and rush lights provided a poor illumination, augmented only by the glow and flickering flames of the wood now burning in the hearth, so that no one noticed Ælfwyn and the others leaving the tables.

Behind the high table, one end of the Hall was partitioned off by a wall of hides fastened to a timber framework and extending upwards towards the roof, but leaving a broad gap close to the vaulted timber roof. Behind the wall of hides was a space with its own hearth in the centre, below a smoke hole in the roof. Benches and chairs were placed, a horseshoe around three sides of the hearth. Sleeping places were arranged along two walls, curtained with sheepskin. At the far end of the space was another hide clad wall, but the hides ending well below the underside of the roof. These were quarters for Ælfwyn and her children, but also, here in this first space, a council room.

The happy noise of feasting was no more than a low rumble of sound behind the thick cow hides. The space was lit by rush lights in tall iron holders, jammed into the earth floor. A small pile of logs was already alight in the hearth, adding to the flickering, amber glow. It was a companionable place, too large to be described as cosy. Ælfwyn sat in a high backed chair, throne-like and extravagantly carved. The other seats were arranged in a rough part circle to either side of her. Wulfmaer, Gytha and Gudhrun to her left, Einaar, Lodin and Theodric to her right. Gudhrun was sprawled in her chair, long legs stretched out towards the hearth, head resting, chin cupped in her right hand, elbow rested on the arm of the chair, a sated feline insolence, sword propped against her left thigh, only her large green eyes showing any sign of alertness. Gytha sat neatly in her chair, feet and knees drawn together, hands folded neatly in her lap. A young woman close to the height of her beauty, demure and yet with a confidence that comes to someone accustomed to authority. Wulfmaer and Einaar could have been two sides of the same coin.

119

Both young and tough, an arrogance and self assurance, leaning slightly in towards Ælfwyn, still a handsome woman, thickening in her middle years, with the calm authority of a mother and a village leader. Lodin and Theodric well-matched, mentors to young warriors, leaders and followers, supporters but not servants, respected for their experience, fit and healthy, but marked with the scars of past battles. It was a balanced group for a council of war.

"Leofraed would you speak?" asked Ælfwyn sensing his desire to say something but with an uncertainty.

"Gentle Lady, we are grateful for your hospitality, which once more I enjoy. It would sadden me to continue in a once necessary deceit, on a day when we start forward together. My given name is Lodin, son of Berfinn. I serve my Lords Ivar and Einarr. Forgive my art this past summer".

"My Lord Lodin, you are well met and gladly forgiven," replied Ælfwyn, a warm smile lighting her face. "I greeted you as a guest before. I greet you doubly today as a friend. You are welcome in our hall." Again that chemistry between them, as at their first meeting.

"My friends, we live in troubled times, my loyalty is to my family, my village, then to my King and to those I call as friends by their deeds. Let us speak as friends. Let us frustrate our enemies and avenge their ills to us".

The Lady Gytha looked to those around her. In her soft voice,

"I am thankful to you all, as will be the King, my cousin." She inclined her head to Wulfmaer and then to Theodric, " You were our strength and comfort in our captivity, for that I thank you". Inclining her head to Einaar, "To you my Lord Einaar and to your comrades we owe our freedom, a precious gift beyond all others". Looking warmly at Gudhrun, "I have a new sister, another precious gift. I will present the plan we make this night before the King."

Einarr told the story from the beginning, his grandfather betrayed and killed, his father and his uncles planning revenge, the reconnaissance a year before, the gathering of the fleet and the voyage to this land. He used his judgement of his new friends to tell them of the armies that would arrive in the North after the winter, and how he and his comrades would march to form the anvil on which the Northumbrians would be beaten by those northern armies. He then outlined Ivar's new plan to assist the Anglian King to defeat his enemies in return for unopposed passage for his army on its march north at the breaking of winter. As he talked, his audience was attentive. There were few questions, but those that were asked showed constructive thought and an acceptance of this as a plan they shared.

Lodin was sent to check the Øvind and her crew, followed to the dock by villagers carrying food and beer for the crew. The night had drawn in, a darkly clouded night. Lodin's small party carried light horns that gave a pale diffused yellow light, the candle light penetrating the horn which kept the flame alive against the cool gentle breeze. As they approached the quay, Hafgrim materialized in front of them, silent as a spirit.

"We thought you had forgotten us Lodin", he chided.

"An easy thing to do, but we bring you food and beer. What have you to report?" Lodin responded.

"Everything is quiet. I have posted sentries on the Øvind and ashore, five of us, the forward canvas is rigged, but I have ordered that there be no lights. How goes the meeting?"

"We met well, they are good people and Lord Einarr has won

them. We will leave horn lights for you to eat by, they will not show through the canvas but, when you have finished the food, put out the lights. Send five men ashore to accustom their eyes before they replace the sentries," instructed Lodin. "I will return now to the Hall. If anything occurs, send one of the crew to me immediately, whatever the time."

The Saxons had passed the food and drink across to the crew in the Øvind, left three of the lanthorns and returned to where Lodin and Hafgrim were standing. The two warriors clasped forearms in farewell and Lodin turned to lead the small procession back to the hall. They walked carefully in silence, the remaining light horns giving barely enough light to pick out the narrow path.

On entering the hall, Lodin found the fire blazing in the great central hearth and the noise of the feasters fallen to a low rumble of sound. Here and there guest and host alike had fallen asleep at the tables. His Saxon helpers returned to their places at table and Lodin entered Ælfwyn's family quarters. He found the party still seated around a hearth that now provided a warm dancing light from the blazing logs. It felt hot after the cool night breeze, an open oven ready for the day's baking. Ælfwyn was still deep in conversation with Einarr and her son. Theodric had left the discussion to rejoin his family, but Ælfwyn's two daughters were talking to Gytha and Gudhrun, almost a conspiratorial conversation, broken by laughter.

Einarr looked up as Lodin came towards the fire.

"The Øvind and her crew are well?" he asked. "Aye", Lodin answered, "Hafgrim has set watches and there is nothing to report. Its quiet, black as Odin's cloak out there, nothing stirs. What would you have me do the morrow Lord Einarr?"

"The Lady Ælfwyn suggests we take horse to the King's court in the morning. I will ride with the Lady Gytha and her maids. Gudhrun will come with us, and you will pick six men for our escort. Wulfmaer will join us, picking six men from amongst his people to complete our escort. I want you to take charge of the remaining crew. Assign men to guard the Øvind, but the Lady Ælfwyn could use as many as you can spare to help with the building work and to improve the defences. Theodric will be responsible for the people of the village. Work with him. We expect to be away for ten days from the morrow. If we are detained longer I will try to send a messenger."

"Aye Lord Einarr it will be done. When do we expect more men?"

"Lodin you will command for me while I am away. Gædda and Dagfinnr will be with you first. As we agreed, Dagfinnr will arrive in the morning and you will ferry him and his men across in the Øvind."

"Should I bring all of them across? It will take time to load and unload the horses"

"I must leave that as your decision Lodin, Swim the horses across if the river permits. Discuss with Dagfinnr what he has observed since last we met. He may suggest keeping some men and horses on the far side to scout further. We must learn more of the ground to the north of the river, but the Lady Ælfwyn and her people can tell you much of what we need to learn.

Gædda and his riders should be with you before night tomorrow, perhaps earlier. Station someone at the burnt village to watch for their arrival. When they arrive you will build a fort on the ridge at the end of the causeway from this village. In two days, perhaps sooner, a ship will arrive with supplies. Once you have unloaded these, the vessel will return to Lord Ivar with any messages you may need to add to these". With that Einaar handed Lodin a parchment rolled in a leather cover and tied with a thong.

"I understand Lord Einarr. Before we set out for this village,

Lord Ivar said he would reinforce us further. Will these men come with the supplies?"

"I do not expect that, my father sends more horsemen. If they have not met opposition they will be here in four days, perhaps sooner, following the south bank and Gædda's route. You must agree with the Lady Ælfwyn how to keep the horses. If there is space, keep them in the new fort, not on this side of the swamps.

Do all that you can to help the villagers. If you need help with building, ask Lord Ivar to send Aggi, or one of his carpenters. He may spare for us some of the buildings that require only assembly. I have asked that he send the Hildr and a crew to carry messages between him and this village. Once we are established here, the Øvind will return to Lord Ivar. When I return you will have completed the fort and we can decide with the Lady Ælfwyn how many men to bring up river to reinforce us further. When you start work on the fort, I want you to build it as a gateway to the village and clear an area of trees twice further than a bowshot inland from its walls. Before winter comes we may need to enlarge it."

Ælfwyn leaned forward to speak. "Lodin we will speak further tomorrow. The party will leave after first light for the King. There are beds for you here in my quarters and you must sleep well for the morrow", she said, gesturing to the curtained bunks along both sides of the room.

With that she rose and withdrew into her private quarters, followed by her daughters.

Nineteen

I t was time for us to think of sleep. I could have continued, but the bairns need their sleep. I was reluctant to end this evening, which had been so grand. Janet has been sweetness for once. She has followed the story, even asked a question or two. Perhaps I have misjudged her. Maybe she is shy and unsure of herself in our household. Perhaps she has found me forbidding in the past. My dearest Margaret always chided me for appearing remote.

I promised myself there and then that I would try to look less forbidding, to spend as much time with them, Janet, Morag and the bairns, as duty allowed. I felt so much happier and less burdened this fine evening. Dearest Margaret had taken a part of me with her. I know that I can never replace that, but here I had found a new joy. I felt stronger, younger.

The boys bowed goodnight, Mary curtsied, then rushed forward to put her arms around my neck and kiss me. Janet lent forward, kissed my cheek and smiled,

"Thank you for a lovely evening My Lord".

Morag kissed me and squeezed my arm.

As they shepherded the children off to bed, the room seemed so much larger and colder in their absence. Jamie limped into the room carrying fresh wood for the fire.

"Jamie old friend, put more wood on the fire, fetch me some aqua vitae, and a pig foot for Kara, I will sit here a while longer", I ordered.

He limped away muttering, after stacking more logs onto the fire, which crackled into renewed life from the glowing red embers.

He returned with the jug of whiskey and a silver tumbler, which he placed on the small table beside my right hand. He was about to speak. I motioned him silent.

"Jamie, I will need you no more this night", I said. "I will look to the fire before I sleep, but I want you to call me at first light."

He wished me goodnight but I knew he was muttering as he left the room. He always wanted to see me retire before he did, but I was not ready for sleep.

Kara nuzzled my left hand. She was so gentle for such a large hound. I gave her the pig's foot, a treat she has always enjoyed. She lay down by my feet and began to crunch her way through it, holding it between her great paws. I looked at the dancing flames and began to talk to my dearest Margaret as I used to do in the last year of her life when we sat together before this same fire and shared the end of a day, not knowing how few days we would share together. How I wished that we had enjoyed more time together. I hoped she could hear me, I could hear her responses as though she sat beside me. I knew that tonight I would again sleep in my chair before the fire and Jamie would mutter disapprovingly when he found me there in the morning.

Part Three -

Ivar's Bargain

Twenty

How I have looked forward to this evening. We will again have a meal together in my rooms. It is more than a week since our last evening meal together. The Winter grows deeper, the wind still cutting from the North, but I had spent some time with my grand children in the days between.

James and Mary had ridden out with me three days ago. We had followed the broad sands towards the English border. It had been a bright and beautiful morning, but so cold. We will see ice in the Firth again this winter and the snow thick on the ground.

This morning we practiced swords together. They are both becoming too quick for me. James is the easier to best. He is too cautious. I will speak with his tutor. Perhaps the dag and the hackbut will replace sword and bow, but not for many years. They are slow to reload, all too easy to lose winding keys and fuses. A boy must master all weapons.

Mary is hard to better. I can still out-scheme her, but she is so quick, she recovers easily from a mistake, and she is daring. She grows and her arm strengthens. In but a few years she will be the match of any man.

It was a welcome break from the English guest who had just returned to his own lands. My son Robert had arrived this week past. His time with Morag and the bairns too short as he preceded our guest by little more than hours. James Frobisher is a gaunt Englishman, of sour appearance, but a trusted ambassador from Elizabeth Tudor. Oh what a delicate game we must play.

He had arrived in an English carrack, escorted by one of our own ships. A outdated vessel but still much used in trade by the English, poor to handle, but capacious. We have often been grateful for both qualities. Our own vessels can out sail an English carrack with great ease and their generous cargo is always a pleasing addition to our store houses. Oft times we are doubly blessed, finding chests of English gold intended for James the Bastard.

For this meeting an anonymous trading vessel was a good choice, able to make use of our own harbour within the castle defences. Inside our walls it will not be noticed. A wise choice to journey by sea, avoiding the dangers of a long ride through lands of doubtful loyalty.

The Englishman has a sharp mind, with the silken tongue of a diplomat. His sour appearance masks a lively wit and, after a few drams of aqua vitae to drive out the cold, he has a fair humour and a wealth of stories. His mission was not an easy task for his mistress. She has sided with James the Bastard. The Tudors intrigued against our own late King, as Elizabeth now does against our young Queen. I canna abide James, but our future is no longer with France. Our Queen has not the wit to see that. She has been raised a French Princess, married to that sickly Dauphin and widowed still a child. Hepburn supports her, but with deep reservations, as do we. So the English Queen fears that our Queen bears a child that she herself will never have. She knows then that child will be the future of both countries, but she fears that future.

Our family has long controlled the gateway between our two realms. We still use the road built by the Romans, north from their great wall. It follows the river on up the valley beyond the Waters of Milk. In the centuries that have followed their leaving, armies and travellers heading north or south must pass through our lands.

Our favour has been sought by Kings and Queens. Elizabeth Tudor is no different. I noted that Frobisher had not been instructed to complain of our harassment of English ships on this visit, perhaps a mark of his mistress' need for our favour. She knows that neither we, nor the Hepburns, are of the Roman Church, or follow the foul Knox, free to pick whichever side we chose. She also knows that we have fought for English gold since the time of Edward Long Shanks, when our fathers helped him beat the Welsh into submission. She also knows that we have stood with the Bruce and the Stuarts against England, that we are good allies, bad foes.

If he expected a firm commitment, he was disappointed. I suspect that he was happy to be heard. His mistress will play the long game, as she does with Spain and the Netherlands. How I wish our own Queen had half her wisdom, a quarter of her art. I will not live to see it, but our two kingdoms will become one, and Scotland will be the richer for it. We must protect our Queen, that she brings forth the heir to unite the kingdoms. Her half brother, that jackal James, is threat to all.

Now that Frobisher has returned to London there will be more visitors from both sides. I was glad to have Robert with me at this time. He is a good fighter, like his elder brother, but he is more the diplomat than Erik can ever be, or should be. Frobisher recognises Robert's talent. This will help us in the time ahead.

To take food with the bairns and their mothers is blessed change from negotiation. I draw new strength from their company and from the saga of our family. It reminds me that the world is little different. We can learn from the experiences of those who went before us. It is the purpose of the sagas that we may learn from those who gave us life, to know that great tests can be met, as they have been in times long past.

It brings me joy to draw nearer to my blood. I see how we are, what our family has been, the future yet to come. This night Robert is with us as we crowd around the table for our meal. Jamie would have set the table in the Great Hall, he sulks that we eat in the turret room, but this is a more intimate place as we relax together. I am pleased that Robert will stay as I tell the story, a story he has not heard since he was a bairn in my father's company.

Morag is her usual cheerful self, Robert, still tired from his journey and our discourse with Frobisher, is more reserved than his usual robust and outgoing character, Janet is again in unusual good humour, the children are boisterous and enjoying the occasion. As we eat, Robert entertains us with stories of his recent journeys. He tells a good tale, his voyage to the Russias has much of novelty, and this land promises great opportunity in trade for our interests. It is many generations since our family last explored the vastness of this infant nation on the margins of the Duchy of Lithuania and the Ukraine. It is a land rich in fur, a route to spices and silks that avoids the traders of the Mediterranean.

Our meal completed, we draw around the blazing fire in my chamber beyond the turret room. Now it is my turn to entertain, to continue the Saga of Einarr.

Twenty One

Einarr was shaken awake by Gudhrun. "Come sleepyhead, the day is begun", she said, with all too much enthusiasm in the early dawn.

He rolled out of the cot, onto his feet, sleep reluctantly releasing him.

"It is not yet light", he complained, rubbing sleep from his eyes and stretching.

Gudhrun exuded energy that he did not yet feel. "Are you going to wash and scrape your face?" she asked, running a finger along his stubbled jaw, "or do I eat before you?"

He followed her through the hall, past those still asleep at the tables. Behind the hide wall at the far end was a rough table on which stood leather buckets filled with cold water for the guests to wash. He dipped his face towards the water and splashed the icy liquid over face and neck. His skin tingled with fresh life. Gudhrun rubbed his face vigorously with a rough cloth. Then she picked up the sharp blade and expertly drew it through the stubble.

"There", she said, satisfied with the result, "do I not make a better job than Agata?"

Agata was Einarr's servant, a slave girl six summers older than he, a gift from his father to tend his every need. Gudhrun never concealed her dislike of the servant, or any who intruded on her relationship with Einarr. A relationship she felt changing. No longer sister and comrade, but something else, something forming, challenging the comfortable past, something she felt but did not understand, something she was afraid of.

The village was coming to life. Some had been long awake, tending to the chores that started each day, even before first light chased away the dark clutches of night. Those who had eaten and drunk too well were struggling to come awake. Within the Hall were those who made the household of Ælfwyn, an extended family of relatives and servants. They shared the first meal of the day, but were joined by any of those from the village who wished to break bread with them. It was a social event, part of the planning for the day ahead. Food, and the inevitable bitter sweet Saxon beer, had been placed on the tables where small groups formed to talk and eat. Where the previous night's meal had been a noisy feast, this morning was quieter, with purpose, almost subdued. Individuals and small groups were coming and going in quiet activity.

Ælfwyn entered the main hall and exchanged greetings with those at the tables as she passed them, making her way towards Einarr and Gudhrun.

"My Lord Einarr, Gentle Lady, you have rested well?", she enquired. "Your horses and provisions should be prepared for the journey." Einarr thanked her again for her hospitality. Gudhrun mumbled her greeting and thanks through a mouthful of food.

"We are ready to leave at the time Wulfmaer and the Lady Gytha advise," said Einaar. "How far think you must we travel to the King?"

"That we do not know with certainty. The Lady Gytha is familiar with the King's progress but his court moves between the Halls of his chosen earls. With fortune and good passage, you should reach him within three days, perhaps four, unless his progress has been changed," replied Ælfwyn.

As she spoke, the Lady Gytha and her maids joined them and Lodin entered the Hall, deep in conversation with Theodric. The two men had become close friends, more like brothers.

"My Lady Ælfwyn, Lord Einarr," began Lodin, "I have been looking over the horses with Theodric and we are unable to find all that you need for your journey. We have discussed this and both agree that you should not reduce the size of your party because we cannot be sure how far you must ride, or what you may find on your journey. Theodric knows the ground. He has suggested spare horses. We have found eight good horses to ride, but you will need another fourteen."

"The solution is simple Lodin," replied Einaar. "Dagfinnr will be with us this morn. Wait for him on the other bank. Select what we need from amongst his horses and ferry them across first in the Øvind. We can then depart while you bring across the remaining horses. It will delay us little and we will have the mounts we need. With Black Gædda and his men arriving by nightfall, you will have more horses than will be needed here. "

"Aye Lord Einarr, it will be done", Lodin responded.

Lodin and Theodric left to prepare the selected horses and to await the arrival of the first horsemen. No sooner had they left the Hall than one of Hafgrim's men arrived to report that Dagfinnr had reached the river bank.

Twenty Two

Since they parted from the Øvind, Dagfinnr and his horsemen had enjoyed an uneventful ride. They had ridden inland on the long thin neck of firm ground and then skirted around the northern margins of the marshland, to ride south once more for the river. As they rode towards the river, the mixed forest of the northern dry lands had given way once more to willow and alder. There was no track, suggesting that people rarely followed close to marsh and river. In places they had to ride inland around the thicker clumps of willow and the sprawl of alder, losing sight of the water. They almost missed sight of the village in avoiding the thicker marsh wood. It was more by luck that one of Dagfinnr's riders saw the mast of the Øvind through a break in the branches. The boat hid the wooden pier, which was the only visible indication of habitation from the northern bank of the river. Twenty paces further, they came on a clear area of ground and found the wooden stake that had been driven into the bank on Lodin's orders, with a rope bent on it, leading into the water in the direction of the Øvind.

Twenty Three

Dagfinnr stood in his stirrups, waved, and called across to the Øvind, to be answered by Hafgrim. Almost immediately he could see activity in the boat as Hafgrim and the crew had obviously been awaiting his arrival. He watched as the lines were cast off the boat. He could see two of the crew in the bow preparing to haul on a thick rope that angled into the water. They pulled hard together and the rope began to snake into the boat. Then it snapped out of the river, suddenly taught, in a line across to the stake, water spraying off it along its length like a wet animal shaking itself dry.

Bringing men and horses across the river to the village was to prove a simple exercise. Hafgrim had rigged up a heavy rope between the stake and the timber jetty, running through pulleys fixed fore and aft on the Øvind, across the slow flowing water, so that the Øvind might be pulled across as a ferry. The boat began to make way across the river. Two more of her crew were standing in the stern, paying the dripping wet rope over the stern. Once the horses had been loaded, the crew in the stern would exchange duties, hauling on the rope, to pull the Øvind back across the river to the jetty, where the horses would be unloaded. This was faster than attempting to row back and forth, making the task easier. Loading and unloading the horses could not have been simpler. A broad gangplank was laid between boat and shore for the horses to be led across, to and from the boat.

The first horses to be landed were led towards the Hall for Einarr's party. As they were checked again, fed and watered, most of the remaining horses were brought across the river. Finally, Dagfinnr and his men were ferried across, leaving behind a small party that would scout further West along the river's northern bank.

Before Dagfinnr and his main party came ashore, Einarr

139

and Wulfmaer were already leading their party through the swamp, to the evacuated village, for the road which led inland. Once through the swamp, the riders were able to break their single file, riding in loose groups. At the centre of the party rode Gytha and Gudhrun, with Gytha's maids. Ahead of them rode the six Saxons, led by Einarr and Wulfmaer. Following them in the rear of the loose column were Einarr's men. The spare horses were spread through the group of riders and carried the supplies for the journey.

The morning was half done, the sun standing high in a great wide pale blue sky, streaked by thin streamers of white cloud. A pleasant day for the ending of summer. The warriors and Gudhrun wore their mail coats and helmets, shields at their shoulders, and each carrying a spear with their personal weapons. Gytha and her maids wore heavy riding cloaks over their clothes. The party was making fair time on the road, which was in good condition, showing signs of regular use and repair. It led straight as its Roman builders had intended, a broad path, with low scrub on either side, before the fringes of trees where the forest began. As they rode on, they passed narrow muddy tracks that joined the road from either side. Each track would meander through the forest to villages, hamlets and isolated homes. Some of these tracks showed little sign of recent use, fresh vegetation attempting to heal the bare muddy wound.

By midday they had reached the first village. It straddled the old Roman road and its collection of wattle and daub buildings housed the villagers and their animals, but also provided a local trading centre. Open-fronted buildings were occupied by a smithy, a potter and other craftsmen. A group of empty pens suggested that this was the market for smaller villages in the surrounding lands. Wulfmaer stopped to talk with the village headman but the party continued at a leisurely pace. Wulfmaer and Einarr had agreed that they would make halt further along the road, where a convenient stream would provide water for the horses.

When Wulfmaer caught up the other riders he had news

of the King, which he shared with Einarr, when he rejoined him at the head of the column. They would debate it further when they halted to rest the horses.

The sun was past its highest point as they reached their planned halt. First the horses were watered at the stream, which bubbled sparkling clear water along the side of the road, before turning away into the forest, following the shallow valley. The horses were tethered and the riders grouped together beside an ancient oak tree. Food was brought from saddlebags, a makeshift meal was taken, simple cold food, meat, cheese and bread, washed down with small beer.

In addition to Einarr's party, two other groups of riders had been riding towards the West. Einarr knew of one group, but not the other.

Twenty Four

Black Gædda and his men had followed the southern bank of the river. They had managed to gain the higher ground after landing on the marshy shore of the lake. It had not been easy. There was no marked path to follow and every step had to be taken with great care as they led their horses. It was with some relief that Gædda scrambled up the steep slope, onto the higher ground, his horse following with less difficulty. Here it was sandy soil with sparse tufts of rough, dark grass, becoming thicker and more regular as it reached across the plain towards a forest. The dry ground was much closer to the southern lakeshore than its northern neighbour was to the lake's north shore. On the southern shore, the marsh ended, dry ground rose from the marsh, a wide area, more than half a thousand paces deep, before the forest started, gorse and heather with clumps of bramble and scattered stands of young trees. This was not encouraging because Gædda's riders would be very visible to anyone watching from the forest. Even a man on foot stood out clearly, a man on horseback was hardly less visible than a flag waving in the breeze.

Gædda turned towards his men who were still leading their horses up onto the higher ground,

"Bjornulf, Arnfinn," he paused and cast his eyes across the riders, "Ah and, Sigbrand, ride to the edge of the trees and scout the forest edge while we wait here. If you see no one, send Arnfinn back to me and continue along the forest in line with us".

"Why don't we all ride to the trees Lord Gædda?" asked Arnfinn.

"If there is anyone to watch this plain, they will only see three riders and may miss us here if we rest our horses", replied Gædda patiently.

Arnfinn was a young warrior with some promise and Gædda was pleased to encourage his questions.

"Lord Ivar instructed me to stay close to the river valley that we might find any threats to the boats. Even travelling with care, we will travel faster than the boats that must follow the river", he said, pointing towards the broad bends that snaked slowly towards the west. "Now go the three of you. Be watchful and report back to me".

Bjornulf, an experienced warrior, led his two comrades south towards the first trees. They rode slowly as though they had no clear destination in mind and no urgent purpose. As he looked back towards the lake shore, the main party was hardly visible and, from the edge of the forest, they must blend into the grass and gorse scrub, but Bjornulf knew that any movement could make them visible. His small group moving across the plain would also act as a distraction because of their movement. As they drew closer towards the trees they would be the only focus for anyone who might be looking out across the plain.

The scrub was soon giving way to small trees and these became larger and more numerous. There was no sign of any people, only the birds and the small animals that frequented the margins of the forest. As the riders reached the heavily wooded area, they looked carefully about them. The trees were mostly mature oaks with broad trunks and spreading branches, still with a full complement of leaves, but mixed amongst them were other trees, with beech trees most common. Care was needed because this land was an area where snakes were common. The adder was shy but would strike if it thought itself threatened, the bite painful if not fatal.

The riders divided to cover a wider area and rode in and

out of the great trees, looking for any sign of a threat to Gædda and the main party. The forest floor was covered by dry, crackling bracken, clumps of briar and grassy clearings, no more than natural glades. Here and there fallen trees rotted slowly into the ground from which they had once sprung and prospered. Having ridden along and in the edge of the forest for four hundred paces, Bjornulf signalled to his two companions as they came into sight and they rode towards him.

"Arnfinn, ride back to Gædda and tell him that there is no one watching us," he said as the young warrior approached. "Tell him also that we will ride along the edge of the trees so that one of us is always visible to him".

Arnfinn nodded and swung his horse towards the lake, urging it to a faster pace. Bjornulf followed him only to the forest edge and then turned west, keeping the first trees close against his left. Sigbrand rode amongst the trees so that he could see Bjornulf most of the time, and be seen in return by him. Between them, they were likely to see and disturb any watcher, but none was to be found. Bjornulf could now see Gædda and their comrades, but with difficulty. It was really only the movement that attracted attention and they were less visible than Gædda had feared, perhaps visible to Bjornulf only because he knew where to look.

As the party of horsemen, and their two flanking scouts, continued west into the dying day, the forest drew closer to the low cliff above the river valley, bringing the two groups together. Soon the trees reached to the cliff and the light faded. The fitful moonlight was dissipated as the mist rose from the river, its tendrils reaching out to the forest. By this time the main party had moved under the canopy of trees, the two scouts once more part of the group. Gædda was soon forced to halt for the night. He knew that they must soon move away from the river to avoid the fort and that could not be done in strange territory without reasonable light. He expected that Ivar would take the fort, but he could not be sure. If the attack was a success, he would ride on with care, sending a scout to make contact with Ivar. If the attack had not succeeded, he would return to the fleet with what news he could gather. If the fort had been taken, his horsemen would watch the approaches, or scout further as Ivar directed.

As the first light broke, Gædda and his men cleared heir temporary camp, mounted and set off towards the fort. He sent Bjornulf and Arnfinn ahead with the Saxon Aldfrid to find out what had happened at the fort. Aldfrid had been taken captive on an earlier raid by Einarr's grandfather. It was not uncommon for a captive to be freed, choosing to remain with his captors as a free man. Although he had lived to the south, he knew the lands around the fort. While Gædda waited in the forest to the south of the fort, the scouting party headed north. Just before they reached the road to the fort, Aldfrid was sent ahead. If the fort had not been taken by Ivar, he could pass for a traveller, collect intelligence, returning to Bjornulf and Arnfinn with news of the Saxon defenders. It was past midday when he arrived at the fort, to be greeted by Red Osten and his guards at the main gate. The smell of wood smoke from the burning hall was still strong. He reported the lack of contact on their ride from the lake. Although this was not positive news, it did confirm that the area to the south and east of the fort did not support any new villages or homesteads and was free of warriors watching the coast.

"I will pass your news to Lord Ivar," said Osten. "he has given me instructions for you to take to Black Gædda. Do you know the village of the Carl Ealdwulf?"

"Son of Caflice?   I have passed through the village, some years ago", replied Aldfrid.

"You are to tell Gædda that Lord Ivar wishes him to ride to the village, studying any places of importance on the way there. Since you passed that way, Ealdwulf's village has been abandoned, but the people have moved into the marsh to an older village. When Gædda reaches the village he will find Lodin who

146

will hear his report and give him new instructions."

"I understand," responded Aldfrid, " till we meet again Lord Osten", and with that he mounted and turned his horse back towards the place where Black Gædda would be waiting.

Twenty Five

Birdoswald, come here," roared Esla, glaring towards the doorway, expecting to see his man obediently rushing in, responding to his command.

The earl was in a foul temper, waking from a drunken stupor, reminded again of the rotten tooth which his swollen gum still clung to obstinately. His temper was infamous, his relatives and servants trying to avoid his sight until he was in better humour, which was not often. There was always something that offended Esla, the black mood being as much a part of him as his right hand. He reached for more ale, drinking from a horn, the foaming liquid spilling down his chin as his swollen mouth tried to conform to the shape of the horn's rim, without any great success. Esla was short and stout. No one could remember him looking different. His body was almost square and his heavy head sat into his shoulders as though his thick neck did not exist. He was dressed in the Saxon tunic, shorts and hose, his chin shaven, his long blond moustaches straggling down to his lower jaw. There was nothing appealing about Esla, who had become an earl through his greed and ruthless aggression. The more he gained, the less satisfied he was, seeing threats against him everywhere.

Birdoswald entered through the open doorway moving cautiously towards his master. He knew that Esla, in a good humour, could turn violently on him without warning, but Esla in a black mood was very dangerous.

"I am here My Lord," Birdoswald piped.

He was a tall and spare man with a curiously reedy voice that achieved a higher pitch in fear. Birdoswald was a natural creature of Esla. His face was distorted as though someone had tried to pull it apart, skin deeply marked by the pox. His dark beady eyes were sunk into the pale, greyish, doughy face, and most of his front teeth were missing, a souvenir of misjudging Esla's mood the summer past. His back was slightly bent and twisted, an old riding injury that gave him a curious gait, as though one leg was shorter than the other.

"My Lord, how may I serve you?"

Esla regarded him coldly. "Birdoswald you pox ridden dog - where have you been hiding?"

"My Lord, I have been guarding the door while you slept, ready to do your bidding. You have only to command."

"I have a small task   within even your small ability," Esla stretched his arm forward across the table, his fist bunched. "Take some men and collect a tribute from that sow Ælfwyn. There are only old men, women and children in her village. Take anything of value,   however small. You should have finished the job before, when we killed Ealdwulf and sacked the village"

"It shall be done My Lord."

Birdoswald edged back towards the doorway, grateful to be away so easily. Through the door he turned and almost tripped over the boy Hunwald who was picking up the cloth that he had just dropped. Birdoswald's well-aimed boot connected with the boy's haunches, sending him flying.

"Fetch me Dreng and Hengist and be quick about it boy"

A second kick missed as Hunwald scrambled to his feet and fled. Birdoswald reflected with satisfaction that there was always someone he could vent his displeasure on. The morning felt better already.

As the thought faded pleasurably, Hunwald returned with the two warriors. Birdoswald was pleased to see them hurry to him.

"I have a small task for you that even you will be capable of performing. Fetch your men. We ride this morning". Turning to Hunwald, "Boy go and find us horses immediately," a moment's reflection, and "then you will come with us. It is time for you to earn your keep and learn the ways of the fight."

It had taken little time for Hunwald to choose horses from the pen and, with the help of the lads who tended to the stables, saddled the mounts and tied a bag of food and a skin of water behind each saddle. Hengist had arrived to supervise, allocating a horse to each warrior as he arrived at the stables. With Dreng and Hunwald there were twelve, each with a horse and with six spare mounts ready for the expedition. Hunwald finished polishing the bridle of Birdoswald's horse as the party awaited their leader.

Birdoswald appeared, brushing fragments of food off his tunic, and made his way to his horse, belching loudly. He impatiently ordered them to mount up, as though he had been waiting for them, and led the party out through the main gateway, onto the road inland. He had no intention of hurrying and the riders made their way at a leisurely pace along the well-trodden path, towards the old road that would take them comfortably towards the village.

They arrived at Ælfwyn's abandoned village as night was falling. They picked their way amongst the burnt buildings, but could see no sign of life. Birdoswald decided to make camp for the night in one of the least damaged buildings, which had been the village grain store. He set sentries and waited for the dawn.

Dreng was sentry as dawn broke. Birdoswald appeared at his shoulder, silent as a ghost in the strengthening light.

"I don't like this Dreng. Where have they gone?"

Dreng pulled his moustache, as if for inspiration. "There is the old fishing village in the marshes", he offered helpfully.

"That's no good to us though is it?" muttered Birdoswald, "it will be the devil's own job finding a way through the marshes." He scratched his head and looked about him. "No we won't risk the marsh, but if we go back empty handed Esla will have our hides."

After long moments of silence he came to a decision, " I know, we will remove all evidence that we have been here and go into the forest. We can watch the crossroads from there without being seen. Perhaps we will find something worth taking, even if its only a few cattle. They can't graze them in the marsh."

With that faint joke, Birdoswald broke into his curious braying laugh.

Birdoswald had checked several times to make sure that all evidence of their camp had been removed, before he joined his men inside the edge of the forest. He moved all but two sentries further back amongst the trees, where they could not be seen from the roads, far enough that careless sound would not travel to anyone on the road. They then sat back and waited. The morning dragged on, broken only by the changing of the sentries. After what seemed an eternity, Cynric ran towards Birdoswald from the direction of the road.

"Riders in the village," he gasped as he tried to get his breath back.

"How many? Where from? Who are they?" demanded Birdoswald. Cynric shrugged and held up both hands.

"Must I do everything myself?" raged Birdoswald, "Dreng, Hengist come with me - and quietly"

The three moved quickly towards the road, but taking care

not to make noise, newly fallen leaves silencing their footsteps, but making it easy to slip. As they neared the edge of the forest, they moved slowly and carefully from tree to tree, crouching as they went. At the edge of the trees there was bracken and thorn bush to provide some screening for a crouching man. They saw Eadbert lying in the bracken and they crawled towards him. He turned and held a finger to his mouth. They crawled even more carefully to join him. Through the bracken they could see, in the direction he was pointing, a line of riders emerging onto the road.

As he watched, Birdoswald was surprised to recognise Wulfmaer at the head of the column, but he did not recognise the riders with him. The line of horses was still strung out, passing between the remains of burnt buildings. Cynric and Eadbert must have seen the first riders entering the village from the marshland. There were horses with packs amongst the riders and it was hard to count them as they were briefly visible in the gaps. Birdoswald had to be patient, waiting for them to catch up with Wulfmaer and the two other riders who had reached the road, then he would be able to gauge their numbers. What made him very uneasy was that Wulfmaer was in the group and he should not be there. Even more worrying was that the party looked to be larger than the group with Birdoswald and they all seemed to be well-equipped, strong, healthy, young warriors.

Eventually, and it seemed a lifetime to Birdoswald, laying on the wet ground, the last riders had emerged onto the road and the column was riding West. Birdoswald noted that there were three women in the party, at the distance he mistook Gudhrun for a man, but disconcertingly there were fifteen warriors. Esla would want to know who the riders were and where they were heading. The village now seemed a dangerous place. There should be no warriors, but there was this large party of horsemen, there could be more waiting at the old fishing village in the marsh. A difficult decision and one that would be wrong, which ever course he set on. Birdoswald disliked making decisions, but he had no choice. If he returned to Esla empty handed, with a story of escaped prisoners and bands of horsemen, he would not be believed. If he waited until the riders were out of sight, which would take some time because they were not riding hard and the road was long, wide, straight, and level.

He could send two of his group forward to scout the village. That would take time and, if the scouts saw more warriors in the village, he knew they could not risk an attack across the marsh. Worse, they might be captured and betray him and their comrades.

He could send a rider back to Esla to give warning that something strange was happening, but then he was already outnumbered by the riders heading west, also perhaps by who ever was in the village. Esla would not take a lack of action well. In his present black mood he would take it very badly.

The only course open to him seemed to be to trail the column of horsemen and wait for an opportunity to surprise them. They would have to camp somewhere for the night. Once they were asleep he could kill the sentries and then take those sleeping. That was the kind of fight Birdoswald liked best, if he had to fight. At the least he would have horses to take back to Esla, perhaps prisoners, perhaps answers to all the questions bursting in his head.

At least there was now no movement in the burnt village. Birdoswald sent Hengist back for their horses and their comrades, with instructions to approach the road with great care. He watched as the riders faded into the distance and moved out onto the road, standing for a better view to the West. He could just make out the end of the column of riders. He signalled Hunwald to bring his horse onto the road. He mounted to see better into the distance. It was safe to call his party out to join him. He decided to send Hengist ahead, to be followed at a distance by Dreng, and then, at a further distance, by himself and his other riders with their spare horses. The hard dry surface of the road would not produce a dust cloud, which was something. If the riders they were trailing stopped suddenly, Hengist should have time to turn back to Dreng and then send him back to Birdoswald with a warning, but they would have to be very careful.

Twenty Six

Unaware that they were being followed, Einarr's party were eating their food and discussing the next stage of their journey. Wulfmaer told them that the village headman believed the King to be at Kett's Hall, which was more than two day's ride, closer to three days further. They could ride on through the night, making regular halts to rest the horses. This was not dangerous because they had a good road for now and, if the night remained clear, there would be the light of moon and stars to guide them. Hunstan expressed some doubt that the horses were strong enough because those borrowed from Dagfinnr and his men had already been ridden hard before they reached Ælfwyn's village. Einarr brought the discussion to an end.

"Friends, we need make no final decision yet. Ahead is a straight and easy road. Until we reach the point where we must leave it, we will follow it in comfort. If light, or road, begins to fail us we can camp for the night. If the horses grow weary, we can look for the first suitable place to halt until they are rested. Let us take horse and continue our journey."

At that, the gathering dissolved, each going to a horse, mounting, reforming in a loose column to continue on their way. Their steady pace was maintained as a reddening sun dipped slowly below the trees, its glow fading into a deepening sky. The stars shone brightly, combining with the waning moon to give good light on the white line of the road as it reached out for the horizon, its surface of gravel and chalk reflecting light from the night sky as though it was fresh lime wash painted with a broad brush. Had it not been for the road, which served a human purpose, they could have been riding alone, the first to discover a new wilderness. There was no drifting wood smoke to indicate a village, or any sign of habitation, no light to indicate human existence, only the night sounds of hunting owls, a barking vixen, the scurrying of smaller creatures, to which was added the sound of the horses' hooves on the hard surface, the jingle of harness and weapons, and the occasional low voices of riders.

With the night at its mid point, Wulfmaer and Einarr agreed to stop and rest until dawn. They had reached an open grassy area, which led down from the road to a small stream. With horses and riders becoming weary, it was too good a place to ride past. To the south of the line of the road was an area of grass and scattered scrub. To the north, the lush grass and gentle slope made an ideal place to camp for the night, with fresh water for horses and riders alike. Einarr posted sentries, the horses were hobbled, and the riders laid out their bedding rolls together. No fires were lit but there was meat, cheese and bread for a simple meal.

Through the night the sentries were changed. One of the Saxons, Berðun, wakened Wulfmaer. Berðun was an experienced warrior of twenty summers who had shared captivity with Wulfmaer. Although a trained warrior, Berðun was a poor man, a short mail coat reaching only to the hem of his Saxon tunic, above shorts, woollen hose and badly worn leather shoes. His helmet was of rough leather with iron bands, but he carried a sound shield and spear, a good sword hung from his belt, weapons issued by Lodin from those seized at the fort. He was suspicious of faint sounds to the South of the road, carried on the light breeze. He was sure that he had heard metal on metal and Wulfmaer did not doubt him. They quietly woke Einarr and it was decided that all of their party would be woken.

Only two sentries would be visible to anyone creeping towards the camp from the south. Behind them were the hobbled horses standing quietly or grazing on the rich grass. Their riders would be invisible behind them. The size of the party would only be known if it had been followed in daylight, the hard surface of the road allowing no tracks. As the ground rose slightly from the south to the edge of the road and fell away in a gentle slope towards the stream to the North, any attacker would be seen by the two sentries before they could see the main party.

Taking advantage of the ground, Einarr, Gudhrun, with two of their comrades, slipped away eastwards from the group, keeping low and edging round towards the road. Wulfmaer had taken three of his Saxons in a similar move to the west. Cloaks were laid on the ground over packs from the horses, realistic dummies between road and horses. Inside the loose ring of hobbled horses, the three remaining Norse and two Saxons, armed with spears, formed a protective ring around the Lady Gytha and her two maids. From their positions to either side of the camp, Einarr and Wulfmaer could see crouching figures stealthily advancing from the south of the road. In the dim light there could be twelve figures, a larger party than that led by Einarr and Wulfmaer, but hoping to catch the travellers asleep in their camp. As the figures cautiously crossed the whiteness of the road, Einarr and Wulfmaer prepared to move round and in behind them, ready to fall on the intruders' flanks. Both groups were unencumbered by shields, the intruders carrying only drawn swords glinting in the pale moonlight, but Wulfmaer's Saxons were armed with spears, their swords strapped across their backs.

As the intruders reached the mid ground between the sentries and the road, Einarr and Wulfmaer fell upon them, taking them by surprise. The attackers wore no mail and Wulfmaer's spearmen accounted for several of the intruders with little sound, other than the muted cries of those fatally wounded. Einaar's group tried to cut out four of their foe, but taking prisoners in a night fight was risky. It was a short but hotly fought battle with only two wounded survivors from amongst the would-be attackers. One had tried to flee, only to be struck in the back by Gudhrun's sword, thrown as he ran past her. As he lay on the ground, writhing in pain, the sword still shivered in his back. Gudhrun moved towards him, placed her left foot on his back and, with both hands, pulled out the sword with some difficulty. Neither survivor promised to last long, bleeding heavily from many sword cuts. As Gudhrun threw her sword, Einarr had leapt in front of the other Saxon and cut him hard at the shoulder, almost severing the arm from the body. Esla's men were no match for two warriors who had trained to fight as a pair and think as one.

The two captives ebbed quickly and refused to provide any information. Wulfmaer and Einarr were little wiser about the strength of the opposition but agreed it likely that those they had defeated were most of the force. There was no evidence of any other group trying to stealthily approach the temporary camp. There was also no clear indication of where the men had come from, but it was unlikely that they would have come far from where their horses and remaining comrades would be.

"We will search out the rest of their party. They must have horses nearby," said Wulfmaer.

His Saxons formed up around him, he and Einaar having agreed that was adequate for the search party. Followed closely by his Saxons, Wulfmaer carefully crossed the road, heading back in the direction their attackers had come from, but keeping low and to the East of the likely route, leaving Einarr and his small group to guard the road. Wulfmaer's party cleared the open grassy ground and reached the scattered brush. Still no sign of horses, or warriors. The brush thickened towards the edge of the forest.

" Is that you Birdoswald?" a young voice called softly from the trees ahead and to Wulfmaer's right. The voice sounded very young and nervous. Wulfmaer signed his companions to fan out to either side.

"Birdoswald?"

"Yes", muttered Wulfmaer in response.

"Have you taken them?"

Before Wulfmaer could mutter a further reply, there was a

cry and a scuffle.

"Its only a boy", Berðun called from where the first voice had come.

Some further scuffling, an oath from Berðun and a muffled cry. Wulfmaer reached him to find he had the boy pinned to the ground. The light was poor but the lad's eyes seemed to be bulging in terror, Berðun's spear shaft forced across his mouth as a gag. While the frightened boy was pinned down, Eadbald, Berðun's younger brother knelt down and slipped leather horse hobbles over the boy's feet. Then they turned him over onto his stomach, face pushed roughly into the ground, and tied his hands behind him with a leather thong.

"Not a sound," cautioned Berðun as he turned the boy round again and sat him up.

"Boy tell me who you are and where come you from. Tell me true. Tell me false and you will lie dead with the other dogs" said Wulfmaer.

"My Lord I am Hunwald from Lord Esla's Hall. Please spare me. I am sent only to tend the horses. I am no warrior."

"What others came here with you?"

"My Lord there were but these and these," the boy replied, holding up his spread hands awkwardly behind him, then again two fingers of one hand. His voice still shaking but the fear passing.

"Know you who I am?"

"N-N- No my Lord. I heard Birdoswald say that we follow Wulfmaer, son of Ealdwulf. Perhaps you are he"

"How long have you followed our riders?"

"My Lord one of our band was watching the village of the Lady Ælfwyn. We saw riders leaving and we followed. When you made camp Birdoswald said he would kill you all while you slept."

"How old are you boy?"

"Twelve summers   I,   I think My Lord."

"My sword does not feed on scraps, but play me false and you will not see the next summer."

Wulfmaer turned and began walking back to their camp. Hunwald was tied onto one of the horses, his hands still tied behind him. The Saxon warriors followed Wulfmaer leading the horses.

Back at the camp, Wulfmaer discovered that the two wounded prisoners had died before they could provide any useful information. Hunwald was now all the more valuable, even though he had not been trusted by Birdoswald with any information, other than what he had needed as a very junior member of the band, which was very little, and what he had overheard, which was rather more useful to Einarr and Wulfmaer.

The captured horses were a useful addition to their resources. It solved the problem of what to do with Esla's dead warriors.

Each body was wrapped in a cloak and tied over the saddle of a horse. Einarr was pleased with the idea because it removed the bodies from the scene of the fight and it meant that, when they left the hard surface of the road later in the morning, their horses would leave prints, showing a group of riders, now grown by thirteen more warriors, the horse ridden by the boy carrying a pack of stones to make its prints look like those of an animal carrying a fully equipped warrior.

If Esla had sent out a second group of riders, this would delay the discovery of what had happened and the larger group would confuse anyone following them. Wulfmaer and the Lady Gytha were confident that the bodies would add weight to their charges against Esla when they met with the King. They were certain that amongst the King's retinue would be friends of Esla who would send him news of the failure of his men. Possession of the bodies would leave no room for doubt of their total victory.

With the first light of dawn streaking the eastern sky, the riders formed up and set off again along the arrow straight road. It was to be an uneventful ride. Leading the additional horses with their grim loads slowed the pace, but they reached the rough track, heading off through the forest, where they would leave the hard road, by mid morning in good time.

Once off the road, Einarr called a halt in a clearing. While they took a brief rest and checked all of the horses, Einarr sent three men back towards the road to look for any signs that they were being followed. Eyvald, a Russ Viking who had voyaged with Einarr's uncle Bjorn, with Eindridi, who was one of the Frakokk's crew, and Eldwyn, one of the Saxons they had freed at the fort, made up this small group. Eldwyn knew the area well and they were not far from his village, which they would pass through on their way to Kett's Hall.

Eyvald was a skilled warrior, his keen eyesight and hearing legendary. Eindridi was worth six in a fight. He was tall and broad, the only warrior who could best the ugly giant Ulf in a wrestling contest. They rode quietly back through the forest towards the old Roman road. Two hundred paces from the edge of the forest. Eyvald and Eldwyn dismounted, leaving Eindridi holding the reins of their horses. If they needed him in a fight, or their horses to flee a larger force, Eindridi could be with them in moments, but their mounts would not be visible through the trees. Eyvald watched patiently, time passed slowly, but eventually he was satisfied that no one was following them. He rose from his cramped position and stretched.

"Come Eldwyn, I see no followers, we will rejoin our comrades".

Eldwyn nodded his understanding and agreement. A quiet man not given to much talk. He walked with Eyvald back to Eindridi and the horses.

"Nothing?", enquired Eindridi, still sitting on his horse. "Nothing", responded Eyvald, "no one and no thing has passed on the road, nor in the trees to either side. I wonder that anyone uses this road."

"Oh it is used oft times. Merchants, soldiers, herdsmen to market," offered Eldwyn, his contribution surprising his comrades, not by its content but because, for him, it was a speech.

In the short time they had known him they had become accustomed to his lack of words, a shrug, a grunt, a movement of his head being his normal response. Even that was rare, as he listened intently to discussions, reluctant to participate. Although he stood aside from the conversations of his comrades, he had already shown that he did not hang back in a fight, stepping forward in determination and skill. His clothes were good, in the Saxon style of hose, shorts, tunic, and cloak, all of finer cloth than a villager could be expected to own, yet not the garb of a wealthy man. His fair hair was long, with narrow plaits to either side of his face, and drooping moustaches hanging below his lower jaw to either side of a square and shaven chin. He had the strength of a warrior fed on the best cuts of meat and exercised regularly in training with shield and weapons. When he did speak he had the accent of nobility, all that marked him out as a noble or a professional warrior, not a farmer with some training in arms.

His appearance contrasted with his two comrades. They both wore leather trousers, woollen shirts and fur jerkins. Neither wore a cloak, these being rolled behind their saddles. Both had long hair and full beards. Eyvald's faded yellow hair was streaked with lighter shades, almost grey. Eindridi wore his hair neatly cut to the shoulder, his beard trimmed, his bright blue eyes peering out from below dark bushy eyebrows that contrasted with his pale yellow hair.

Together, the three had the air of competent warriors but, although they carried swords, dirks and shields, none wore a helmet, mail coat, or carried a spear. Helmet and mail coat were bundled into leather saddlebags on each horse, spears had been left with the main party, watchers relying on nimble speed and good eyesight, taking cover and avoiding a fight.

They soon caught up with their main party and reported to Einarr and Wulfmaer that there was no one following. Their comrades had been taking a steady pace, still leading the captured horses with their grizzly loads. The forest was thick with oak trees, bracken, and a mixture of birch and ash trees, the rough path winding between the trees, kept bare by the passage of other travellers. As they rode, they passed close to isolated huts of foresters and charcoal burners, sweet wood smoke drifting through the trees.

By mid afternoon the air was becoming hot and humid, suggesting an approaching storm. The trail they were riding was becoming wider and showing greater use. There were scattered huts to the left, as they rode on, the huts became more numerous, becoming a village. A small group of villagers formed beside the track to greet the strange riders. At the front of the group was a young man who could be Eyvald some years before. His face broke into a broad grin as Eyvald rode up the column of horses towards him, jumped down from his horse and embraced his younger brother Leofgar.

Eyvald turned to introduce his companions. Leofgar invited them to spend the night in his village. He could offer only a modest feast, but it was hot food and somewhere dry to sleep as the storm swept in. The hall was small but more than adequate for villagers and guests. Eyvald asked his brother for the use of a barn and compound to unload the packs from their horses and to feed and water their mounts. The bodies were lifted down and placed together in a row inside the barn, the other packs stacked away from them. Four of Einarr's warriors were given the task of guarding the barn. As yet the bodies were not pungent but they were beginning to smell, thanks to the warmer day.

Einarr learned from Leofgar that Eyvald had left after a violent quarrel with their father. In his place, Leofgar had become Alderman after the death of their father Pendraed a year past. Leofgar was unsure why his brother and father had disagreed so strongly, but he wondered if Eyvald would now stay and take his place as Alderman. Although he was pleased to see his brother well, he had become accustomed to his position in the village. For his part, Eyvald assured him that his future was now elsewhere, he might visit again in the future, but had no intention of settling back where he had started.

Unsure of where his brother stood in loyalty to the King, Eyvald and his comrades avoided discussion of their journey or their business. Eyvald led his brother to believe that their party were mercenaries, travelling through the King's lands, but he did not volunteer any useful details. Leofgar displayed little interest in their mission and played the host well. As the villagers had no contact with the four Norse guarding the horses and cargo, the riders consisted mostly of Saxons and several of these were from villages not far away. Wulfmaer and Eyvald led the conversation for their comrades and the King's cousin was known by sight to some of those in the Leofgar's village. Armed bands were not unusual travellers, including some, in a party of riders, who may have had different origins from lands far away. It was easy for Leofgar to assume that his brother was on a mission for the King, perhaps escorting the King's cousin and her maids, and unable to share any information about the nature of that mission.

As the feast came to its conclusion, Einarr and his comrades slept in the hall around the dying embers of the fire. This was all that they required and much improved on the prospect of sleeping without shelter during a storm. In the morning they woke refreshed and stepped out into a clear cool day. From the many large puddles around the buildings, it had rained hard during the night, the water draining slowly through the sandy soil.

Einarr and Wulfmaer first checked the guards and the cargo in the barn. No one had approached the barn during the night and everything was in order, ready to be loaded back onto the horses. As their comrades emerged from the hall, they made their way to saddle the horses and secure the loads, ready to leave the village.

Leofgar and a small number of senior villagers saw them on their way with their best wishes and the expressed hope that Eyvald would visit them again. For the two brothers, there had been genuine pleasure at their meeting, but Eyvald suspected that his brother was pleased to see him continue on his journey. For Einarr's party, the feast and the accommodation had done little to delay their journey, and much to make it easier. Had they not had a village to break their journey in, they would still have had to make camp until the storm played itself out, but suffer a wet, cold, uncomfortable night without adequate shelter.

Although none of their comrades were certain who might support the King and who might rebel, they had not left any useful information to an enemy and what they had told their hosts was misleading. In return they had learned that the King, with his court, was indeed at Kett's Hall, Leofgar had only returned from business there two days before, and that they could expect to reach that village before nightfall.

They made several short halts, to check on their horses, taking a break for food and water where their path forded small streams. The trees were still mostly in full leaf and the sunlight filtered down through their canopy. They could not be sure of time, but it must be well towards nightfall, judging from the angle the sunlight cast. It came as a surprise when they reached Ketts Hall. The forest suddenly gave way to pastures, there was no warning, no gradual thinning of the trees. They had burst into another world. Einarr had expected a small hamlet, or a hall surrounded by scattered farms. What lay before them was a large and prosperous village.

From the trees, pastureland reached to the foot of wooden palisades that enclosed many huts, and several larger buildings. The path ran directly to a small gateway without towers, obvious only because the gates stood open and welcoming. Beyond the gates, paved roads connected the buildings. Mostly, the roads were of chalk and gravel, wide enough for a cart and oxen to pass, hard from years of traffic and layers of new chalk and gravel. It was almost a town. There were homesteads, most with animal pens alongside them, the domestic animals of the household, a cow for milking, a few pigs, some sheep and goats. Chickens and geese wandering free, picking up choice morsels from the ground around the buildings.

Einarr could see that they had entered through a smaller road that ran directly across the palisaded township, it really was too large to be called a village, cutting a much broader paved road that formed with it a cross. The wider road went out through gateways that were overlooked by wooden towers, in which sentries could be seen. Each of the four quadrants of the village was divided up by smaller pathways, some of chalk and gravel, but many were paved with wood. Where the two cross roads were straight and level, the smaller paths followed less regimented routes, in places winding their way around buildings that were larger than their neighbours, spoiling any attempt, if attempt there had once been, to form precise grids. The buildings varied greatly, not only in size, but also in structure. From their entrance towards the crossroads, Einarr's party rode past what might be the poorer houses. These were round huts with steep conical straw roofs. The walls were smooth plastered, the only piercings being the entrance doors. Some were clearly storehouses, but others sheltered families. Towards the crossroads stood larger houses. These had straight walls, some smooth plastered but others showing the heavy timber frames of substantial homes, a few being clad in oak planks in place of the more common washed wattle and daub plastering. The wash varied from building to

166

building. In some it was a dazzling white but on most it was coloured yellow, brown, or pink, in all shades of those colours. Here and there were some of the inhabitants, children playing and women attending to homely chores. As the riders passed, they paused in their activity to watch with curiosity, before returning to work or play.

As the riders approached the cross roads, they could see that the northwest quadrant comprised a large clear gravel area in front of a substantial timbered building. The Hall had stood there for many years, its timbers decorated with carvings, a lower palisade, twice the height of a man, stretching out on either side, round to the outer walls that rose the height of a man and a half higher. Within its palisade were a variety of smaller buildings, stores, quarters for servants and workshops, their roofs visible above the palisade. Facing it, the forth quadrant appeared to be given to the homes of merchants and craftsmen. Several of the buildings fronting to the main road being low open-fronted barns, housing potter, wheelright, cooper, blacksmith and carpenter, all busy with their work. Most of the visible people were working in this area. The quietest area being the quadrant in which stood the Hall, the principal building. Einarr was surprised that there was no guard at the entrance to the Hall and feared that the King had moved on to another village or hamlet.

As they reached the crossroads and the clear area in front of the Hall, the rough column of twos, in which the riders had been formed, spread to allow Gudhrun and the Lady Gytha to ride forward to join Einaar and Wulfmaer, Gytha's maids following behind them. Several of the craftsmen came to the fronts of their shops to look at the group of riders with a keen interest.

The leaders rode slowly forward towards the main entrance to the Hall, their comrades grouping loosely together by the cross roads, the smell of blood and death hanging heavy around the pack horses, the day having been much warmer than expected.

The leaders came to a halt before the wide doorway to be met by a man of middle years, by his clothing and decoration, a man of some substance, but not with the presence of a warrior. He had a look of disapproval and uncertainty contending on his face. He had the manner of a merchant, or an official, keen to take his wealth, or his master's position, as indication of superiority. Before him were riders he did not recognise, dust coating their cloaks. As he was about to speak, the Lady Gytha pushed back the hood of her cloak and the man's manner changed instantly to deference.

"Good day Saba, where are your master and my cousin the King?" enquired Gytha, using the man's nickname, his given name being Sabert.

"My Lady, the King and my master are hunting. They will be back shortly before the light dies", replied Sabert, wringing his hands together as though trying to wash off some hideous stain.

" I am sorry that we did not know of your arrival. Forgive our poor welcome. Will you come into the Hall that we may offer refreshment".

As he spoke, his hands ceased their symbolic ablutions and began flapping like nervous doves behind his back. Two young boys and a girl hurried out from the Hall at the directions indicated by the hands, taking the reigns of the horses. Einarr, Wulfmaer and Gudhrun swung down from their mounts with a practiced ease. Gytha was helped down from the saddle by her maids, who shook out her cloak and tried to brush off some of the accumulated dust.

Sabert gave every indication that he expected to be introduced to Gytha's companions, but she took off her gloves to swish dust from her cloak, moving imperiously past him towards the Hall's interior, Wulfmaer to her left, Gudhrun and Einaar to her right.

As she passed him, "Thank you Saba, food and drink

would be most welcome while we await the King's return. Send grooms to tend our riders and their horses".

Sabert knew well how far to play his self importance and stepped back, turning as they passed him. The Lady Gytha knew the Hall and made for the centre of the main room with its great tables and chairs. Where Wulfmaer's Hall at the village of Depenham had been a simple barn-like structure divided into three main areas by cross frames clad in hides, Ketts Hall was an altogether grander building enclosing a large courtyard with several annexes and extensions added to the original building.

Gudhrun was surprised and amused by the way that Gytha had addressed Sabert. It was so very different from the Gytha she had quickly come to know, relaxed, friendly and informal with all, servants, or well borne. To Sabert she had been curt and overbearing, the Lady to the meanest commoner. As they sat and Sabert scurried off to order refreshment, Gytha turned to Gudhrun with a smile,

"Sister, he is an awful old bully and much above his position. If I did not bring him up short, he would try to treat us like servants under him. He is Lord Cynegils' steward and believes himself the earl when his master is away," she confided. "Hope the food is served well, or I must hound him further. I confess that I am not much accustomed to long journeys sister. I do not have your endurance. Oh how I wish I could dress as you and have your tolerance of hardship."

" I go where Lord Einarr goes and live as he does, as we have from children. I know no other life but I sometimes wish it to be different," Gudhrun confided in return.

Sabert scurried back into the room, ushering a clutch of servants before him like a mother hen with chicks. They brought bowls of fruit and jugs of beer, which they laid before the visitors. From outside came the sounds of commotion and horses. The

King was returning from the hunt. Sabert and his helpers rushed off to fetch more food and beer.

First through the doorway was a young man of not much more than twenty summers, of average height for a Saxon, his hunting clothes dusty and stained from the chase, but obviously of the best materials. Gytha had stood as he entered the Hall and stepped quickly towards him, the others of her party rising from their chairs. As she approached him, the man smiled broadly and opened his arms to embrace Gytha warmly. She took his arm and drew him towards her friends, other huntsmen coming in through the doorway behind them.

"My Lord you know Wulfmaer, son of Ealdwulf, who has served you, as did his late father," said Gytha, introducing the first of her party. King Edmund reached forward to clasp arms with Wulfmaer.

"Where have you been Wulfmaer? We feared you met with mishap," the King enquired, "These are dark times and we have lost so many faithful friends this sorrowful year".

Before Wulfmaer could respond, Gytha turned to her cousin, "My Lord, we have so much to tell you, to warn of a danger and to offer a plan. I have been held prisoner by a man you thought a loyal friend. He also took Wulfmaer and his warriors into captivity. With those others here, Wulfmaer has helped me to survive and to be free again."

She then introduced Einaar and Gudhrun. King Edmund appeared shaken and angry by the insult done to his house and his warriors by his cousin's imprisonment but, with that, was the same joy at reunion that had characterized the arrival at Wulfmaer's village. He was intrigued by Einaar and Gudhrun but reassured by the obvious friendship between them, his young cousin and Wulfmaer whom he recognized as a promising young warrior and leader.

"You will feast with me this night, but we must first consider this insult done my house. Cousin, tell me all of the story." Then Edmund hesitated, "No,   First we must attend to your riders and those stinking packs outside." With that the King turned to a sturdy warrior who had followed him into the Hall.

"Ceolwulf," Edmund commanded towards the open doorway. A tall well-built Saxon, the captain of the King's bodyguards, the carl Ceolwulf was an imposing figure. Half a head shorter than Einaar, he was broad and sturdy, a professional soldier of obvious experience.

"Majesty?"

"Ceolwulf, bring the riders we saw outside, with their pack horses, into the compound and take them across to the old grain store. We will meet you there," ordered Edmund. To Gytha,

"Cousin, we will look at your prizes away from public eyes. With your companions, follow me."

With that Edmund headed across the room to a door that led away from the street and into the walled compound behind, to the side of the Great Hall. As they came out into the enclosed area, the horses were being led through the gateway and across the open space to a long rectangular building with high whitewashed plastered walls. Ceolwulf led the men and horses through the wide double doors, which were pulled closed behind them. Edmund made for a smaller door at the end of the building.

Inside, Edmund ordered the bundles on the ground and walked down the line, unwrapping each head in turn, a grim expression on his face. He unwrapped the figure half way down the line and stiffened.

"I know this dog!!   Birdoswald!!   He serves Esla", Edmund said loudly, with evident anger, more to himself than to the others there. He flicked the cloak back over the face of the dead Saxon and continued to the end of the line of bodies.

"Ceolwulf, fetch a cart and trusted men. It is almost dark. Take these vermin for burial in the forest." With that he walked back to his cousin and her friends.

"Cousin, now we will talk of these matters, but first send your riders to the retreat where they will be fed and can rest."

Gytha gestured to her maids who were standing with the warriors. They came to her and she instructed them to take the warriors to the retreat as the King had commanded.

The retreat was a long low building, within the walled enclosure, that served as a guest house for visitors. Its several rooms were plain with bare earth floors, providing simple shelter with curtained cots along its walls, rough boxes with hay and moss, covered by sheepskin, but comfortable beds for tired travellers. She instructed Agatha to arrange food and drink for the party, but to keep apart from any others who might be in or near the retreat.

Ceolwulf had called servants to attend the guests. As food and drink was brought to the warriors, grooms took their horses to the pen beside the retreat. The pen was built onto the enclosure wall, part covered by a simple low thatched roof that sloped from close to the top of the wall. Within the pen there were water troughs and racks with fodder. The grooms took saddles, bridles and packs to a room at the end of the retreat. With their comrades and horses cared for, it was time for hard discussion.

Edmund gestured for Gytha, Wulfmaer, Einaar and Gudhrun to follow him outside, but stopped beside the building, showing no sign of returning to the Great Hall. The light was fading fast.

"We will talk here, where there will be no disturbance and where no one can approach without our knowledge," said Edmund.

Then Gytha told her cousin, the King, the full story of her imprisonment with Wulfmaer and the others, how they had been freed by Einaar's people, what had befallen Wulfmaer's village and how they had survived the attack by Esla's men as they rode to meet the King. Edmund said little during the telling of the tale. His expression was grim and serious by parts. He asked few questions, some to Gytha and some to Wulfmaer and Einaar.

As they talked, Ceolwulf had returned with men and an ox cart to remove the bodies from the old grain store. As the King listened, servants had set lighted braziers in the enclosed yard, providing in the growing darkness a fitful light that hardly reached to where the King stood. Only when Gytha had finished her story did the King show any inclination to move from where they stood. First he stood in thought, slowly stroking his chin and looking to the ground. Then he shrugged himself back to Gytha and her friends.

"Cousin, what you have told me gives me great concern, Anger at the treatment of our Royal House of Wuffings. Joy for your deliverance safely to me. Concern that I reach the best decisions. There is much to think on." He looked towards Einarr, "Lord Einarr you will understand my gratitude to you and to your people. You will also understand my caution. I will not give my decision now. First we will feast and celebrate the safe return of a much-loved cousin. We will talk no more this night of these matters. I will sleep on this, consider it further in the morning and we will talk again later on the morrow." With that he reached out his hands to Gytha and Einaar in friendship. "Come, let us eat," he concluded.

The small party returned into the Great Hall through the door they had earlier left by. There was a bustle of activity and the

173

large space was well lit by torches held in iron brackets reaching out from the walls. At the North end of the room a long table, placed on a raised wooden floor, stretched almost from wall to wall. Behind it stood high-backed, carved chairs. To either side, tables had been placed in lines along the walls, narrow breaks between each table and with benches down both sides. The southern wall also had a line of tables, but with larger gaps between them. Standing beside the unlit hearth in the centre of the room was an older man, perhaps of fifty summers, richly dressed. Of average height, he looked shorter because his back was stooped. He greeted the King and looked at the others with him, silent query on his face.

Gytha stepped forward, "Lord Cynegils, we are pleased to see you once more. You look well. We thank you for your hospitality. You know Lord Wulfmaer, but my dear friends are strangers to you. Lord Einaar is the dearest of friends to us and the Lady Gudhrun is as a sister to me."

Cynegils, if he was in any way surprised, hid surprise well. "You are all most welcome to my humble home," he responded warmly, " Come seat yourselves".

Edmund took the seat at the centre of the raised table. As host, Cynegils sat on the King's right. To his right sat Gytha and to her right sat Gudhrun. To the King's left sat Einaar and to his left sat Wulfmaer. Only when they were seated, did other Saxons take the remaining seats at the table. While the raised table was filling with diners, others were coming into the Great Hall and taking seats at the other tables. Einaar was surprised that there were very few women present and those that were seemed to be servants. The Saxons seated at the raised table were all warriors, except for one who was a priest. By their dress and manner, they had the look of leaders. Those at the tables before them were mostly warriors, with some merchants and craftsmen, and a few more priests in their rough black clothes. This was a rather more subdued gathering than those feasting at Wulfmaer's village. Servants were bringing in food and beer but there was no rush to consume it. There was a hum of conversation but that was subdued also.

The priest stood, the diners fell silent, he mumbled something in a language that Einarr was unfamiliar with. As he finished speaking and resumed his seat, the conversation became louder and the diners began to work their way through the food. Even so it continued to be a strangely ordered gathering, although there were several stealthy glances towards the raised table, as those before it wondered who the new guests were and wondered also why a young and lowly carl was accorded the honour of sharing the King's table.

There were many rumours about those who had arrived with the Lady Gytha, she at least was well-known to most in the large village, but no certain knowledge of her companions, although some of the warriors recognized Wulfmaer. The woman sat beside the Lady Gytha was a considerable mystery. She was a great beauty, but her dress was strange, no jewels to decorate her, a loose yellow shirt of leather, studded cuffs at her wrists, and dark brown leather trousers, in contrast with the Lady Gytha's feminine dress, the gold of rank about her neck and wrists. It was a hearty meal taken in some seriousness and quiet purpose.

There was little conversation at the raised table. Edmund made some inconsequential remarks to Einarr and then to Cynegils. Gytha and Gudhrun were in animated conversation, Gytha also making some polite conversation with Cynegils. Einaar and Wulfmaer exchanged a few words when free to do so but no one shouted across from one table to another. The platters of food continued to be presented by servants and empty platters removed. None of the platters were heaped with food but contained a modest mound. Each diner took some items from the platters and placed them on a smaller plate in front of them, so different from the happy free-for-all that Einaar was accustomed to, where the table served as a plate for the diners. Although it was so strangely subdued, there was nothing to fault the food, it was a selection of many different things. There were platters of shellfish and herring, legs of chicken, platters with strips of chicken flesh, slices of pork and bread.

As the food dwindled, and no more platters were brought in, Cynegils rose from his chair, silence fell over the company, and he began to speak.

"Majesty,   Friends,   tonight we again welcome the Lady Gytha as a cherished guest".

Before he could finish speaking the diners began thumping the table tops, making a thunderous sound. After the subdued eating, the noisy enthusiasm was startling. He raised his arms and the noise subsided.

"You will know that others have come to council with the Court. Lord Einarr and Lord Wulfmaer are most welcome guests"

This was followed by a more polite pounding of the table tops and Cynegils resumed his seat without introducing Gudhrun.

Gytha touched her hand and said quietly, "If I was not the King's cousin no mention would have been made of me. I think this is different from your customs."

Gudhrun smiled, "Not so very different. As a warrior sharing with Einarr, I am treated as any other warrior according to rank. We live in friendship as Wulfmaer's people when each family attends a feast, even children and, Yes, it is as noisy and happy. Why are the people here so cautious together?"

"A good question dear sister. There is more polite reverence for a King, than your people show for Einarr's father, even though I understand the Lord Ivar commands a greater nation than all of these islands. We are subdued with the presence of that miserable old priest Caedmon," she confided, gesturing towards the old man at the end of the table who was staring into the middle distance with a sorrowful expression that suggested great loss.

"My cousin became King still a boy, and Lord Cynegils was his adviser. He is still listened to with great respect by the King. Of those with us on this table are the bodyguard of the King, but they are also nobles with their own people. There is some suspicion as Wulfmaer sits with us and many will wonder what service he has performed the King for one so young and of low rank."

Gytha then explained to Gudhrun how each village provided warriors to support the King for half a year, their trusted leaders serving as bodyguard to the King and commanders in battle. If there were no conflicts, the warriors remained in their villages at the King's call. Each period of duty was followed by three periods at leisure, unless war threatened. Through the year, the King toured the Halls of his nobles, bringing justice and listening to any complaints. His own Hall was in the forest at Rendlesham, but he spent little time there. Ketts Hall was a favoured place. Closer to the centre of the kingdom, it served as a meeting place to consider the fortunes of the realm and to debate actions. Further inland lay the Abbey of Banleuca which was almost a rival court for the priests. Gudhrun had difficulty in understanding the religion of the Saxons.

Gytha was not entirely helpful because she was not a true believer. When Gytha's forebear, King Redwald, had been buried more than two hundred summers before, he had converted to the priest of Christ, but his burial was lavish and pagan, as befitted the High King of the Saxons, a new-built boat, equipped with all he would require beyond life, buried beneath the sandy soil of the coastal margins. Then, the Kingdom of Anglia was the greatest of the Saxon Kingdoms, in peace and wealth. In the summers since, the priests had grown wealthy and strong, but the people still held many of the old beliefs.

As Gytha attempted to explain, Gudhrun became more confused. There seemed to be two very different cultures entwined. The customs of the villages and of King Edmund were familiar to her, as was the language, little different from her world. Ælfwyn's village was little different from those she knew from her growing. All were equal and those who led did so by common consent. These priests appeared to have different customs, and their own language, an alien culture that did not seem to accept the cheerful freedoms of the People. If they were all like the gloomy Caedmon, Gudhrun could see no merit in their world, or in their gods.

For Gudhrun and Gytha the meal passed quickly because they were diverted in their own conversation. For Wulfmaer and Einarr it was a slower and more tedious occasion. They both wanted to observe and learn, which precluded a friendly discussion between them. Their neighbours attempted some polite small conversation and several of the company wandered around the tables, stopping for brief conversation with those they knew, but few approached the King's table. It was therefore almost a relief for the two young warriors when the King stood and the diners followed him to their feet. Edmund nodded politely to those who had shared his table and then walked from the raised flooring through the hall and out through a small door at the end of the room, acknowledging those he passed. As he left through the small door, those standing at the tables began leaving the Hall. It all had a strange quiet formality for Einarr and Gudhrun, although Gytha and Wulfmaer were familiar with the customs.

Gytha led her companions out of the Hall into the compound and across to the retreat. The compound was still lit by braziers which gave a flickering yellow light. A small room at one end of the building had been allocated for their use. There were curtained bunks along each wall, enough for ten people. Gytha's maids had prepared four bunks along one wall for their mistress, Gudhrun and themselves. Einarr and Wulfmaer had five bunks on the opposite wall to choose from. They gratefully climbed into their curtained beds and were soon asleep, the fresh straw and moss making a soft mattress below the sheepskins, the rough cloth curtains keeping out the colder draughts, the scent of herbs, mixed with the moss and straw, producing a calming aroma.

Dawn broke and a new day was begun. The weather had turned, bringing in a cold dark morning, the heavy rain slanting across the walled compound in sheets of water, driven by a bitter north wind. The compound was already pocked by puddles, the rain taking its time to penetrate through the light sandy soil. The horses huddled together under the narrow roof of their pen, their coats plastered blackly against their skin, steam rising from those more sheltered from the rain. Gudhrun led the dash across the compound to the Hall, but they were all soaked by the time they reached the door, rain pouring off the roofs in solid curtains to rival any waterfall. Inside, the Hall was lit poorly by rush lights, little natural light penetrating the gloom. Edmund was seated at the raised table and called them to sit with him. There was no one else to be seen, other than one servant, who scurried away to fetch food for them. Edmund cast a forgotten, slightly sad, figure alone at the broad table, the spacious Hall stretching away from him. Even with his four guests, they were dwarfed by the space. There was fire in the hearth at the centre of the long room, its growing flame adding to the poor illumination from the rush lights, making the space more welcoming.

"You are well rested?" Edmund enquired of the four, but, continuing before they could respond, "I have slept little. I must confess that I have long doubted Esla's loyalty but his actions still shock me. The Mercians and the Northumbrians have long wanted to swallow this kingdom, when once they were vassals to Redwald and these lands. I would be hard pressed to withstand an attack from our neighbours, aided by traitors within our borders. Esla is not alone, there are some even who shared food with us this last night who would join him. Your people have already aided us Lord Einaar and we can be allies against a common foe. I do not need further reflection. It is the right decision. Now we must make plans together."

Huddled together the group retraced the conversations that had before included Ælfwyn. Einarr explained the plan his father had made for the coming year and they shared their knowledge of Esla and the Northumbrians. Edmund realized that the large stock of new weapons at the fort meant an army was to be formed against him. What none of them could be sure of was how far Esla's plans had developed, or how large the army might be.

Esla could be planning on training more warriors from the people on his lands, but Ivar had learned from his prisoners that they had been expecting warriors to arrive by boat through the winter. It would make sense to reinforce Esla by boat for the same reasons that Ivar had planned for his own campaign against the Northumbrians. They could not be certain, but this could mean that the Northumbrians planned to launch an attack, aided by Esla and other traitors, at the end of winter. Ivar and Edmund must attack first, when Esla was weakest, before Ivar himself needed to march North against Northumbria at the end of the coming winter.

Edmund reached that same decision.

"My friends, we must strike Esla before he can begin his own plan. As long as King Ivar holds the fort, he denies the river to our enemies. Once Esla has been dealt with, we will know more of the plans that involved him and we may learn who in my kingdom has plotted with him. If the Northumbrians send men, we can deal with them as they land. The vital task is to remove the threat Esla poses."

"Majesty, how can we be sure of our own forces?" asked Wulfmaer.

"Yes, I had wondered about that," added Gytha to the discussion.

"Sadly, we can be sure of no one," answered Edmund after

only a moment of reflection, "that is a lesson you must learn Wulfmaer, as a leader. I wish I could be sure of those who have long supported my house, but I know that some will waver and some may already be set against me. I am grateful that I can count on you. I hope that my worst expectations are unfair and that few will side with the Northumbrians"

"Majesty, I must return to my father. May I take Wulfmaer with me?" asked Einarr.

"Yes. I would that you return with all your party, including my cousin. I know that she will be safe with you. It will remove a possible hostage from the reach of my enemies and allow me greater freedom. I will remain at Ketts Hall until I can muster an army to join you. By the next new moon I will meet King Ivar at Bertwald's Bridge. 'Til then we can exchange messages as we need. Your horses are well rested and supplies have been packed. I ordered it before first light. I will leave to hunt and take my court with me. You will be able to leave quietly after we have ridden out, but do not take a direct route from here. There may still be spies in this place." With that, Edmund bid them a safe journey.

Einarr and his companions left the King, still a melancholy figure, sitting alone at the high table. They emerged into the courtyard and dodged the growing puddles as they ran for the welcoming shelter of the retreat, but the heaviest rain had passed.

They could now prepare for their journey and wait for the hunt to leave, taking the King's loyal supporters and disloyal traitors beyond sight. Einarr knew that there might still be traitors amongst the townspeople, but all they would see would be a party of mercenaries leaving by the North Gate and the forest on their way to hunt more bandits in the wide expanse of marshes and lakes, unaware that Einarr and his comrades would be working their way through the forest to skirt the town that was Kett's Hall on their return to Depenham.

Twenty Seven

Sleep does not press me, even the twins are fully awake. I have enjoyed a most attentive audience this evening. I was surprised and pleased to see Janet taking much apparent interest in the unfolding tale. Only Robert is showing signs of sleep, but he has not recovered yet from his journey and from our discussion with the Englishman. I confess that, had it not been for Jamie, I would be unaware of the late hour. His visits have become more frequent as the evening draws on. Each time he takes longer to attend minor chores that have no need, and he makes more noise in undertaking them. He stands by the door, trying to catch my eye, before giving up and withdrawing.

It has pleased me to see how my audience is becoming involved in the story with each evening that we spend together. We are exploring a great adventure together. It has come to mean so much to me. It is a deep pleasure and a peace that I have not felt for so long, perhaps not since my own childhood. The story is the stage, but we are all as much players as the characters from the distant past. I am struck by how much our life is like the lives of those who have gone before us. The joys, the terrors, the betrayals, the disappointments, the peace, the conflicts, all so much the same for the past, as for today. Then there is a restlessness that runs as a thread through our generations. As I bring the story to an end for this night I see a reluctance on the faces before me. As we bid each other a good night, there is a reluctance to part.

Before I realize it, I am alone. I finish the drink that Jamie has left for me. Tonight I will sleep in my bed, a deep and peaceful sleep, to dream of happy days, my dearest Margaret and my family.

The fire has died in the hearth, the rush lights extinguished, the candles snuffed, only the solitary candle in its dish to light my way. Kara has awoken and follows me like a silent shadow, to take her guard post against the door of my sleeping quarters. I feel a great peace and satisfaction for the first time since my Margaret died. I know now that she will always be with me beyond the end of days to the rebirth of Ragnarock, the promise of the Phoenix.

Part Four: -

Deception
And Confusion

Twenty Eight

It has been a deeply worrying day, yet I am looking forward once more to a family meal in my quarters. The matter that troubles me most is that I have grown careless and it could have cost us much.

I must own to myself that it was not just my error that troubles me, but that which I cannot explain to my satisfaction. A Border life is never easy, yesterday's comrade can as swiftly become today's bitter foe. The lesson that was drummed into me as a child was that no one can ever be trusted completely. I learned to see good in others, but prepare for treachery, not just with people, but with places and events. Today I saw that I had let down my guard. I can make excuses, but it must never happen again.

It was a fine morning even if this winter drags on interminably. I have never known a time so cold and so firm a grip. I intended to ride out alone along the strand. Time to think, when there is much to think on. Jamie had saddled my favourite horse. A pair of dags were holstered before the saddle, saddle bags behind contained food and drink should I ride longer. I have come to enjoy again a casual ride along the strand. It relaxes me and I can think of many things without disturbance.

Jamie does not like me to ride alone. I have noticed before that he has ordered horsemen to ride behind me at some distance. They have become adept at this, giving me the illusion of solitude, but close enough to give me aid should I need it. The first time I saw them trailing me in the distance I was minded to turn around and give Jamie my displeasure, but then I knew he meant only good, saw his duty to me, and arranged an escort that was discrete.

This morning, as I climbed into the saddle I heard the little clipped steps of a pony. Mary came into the courtyard, leading

Heather, her favourite pony. I tried to look stern and forbidding but failed.

"Gran Faddi, will ye no grant me the boon that I may ride out with you?"

"Aye blossom", I replied, - how could I refuse her?

We rode out through the postern gate, across the causeway and East along the strand. It really was a grand day. It was cruel cold, but beautiful. The wind of last night had died, the sky was a clear pale blue, the sandy shore a warm gold and the sea caressed the beach with gentle rolls of breaking waves. There were birds in the sky. Over the water gulls were scanning the waves for signs of food. Inland, a kestrel was hanging motionless in the light breeze, waiting to dive on prey. On a day like this there is much to be joyful for. Perhaps that was the start of my mistake. It was a day of peace, an ageless tranquillity that this shore had known since the beginnings of time, a respite from the clash of storm, the dismal grey of heavy rain, the torment of tempest.

We rode on in companionable silence, I looked round once and saw our distant escort. Mary rode on my right along the shore. She had brought with her a fishing lance but showed no inclination to search the tide pools and lagoons that were forming on the falling tide. She has such maturity for one so young. She knows when to talk and when to be silent. I feel so comfortable in her company and it is strange that I can think as freely as if I was alone.

From time to time we stopped, looked out across the Firth, and exchanged casual conversation. Mary has confidence beyond her years. I can talk easily with her as to a full-grown woman. She makes me feel that she wants to hear what I have to say and to understand. I find myself talking to her as an adult with that same interest. Over the recent weeks when we have been together I have seen her reaching out to the future as I saw my dearest Margaret when we were both young.

Perhaps I make an excuse, but this combination of

working through my thoughts, and talking with Mary, separated me from our journey. I was unaware of the passing scenery for much of the time. We could be halted, or still riding. In my detachment I missed what Mary had just said. I learned towards her to hear her better.

The breath of death passed me close enough to feel it on my cheek. I knew it was the stone ball from a hackbut. I turned low in the saddle, drew the dags, their heavy steel cold through my gloves. I had brought them from Germany. I was proud of their advanced design, each with two barrels and each barrel with its own wheel lock. I pressed the first trigger on each and sparks flew from the wheels. They both fired at the smoke that hung over the coarse grass inland. I turned both dags and fired again. I did not expect to hit a target, all I could see was the drifting smoke from the assassin's shot, but to delay the killer in reloading, whilst I rode down on him, through the smoke from my firing.

Before I could do more, Mary had dashed in front of me and towards the smoke, her lance raised in her hand. From there I doubted my own eyes - I still do.

A figure rose from the grass, sword in hand, as she charged into that grassy bank, sand flying from the hooves of her pony. It must have been a trick of light. She and her pony seemed to grow, to glow in a bright light. I saw the arm pull back and then thrust down at the figure. I was riding after her as fast as I could, my sword drawn, fearing I would be too late.

In my mind a voice softly spoke, "My love for ever".

I reached the assassin moments after Mary, my sword raised to strike him down. I saw that one of my four shots had hit home, his bloody left arm hanging down, almost severed above the elbow. A lucky shot that had prevented him from reloading the hackbut, which was flung behind him. He was no longer standing, but not yet lying on the ground. Mary's fish lance had been driven through his torn throat, into the ground behind him, supporting his body as it learned back.

If I had not seen it, I would never have believed it. I was unsure even then that I could believe my eyes. A full grown man at full gallop could have driven a spear through another's neck like that, but a fish spear is not a single point, its trident intended only to firmly hold the fish in its grip, its metal shaft intended only to support the weight of a generous salmon. I could not credit that a young girl, riding a pony, could have done that.

As I looked in amazement Mary trotted her pony back, it having carried on past the dead assassin with the momentum of the charge. She looked at the man with as much amazement as I.

"But Gran Faddi, that is my spear. How did you take it?"

"My brave dear child I didna. It was you who struck the blow and saved us"

We sat our mounts and gazed together at something we did not understand. It surprised me also that she was not affected by the sight.

I reloaded my dags, looking around for signs of a further threat. I used the spanning key on each lock that the dags be ready if the need be.

I shrugged my mind together,

"Come let us ride for home. There may be others here who would do us harm."

I reached across and caught her reins to turn her with me and we rode slowly back towards home and the escort that was galloping towards us.

Two of our men broke away to turn in behind us, while their comrades rode on towards the dead assailant, to search for others who might have been with him.

Mary rode quietly beside me as though nothing had happened. I confess that I was shaken. Shaken and angry, but angry with myself as much as for the man sent to kill. Almost within sight of our home, someone had sought to do me harm and only an accident had saved me, an accident and an unbelievably brave child.

When we rode into the courtyard, Jamie was waiting for us. I dismounted and helped Mary down from her pony, while Jamie held our mounts. I hugged Mary and she hugged me. She was unharmed and unaffected and this made me thankful, but it also troubled me. I have been no stranger to the fight and I knew that what had happened should not have been. We walked towards her family quarters, my arm protectively around her shoulders. Morag stood at the door a questioning look on her face. She realized that something had happened. Mary was not injured, or upset, there was only the air of disturbance hung around us, a cloying cloak, that Morag could sense.

I passed Mary to her mother.

"We will speak later Morag, will you tell Robert to join me in my quarters?"

She made no question, nodded her understanding, and led Mary through the doorway, as I turned for my quarters.

When Robert joined me, I told him what had happened, or at least a part of it. I told him of my pride in Mary's great bravery. We were both much moved. We discussed the meaning of the assassin. Greater precautions were needed. I knew now that my regular rides along the coast had become predictable. I cursed myself for such negligence. Even so, it could not have been either chance or careful planning alone that had placed the man where he was, hidden in the grass awaiting me. We agreed that Robert would send out horsemen to search for others lurking in wait, and that I would from today ride out only with a close escort and riders ahead of me.

We agreed that Robert would depart earlier than we had

intended. I was reluctant to send him away, to deny him the precious days with his wife and children, but events seemed to be turning faster. I should face the threats here, knowing that my sons were away and able to avenge any outrage. Unless we discovered others, we could not yet tell where the threat came from. I did not know the assassin and he was in no position to provide any information. His body had been brought back so that all of our people could see him, that someone might recognize who he was and from which family he came. I did not hold great hopes. From his dress he was from the Netherlands, his arms German, but that could be to deliberately mislead. We could guess which group had sent him, but they had chosen someone not from these lands.

I spent the remainder of the day instructing our men in greater preparation. We would review all of our defences once more that we might find any weakness. We would increase our guards. No one would leave our walls without some protection, neither would they leave without informing the guard where they were headed and when they expected to return.

When Jamie came to ask what I expected him to arrange for a meal, I was surprised how fast the day had flown. I told him to prepare a family meal in my quarters. It was something that I was now looking forward to, almost a desperate wish for domestic normality.

Morag had visited to tell me that Mary was well and to talk about what had happened. There were no recriminations, no sulks, as there might have been had Mary been Janet's daughter. We were both relieved that the girl was unharmed by the event and proud that she had demonstrated such courage instinctively. We had both known that she was a bold child, but boldness can still fail the test of battle, as it has for many a strong young man in his first combat, but there is no shame in that. We all face first danger to find our reaction.

When they arrived for our meal, Mary stepped forward first and put her arms around my neck, kissing me on the cheek. I was so delighted that she had shrugged off the near disaster, that she seemed once more an unaffected child. The others came into the room behind her and she was the guest of honour. I had feared that this meal might be subdued but it was livelier than any before. We were all talking and laughing as we worked through the dishes brought in by Jamie and Annie.

Then we came down the steps into the meeting chamber to gather around the hearty fire, to drink our mugs of punch. I could not have asked for a happier gathering. It had become a great celebration, a thanksgiving for a threat averted and a safe return.

This flowed naturally into the continuation of the saga. Again, I found myself as much a listener as a storyteller, enjoying the unfolding tale as it wrapped around me like a much-loved cloak.

Twenty Nine

Ivar and Peder were returning to the fort. They had found a suitable wooded grove and made sacrifice to the gods. It was the first time since they had landed and taken the fort. Peder was anxious that they make their thanksgiving for their good fortune, to seek knowledge of what lay ahead

First Ivar had attended to the establishment of their people. Small scouting parties had been sent out in several directions to learn more of what surrounded them. Extra buildings had been erected within the massive walls of the fort. Some would serve as stores and others to provide shelter through the winter for the warriors gathered there.

They were still some distance from the fort's gate when Tryggvi reached them. He had run hard to find them and the message he carried was interrupted as he gasped for breath.

" Lord Ivar,   ships   in the river   sent to   tell you...."

Tryggvi gasped the message out, long pauses for breath, rushed groups of words, but the meaning was plain to Ivar and he began to run towards the fort, pulling Tryggvi with him, Peder keeping pace with both.

Just inland from the coast, a picket had lain hidden in the reeds, their small boat tied up on the bank close behind them where the river doubled back on itself. As soon as they saw the first boat heading upriver towards them, they had hurried across the narrow marshy strip to reach their boat and row for the horsemen who were awaiting to take a warning quickly to the fort, avoiding the serpentine river by sending a rider on the higher ground that cut straight across to the fort.

Once at the fort, the messenger made his report to Red

Osten, while the picket hid with their boat in the reeds to watch the approaching ships as they made their way inland. They would then send a second messenger as soon as the last ship had passed their hiding place.

Osten lost no time in sending Tryggvi to find Ivar to warn him of the ships heading towards the fort. The speed with which the messenger had ridden to the fort gave ample space to prepare. A rider was not just faster than a boat being rowed up a river, but he travelled a very much shorter distance by using the straight path along the higher ground as the river snaked its way slowly inland to the lake and fort.

As a skilled commander, Osten began making preparations without waiting for Ivar. As Ivar ran over the bridge, the fort already looked deserted in the falling light of late afternoon, much as it had when Ivar had watched it so carefully all those months before.

Osten was waiting for him just inside the great gatehouse, ready to report on what had happened since Tryggvi had been sent out with the original message. As Ivar had expected, Osten had followed the plan, prepared shortly after they had landed and taken the fort from the Saxons.

The sentries on the walls lay so that they could watch the lake or ground in front of them. Sentries walking the walls would have signalled, to any who knew how the fort had been used, that something had changed and change was not reassuring. All of Ivar's warriors were alert and silent at their posts around the fort. They were arranged in squads, hidden by the buildings from anyone entering by the main gate, but ready to rush to the aid of the squads waiting behind the gate towers.

Ivar had climbed to the walkway that was set on top of the walls behind a low parapet. By lying down on the walkway, he could look out onto the lake through one of the slits that pierced the parapet. Although he could see across the broad expanse of the lake, anyone sailing across the water would see no one on the walls. It had been one of the first tasks, on their first day, to piece the walls for lookouts. Ivar had been surprised that, in all the years the fort had stood there, no one had thought of it. Perhaps the Romans had felt no need for hiding sentries, confident in their knowledge that the massive walls and visible sentries were adequate discouragement for any potential attacker. They would have asked, "Who would challenge a Roman Legion?"

The tiled roofs at each corner tower provided shelter from the weather for sentries, suggesting that the original builders considered the comfort of the sentries, leaving only the soldier patrolling the wall between each tower to suffer the discomfort of the cold winds and rain. Ivar knew that the availability of relative shelter would have discouraged a sentry from leaving that comfort to patrol the more exposed walkways. Within the shelter of the roofs, there would have been artillery. Ivar had seen this in the southern lands, where the Emperor had ruled as a Roman, in Roman ways. Those weapons had long since been absent, probably removed by the Romans when the last Legion was withdrawn.

Today, Ivar would have to rely on spear and bow, until an attacker came within range of sword and axe. He hoped that the approaching boats were unaware that the fort was under new control, that they would approach, to be surprised, overcome by a stealthy defence. He had planned carefully, but there were limits. In battle there was always the unexpected to challenge the more carefully drawn plans.

His remaining ships had been taken inland so that they were out of sight from the lake. The ships closest to the fort were fully manned, with the others moored behind them as a boom across the river. As the work within the fort had progressed, there was little need to use the longships for accommodation. Leaving crews only for a small number of ships that were to be held at readiness. If the approaching enemy intended to pass the fort, to continue inland, their way would be blocked. Behind them a chain would be raised across the river, preventing their escape towards the sea. If they became trapped, Ivar could quickly send warriors from the fort to reinforce his ship crews.

If the unknown visitors reached the lake and took fright, a

second chain would be raised across the river by the hidden pickets, cutting off any escape to the sea. Ivar could then send his ships after them, overpowering the invaders, preventing them from giving alarm to any comrades who might be following them.

The more difficult position would be if the attackers came ashore, but did not enter the fort. Ivar had positioned a watcher inland from the fort, who would be able to warn their own waiting ships should it not be possible to send a messenger out of the fort to them. Their own ships could then sail back to the fort and attack the besieging force from behind, trapping them between the fort and Ivar's longships. The weakness was that the attackers might be stronger than Ivar's ship crews. It would have been better to have had artillery in the fort to even any odds. Ivar had been prevented from building these mighty weapons by a lack of skilled warriors. The People did not have the skills of the siege, but they were learning. He intended to work on this during the winter months when they could build catapults, giant bows and fire tubes. For now he must use what resources he had.

His thoughts were interrupted by another messenger who had just arrived to tell him the size of the force coming up the river. There were twenty ships, several small, and most carrying cargo rather than warriors. If the pickets had counted correctly, and Ivar knew he could rely on them, the force was very much smaller than his own. As the messenger completed the information, the first masts could be seen approaching the last bend before the lake.

The ships came on towards the fort and began to move out of single file to approach the quay. There was nothing to suggest any alarm amongst their crews as the first ships slowed and drifted towards the fort, men standing ready to jump ashore to secure the vessels to the quay. The first six were alongside and the next vessels drifting in towards them to moor to their sides. That would make unloading easier but, more importantly, Ivar knew that vessels rafted together side by side would be much more difficult to get underway again. The arrivals were helping him to ensure that every ship and crew member could be trapped.

The last vessels were mooring to their sisters and groups of men were forming on the quayside, looking relaxed. A party of six sailors was headed for the main gate to announce their arrival and, doubtless, to seek help to unload the cargos. As they entered through the main gate, they saw three men loading a cart.

"Greetings we come from King Aelle of Northumbria," called the leader of the six.

"Greetings from my lord Esla", answered one of Ivar's Jutlanders who was fluent in the dialects of the Saxons.

The two men advanced towards each other and warmly grasped forearms in greeting.

"We have brought men and supplies as Lord Esla requested," said the Northumbrian. "Can you spare some men to help us unload?"

"Aye, but will you not take food and drink with us while I send men to the boats?" responded the Jutlander, putting his arm round the Northumbrian's shoulder, motioning his five comrades to follow, leading the party towards the first hall.

The party entered the hall and were quickly subdued by the Jutlander's comrades who had been waiting within. It had all been so easy, but this was just the first stage of Ivar's plan. As soon as the Saxons had been disarmed, bound and gagged, the Jutlander was sent out with twenty of his fellows to help the Northumbrians unload their ships.

The Northumbrians had already begun to move cargo across the rafted boats to be piled in mounds on the quay. The Jutlander, Hunbogi, and his men were soon helping the Saxons to unload their cargo. Ox carts began arriving from within the fort to take the cargo inside. Hunbogi sent small parties of Saxons into the fort with each ox cart making an invitation to take food and drink. None refused the welcome break that was offered. As each cart vanished into the fort, the Saxons accompanying it were silently overpowered.

The cage built by Esla to hold his prisoners was soon filled with his would-be allies. On the quayside, the number of Saxons remaining had reduced and the boats in the outer line were empty. As each boat emptied, Hunbogi sent it to moor at the island in the centre of the lake, further reducing the number of Saxons on the quay. As each empty boat prepared to make the short passage to the island, Hunbogi made certain that they received a generous supply of food and beer.

It was almost dark as the last boat was unloaded and sent away to join the others. Those Saxons still on the quay were brought into the fort and overpowered, leaving no more than a hundred with the boats moored at the island. The deception had been completely successful, the prisoner cage was full, groups of prisoners, who could not be forced into it, bound and guarded in the other buildings. That left only the skeleton boat crews to deal with and Ivar decided to leave that until first light. Attempting to take them in the dark risked unnecessary injuries to his own men.

To make the morning's work easier, Ivar sent some of his own boats quietly past the island to completely block the way to the sea. The remaining boats were positioned ready to sweep out of the river into the lake as the day was dawning.

In addition to four hundred prisoners, taken without a single casualty amongst his own warriors, Ivar had a large cargo still to be inspected. There had been no time to look through it, or to pack it away inside the new storehouses that Ivar had built inside the fort's massive walls. As each cart had arrived, the Saxons had helped to unload the supplies into mounds before being led into the second hall and overpowered, the empty cart returning for its next load. As a cart returned, those of Ivar's warriors who would pass for Saxons were sent back with it to speed the unloading. They had been carefully selected well in advance of being needed and as the numbers of Ivar's men on the quay increased, and the numbers of Saxons decreased, the advantage rapidly moved to Ivar, should the Saxons become alarmed. That they did not sense danger to the end was a great credit to the men selected by Ivar for such an eventuality, and to the careful training in the weeks before.

Hunbogi had done well, Ivar recognizing his abilities, marking him for important future tasks. The size of the force brought over had meant that there were many Ivar did not know, or even recognize. He had relied, as every commander of a large force, on his lieutenants. These were longship captains he knew well, knew he could rely on. The small group of senior captains were proven comrades who inspired volunteers to join their crews. Those boat captains below them were not all well known to Ivar, but he could recognize them, knew their reputations and their names.

Hunbogi had been selected because he had travelled amongst the Saxons, was fluent in their dialects, could pass close scrutiny as a Saxon. He had demonstrated in training that he was a natural leader, respected by the other warriors selected to deceive any Saxon visitors. The selection had been left to Lodin in the months of final preparation before the fleet had sailed.

Many times, Ivar had triumphed by using deception against his enemies, although not always with such complete success as on this afternoon. True, there was still the matter of overcoming the remaining Saxons on their boats, but this should present little challenge. Overwhelming force, that Ivar could range against them, would encourage surrender. As the Saxon crews were only sufficient to move their boats across the lake to moorings, they would be unable to handle their craft and fight, but Ivar would send fully crewed boats against them and, if a Saxon boat did manage to break away in the confusion, it would only meet a number of Ivar's boats in the river on the seaward side of the lake.

With everything prepared for the morning, and no other threat visible, Ivar could concentrate on checking the unloaded cargoes and questioning prisoners. Having so many prisoners, their numbers must be reduced. A pity, but, with the weather deteriorating into early winter, there was no benefit in sending prisoners back to Heddeby as slaves. Peder wanted to use some of the prisoners as sacrifices to the gods. Well, he could have some, they would be a powerful offering as they bled out, hanging from the trees in the grove Ivar and Peder had selected to honour their gods, but that would still leave a great number.

A fully crewed warship would have at least forty warriors and the largest ships would carry a hundred men and more. The Northumbrians had sent smaller trading vessels and the larger vessels had carried forty men, but they were not all warriors. Many were sailors who plied the coast as traders, most of those on the island were sailors. Even so, a force of some five hundred men was a large force. Ashore, a war band was usually between thirty and sixty strong, armies were often fewer than five hundred strong. A smaller armed group was often a group of bandits, of which there would be a number roaming any kingdom. For Ivar to remove five hundred men from the fight to come was a blow to Esla and his Northumbrian allies, but it could also be a burden on Ivar's resources. Sending most of them back to Hedeby as slaves would require larger crews to control the prisoners and man the ships. Keeping the Saxons at the fort as prisoners would require warriors to be used as guards and consume valuable food and supplies. That left Ivar only with the choice of killing all the prisoners, or keeping some as potential supporters after their changed allegiance could be measured, but first they must extract all the information they could from their prisoners.

Ivar placed Osten and Hunbogi in charge of the interrogators. One of the halls was set aside for the purpose and prisoners were brought to the hall to be assessed. Those considered of no value would be taken out and killed without further delay. At first light, the bodies could be loaded onto carts and taken to a mass grave. Some Saxons would be happy to join Ivar's men and could be separated from the others, but kept under guard. A small number would be able to provide important information.

The interrogations proceeded briskly. Any Saxon who showed defiance, or could be seen to have no value, was rapidly identified, taken out, gagged, their hands bound, to be killed. By the middle night, eleven Saxons had been separated as potential new comrades. Peder had selected twenty for sacrifice from those marked for death, seven had been taken to one side for further interrogation as leaders with important information, and the remainder had been killed. Reviewing progress with Osten, Ivar discovered that the total number of prisoners was four hundred and seventy three, with perhaps a hundred more still to be taken in the morning from the boats.

"Osten, you still have much work to do with the prisoners. I wish to be present when those of value are questioned again. Do you wish to rest your men?"

"Lord Ivar, we will continue but I will send some to rest by turns. In a few hours we will have fresh prisoners. I want to be sure we have not lost any of value, the remaining numbers present no difficulty in guarding. The work could take days more, although from what Hunbogi observed, those taking the boats to moor at the island were seamen considered by the Northumbrian warriors as lesser men, little more than slaves."

"Good Osten, we will talk more in the morning when the remaining Saxons are taken from their boats".

Red Osten watched Ivar make his way back to his quarters. He knew that his leader would not sleep until the work was completed.

Thirty

E inarr sat by the remains of the fire with Gudhrun. They leaned together, not asleep, but not fully awake. The journey back from Kett's Hall had been easy and unhurried. They had come down onto the old Roman road further West than they had left it on the way to Kett's Hall. Having circled around Kett's Hall after leaving by the North gate, to deceive any watchers there, reinforcing the circulated story that they were mercenaries hunting bandits in the Great North Marsh for the King.

They had lost time circling around, but made up for the loss on the good road, bringing them to within a day's ride of Depenham. The straight highway looked no different. There were no villages, no signs of life in the woods on either side.

They had decided to break their journey once more, then continuing to Ælfwyn's village, to arrive before nightfall, the days now becoming noticeably shorter as winter approached. Once at the village, they could decide whether to ride on to the fort, or sail down the river in the Øvind. Einarr knew that it would be quicker to use the horses on the Roman road, but it meant travelling through Esla's lands with risk of ambush. Still, it would not take much longer by river if they left on the tide and rowed hard. They might even be fortunate with the wind in their favour.

Camped beside the road, Einarr's party had sent two warriors a few hundred paces West along the road and a further two were sent East as pickets. With two guards in the camp, that would prevent them being surprised by any attackers. By changing guards, this allowed everyone to rest and sleep adequately, the fire quenched as the light was lost. It was a cold night, but the ground was dry and the clear sky was lit by the stars.

Wulfmaer and Eyvald had the last guard duty in camp.

Wulfmaer had gone to check both sets of pickets mid way through their duty and found them with difficulty as they sat in the brush to either side of the road. It had been an uneventful night. Wulfmaer had sent Eyvald to call back the pickets as first light broke and went round his sleeping comrades, waking them for the new day. The sky had clouded and a dismal drizzle fell lightly in a faint west breeze. It was not a day to raise the spirits, leaves falling from the trees, the advanced guard of winter moving over the land.

Einarr came awake, Gudhrun's elbow in his ribs. "How did she always manage to wake first?" he asked himself. It was something that irritated him, but not so much as her perpetual cheerful enthusiasm at the start of a day. Einarr could wake rapidly in the face of danger but he otherwise came slowly, reluctantly, to wakefulness.

Breakfast was a rushed affair. Each member of the party had food from the kitchens at Ketts Hall, bread, cheese, cooked meat, fruit and beer. This served for every meal on the journey. Nothing had to be cooked, making a fresh fire unnecessary. The party mounted and formed into a group, some still eating their hasty meal, keen to make Ælfwyn's village as early as possible.

The riders set off at a smart pace, their horses hooves ringing out on the hard surface of the ancient road. They passed the site of their brief battle with Esla's men, through the straggling village that served as a local market, and were soon approaching the cross roads where they would turn through the marsh to Ælfwyn's village. They had taken only two short breaks to check their horses, their mounts showing no sign of tiring. The road helped greatly, being smooth, level and firm.

As they reached the crossroads they found that Black Gædda had set men to form a picket in the buildings that remained from the ransacked village. There were some repairs, making the buildings more comfortable, but care had been taken to hide the fact that they were once more in use. Behind, and growing into the damaged buildings, was brush and young trees, a fringe in front of longer-established and mature woodland.

Where Einarr and his party had expected to continue to ride through woods to reach the marsh, they were surprised to find a completely cleared area in front of new palisades. It did not seem that they had been away long enough for such a transformation. As they approached the gate towers, they were again challenged and identified. Einaar recognized some of Gædda's men amongst the guard. Satisfied, the sentries swung open the high gates to allow the riders entry.

Einarr could now see that this impressive structure was based on the prefabricated fortifications that they had brought with them across the Poisoned Sea. Lodin and Ælfwyn had used their people to assemble the wooden sections into a fort and walls leading off to both sides, curving back towards the marsh. Once the basic structure was complete, it took only two days, men were then set to work, clearing the area beyond the walls towards the evacuated village and the Roman road. The trees cut down in the clearance were roughly trimmed and used to build a rustic palisade, linking the fort to the marsh, creating a large compound. The space, between the two rows of trees that formed the palisade, was then packed with earth, creating a ditch in front of the rough outer wall, to make the walls higher and a greater obstacle. With clay smeared liberally over the rough timber, the walls blended into the landscape.

To make a fully effective fortification, it would have been necessary to build a second fort facing to the causeway, twin to the fort that now faced towards the Roman road, through the marsh, connecting it to the newly established walls, with towers at intervals in the wall. The result would be a strongly defended compound to rival the great Roman fort that Ivar had captured at the beginning of their campaign. The wooden walls could not compete in strength and height with the walls of the ancient fort, but they could enclose a similar expanse of ground and prove more than adequate against sustained assault. That additional construction would require more resources than were available. For now, a rough picket fence served as simple protection along the edge of the marsh between the two more substantial walls to both sides of the fort. With the soft and flooded ground leading up to it, the picket fence made a more formidable barrier than it appeared, as did the rough gate that was dragged across the opening to the causeway.

The fort was not much more than a gateway between towers, a second gateway and towers, facing towards the marsh and river, being connected by high, double palisade walls. A simple fortification that would slow an attacker and provide a strong point. A handful of warriors could hold such a fort against much greater numbers, but the space it enclosed was sufficient to accommodate buildings for more than a hundred warriors and horses, still having space to spare.

Behind the fort was an area already being cleared that would provide protected ground for crops and grazing, space for stables, storehouses and other buildings. Although there would be much work to fully complete and consolidate the fortifications, there was already an effective screen, with space to accommodate the horses and warriors that greatly expanded the village population. Ivar had taken the opportunity to send more warriors to the village and this risked overwhelming the Saxon villagers.

Lodin had decided to quickly create fortifications that would provide an effective additional screen to the landward side of the marsh and enable him to separate his growing garrison from the villagers to avoid friction. Having achieved that he could then spare men to help the villagers speed up the construction or repair of the homes they so desperately needed to help them with their preparations for winter.

Ælfwyn's earlier fear that Ivar's army would impoverish her people proved unfounded, the reality was that Ivar had started sending more supplies up river than Lodin's warriors required, giving the villagers an unexpected improvement in food supply. With winter establishing itself, there would be little Lodin could do to help the farming but, as time permitted, his men could clear new areas and complete the building work the village needed. He intended to set up a forge and other craft services that would provide for his needs to maintain his own equipment, also providing for the villagers' future needs. He had become personally committed to the village, or perhaps to Ælfwyn. He could see this becoming his home, his trader's instincts recognizing the potential to develop a trading centre and a prosperous community, where before the villagers had, at best, only subsistence and hard work.

Einarr and his party were amazed at the speed with which the transformation had taken place during their absence. They passed out through the rough gate onto the causeway, their horses now showing signs of tiredness as they plodded on through the water and mud towards the island on which the village was built.

This was the second surprise. Rising up out of the marsh was another fort, its gates open, Lodin and Ælfwyn waiting to greet them. This new structure was set into the palisade wall that had been built around the village, replacing the simple gate, through which Einarr's party had set out for Kett's Hall. The new fortified gateway was still invisible from the river but, from the platforms atop the towers, a sentry could look out across the marsh to where a fortified gate would be constructed in an improved rear wall to the outer landward defences. Until the materials arrived, the sentries could see the tops of the towers in the fort that looked out towards the abandoned village. With this view, the approach of an enemy on the river, or from the Roman road, could be signalled to the other defences without the approaching foe being aware.

They rode up to Lodin and Ælfwyn, on the dry ground before the gate, Einarr still in the lead, but the other riders bunching around him, some already dismounting.

" Greetings Lord Einarr. How like you the magic since you rode out?" inquired a grinning Lodin.

"I see it.   I must believe it.   You have done well in our absence", responded Einarr, jumping down from his horse.

"Ah, not all to my credit. Much was brought up river the

day you set out. Agmundr Ingimundsson and his elves arrived with the materials. If they needed trees felled, and brush cleared, we did that, but they joined all the pieces together in sections. Then our men pulled on the ropes to raise the sections and Aggi fastened them together".

"I could not believe it," said Ælfwyn. "We took our cattle out to pasture and when we returned there were these great towers and walls. What would have taken us many seasons, your men achieved in days and they have helped us to build all the homes we hoped to build next summer. My people owe you so much. Everyone will have shelter and warmth this winter. We have new store houses filled to the roofs with fodder for our livestock and food for us."

"We are as surprised as you Gentle Lady," replied Einarr, "It pleases me that we have been able to help you and your people.

As they spoke, villagers came to lead off the horses, to feed and water them. Ælfwyn bade them follow her to the hall. As they walked, they passed new buildings, some in the Saxon style and others wood-planked, of the type designed and prefabricated by Aggi. There were new pens for animals, the village looking prosperous and so different from when Einarr's party had left to find the King.

They entered the hall behind Ælfwyn, to find food and drink already laid out on one of the long tables. Hildelith and Cyneberg were there to greet them. It was beginning to take the feel of that first night when Einarr and his party had brought home Wulfmaer and feasted with his family and the villagers. So much had happened in so short a time.

Einaar realized that the first feast had consumed much of the village food reserve, a generosity to honour valued guests. Then the hall had been the only building where the villagers could come together and relax from their toils, sharing their scarce food supplies. Now, an enriched village had no worries about how they would restore their larders.

Tonight, villagers and Ivar's warriors would come to exchange news and meet old friends. Where the feast had been joyful chaos and noise, this was more businesslike. It was a series of social gatherings, and Einarr and his close group were able to talk with Ælfwyn, her family and her advisers, seated around the table. Through the evening, Einarr and Wulfmaer described all that had happened since they had set out to meet King Edmund. They had an attentive audience. It was late into the night when they finished recounting their saga, hearing what had happened at the village and what news had come up river from Ivar.

Although Einarr's expedition had been isolated from the village and Ivar's main camp, there had been a regular traffic between the village and the Roman fort. Scouts had been sent out from both locations and between them. Supplies and craftsmen had travelled between the two sites by river. Einarr learned that more ships had arrived to join Ivar. Some were from the original sailing, straggling in after being blown off course, or delayed for repairs. Others were fresh arrivals that had not been ready to leave with the main fleet. As Ivar was returning unwanted ships, a flow of news was possible between the Great Army and the homelands. That flow of ships would slow and stop as the winter storms swept in, but the longer the trade could continue, the better prepared all would be for the campaign that was to follow from the end of winter.

Einarr learned that his father had decided to build forts between the Roman fort and Ælfwyn's village. This would provide strong points, between which patrols could ride, to allow a patrol to seek shelter, or be reinforced rapidly, if attacked. These forts were built on either side of the river. Where two small forts faced each other there was a rope ferry to allow reinforcements to cross the river quickly. This was not part of the original plan, but the addition of a friendly Saxon village, and almost no casualties, made it possible to hold a much larger area than originally expected. It also avoided crowding out the fort which, though it was very large, was not an infinite space. Now with the prospect of a number of winter skirmishes with Esla and his allies, greater thought had to be given to maintaining the Great Army until it was time to march North.

Lodin had built onto Ælfwyn's village a major fortification. As time and resources permitted, he would further strengthen the defences, but the construction was already strong enough to resist a considerable enemy force. His ambitions for the enlarged village were providing the workshops that would allow weapons to be made and repaired. As he described their progress, Lodin impressed Einarr greatly. Even with the help of Aggi and his pre-fabricated buildings, what Lodin had achieved in days was remarkable.

"Tell me Lodin, why you have neglected the quay?" asked Einaar.

"Not neglected Lord Einarr," responded Lodin. "Aggi is already considering how we should improve the quay, now that it is being used so frequently, and by larger ships. I have also been thinking of ways to make more use of the river. There are two matters of concern."

"I am grateful for all that your people have done for us Lord Einarr", interjected Ælfwyn. "Even with more people and time, we would never have built what Lodin has constructed here. We do not have the knowledge and the skills. I have wanted to repair the quay but, with our small boats for fishing, it was a lesser importance than shelter and tending our crops."

Einarr considered for a moment. "Gentle Lady we can provide the people and materials", turning to Lodin, "What are your concerns Lodin?"

"Lord Einarr, as you know from our first arrival, the old and poorly kept fishing village matches the quay and is all that can be seen from a boat passing on the river. If we build a new quay that is adequate for our ships, anyone passing will wonder why someone has made such effort to build a quay that would serve a township. Aggi thinks that he could make a stronger quay that does not display its strength, but matching the appearance of the few old fishing huts".

"Yes, I understand that," replied Einarr, "but from what you have told me of my father's plans to build forts along the Roman road, we will no longer be invisible. We could never have hoped to remain unknown, but the events of the last few days have announced our presence to a close enemy, perhaps to the Northumbrians, as we do not know how well Esla communicates with them. Esla will know now of the loss of the fort and of his warriors. From those plotting against the King, he will know that time is running out for him and he can no longer expect to strike by surprise. We must believe that he has sent messengers to tell the Northumbrians and plead for their early support."

"You are right Lord Einarr," said Ælfwyn. "Esla is no fool and he must know now that a great force already opposes him. He must have sent spies to gauge your strength, to see what forces are here in this village."

"That answers your first concern Lodin, what of the second?"

"The second is time and resources, with the winter drawing in."

Lodin paused for a moment before continuing. He drew in a deep breath. Now, he decided, was the time to talk about an ambitious plan that had been forming.

"Lord Einarr, it would not require great effort to repair the existing quay for small boats. It would be an easy matter for Aggi to disguise the repairs. To rebuild the quay for regular use by our

213

ships would require a great effort and greater visibility. There is still advantage in not advertising our strength. I have also been thinking that perhaps we will now be here longer than we expected. If the Northumbrians send forces to assist Esla and the other Saxons who scheme against their King, we may fight in these lands the battles we expected in the North. Now that we ally with the King, this would be a good place to serve us as a port for our supplies. I have thought of a plan to support this."

"Set out your ideas Lodin, and I will take them to my father. I agree with you that our plans are already changing since King Edmund agreed to ally with us." As he spoke, Einaar leaned further towards Lodin with strengthening interest.

Lodin reached into his jerkin and withdrew a roll of vellum. He unrolled it on the table, brushing aside remaining food. He placed his dirk on one corner of the skin and drinking mugs were placed on the other corners. Einaar could see that this was the working plan for the fortifications. What he had not noticed before was that a stream snaked down from the Roman road and joined the main river to the West of the island on which the village stood.

Lodin described how the stream could be widened from its confluence with the river, inland to the point where it almost reached the Western palisade from marsh to the new fort. If the stream was dug deeper and wider at low water, deep to a man's waist, better to his chest, it would be deep enough even for their larger ships at low water, allowing vessels to come into the new port at any state of the river. While the stream was being improved, docks could be cut beside the palisade and a new palisade would be set up around the docks. As that work was being completed, a new fort would be built facing into the marsh at the causeway.

"A worthy plan Lodin. Make a start tomorrow on the digging of the docks with the men you have to hand. List for me the additional resources needed and I will ask my father to provide them immediately. List also any items that Aggi must prepare, and make me a copy of your map. At first light I will take the Øvind down river to the Roman fort. I will take Gudhrun and the Lady Gytha with her maids. Give me a full crew and I hope to return within two days. If I am to be delayed, I will send word back with the Øvind and instructions for your work on the port. Now we shall rest before our journey".

With that, Einarr stood and the council broke up for the night.

Lodin looked at his young leader with great approval. Before, Einaar had been a young warrior learning from others. In a few short months he had become a Prince, a natural authority, an acceptance of his powers, to be followed readily by those around him.

Thirty One

A cold wet morning had greeted them as the Øvind was got underway, sleet mixed with a cutting rain. A small party, including Lodin and Ælfwyn, had seen them off. The strong Westerly sent heavy rain slanting into the vessel, but in compensation pushed the Øvind eastward towards its destination. The village quay was rapidly lost from sight. There was little for the crew to do as the bow cut through the ruffled waters of the river. Today was work for the steersman and those following his tacks on twin sail lines. The wind was directly behind them for much of the way, the sail hauled only to keep it taught and filled as the river wound to the North or South of true East in its serpentine route across the flood plain.

The Lady Gytha and her maids retired to the relative warmth of the dry space below the aft deck, but Gudhrun remained on the foredeck beside Einarr. It was cold and wet beside the stem and its great, carved dragon's head, but it was exhilarating. The lightly loaded Øvind sat on the water rather than in it, skimming across the surface at great speed. The speed seemed all the greater as the riverbanks shot past on either side. Einarr was pleased that he had decided to take the river rather than ride the shorter distance along the Southern bank of the flood plain. He had considered this the safer route, but it was also the most comfortable. Riding through the driving rain would have been miserable, tiring for horses and riders. He chose to stand on the foredeck, enjoying the passing view, but the crew had rigged sail cloth between foredeck and mast to create a dry area for those not involved in sailing the vessel.

Old Gisi was steersman and captain for the voyage. Immune to all weathers, he stood to the steerboard, ignoring the lashing rain and the occasional flurries of sleet and snow. He expected to reach the fort in the daylight, believing the wind would hold all day and more. It would have been no faster on horseback, in the increasingly heavy rain it was more likely that horsemen would have had to stop to rest their animals, with no shelter other than the trees which were already shedding their leaves for the winter. Einarr and Gudhrun seemed as immune to the cold and rain, standing together, water streaming off their heavy cloaks, their heads covered by hoods, as the Øvind raced on towards the great Roman fort, passing the small forts and ferries set up since Einarr had first headed inland to the village and on to King Edmund. He noticed that the small forts were little larger than the area of three village huts, providing stout walls and walkways inside the walls, but with a thatched roof that protected the occupants from the weather.

The light was fading fast as they rounded the last bend before the fort. Even the turning tide had not slowed their progress. A convenient and distinctive cluster of large willows on the North bank had alerted Gisi to the closeness of the lake, although he was coming to know the river well, having made several journeys along it during the last ten days. He felt he knew it well enough to sail at night provided there was at least star-light to illuminate the way dimly. The willows provided a welcome reminder of position, giving time for him to take in the sail and set the crew to the oars for the final stretch. The oarsmen pulled steadily, the Øvind passed longships moored to each side of the river, the crews exchanging greetings as they passed by.

As they rounded the final bend, the fort came into sight, the Øvind was making way smartly under oars, ready to make a well-timed approach to the quay. The temporary cover over the fore part of the main deck had been folded and stowed. The oarsmen backed water to time the approach to the quay and Einarr noticed a number of strange vessels moored to the island in the centre of the lake.

Einarr and Gudhrun stood proudly on the foredeck with the Lady Gytha and her two maids as the Øvind coasted the final paces to make soft contact with the stone quay, oars already tossed and stowed on their racks. The rain had given way to squally showers, but this was ignored by the party on the foredeck. Soon they would be ashore in the shelter of the fort and its buildings.

Ivar had himself formed the reception for his son on the quay. As he greeted Einaar and his small party, Gisi made certain that the Øvind was safely moored to the dock and dismissed his crew.

Ivar was anxious to hear how Einaar had succeeded in his first diplomatic task. He already knew that the Øvind and her company had been well-received at Depenham. He had sent the first supply ship up river a day after Einarr had left to take Wulfmaer home. It had taken longer for the loaded vessel to reach the village, but it had been preceded by a small fast boat that arrived shortly after Einarr had ridden out to meet King Edmund. It pleased Einarr that his father showed such confidence in the untried diplomacy of his son that he had dispatched the first supply ship before receiving news of the meeting with Ælfwyn.

Einarr gave Ivar a full report of all what had happened since he left the fort for Depenham. Much of the early story was already known to Ivar, from the regular exchange of news with Ælfwyn's village. Ivar still wanted to hear directly from his son. After Einarr and his party set out for Kett's Hall, the story was new to Ivar. He listened intently but made no attempt to interrupt the flow of the Einarr's account. It was clear that his confidence in Einarr was well placed, he was proud of his son's achievements, pleased that Einarr gave such a clear and detailed account of all that happened during his expedition to the Saxons.

While Einarr recounted their adventures, food and drink had been brought to the table they sat around, in the hall that had been taken for Ivar's quarters. Red Osten and several other captains had joined them as Einarr presented his report. When he reached the time of their less eventful return journey, Einarr paused.

"Lady Gytha, thank you for the help that you have given us. You will be safe here with us," said Ivar, turning towards

Gytha who had been listening to Einaar recount the adventures they had shared, then turning to his left,

"Tryggvi, go to the new hall and prepare it for the Lady Gytha's use," Ivar commanded.

The new hall had been built on the site of the hall destroyed when they captured the fort from Esla's men. It was smaller than the original building, constructed from the materials Aggi had prepared for shipment with the fleet. It was still a large building for Gytha and her maids, more to respect her status as King Edmund's cousin than to provide her with essential accommodation. Conveniently, one third of the building had been divided to provide the private quarters of a high lord.

"Gudhrun," said Ivar turning to her, "I give you a special duty. You will share the hall with the Lady Gytha. I want you to select servants and warriors to complete the household, to serve and protect our honoured guest."

"Lord Ivar, I will be glad to take this duty. May I ask my lord that I will be allowed to also continue my duties as a warrior with Lord Einarr?" responded Gudhrun

Ivar nodded his approval and turned again to Gytha, "Lady Gytha, I trust that this will meet with your approval. For now, Gudhrun must select warriors from our people, but you may wish to ask the Lady Ælfwyn to provide warriors and servants. You can send a message back with the Øvind tomorrow and I will order her captain to return quickly with those the lady Ælfwyn provides to staff your household."

"Lord Ivar, you are most considerate. Gudhrun is as a sister to me and I thank you for your kindness. As to servants and warriors, I am most grateful for your kindness in providing these immediately. If the Lady Ælfwyn is able to lend me warriors and servants, I shall be less a burden on your hospitality, but I would not want to place an urgent duty on the Øvind. Perhaps, when it is next convenient, she could carry a few of the Lady Ælfwyn's people to augment my household."

Einarr observed the exchanges. He was pleased that Gytha had been so skilful, recognising that Ivar was both generous, and maintaining control of Gytha, almost as a hostage. By requesting some Saxons to add to her household when next the Øvind could be spared to transport them, Gytha had acknowledged Ivar as her protector and host.

"Einarr, please continue with your account, I want every detail from you," Ivar instructed.

Einarr continued by recounting their return journey from Kett's Hall to the Roman fort. He concentrated on a review of the new fortifications at Depenham and Lodin's request for additional resources. The idea of building a port inland appealed to Ivar. It would relieve the Roman fort and distribute their resources, but without altering the plans for the coming year, rather it would assist the plans in placing a part of the army further inland along their line of march, but he could see many new advantages.

Ivar had yet to negotiate a formal alliance with King Edmund. He could now see that the Saxon King was unlikely to survive without his assistance. That should be worth more than just safe passage to fight the Northumbrians!

Ivar was already thinking beyond those battles. Here was an opportunity to reach a more durable alliance, securing two ports for future trade, bases to sail against other Saxons, something his father Ragnar had been considering before his death. That the Lady Ælfwyn had formed a strong bond with Lodin and his own son, and Gudhrun had formed a strong friendship with Gytha and Wulfmaer meant that there was a special alliance with Depenham, its new fortifications and facilities.

If Edmund would create Wulfmaer an earl in place of Esla, that allowed Depenham to become an allied port, shared between Ivar and Wulfmaer. The Roman fort would command the river to the new port and Ivar would insist that it be under his full control, together with the island in the centre of the lake. Since the capture of the Northumbrian ships, Ivar had seen potential in the island as a defended mooring, the Roman fort having a short remaining quay.

Thirty Two

The quays had been surveyed in the week after Ivar had taken the fort. The reports had not been encouraging. Although the fort enclosed a great area, and Aggi had built storehouses and halls, the surviving quay slowed the unloading of ships.

The stone mason Julius was an East Roman who had worked for the Emperor, building fortifications and repairing harbours. He had great skills and experience in working with stone, joining Ivar's father Ragnar to advise on defeating stone-built defences. He was a neat stocky man, black hair streaked with white, face lined and hardened from years toiling in the dust of stone working. His recommendation to Ivar was that the surviving quay should be repaired, but no effort should be expended in rebuilding the two additional quays.

"Lord Ivar, I have surveyed the walls and quays. The walls require no work, the surviving quay requires only small works. The other quays are so far decayed that it would not be a matter of major repair, but of building new quays in their place. You know I have few in our party who can work with stone, we know nothing of local stone, other than that it would require transport from some distance inland. I cannot recommend that you order this work to be done. If you decide it should be undertaken, I must advise that it will take a considerable time to complete, well past the approaching winter. If you accept that we should only repair the surviving quay, I can salvage all the stone required from the decayed quays"

Julius paused, but Ivar showed no sign of asking questions or giving orders.

"Lord Ivar, to the difficulties of major construction in adding more quay space, there is the matter of defence. You post sentries at all times in the fort, and on the river approaches. With these preparations, no one can take this fortress by surprise and stealth as you did. The surviving quay is well covered from the main gate. The bridge will not support a large attacking force from the land, but the addition of new quays will stretch the defence."

"Your points are well made," said Ivar, stroking his chin thoughtfully. "Continue."

"Thank you my lord. You had asked me to consider artillery and defences. I believe that you will be best served by having Aggi erect wooden platforms inside the fort's walls at each corner. We would then build ballistas, catapults, trebuchets, and great crossbows on the platforms to cover the approaches to the walls, allowing any approaching boats to be destroyed before they could land warriors. Fire projectors would be mounted on the stone walls between each corner."

"Have you sufficient people to build the artillery Julius?"

"Yes Lord Ivar. If we build wooden platforms, Aggi has people who will do that work well. They will then be able to help my people to construct the engines of war."

"I will order the work to begin," said Ivar. "Tell me now what can be done with the island."

"I have surveyed the island. Had we men and materials, I would recommend the use of stone, but wood will allow us to begin work now. There is no shortage of suitable trees in the forest, and your warriors would add to our skilled wood workers. I spoke of this with Aggi. He suggested that he could spare three of his craftsmen to supervise warriors selecting and cutting trees, making the components that we need to fortify the island."

Julius unrolled the vellum map of the island. At its North end, the island was a hill rising out of the lake, a rough circle of dry land, at its narrow summit, almost half as high as the tops of the fort's great walls. The hill had a covering of trees, many had already been cut down but the remaining trees must be cleared. In all, this part of the island would have almost supported two Saxon hides, if the flooded area, nearly surrounded by the curving spit, was included in the calculations. From its South East edge, a spit of land extended, curving round towards the West, a natural but shallow harbour.

A stick of charcoal in his left hand, Julius began to add detail to the map of the island as he spoke.

"Lord Ivar, here near the top of the hill is a well with sweet water. I recommend that a palisade be thrown up around the base of the hill with a single gate here," sketching a gate with towers in the crook of the spit.

"The outer stand of timber should be driven in at the water's edge. A second stand of timber should be set up two paces behind the first. Earth will be used to fill the space between. Most of the earth required can be provided when reducing the height of the hill to provide a broad level area. In front of the gate, there will be a timber quay. Along the Eastern side of the spit, we will build a single stand of timber in palisade, continuing the arc round to a tower. A second tower will be built ten paces from the first and the palisade continued round to join with the double palisade of the hill. We have measured the tide's range and, at low water, the area inside this single palisade is as deep as the waist height of a man so your ships will be afloat even at low water. Rafted together, there is space for more than forty of your largest ships".

"You have done well Julius. We can cover the gate from the North East corner of the fort. From the top of the hill we could cover the fort's quay," observed Ivar, tracing an arc from the fort to the harbour palisade sketched on the map, then tracing an arc from the island hill across the fort's quay.

"Yes my lord, although a war engine on the hill could be used to threaten the fort." Julius paused and stepped from one side to another as though viewing the island rather than a map.

"Ah! I have it. I could build you a watch tower atop a platform on the hill's summit. A trebuchet facing towards the sea. Below the platform we would stow barrels of oil and kindling, dry from the weather. If ever the island was at risk of being taken, the oil could be fired to destroy tower and war engine."

"I could not have suggested better," approved Ivar, "but there are further detailed improvements that could be made. You will provide a windlass in each tower at the port's entrance to work a chain boom," Julius nodded and smiled, "if you build a windlass on the fort's quay, a rope ferry would speed the movement of ships between the quay and the island. We need a strong garrison on the island and the well provides for many men. For now, the warriors helping to build the island's defences can live aboard the ships moored there. As soon as we have completed the palisade around the hill, put up frames against the walls, make shelters with sailcloth for men and supplies. You can use sails from some of the ships in the harbour. Later, we will replace the shelters with permanent buildings when the defences are complete."

Ivar was pleased with the progress that they had made in developing his original plan. Being able to securely moor longships at the island would allow him to keep the skeleton crews that would otherwise be required to sail them home. If the winter was not harsh, there would be regular sailings between Ivar's winter camps and the homelands. The ships' crews would provide a guard at the fort and island when he led his main force

226

North and into battle. It would provide a secure place to land additional men and supplies, if needed, and provide a strong base to fall back to if the campaign in the North went badly.

Ivar's brothers would not have made any effort to develop beyond the original plans, which were already more complex than they liked. They would have spent their winter working through their supplies of drink and food, venturing out only to hunt and terrorise any local villages. In the Spring they would have assembled their warriors and begun the march North. Ivar thought beyond today. He realized that the days of raiding would become more difficult. The signs were there already for those who would see. Opposition would increase and a raider was always at a disadvantage from any natives raised against him. The only advantage was surprise and what surprise could there be from raiders who repeated earlier raids?

Ivar had long been thinking of settlements and trading posts in other lands. It was always possible to find land that could be settled. It was always possible to establish a place of trade. To build fortified trading posts, to form alliances with the local leaders, providing a new opportunity. It also created a base from which to launch raids further than they had raided before and where the people of those lands were not familiar with their way of raiding. Now, almost by accident, these half formed ideas were coming together with the prospect of a permanent and strongly protected base and trading centre. There was still work to do in forging a strong alliance with King Edmund, there was still the original objective of taking revenge against the Northumbrians. Even the original objective was starting to change in Ivar's mind.

Thirty Three

Esla roared again, pounding the table with his fists. He was missing Birdoswald, not for any sentimental reason, but because he had always been there to accept his master's displeasure. The earl was alone in his hall, servants, family and warriors all avoiding him. This was the third day that he had raged blindly and there was a pile of furniture fragments to bear testimony to the depth of his anger. That his supporters had taken every effort to avoid him demonstrated a level of wisdom because Esla was liable to destroy anything, or anyone, who came within his reach. He saw only through a red mist and his mood was not assisted by the continuing toothache.

The messenger who had arrived from Kett's Hall carried an incomplete warning. It was the cryptic message of a very worried co-conspirator, carried in the messenger's memory. The man was lucky not to have been struck down by Esla but he had been sent back to find more useful information.

By bringing Einarr's party inside the hall's compound, Edmund had denied any potential rebels full knowledge of the party or the decomposing bundles lashed to the pack horses. The removal by cart, the burial at night in the forest, had been effective. Much might be suspected, but there was no certainty about the exact nature of the stinking cargo, or of the numbers of bodies that might have been brought there, or why they had not simply been left where they fell. By keeping the party in the retreat, little was known about who they were or how many were in the party. Again, much could be speculated and the rumours that were circulating further confused potential intelligence.

To add to the confusion, the King had deliberately planted the rumour that he had sent a small band of warriors into the Great Marsh to the North West of Kett's Hall to deal with the robbers who had fled there. This was a credible story because, for generations, outlaws of various kinds had made their home in the vast expanse of marsh and shallow lakes into which several rivers drained. It was a wild hostile place, dotted with small islands and many dangerous tracks, a maze that could swallow an army. The only way to deal with the inhabitants was to hire a mercenary band and leave them to seek the outlaws. Having found and killed a number of outlaws, the mercenaries would bring back the bodies as proof to earn their pay. It was possible that this had nothing to do with Esla, or Birdoswald, or their planned treachery, but, as Esla's friends at Kett's Hall knew nothing of the mission given to Birdoswald, there was no link to direct the speculation.

When the King went out to hunt, Einarr's party had remained within the compound. When they rode out after the King had left for the hunt, they rode North before circling back through the forest to return to their original starting point. That added credibility to the story the King had planted, because mercenaries would return to hunt for more outlaws. As Einarr had been careful to avoid any isolated huts or hamlets, there was no new intelligence filtering back to Kett's Hall.

Esla knew that it all had something to do with the failure of Birdoswald to return as instructed, but the question he kept asking himself was:

"What does it all mean?"

The riddle was driving him mad. He had suspected that Birdoswald had decided to stay away, and he might have nothing to do with the news from Kett's Hall, but Esla did not like or trust coincidence and it did not much assist him because Birdoswald had been the only person he trusted to organize patrols that kept an eye on those within his lands. He was coming to understand how his treatment of Birdoswald had been unwise but that only made him rage further.

He needed to find out what had happened, what might still be happening, and how it could affect his plans. He could hardly set off on his own, but he was at a loss to find anyone who could be relied on. He was no coward but, until he knew more of what faced him, he could not expose himself to risk of capture by whatever threatened him. The patrol that had failed to return could have met with any of several fates. It was small enough to be taken by bandits and there were gangs that roamed the kingdom. From their patrol route they would have met another force somewhere in a short ride to either side of the old Roman fort, but then again they could just have decided to avoid Esla's rages and kept riding to start afresh with another earl. All of the members of the patrol were professional warriors and none had families, so there was nothing to hold them to Esla beyond fear of any consequences that might follow them, from a lord who was known for his delight in vengeance and his ability to hold a grudge for ever.

"No, there is a hostile force out there and both the patrol and Birdoswald's riders must have been taken or killed," Esla told himself.

That revelation was no more comforting because it left unanswered the 'who', 'where', 'why' and 'when'. Also unanswered was the question of what should be done about it. He would look a fool if he started sending messages to his fellow conspirators without having something to say beyond wild guesses. He had already sent messages to the Northumbrians and his comrades to urge that the planned confrontation with the King be brought forward. He knew that weapons and supplies were due any day from the Northumbrians, that this might include warriors and that a second group of ships might arrive not long after the first.

Had Edmund suspected or uncovered the threat from his rebel earls? Did he know of the involvement of the Northumbrians? It was possible and it could explain why he remained at Kett's Hall that was in the centre of his most loyal supporters. That had been worrying the conspirators because they originally planned to ambush the King and his bodyguard when

231

he rode East, back to Rendlesham.

If he continued to stay at Kett's Hall they might have to take the battle to him on formal lines with increasing risk to the conspirators.

Then again, Edmund might have new allies, or perhaps he had hired a band of mercenaries. There were always professional warriors for hire. There were so many possibilities, but only one reality. Esla kept turning the questions over in his mind and hoped for some solution. He came back time and time again to the 'how' and the 'who' in answering the questions.

The solution proved to be so simple. He was amazed that it had not occurred to him at the beginning. Perhaps this rotten tooth was the real problem, a nagging pain that intruded into his thoughts. No matter, the solution was found now. What had given him the idea was his cousin's husband, Baldred, who had made the mistake of entering the Hall.

Baldred was a poor relation, old before his time and poorly dressed. The least suspicious person to gather intelligence. No one could look less like a warrior. Baldred was a trader, on a small scale, good enough only to make a meagre living. He was also very loyal to Esla, one of the few people the earl could trust, not that he trusted anyone.

"Baldred, how good to see you, I have a small commission for you", said Esla trying hard to look good natured and generous. "I want you to ride out for me to seek some information."

Baldred approached the table, but even he was keen to keep beyond the easy reach of Esla. As he came closer, Esla dropped his voice to a conspiratorial whisper and gave his instructions. He also gave Baldred a purse with some coins as an advance payment, promising to compensate him further on his return. Baldred was cautious because this was great generosity for Esla, suggesting that the task was to be more difficult or dangerous than presented. Still, the payment was not to be dismissed at this time of the year when travel would become more difficult as the winter followed with its storms and cold. With the second promised payment, Baldred would enjoy a comfortable winter and not need to set out until the conditions had improved again.

Baldred had returned to his wife and home to saddle his old pony and collect some supplies. Mathilda, his wife, urged him to be careful as she made up a bundle of food for him. She knew her cousin too well to trust any sign of generosity. Still, the money would see them safely through the winter, making the risk seem worthwhile.

Now his pony plodded on, reversing the route followed by the northern patrol. He had ridden on through the small village that was the first sign of habitation after leaving Esla's Hall. Baldred knew that this part of Esla's lands had few people and fewer villages. Its mixture of rivers, marshes and sandy soil did little to assist a farmer and the villages were small and poor. There was no indication that any misfortune had befallen the village. It looked worn and ill cared for, that it could have been sacked by a passing war band, but Baldred knew that it always looked like this. It was a modest collection of huts, some round and some square, nothing remarkable. It was neither a wealthy village nor a place of grinding poverty, in every respect unremarkable, limping on from one year to the next, set back by drought and flood, plague and famine, but always struggling on against the adversities. Baldred had acknowledged the two men he had passed. He recognized both and they recognized him, although he struggled to remember their names. As he passed the second man, he slowed almost to a halt and asked when he had last seen the patrol. He learned that the patrol had not been seen for some days but the villager was unsure exactly when.

So Baldred had established that whatever had befallen the patrol, the location of misfortune was further west along their route. Ahead of him was the old fortress. His pony carefully stepped along the winding road that would shortly descend onto a straight road that ran past the fortress. As the track descended and curved towards the great stone walls, he would briefly see out across the lake before his view was cut by small groups of trees, then he would be onto the hard straight road and the fortress would leap into view. He gathered his packhorse closer to him, a steady animal, no younger than the pony he rode, but still able to carry a full load. Today it carried some trade goods in boxes on either flank, an old cloth tied over them. A suitable disguise for a spy, authentic to Baldred as his normal appearance when heading to a market. He had carefully selected the contents of the load. Although he had a commission from Esla, it did not mean that he could not make a profitable trade should the market present itself.

The sound of horses approaching alarmed him. He had only enough time to move off the track and hide with his animals in the scrub and trees beside the lane he had been following. A small band of warriors rode past. He could not see them clearly but they appeared to be young and healthy with good equipment and their horses were in their prime. Baldred now faced a quandary that he was not well equipped to consider, never having been trained as a warrior. Having been forced to hide from one group of horsemen, he could meet a second group and not have time to get off the track and out of sight. Even if there were no other armed riders following the first group, he had no way of knowing how far the group he had just avoided might ride before turning back. He might have less time to hide if they approached from his back.

Had he not been forced to hide, he would now see between the stands of trees across the lake to the large island in its centre. He might not see clearly but there was activity and the masts of ships. He would know that this was not what he should expect to see and he could slow his pony, keeping a careful lookout. He could have stopped and taken a careful view, or even left his animals and walked to the lakeside, but he was now to make a decision that would deny him this intelligence.

To Baldred's left was a narrow and rough track that was little used. He decided to follow this track to avoid any further patrols. He could see little to either side of the track as he led his horses quietly along it, but he would be invisible to anyone using the broader track that he had just left. A twisting path, the track led tortuously down towards the Roman road. He could now see that road through the scrub as he came steeply down towards it, some distance from where the wider path would have joined it. He scanned carefully to left and right but saw nothing to alarm him.

Now on the start of the straight road, Baldred maintained a steady pace. He passed the clumps of trees, now grown almost into a line since he had last ridden this way. The trees suddenly stopped and the fortress appeared to leap forward. At first it seemed as it always had for many years. Then Baldred noticed movement on one of the great towers and realized there were sentries, another surprise and something that he had not expected. He faced a difficult decision. He could ride up to the great doors of the fortress, expecting to find it occupied by Esla's people, but if he was suspected, he might be taken prisoner or killed. Baldred had no liking for those possibilities. As he rode past, he could not afford to look keenly towards the fort but must ride slumped in his saddle as a weary traveller might.

He could see a strange ship tied to the quay, but it was like any trading vessel that Saxons might sail along the coast and up the rivers to the markets of the larger villages and towns. This was the third surprise, but he would learn little more unless he was challenged and that might be the last thing he saw. There was no one on the road ahead and, as he rode past the end of the bridge to the fortress, the great doors were firmly closed, no one stood sentry outside. It was a dull wet day and for a moment he doubted that he had seen a sentry on the first tower, but now he could see movement on top of the gate towers. He made no reaction and allowed his pony to plod on, the packhorse following on its lead.

It seemed an age before he rode past the first welcome trees that would hide him from the fortress. He breathed a sigh of relief. There was no one on the road, no cry of challenge, and then he was beyond real risk. He might still ride into a patrol from whoever was occupying the fortress, but more likely to be ignored as a harmless trader because a patrol would assume he had satisfied their comrades in the fortress. Although he had relaxed, he now faced an even more difficult decision.

Esla had told him to take no chances and to make sure he returned as quickly as he could, should he discover the fate of the patrol, or see anything unusual, but Esla might not be satisfied with what little he had learned. Should he ride on to Depenham to learn the fate of Birdoswald? Every step his pony took could be carrying him into a new danger. He could now see the track that was the shortest path back to Esla's Hall.

He faced the same decision that Birdoswald had faced at the old village of Depenham. He had learned something that should be of great interest to Esla, but there could be more of even greater interest and importance. Where Birdoswald had seen strange riders, his party was of much the same strength and, at that point, held the benefit of surprise. He could ignore the riders and go through the sacked village to find out what had become of the villagers, perhaps capture something of value, or learn something important, but there was always a risk that he faced a larger band of warriors and a hostile village that had to be reached by a difficult causeway.

If Esla had treated his people with respect as a reliable leader, neither Birdoswald nor Baldred would have faced such a difficult decision. As it was, they were afraid of placing themselves at risk and uncertain what Esla really wanted to hear. They could be confident that he would find fault with any decision they took. The result was that Birdoswald had decided to follow a similar sized band of warriors and hope to surprise them at night. If he succeeded, he would have prisoners or bodies to take back to Esla and horses with their equipment and any cargo. In deciding on that course, he lost the opportunity to scout the area and identify what the real position was. That would have provided real intelligence and still allowed time to catch up with the riders he had observed leaving the marsh and heading along the Roman road to the west.

Similar though the choices might be, Baldred knew that he was alone, any warrior he met would be stronger than he. His only defence was to convince them that he was a trader on his way to a market. That might succeed, there was no guarantee, but every possibility that a warrior might take no chances and kill him out of hand. Each step his pony took carried him closer to the point of decision. He looked around but saw nothing new to help his decision.

He was almost past the track that headed eventually to Esla's Hall. Impulsively, he turned his pony and packhorse into the track and picked up his pace. It was the lesser of fears. He still needed to decide on what to tell Esla, but he would have a night's sleep to help him. When he found a place to halt, he decided against making a fire. Even if the light of the flames did not reach some hostile, the smoke might. He ate some of the cold food Mathilda had packed for him and rolled himself in his cloak. The ground was still damp but at least it had stopped raining. He would wake at first light and continue his journey home. Sleep came quickly but there was no dream to help him shape his story for Esla.

When he woke he felt refreshed and his problems all seemed smaller. The wind was chill but it was still dry and he ate some more food before setting out. He also made sure that his pony and packhorse had eaten the oats he had given them and drunk their fill at the small stream where he had camped. There was no need to hurry and he had still to sort out the story for Esla.

As he turned the events over in his mind they fell into a new order. In his mind, he had just hidden himself in time, as warriors rode past not far from the first village. They were young, strong, and well-equipped. They were Saxons but not known to him. He had hidden because he knew only that horsemen were coming towards him, but once they had ridden past, there was no benefit in making himself known to them because they could be friend or foe. His creativity built on this imagined close encounter, providing detail that he had not seen. In evading the riders, he had joined the Roman road further to the west of the point where the normal track joined it. That meant that he had not seen the ship masts and activity across the lake at the large island.

The line of trees and scrub had hidden that view. He now remembered the fortress differently. He saw two Saxon ships tied up to the quay, the only sign of life being sentries patrolling the tops of the great walls. It would have been wise to avoid riding past them along the road. His mind built a picture of small tracks and paths south of the straight road. They wound towards and then away from the road. They took him past guards and small patrols, an invisible observer. With all of this activity, it would have been unwise to attempt to rejoin the road or to travel further westwards. Then he had come across a larger track that he recognized as leading back eventually to Esla's Hall. The story was becoming robust and new detail was added here and there. Soon it was a product worthy of telling around the winter hearth.

By the time that Baldred had reached the small hill overlooking Esla's Hall, and the collection of buildings that made up a small village, he was the hero spy, carrying vital information to his master. His bravery was beyond calling and no one could challenge his decisions. As he once more travelled through the account, he had learned much and it was vital that he should tell Esla what he had learned with the least delay.

Luckily for Baldred, Esla's toothache had finally subsided and he felt suddenly at peace with the world after days of nagging pain. When Baldred strode confidently into the hall, at contrast with his customary hesitant shuffle, Elsa did not notice today an event without recent parallel, Esla would think well of all.

"Ah Baldred, you have news for me?" enquired Esla in a kind voice.

Even so, the question almost destroyed Baldred's composure.

"Yes indeed my lord," came the reply. "I rode out as you bid and all was well to Saxulfingham. I asked the villagers if they had seen our patrol and they thought it was many days since it last passed through their village. I rode on carefully and heard horsemen approaching on the track. I hid and watched them pass by. There were twenty riders, young and all warriors, well-equipped and Saxon, but I did not recognize any of them. When they were gone I returned to the track and rode on cautiously. Before the straight west road, I heard more horsemen and hid again. This was a smaller patrol, but similar to the first with Saxon warriors I did not know. As I was about to return to the track I heard them riding back and stayed in hiding. I did not know how far they had ridden ahead of me, or if they might return. To make certain that I would not be taken prisoner and prevented from returning to you with my report, I carefully walked my horses through the scrub and trees, stopping frequently to listen for horses or men. I worked my way down towards the West road, tethering my horses, I crawled to the side of the road. I could see no one else on the road or in the trees opposite me. It seemed safe to gather my horses and come down onto the road.

I knew the fortress would be to my left and not far away. Once on the road I made my way towards the fortress. As the trees thinned, I could see the walls and two ships moored to the quay. As the first tower came into sight I could see a sentry, then the gate towers with more sentries. I rode slowly on, the hood of my cloak hiding my eyes from the sentries. Then I was screened by the next trees but I could hear people and horses on the road ahead.

I found a small disused track heading South and left the road, hobbling my horses in a small clearing, returning carefully to the West road. I was in time to see six warriors riding back towards the fortress. I now knew that there were more than twenty warriors set to patrolling the road and tracks to the south of the fortress and there were at least twelve more standing sentry in the towers. Although I recognised no one, they were all young and healthy Saxon warriors. With the two ships, there may be two hundred in the fortress. But no attempt had been made to close the road and tracks with guard points.

I made my way back to you my lord as quickly as I could

that you may decide what actions now to take. I could return if you wish, try to gain further information, or ride to Depenham to see what can be learned there." With the ending of his story, Baldred looked cautiously towards Esla to gauge his reaction and duck anything that might be thrown in his direction. He was surprised to see Esla still in unusually good humour.

Esla smiled, a rare event, "My dear cousin, you have done well. Take this token of my appreciation of a difficult task performed loyally."

With that, Esla passed a large leather bag of coin on the table, pushing it towards Baldred.

Baldred slid the bag towards him and looked for a way out before Esla changed his mind and manner. "Thank you Lord Esla, you know that you can always rely on me. With your permission I would wish to go to Mathilda that she knows I am home safely."

"Of course cousin and please send Mathilda my best wishes." Baldred needed no further encouragement to leave Esla. If there was anything more dangerous than Esla in apparent good humour, Baldred could not bring it to mind.

Thirty Four

The great gates slammed shut behind the messenger Ivar had sent out to King Edmund. He had chosen one of Wulfmaer's Saxons and sent him on the Øvind, which was taking a further cargo of supplies up river to the Depenham. There, the Saxon would be given a horse and an escort to ride on to Kett's Hall.

Ivar had debated with himself on the course of action. He had been tempted to send Einaar but there might be greater need of him here. Since they had first made landfall everything had gone better than his most optimistic hopes. Ivar knew that this could mean a harder shock when the tide turned on their good fortune. They were still three weeks from the planned meeting with King Edmund, but Ivar had learned from a Northumbrian prisoner that a fleet was due to follow on their delivery of arms and supplies, Esla having persuaded the Northumbrian King that they should attack King Edmund before winter closed on them. It was already growing late in the year for a campaign, but Ivar could see the merit of a short sharp attack without the threat of a counter attack before the next Summer. It hinged on how large an army was sent down to aid Esla. Unfortunately the Saxon prisoners either did not know the details or were prepared to die rather than reveal all that they knew. Whatever their motives and loyalties, it mattered little because the result was the same and denied Ivar the intelligence he needed.

He had decided to send what information he had gathered to Edmund, but he knew that his force would most likely face the invasion with their own resources. Then, if they triumphed, most probably when they triumphed, to join Edmund in a sharp campaign against Esla and any other earl who was believed a traitor. In the confused situation Edmund faced, there was the risk that some traitors would escape identification and punishment, with an equal risk that the innocent might suffer unjustly. Ivar knew that the real risk was his prospects for success in battle before he could join with Edmund.

It was most likely that the Northumbrian fleet would head directly to the fort that they might still believe to be in Esla's hands, but Ivar could not afford to make this assumption. Esla must be aware now that Ivar's army had taken the fort. He might not realize how large a force had been landed, but even that might not be a secure assumption. No, Ivar had to assume that the enemy would know his strength and positions. If he was wrong, that only improved his prospect for victory.

From his recent experience as the attacker, Ivar knew that the lake close to the sea was able to hold a large number of ships, but that was little advantage because of the difficulty of coming ashore through the treacherous mud and marsh that were the margins of the lake. Where he had needed only a small number of ships to attack the fort, the Northumbrians would be forced to bring as many ships and men as possible to attack the defences, with the garrison well-equipped and ready for the assault. They would be limited by how many ships they could bring up the twisting river, even in daylight. Where they were assured of a strong defence against them at the fort, the island was now fortified and the river could be closed against them before and behind their ships. Bottled up in this way, they could be worn down and prevented from landing warriors to march to Esla's assistance.

Julius and Aggi had been working furiously on completing the new defences and heavy weapons. The result might not be as pretty as they would have liked, but the defences would be reliable. Julius would have preferred to have built in stone and Aggi would have wished to drive the palisades around the island further into the mud and soft ground, but both craftsmen knew that they must complete an adequate defence quickly and be prepared to rebuild later for a durable defence to rival the strength of the old Roman walls.

The work at the fort had been easier than expected

because the walls and towers were so well-built. Aggi had been able to avoid extending the decks of the towers. Once the sheltering roofs were removed from the corner towers, there was sufficient space to mount the giant crossbows and the trebuchet. Where Julius had intended to build fire tubes in the Greek style, Ivar had devised a simpler method. A number of leather pipes had been hung down the walls and been buried, to project above the water from the face of the quay.

All that was required was a tub of flame liquid that could be poured into a funnel at the end of the hoses atop the walls. They had tried one hose the day before and the result was terrifying. The mixture had run down the pipe and onto the water to be ignited by a flaming arrow shot from a tower. The stone facing of the quay was scorched but any ship that had been approaching the quay would have been consumed in the flames. There was no need for complex machinery and bellows to project flame from the tops of the walls and the attackers would be unaware of the danger until it was too late.

The defences on the island required much greater time and effort. One group of warriors had been put to cutting suitable trees. Another group moved the timbers to the lake and floated them out to the island. Each trunk was rough hewn and put in position. The island's shore was cut with a ditch at low water that allowed tree trunks to be set into it and roughly driven. Supports were nailed to the trunks and a second ditch started behind the first to take an inner wall. The space between was filled with earth, rubble, and pieces of timber, until it formed a narrow sentry walk. Each day more trees were positioned around the island's shores until they met the first timbers driven into the ground. Each day seemed to see more trees installed than on the day before. It was hard work but the young warriors were fit and needed working to keep the edge to their power.

The feverish work on defences at fort and island were matched by work on the river. Where the river entered the lake from the landward, a barrier was built from the oldest ships. Those nearest the bank on each side were moored to newly mounted posts and more ships were tied firmly to them, advancing from each bank towards the centre of the river. The gap left was four boats wide. Into this gap was hauled a raft fixed to four old vessels. This raft provided a fighting platform that could be pulled aside to let a ship through into inland waters.

Ivar would have liked to construct a similar barrier to block the seaward river as it left the lake. The construction would have presented no difficulty, but where the landward barrier was invisible until a ship tried to enter from the lake, the seaward side of the lake provided no cover from which to hold the elements of a barrier to be erected after the enemy had sailed out of the river on the seaward side. Ivar needed to allow enemy ships to sail into the lake before their escape route was blocked. Drawing the enemy in and onto the defences was the only way of knowing how much damage the defenders had done. Any ship that escaped could later prove dangerous, seeking out a route that no one had thought of because the river was so obvious.

As the hurried work was completed, there was still no sign of an approaching enemy. Ivar increased the number of scouting parties on the high ground behind the fort. In preparing for the Northumbrians, it was vital not to neglect an attack from Esla or one of his fellow conspirators.

There was little left to do, but to await an attack that might come during the days ahead. Red Osten had been given charge of defending the fort and he drilled his warriors each day to ensure their efficiency. Between the drills, his comrades filled their time in burnishing the blades of their weapons, oiling their mail coats and repairing or replacing any weapon or clothing that was not in perfect condition. They were helped by those women who had accompanied the fleet and who were mostly employed in the camp's housekeeping. They were all skilled enough to join the defenders, but few regularly fought as Gudhrun did. The same rules applied to the very young girl or boy who had sailed with Ivar. Their place was to experience, learn and support, but they would join the battle line if needed and give good account of themselves.

Thirty Five

Once more it is time to bring the story to a temporary halt. Each time the evening stretches further as we all become immersed in the adventure of Einarr. I wish that the breaks between each evening were shorter and it will be so. Winter has been tightening an already firm grip. We are still far from the Festival of Light and further from the renewal beyond the end of winter. The days are short but will become shorter still. The storms roll in along the Firth, or pour over the hills and forests to our North. There is ice now in the Firth and every promise that it will become colder.

As winter deepens, there are fewer things that we can do. The cattle are long in their winter quarters. The food stores have been filled and now begin to empty. We can survive a long winter in comfort but I feel our enemies gathering. The assassin of this morning was a cold reminder that even in our own lands we are not completely safe. I do not expect armed bands riding against us, at least not before the weather improves, even then they are not likely. For now each faction watches the others. Each searches for weakness to exploit. The assassin is the likely weapon. Elizabeth Tudor carefully weighs her options. She fears a strong French alliance with her cousin Mary,   James the Bastard is her protection against that. She knows that there are those who are comfortable with England but distrust James, as does Elizabeth. Had she trust in him, she would not send gold alone but soldiers to fight alongside him, warships to patrol the routes from France.

As I recount the saga of Einarr to my family, I see we still live the plan of his father Ivar. Much has changed, but so much remains. In all the centuries that have passed, we are still in many ways outsiders, living between others. Close to us are other families who have similar roots, families we have fought alongside, and against, as the tides of fortune have washed along the Firth, between the forces of Scotland and of England.

The twins are still awake but not for much longer. Robert
has been listening to the tale, but I sense he is pre-occupied with
his own thoughts. He would rather remain with us, but he
understands that our protection is to have my sons away from
harm here, surrounded by their men and protected by the sea. We
are fortunate that our enemies prefer to fight by land. If this
winter continues fierce, the routes through the hills will be filled
deep with snow. By the time that spring forces its way through,
the situation may be much changed.

I noticed Janet put few stitches in her embroidery this
evening. She listens now with growing interest to the saga. I feel
perhaps we have a new beginning, a new understanding. It pleases
me. She has been more cheerful these recent days. I see now that I
have misjudged her in parts. She has not the sunny ways of
Morag, but that is her uncertainty. I realize now that she frets
when Erik is away. Morag is able to take each day on its own
terms, seeing the best and the brightest it has to offer.

"My lord, thank you, a wonderful evening, much
enjoyed," offers Janet as she gathers her children. Her face breaks
into the warmest smile I have ever seen lay on her features.

"Goodnight Faddi," says Robert with a solemn bow.

"Goodnight Gran Faddi," copies James. He is already,
quite the young man.

"Goodnight Gran Faddi," chorus William and Gilbert,
cheerfully, but sleepily.

Then Morag and Mary come forward to me, putting an
arm on each shoulder and kissing my cheeks.
Then I am all alone, save for Kara. The walls of my
chamber seem to move away from me. It is a void. Kara is

reluctant to move away from the dying fire. The hangings dance in the chill drafts. The wind howls around the turret and tower. The rush lights hiss and splutter.

It has been such an eventful day. A warning of what may yet be to come. I relive the morning in my mind and can still make no sense out of it. Did I see what I thought I saw? I feel need to talk of it with my dearest Margaret, her face in the dying embers of the fire.

As my thoughts fight for order, Jamie enters the chamber, carrying a tray with my favourite whisky. He has given up trying to talk me to bed before he retires. He shuffles now, age catching up with him. I am glad that I still walk straight, but perhaps my time for frailty is at hand.

"My lord, would you have me do else?" he asks, with less firm enthusiasm, already expecting my reply.

"Thank you Jamie auld friend, no, you may retire and attend me in the morning at first light."

I feel guilty dismissing him. I know he wants to see me abed before he joins his wife. I want him gone, to return to my thoughts, but his loyalty and service to me deserves better. I must be softening in my old age.

He retreats, closing the door behind him and I am again alone. The chamber seems enormous. There is no silence but the noise is all familiar and fades from my attention, even Kara's contented snoring as she takes the heat from the fire.

"My love," I begin to the ghost in the flames, "I have so much to tell you this night."

I feel her presence, her calm good sense. I know that she will help me to unravel the morning's mysteries.

I am glad that even death cannot deny me her support and

wisdom. As we converse it is outside my mind, between two people, even if one of them is in the flickering light of the flames that illuminate the fireplace, intruding across the chamber. In all the years and all the partings, we have grown so close that I know what she would say to me if death had not called her. The conversation was already there in my mind and my soul, awaiting the time when it would be needed.

I know not the point when sleep catches me in its arms because my deep conversation with my dearest Margaret continues into my dreams and mixes with the visions of those who have gone before, sharing now their experiences, their hopes and their fears in the family's saga.

Part Five: -

The Gatherings

Thirty Six

This morning I had watched the Black Hawk leaving on the high tide. I stood atop the tower in the meagre shelter of the pharos. The heavy sleet and snow was blowing across the tower at such an angle it seemed unlikely ever to touch ground or water. I had said my goodbyes to Robert when he boarded the ship and made my way to the tower's roof that I might see her safely into the Firth. I might not have taken the trouble, because she was a ghostly outline almost as she cleared the boom and made her way out into the channel. I stayed until all prospect of a sight had faded. Her gallery had come into view between squalls, becoming fainter on each occasion.

I turned to the stair and the sleet lashed my face like lances of fire. I was grateful for the cap and coat of leather that had protected me from the cold and wet. Ducking below the stone doorframe the temperature rose immediately, although there was ice hanging from the lintel. As I closed the door behind me it felt like walking into a fire, my face burned as warmth returned to it and the agony of warmth returning to my gloved hands took me by surprise.

First I would stand before the fire in my chamber and let the burning logs drive the last of the chill from my bones. I promised myself that, and a dram of aqua vita to make sure I had thawed to the core, that warm blood coursed through my body.

I was not surprised to find Jamie waiting patently for me, food and drink beside my chair before the fire. I saw he had stoked the flames and the heat made my clothes steam. I had not realized how cold and wet I had become. Jamie had anticipated my needs well, as he always does, and fresh clothes were waiting, draped across a bench near to the fireplace.

Having changed into the warm, dry, fresh clothes, and taken a hearty swallow of the fiery pale golden liquid from the silver mug, I felt a different person from the bedraggled, frozen wretch who had staggered down the stairs from the roof. My mind was active, but I realized that there was no matter pressing for my attention. Today there was little to occupy me. There were no expected visitors, no matters to judge, nothing to occupy me industriously.

I could read a book. It was something I rarely had time for, almost a rich indulgence. No!! That would not do, I have a need for something more active. I went to the turret and looked out through an uncovered window. There was no activity outside, The heavy showers of sleet and snow continued, snow taking over from the last of the sleet showers, ice hard on the ground, discouraging any task outside. Even within the shelter of our outer walls, no one was abroad, the snow thick now on the ground, the sleet given way completely to continuous heavy snow showers that covered the ice thickly, making the ground treacherous.

"Ah! I know, I will seek out James and Mary at their studies," I exclaimed aloud.

I knew that today their tutor would be attempting to improve their Latin, something I always found tedious. It is important that they learn of life and classical matters, but I felt a mischievous urge to interrupt their studies. When I was a boy, an uncle used to interrupt my studies on a day like this. I understood now what drove him and made him a popular uncle to me.

I went down the stairs from the tower and through the doorway that opened into the Great Hall. Today it was a gloomy barn, its high vaulted ceiling vague in the poor light. It felt cold and damp from disuse. I must tell Jamie to have fires lit here even when we will not be using it. We could always have unexpected guests and I will not let them see that we rarely use this space. At least it had been cleaned recently and fresh rushes spread on the flagged floor.

To one side, at the far end of the hall, was a small doorway that led through into a series of rooms that included the classroom where my grand children came to be tutored. Next to this room was a larger room where the other children of the castle and the surrounding farms came to learn to read and to write.

It was introduced first by my dearest Margaret. She was always determined that all of the our people would be able to read and write and to use numbers. In these basic lessons, she had engaged a special tutor. When she first invited our people to send their children to the school, they had resisted, their children taking tasks on the farms and in the workshops to help their families. I had reluctantly ordered all of our people to send their children to the school in the winter months in the short afternoons. That cost the families much less because winter tasks were fewer. I respected their need for extra hands at planting and harvest, and in tending the livestock.

In time, parents came to see the school as a benefit. Three of the children had shown special promise, two becoming doctors and one a lawyer, returning to our community when they had completed their studies, bringing skills that were most welcome. In this winter, the school had grown and Margaret would have been so pleased to see the numbers grow to fill the schoolroom. My grand children took lessons with the other children in the basic skills, but they studied with their own tutor to learn languages, gaining classical knowledge and the skills required of leaders. Where we found promising students from our community, they took some extra lessons with my grand children, but this winter there were no children joining them.

I entered the room. James, Mary, William and Gilbert were seated at a long table. Their tutor was looking over their shoulders to see how well they were progressing with the tasks he had set them.

James Urquart is a spare man of average height who dressed in French cloth. He came to us much commended, having studied in Scotland, England, Germany and France. He was a serious, but kindly, man who had patience to help the slowest child to keep up. More than that he was an inspirational teacher who coud infect his charges with a passion for study and books.

He had been with us now for four years, a great improvement on the tutor before him. Even so, I was cautious of him. I could not fully trust a man of his education who chose to teach children. It was not unusual for secretaries and tutors to be spies sent by enemies.

Even so, he impressed me with his learning and his desire to learn about that which was mystery to him. He had asked that one of our captains might teach him navigation at sea. He had joined me on two short voyages. I was pleased to see him as able a pupil as a tutor, learning quickly and mastering the skills of navigation.

"Master Urquart, I have come to take two of your charges to practice arms. First tell me how they are progressing under your care."

"My Lord, William and Gilbert must work more diligently. They show great potential but little application. They are all too easily distracted. James and Mary are much stronger students, although it was not always so with Mary. She was once as easily distracted as her younger cousins. These last two years she has worked hard to rival James in languages and numbers. Of James, I believe we have a scholar. He exhibits a most open mind and a quickness in mastering new things. Your lordship may wish to send him to the great universities in time."

"Master Urquart, I am grateful for your observations. I will discuss James' future with my son when he returns. If we decide to follow your advice we will want your suggestions as to which universities and at what time. You will consider this to best advise us. Now I will take James and Mary to arms practice."

Urquart bowed deeply as I left the room with James and Mary. That deference was the due of a King or Queen, but overblown for an old warrior like me. I was more accustomed to a brief nod, it unsettled me, but then I would look now for danger everywhere. I also forget the more formal behaviour in the English Court. At the Holyrood it has long been common for any Lord to approach the King and converse as equals. That would not be the way in England and much less in France. I wonder how our young Queen finds the informality after her upbringing in the French Court.

It was but a short walk along a covered path to the practice ring. The building has stood for generations and been put to the same purpose in each generation. It is a long timber framed building, a roof of thatch, the lower parts of the walls of stone, with the timber frame resting on those low stone walls. When it was first built, a low wood partition had run almost the full length to allow the joust to be practiced. Once heavy horses, clad in armour, armoured knights on their backs, had thundered up and down the full length of the building, great lances cradled in the knights' arms. When I was but a boy, the divider was taken down, the days of armoured knights numbered. Today swing joys stood near to the ends of the room. A rider could attack either with lance or sword, a padded leather ball on a chain attached to catch any rider who struck the swing joy's shield, but forgot to duck low. The sandy floor was a good surface to practice with horse or on foot.

Today we would practice sword and dagger in the Italian style. I am becoming old for such sport, which calls for excellent balance and fast responses. I notice that James is proficient but not outstanding. He lacks the imagination of a fighter. It is not that he lacks a quick wit. With a mechanism, he can work out how each part operates, with impressive speed of reasoning. Perhaps he is just too honest and logical. A good fighter can deceive and strike, seeing the moves and counters, imagining the moves that will follow. Seeing an opening that will not show itself to others for several moves. I canna fault his precision but it is that which makes him predictable to a skilled opponent.

Mary has a fighter's imagination. She lacks some of the precision of James, long practiced, but that makes her harder to read. A move that should follow from a manual of arms is replaced by a move that she has thought out for herself. Her speed is impressive and too fast now for me. I am finding that even my experience cannot compensate. She has yet to best me, but she is very, very close. One day, soon, she will defeat me. James, she can unravel as she wishes and it begins to irritate him. He has learned every strike and counter in the book of arms. He knows every weapon. He can work out which blow, with which weapon, will be effective. Yet here is his younger cousin, a girl at that, who can step outside his strike and counter with a move that is not written in any book. All is done with little apparent effort, almost casual, and yet a counter appears as the strike is made. I can see her thinking moves ahead. In a short time I will not always be able to read that.

It is not yet mid afternoon, but the light fades already, when I call halt to our practice. I am close to exhaustion and struggle hard to conceal it, a vanity on my part. James is also well worked and showing fatigue. Mary seems as fresh as when we started. It gives me cause for thought.

Urquart may be correct. Spending time teaching James to command ships, and men, may be a waste. In times to come the warrior with the strongest arm and fastest eye will not be the automatic victor. It will be the man who can command machines. The gun will be stronger than the bow and its reach will be longer. Already, as I so nearly found, the assassin will prefer to fire from cover, the old choice of sword and dagger a thing of the long past. The old skills of the master mariner will not die, but they will be aided by new machines, some of which we canna conjure in our dreams today. James is part of that future. In his life, much will change and, in his children's time, what he learns now will become the natural choice in future years.

When Erik returns we will sit and talk of the future and how best to train James. He will need to learn the handling of ship and crew, the leading of men in battle. In his time men will voyage far as they did in the time of Einarr and in other ages long past, lost to memory. I wonder at the ignorance of those who praise the great 'discoveries' of new lands, lands which were known to our people five hundred years and more before. I doubt that they had discovered these lands either, only learning again what was once known and then lost in time. I see in the Black Hawk the power and endurance to sail great distances, the weapons to out-reach and out-fight an enemy. Before James ends his days, the Black Hawk will be outclassed by new vessels, vessels that James will scheme and shape.

Mary will be the greater challenge. I see clearly now that she is a warrior. She is Gudhrun, but our society is different now. Those few neighbouring families who have the same roots our family owns may not provide a husband. Those families we call kin from different roots do not understand a woman as Mary will grow to be. I know now that I could teach her to command a ship, to navigate, to lead a crew. I also know that one day few men could stand against her. I know not how best to proceed. I hope and trust that events will present a solution that will allow Mary to enjoy her life ahead, with few sorrows, fewer compromises. I hope that she will find a husband who will sustain her through a long life.

Now I must observe and consider. How fortunate that Morag is, such a happy soul, grounded in good sense and kindnesses, with the inner steel to stand against adversity. I must make time to talk with her about a daughter who can be so great, if we can but make the opportunities for her strengths to exploit.

"Gran Faddi, you are in a land so far away," observed the object of my considerations.

"Ah yes dear child," I responded, searching for something to say that sounded credible, "so much to think on. I have enjoyed our practice of arms. A chance to set my thoughts to something immediate. You have done well today. I am proud of both of you."

With that I place a friendly hand on their shoulders. I notice James relax and I understand that he had felt out-classed by his cousin.

"James, I see a steady improvement in your skill at weapons. I am content that you handle a sword capably. I would now that you concentrate on learning the use of guns and their making. I will talk with your father on his return. Your tutor recommends that you study at the great universities. Have you considered what you wish to do?"

"Gran Faddi, I will as you and my Faddi command. I would like well to study further. There is so much that I wish to learn, but I want to learn of practical things that will benefit our people. I want to create new things."

"Well said my boy. Each generation should build on the foundations laid by those who have gone before."

I am pleased and surprised by his maturity. As I come to know my family, each layer peels to display another layer below. I am on a voyage of discovery without the need to leave home.

Now, in almost an instant, it is time to dine and to recount further the adventures of Einarr. I resent the fleet passage of time, but I look forward so keenly for our evenings together. The winter advances, reluctant to ease its grip. Soon it will be the spring of bright hopes and the season of campaigning. I fear that our Queen slides towards a tragic pass, that campaigns will feature more than has been usual, even in the violent years I have lived through.

Gathered for our meal, and then before the fire for Einaar's saga, it all seems so far away, but it will press in upon us all too soon. For now my sons' children and their wives make a joyful evening, it gives Jamie and Annie as much joy to serve us, although you would'naye know it from Jamie's long face. When I was a boy my Faddi taught me that a servant takes joy from the progress of a master and from the master's joy, that a master should always create the world where his servants are happy. In our community there are no hard lines between master and servant, but the sense of family. Jamie is now as his father had been in my youth. Their family as much a part of us. In the strife of the borderlands, we shared loyalty and comfort, having to watch those from outside our community. That much has not changed down the ages. Each of us has our tasks and duties complimenting all within our society. Now my pleasure and duty is to continue the story of Einarr.

Thirty Seven

Edmund had received the messenger from Ivar. Eldwyn was the ideal choice as the messenger. Although he spoke rarely, he had a prodigious memory. He was able to speak Ivar's message as though he was reading from a book. Every detail was remembered and he had no need for written documents.

King Edmund had decided to receive him in the main hall with only Cynegils and Ceolwulf present. Edmund was confident that both men could be trusted. He valued Cynegils advice and Ceolwulf, as captain of his bodyguard, would carry out any order that Edmund gave him, whatever the cost. As Edmund wryly thought, if he could not trust these two men his position was in great peril. More positively, Cynegils had always been his advisor and had no reason to become disloyal. Ceolwulf was more than just a bodyguard, little older than Edmund, he had been the King's friend from childhood. They had played together, hunted together and, since Edmund had become King, Ceolwulf had been at his side, ready to defend him from any attack.

The unhappy task was in trying to decide which of the other nobles could be relied on. He might have first decided who was most likely to betray him and, in other circumstances, would have considered the friends of anyone known to be an enemy. The difficulty was that Esla had no friends and most of the nobles would have avoided him, but that did not mean that they would not become allies if they saw a benefit in that. A further complication was that many of his nobles, or members of their families, had married into Mercian and Northumbrian families over the years. Most marriages were within the kingdom and with neighbouring families, but there were still some strategic alliances in each generation beyond the kingdom. In most cases that meant nothing in a peaceful realm, but in the troubled times they lived there would be many situations where an alliance with Edmund's enemies could be highly profitable.

The news and request that Eldwyn had carried from Ivar required Edmund to begin making decisions and preparing for battle. In this he faced two challenges. Firstly, a traitor would send information to Esla and the other plotters. Edmund would need great care in deciding how much information should be shared with each noble. Secondly, he had to decide the order in which his army would face an enemy in battle. The fight was usually bloody and offered little decisive advantage to either side because men and weapons were usually evenly matched. There might be some advantage in the field of battle but it was not uncommon for two armies to deliberately choose a field that favoured neither. Battles were most frequently won because a noble defected to the enemy lines, fled the battlefield, or failed deliberately to arrive in time for the fight. If the King knew who could be trusted, he could choose the place and time of battle with confidence. If he did not know who could be relied on, there was a great risk in engaging the enemy and finding that promised support did not arrive, or withdrew at a critical stage of battle, exposing a weakness that the enemy could exploit to turn his warriors into rout. In the worst case, an ally might suddenly turn on his neighbours in the battle line, cutting into their exposed flank while their attention was on the enemy to the front.

Edmund had hoped that he still had time to probe his supporters and identify those who might offer suspect loyalty, but Ivar needed rapid decisions and an earlier commitment to battle. If truth be admitted, Edmund had been postponing the time of decision. Edmund, never the most decisive of rulers, was always reluctant to grapple with difficult issues. This was the real reason why he had postponed decision to the following day when Einaar and his comrades had laid out the treachery of Esla before him.

To make the pressure even greater, Ivar would need to retain a strong force at the fort to take on the expected Northumbrian fleet, the size of which was unknown to him. The original expectation had been to bring Esla and his allies to battle before any Northumbrians arrived, but there was now a probability that Esla might still be engaged as they arrived, or even be reinforced before Edmund could bring him to battle.

The one advantage was that Ivar now held a very strong position that the Northumbrians were unaware of. That meant that any Northumbrian fleet would arrive as Ivar had, making their way up river to the fort. They might even be unaware that it was no longer in Esla's hands. Had they already received accurate intelligence from Esla, or one of the other plotters, they might not send a fleet before the winter set in, or they might make landfall at another point which would then make them very dangerous.

As Ivar and Edmund knew, a fixed defence was only effective if the enemy attacked and found it stronger than their force. Those long years before, the Romans had chosen the site for a fort , built it strongly with great skill, provided its garrison with two deep wells for an uninterrupted supply of water without the need to venture forth for fresh supply, and enclosed a space that could accommodate a strong force with food and weapons to withstand a protracted siege.

If the enemy landed in another place and marched on a different target, they rendered the fort useless and the fort's defenders would have to leave their prepared position, marching to meet the enemy at a place not of their choosing, perhaps not to their advantage.

Edmund had few choices but much scope for making a bad decision. In the time available he did not have the luxury of selecting trusted supporters and sending them out to watch all the possible landing places. In any event, he did not have the numbers of people to watch his long coastline. An invading fleet was most likely to sail up a river to points where the army could threaten the centres of population and wealth. Battles were most likely to be fought at points where rivers could be easily crossed, but there was no guarantee.

Edmund was unfortunate to have a long coast line with many gently shelving beaches that would allow a forewarned enemy to land on the beaches and march inland without facing high cliffs or other obstacles. Once ashore, the enemy could chose their line of march which might be in any direction that led inland. Of all the possible situations, the least favourable would be for the Northumbrians to make an unopposed landing, then marching inland to join with Esla and the other traitors, without Edmund being aware of their arrival. From that point, Esla and his allies could choose the place of battle.

Cynegils and Edmund debated the possibilities and seemed as far from decision as when Eldwyn had delivered the message from Ivar. Edmund was by nature cautious and reluctant to fix on a new path, but Cynegils was surprisingly unskilled in martial matters. He had very little experience of battle and his abilities lay in the management of land and the search for knowledge. At a time when earls were the professional soldiers of the realm, Cynegils owned a library of thirty books and hoped to add more to this huge private collection of knowledge. He was also deeply religious. In advising the young King, he was most effective in guiding his approach to administration and justice, but others were needed to advise on battle. The difficulty facing Edmund was that those best able to help him reach military decisions were also suspect, potential enemies, actual enemies.

It was Ceolwulf who broke the circular discussion. He was the practical warrior who had chosen the members of the King's bodyguard. For him, life was all about the hunt and the battle. He could have been Beowulf of legend. He would eat and train for battle, his leisure the hunt. He was not the finest strategist, or even tactician, in Edmund's realm, but he was competent and Edmund knew that he could trust him completely.

Ceolwulf quickly set out the key points of Ivar's demands and the strengths and weaknesses of Esla. Of the Northumbrians he knew little, beyond the reality that they had greater wealth and numbers than Edmund commanded. He knew more of the Mercians and knew that they held no love for the Northumbrians who had long been their natural enemies. Ceolwulf believed that they would hold back until they were more certain of the winner, before committing to conflict. This led him to believe that the immediate threat was still from Esla and whoever might ally with him against Edmund.

Ceolwulf advised that Edmund should match Ivar's demands for joint action and raise the core of his army immediately from those supporters close to Kett's Hall, where loyalty was most dependable. He reasoned that Edmund could summon other earls to his support, requiring only that they meet with him at Bertwald's Bridge, telling them no more than that he required them to defend with him the kingdom. If any were inclined to side with Esla, they would know nothing of the force they were going to meet with, or the force that they would be required to fight. If they were part of the treachery, they might see the opponent as Esla only because Bertwald's Bridge was on the edge of Esla's lands, but even this was not certain because it was also the point where they would most likely assemble to fight an invader from the sea. More, it was one of the rally points that all knew. In past times, armies had assembled there before striking out in the direction of an enemy, which might be in any direction from the meeting place.

Ceolwulf had reviewed the situation logically and drawn naturally to the conclusions. For Edmund this was a comfort because he was not so much having to take hard decisions, as agree with a logical presentation of natural actions. The decisions were part of those actions and required no further thought.

Edmund was now able to send Eldwyn back to Ivar, carrying Edmund's commitment to meet Ivar at Bertwald's Bridge on the day requested. He could now order the immediate preparation of the initial force and pick up additional warriors at points along his route from Kett's Hall to Bertwald's Bridge, knowing the size of his initial force and the probable size of the army that would assemble at the bridge. Those who failed to meet at the assembly points could be assumed as rebels, at the very best, to be of doubtful loyalty.

Thirty Eight

While Edmund was making his decisions and giving Eldwyn the message of commitment to take back to the fort, Ivar was making his own more complex plans. Where Edmund had found the taking of decisions difficult, Ivar made decisions swiftly, with conviction, importantly, those decisions were most frequently very good.

Even as Eldwyn had set out with Ivar's message for Edmund, Ivar had been sending out observers to establish posts from which they could watch the possible points of danger. Some of the observers, tasked with watching the river from its outfall into the sea, consisted of two teams. Two of each party were hidden by the riverbank to directly watch the river to their East. Close by, the second team of six or eight warriors waited. Periodically two warriors would go to relieve their comrades hidden in the reeds. If any activity merited the sending of a message to the fort, one watcher would remain hidden while his comrade was to quickly reach the horses, riding off to the fort with all speed, while his place was taken by a warrior from the second team. As he rode hard for the fort, he passed other groups of watchers and his passing alerted them to an event further East from their positions.

This chain of watchers covered the most likely route that a Northumbrian fleet would follow inland to the fort. The chain guaranteed a rapid delivery of intelligence but required more than a hundred warriors. As the messengers could ride out of sight from any invasion fleet, it was practical to send them back to their watch team after they had delivered the messages. The more difficult task was to cover the land to either side of the river and along the coast. Ivar could have expended most of his warriors in this task because of the distances involved. His Great Army may have been exactly that, in the terms of campaigns and formal battles, but it could soon be dispersed thinly if it needed to cover any great area. The only option available was to send out overlapping patrols of horsemen, with no more than six warriors to a patrol.

The patrols had been selected and sent out. Ivar had gambled on any Northumbrian fleet either coming up the river to him, or landing on the coast within a day's march of the river. That allowed him to use no more warriors for the patrols than the number already committed to the river watch. Even so, two hundred warriors was a significant force when armies might consist of less than one hundred men. The Saxons described an army as being a force of more than thirty five warriors, although that was a convenient way of differentiating warriors from bandits, who would most times be gangs of fewer that thirty men.

He knew that invaders were unlikely to bring horses with them when they expected to join up with Esla and others who could provide what horses might be required. The patrols to the North of the river could concentrate on covering the coast and the other smaller rivers. Those patrolling to the South of the river would watch not only for the arrival of a Northumbrian fleet but also for Saxons loyal to Esla, with the patrol line extending inland to the fort, joining up with the patrols operating out of the chain of small forts and ferries established by Ivar between the fort and Depenham.

The experience of sailing the Øvind between the fort and Depenham had encouraged Ivar to think of sending boats further inland. He now had six of their smallest boats sailing patrols on stages of the river as far as it could be easily navigated. He now knew that Depenham was the mid point between the fort and the limit of easy navigation. The six boats were smaller than the Øvind but larger than the Hildr. Having explored the navigable length of the river, their patrols had been set so that each boat would meet its immediate neighbours at least once each day. It would have been possible to operate the line of patrol further inland, but Ivar wanted the vessels to be able to turn easily and sail back to the fort without having to put any of the crew ashore to help turn a boat in a narrow stretch.

The furthest boat, at the furthest point of its patrol, could be turned by oars or quant poles without touching the banks. With favourable wind, a boat could also turn under sail with some help from the oars. After a few days of experience on their patrol routes, the crews could confidently sail at night on all but the darkest, stormiest, nights. The warriors were happier on their boats than ashore. It would be easier and safer as the winter closed in than using foot patrols or horsemen. Although even the smallest boats in the fleet were double-ended, it was more difficult to row stern-first for any distance. It was so much better to turn the vessel around. The danger of putting crew ashore in a narrow river, to haul the boat round by ropes, was that they were vulnerable to attack while ashore. For a boat to have made that turn almost certainly meant that the enemy was very close, within arrow range, or closer.

With these groups of intelligence gatherers and the defences at the fort and at Depenham, Ivar and his Saxon allies from the village were in a strong position to resist any attack. They could work on their defences through the winter and into the coming year, but the most important work had been done. Ivar had never intended to rely on finding shelter where he could, with the ships providing accommodation in the absence of suitable shelter ashore, but he had never counted on the good fortune that had attended his campaign.

The Roman fortress now had the added protection of artillery and a fortified island in the middle of the lake. That in itself was an enormous advantage, but it was now further protected by sentries and patrols stretching out to the coast and inland beyond Depenham. As reports continued to come to him of the work to strengthen the village and build there a real port, he knew that there were now two strongly defended locations that could support each other. An attacker would have great difficulty in approaching both locations at the same time, but to attack one was to warn the other and enable Ivar to send out a strong relieving force that would turn any besieger into the besieged, sandwiching the would-be attacker between two forces and assuring his defeat.

The weather had also been considerate. Since they had first landed, there had been periods of rain but no violent storms. Winter was arriving slowly and with stealth. This had allowed Ivar to arrange for further supplies and equipment to be sent across the sea to him and the ships that had brought these supplies had provided a useful test of the watchers hiding along the river. Ivar was receiving reports of the arrivals hours before they reached the fort. The only consideration to give Ivar any anxiety was the expectation that eventually their good fortune must run out. The longer good luck attended them, the better they would be placed at a time of adversity.

Thirty Nine

For Edmund, the last few days had been less comfortable than those that Ivar had experienced. It had taken three days to assemble and equip the force he had formed from local supporters, longer than he had expected. Ceolwulf had first collected those warriors within Ketts Hall and the immediate villages. That gave him only one hundred warriors, another fifty villagers with some military training and thirty villagers to take care of the wagons and pack animals. He then sent out messengers to a further group of villages to send their men to Ketts Hall. By the end of the three days, Edmund had command of two hundred and seventy warriors and trained men, with a baggage train of a further sixty five men and women, with wagons and pack animals. That was an impressive army, but he could expect to face an enemy of a thousand warriors, perhaps more.

Edmund would make better time once he reached the Roman road, but progress would be slow until they reached that hard level surface. It had been raining steadily and the dirt tracks were very wet, churning into gluey mud under the feet of men, horses, and carts. Most of his warriors were on foot and that slowed the speed of the column as it snaked along the network of rough tracks. A herres road was not a military road to match the ancient highways of the Romans, just a track that could accommodate two lines of riders abreast.

As they advanced towards the meeting point with Ivar, small groups of warriors joined them, extending the column and slowing progress. Ceolwulf had sent messengers out to those carls who were further from Ketts Hall, but believed to be loyal to Edmund. As they neared their destination, the size of the opposition could be better gauged by the absence of carls who should have answered the call to join the King. Ceolwulf knew

271

that most of those who ignored the call would not join the enemy force, but would wait to see who emerged as the winner. On the second day of their march Ceolwulf could see that some carls had already failed to answer the call. A few might join them later, after genuine delays, but it was not a good sign.

After five days they were approaching their meeting point, but a third of the expected reinforcements had so far failed to arrive and Edmund could only hope that there would be supporters waiting at Bertold's Bridge. They could have made the journey in a shorter time, but their pace allowed time for supporters to join them on their march, allowing the force to arrive without undue exhaustion. An army that force marched often paid the price of tired warriors who were less able to face an enemy that had rested and waited for them to arrive on the battlefield. All that Edmund could hope was that those who had joined him were loyal and would remain loyal.

Ceolwulf found himself having to reassure his King at every opportunity. He could see that Edmund was depressed by the weather, the size of his force, the prospect of other supporters arriving at the bridge. He needed the King to have confidence and he had to make every effort to ensure that others in their party did not see their King's concern. It was not an easy task. Had it not been for their long friendship, it would have been an impossible task. It was not that Edmund lacked courage in battle, but confidence and enthusiasm was needed now before battle was joined and Edmund naturally dwelt on the dangers and doubts that a leader had to shrug off and stand above.

Ceolwulf had to accept to himself that the King's doubts and uncertainty might be justified as they approached the bridge in the falling light. Waiting for them was a pitifully small group of warriors, most on foot, a few with horses and little sign of a baggage train. More might arrive by the next day when Ivar and his army were expected, but the force supporting Edmund was less than half the number he could have expected. As some of those present might not fully support the King, the situation justified concern. It was now likely that Ivar and his warriors would form the major part of the joint force and that would place Edmund in a vulnerable position, with a serious loss of face.

Ceolwulf and Edmund had originally intended to arrive a full day early so that Edmund could examine his force and make sure that it looked strong and well-equipped, a real army rather than a collection of carls, each with his own group of supporters, little more than an assembly of gangs. Immediately, the wisdom of Ceolwulf's efforts to start with a well-stocked baggage train became obvious. Many of those joining the march, as it progressed, and those waiting at the bridge, had travelled light and some of the trained men were not even equipped with adequate weapons. At least they could be fed and issued with weapons from the King's baggage train.

It was not all disappointment. Edmund could see carls that he had hoped and believed would join him and the warriors were well-equipped and formidable. Even some of the trained men looked the part, with weapons, shields and mail coats, some with their own ponies or horses, but there was no disguising the lack of numbers and the poor condition of many of the trained men. Every village had its freemen who trained at arms and were often indistinguishable from the warrior class. However, much depended on the village and its level of prosperity. The poorer villages often made up the numbers of men owed to the King by including serfs amongst the trained men, failing to provide adequate training and failing to equip the men adequately with arms or armour. The poorest villages had very few horses, fewer to spare for a military expedition and no animals to spare for a baggage train. With the poor state of many herres roads and rural tracks, carts needed the strength of oxen, but this reduced the speed of an army.

Ceolwulf could see the inadequate state of several groups of supporters, but the lack of provision did not mean that their support for the King was equally lacking. Ceolwulf knew that many who were absent had prospered under the King's rule and were well provided to deliver the support that they owed. Some of the least well-equipped would fight with loyalty and fervour. His first task was to see what could be done to improve their equipment and ensure that they were well fed. There was nothing he could do about any past poverty they had suffered, but a full stomach would do wonders for them.

As the new day broke, it was another wet dawn with dark low cloud and a freshening wind, but the King's force already looked better. There had been enough weapons and shields to issue to all those that had arrived without. There had been some spare clothing and plenty of food. The warriors all looked strong and ready for the fight. The trained men looked much more the part, and the depletion of the supplies brought by the King meant that some of the pack animals could now be ridden by warriors and trained men, providing a larger fast force for reconnaissance and flexibility.

By the middle of the day, Ivar arrived with his warriors and the prospects looked infinitely better. The price of this improvement was that Edmund was now the junior partner. Ivar had gone out of his way to complement Edmund on the excellence and strength of his army, but it could not disguise the reality that Ivar's force was superior in numbers and equipment. Edmund and Ceolwulf knew that this strong ally provided a much improved prospect for the success of their forces, but they also had to accept that when their opinions were divided they would be forced to follow the path that Ivar preferred. It was a difficult position and promised some humiliation in the future when the time for negotiation arrived.

Forty

Ivar had decided to take five hundred warriors to meet King Edmund. This left a strong garrison for the fort, the river watchers and mounted patrols. In addition to this, there were those warriors manning the remaining boats, the small forts and ferries, and a strong force at Depenham. Joining Ivar and his warriors, a small force of forty Saxons, led by Wulfmaer, had been drawn from Depenham and some of the hamlets nearby. What made the army more impressive was that all the warriors were mounted and the columns of men included packhorses, enabling the force to move quickly, carrying food and water with them. There would be no need for foraging.

The army rode in two columns, ready to merge into a single column where the road narrowed. The pack animals were distributed through the column and each warrior carried his personal supplies and equipment with him. All wore their armour and helmets, shields carried on their shoulders, swords from their belts or attached to saddles. It was a force that was ready for immediate action, and the weak probing shafts of sunlight glinted on metal as they swung out of the fort and onto the Roman road. Soon they would leave the straight hard surface and ride along the Saxon herres routes, which were often little more than rough tracks, in places no longer wide enough for two horsemen to ride comfortably abreast.

For any watcher this was an awesome sight. Such an army was rare in the three kingdoms of the Anglians, even without so many horses. As a mounted force its like had not been seen for many years, perhaps not for generations. Even Edmund's smaller army was a brave sight. When the two allies joined together, they would present a major challenge to the expected enemy forces. As Ivar's men rode onward to the meeting place, there was the steady drumming of the horses' hooves, the clinking of metal fittings to the harnesses and the weapons. The shields provided a splash of colour, to which was added the flags and banners fluttering from poles and spears. The unhurried progress added to the impression of latent power.

Ivar rode at the head of one column, Einarr alongside at the head of the second column, with Wulfmaer's Saxons close behind Einarr. For the most part, the roads allowed the two columns to advance alongside each other and still have space for single riders to move along the columns with messages. There were smaller groups detached from the columns to range ahead and to the sides of the advancing army, scouts alert for any sign of an opposing force, or hostile watchers.

Ivar was pleased with the steady pace of their march, knowing that it would bring them to the meeting with Edmund in the middle of the agreed day. The riders and mounts would arrive in good condition and good order, being ready for battle at an instant. Unencumbered with a baggage train, Ivar had the freedom of choice in setting a pace and in responding to the unexpected. The greater problem was in planning the rests for the host. The numbers of men and horses meant that the army could not make a short halt as one unit. To allow horses and men to be rested and watered regularly, the two columns were divided into groups. This meant that as a group fell out from its column, its place would be occupied by another group. When it caught up with the columns, the order would be changed but this was not important. When night fell, the army would halt and camp in its groups with patrols moving around the encampment, ready for any eventuality.

Ivar knew that this campaign would be excellent training for the battles of the coming year. The nature of his army meant that riding in an organized formation was a new experience for most of his warriors. They were also unaccustomed to taking part in such a large group, advancing across land. For most, their previous experience of fighting had been as a boat's crew in company with a small number of other boats. Most of them were experienced riders but rarely had they been part of a group of more than fifty or, even less commonly, in an army of a hundred warriors. As it was equally rare that horses would be carried aboard ships, warriors carried saddles, bridles and stirrups, but had to find and take horses where they landed. The result was that a large raiding party would be unable to find enough horses for all of the warriors and a typical group would have most of its men on foot. If a large battle was to take place, the fighting would normally be on foot, any horses being held behind the fight or used to scout for reinforcements attempting to join the enemy. For Saxon and Norse alike, the horse was a method of faster travel and not as cavalry.

Ivar did not yet know if he would find sufficient mounts after the winter for all of his warriors when the time came to march North on the Northumbrians, and he would have to take a baggage train, with oxen drawing carts, but he hoped that he could learn from this campaign against Esla. A large mounted force greatly increased the consumption of supplies, but it provided flexibility in choosing a battle and avoided the risk of arriving at a battlefield, exhausted by a long hard march. Fit though his men were, they were more comfortable aboard their boats, than they were to marching distances across an unfamiliar terrain.

Ivar would hold one advantage in the coming year. He had expected to retain few of their ships because of the need to find warships and transports to carry the other two armies across the Poisoned Sea. He had needed to plan for a loss of ships that had not been suffered and they had also captured the Northumbrian supply ships. It made little difference to the campaign against Esla because it was a campaign on land but, in the following year, Ivar would have the choice of using his ships to carry a part of his force North to join the main force that would march through the lands of Edmund and into the territory of the Northumbrians.

For Ivar, this fight against Esla had much advantage. He could expect his Saxon allies to take at least a good share of any casualties when battle was joined. His loses since the arrival of his fleet had been very light, far fewer than he had planned for. He could expect that he would still have more men after the defeat of Esla than he had originally expected to enter the winter with. In return for a low cost, his power over Edmund would increase greatly in any future negotiations. It was not that Ivar intended to become the all-powerful conqueror. He had arrived with no territorial ambitions, only a burning desire to avenge his father's death at Northumbrian hands. What had been growing in his mind was an idea to establish trading agreements and the establishment of trading centres, such as Lodin proposed for Depenham, where Norse and Saxon could build a prosperous market place that they could defend together if required.

As his columns advanced towards the meeting place, Ivar could consider some of these opportunities. He could not know how much time he might spend in company with King Edmund because they could not be sure where Esla would be brought to battle. Marching together, or sharing a camp, meant discussion and companionship. Ivar intended to have plans to discuss and negotiate as the opportunity presented itself. From what Einarr and Wulfmaer had told him of their meeting with Edmund, his reluctance to reach a quick decision unaided made him vulnerable in negotiation with someone who could present a series of solutions that reduced his need to reach decision. Ivar determined to collect a series of plans in his mind that could be presented in whatever order best suited an opportunity in discussion with Edmund. This was Ivar's great strength as a leader. He could develop complex tactical and strategic plans, then think on his feet to exploit each advantage to take forward parts of the plans, building towards the complete solution.

When he looked back down the columns of warriors he could take deep satisfaction in his progress. His men and women were strong, but independent, and he had achieved much in bringing them together and keeping them focused on working to bring all of his planning to a great success. Many of them were very young but they were strong and experienced. All in this army could be depended on, none would weaken before an enemy. Unlike Edmund, he knew that there were no rebellious factions to betray him, or falter when tested.

Ivar had his bodyguard close behind him. He and they all wore their coats of mail and helmets. It was the same down the following column, but few wore mail coifs above padded coifs. The day was too warm to wear full battle clothing. Many had also avoided the padded coats beneath the mail that was normal in battle. Riding with mail over shirts and trousers was more comfortable and provided some protection in an ambush, but in the battle line the added protection of padded coats and coifs was important. It reduced the risk of an arrow or sword thrust driving the mail links into the flesh behind, with the risk of an infected wound that might prove fatal days later. The padded clothing also absorbed the impact of a blow, and was not too restricting when a battle line had to stand and trade blows from outside shields with the opposing line but, on horseback, the protective clothes were too hot even on a cool day and uncomfortably restricting.

Shields were a necessary impediment and warriors became accustomed to the weight across their shoulders as they rode. For many, they hung their swords or axes from the saddle, easier to draw in ambush and greater freedom for the rider. Helmets were more inconvenient for some than for others. The simple iron-bound leather helmets of the poorer warriors were not heavy and usually worn without a mail coif beneath. The more elaborate helmets of the wealthier warriors were less convenient and rarely worn while riding. Einaar had hung his heavy helmet from the saddle in a bag made of fishnet, as had others with full helmets that covered much, or all, of the face and neck. Some would also wear a mail coif in battle over a padded coif, others would wear only a padded coif, depending on the heavy metal that covered head, face and neck to protect against sword and arrow, but needing the padded coif to absorb blows and make the heavy helmet more comfortable. These warriors would ride bareheaded, relying on their hooded cloaks to protect against wind and rain. There was greater variation in dress because Ivar had carefully picked his army for this campaign to mix the younger, less experienced, warriors with the most experienced, and with his most seasoned supporters. It would have been easy to select only the most experienced and mature warriors, but this was an opportunity for the youngest to gain experience and for the fort to retain a similar selection of skills, providing a strong garrison to resist any attack.

Once again, the army had met an old Roman road on the final stretch before the bridge. The wider surface was still in good condition, straight and level, designed to allow two carts or chariots to comfortably pass each other. Once, Roman engineers would have kept a uniform surface, but the Saxons had patched where needed, there were some potholes in need of filling, but it was an easy route to ride, allowing the two columns to become less formal as riders took advantage of the greater width than the Saxon herres roads offered. Where the Saxon roads snaked around obstructions and followed the contours of hills, the Romans had carved a straight line through all obstacles, throwing up bridges rather than accepting fords across streams, and grading the road to avoid steep inclines and declines. Here, the road rose gently and then began to cut into the rising ground, before falling away gently to Bertwald's Bridge and the broad meadows that flanked the river it spanned as a bridge of nine stone arches.

As Ivar's army approached, they could see Edmund's army camped on the same side of the bridge. Smoke drifted from their camp fires. They looked impressive in their numbers but closer inspection would disclose some of their deficiencies. They had only a few horses tethered in their lines, lacking the mobility of Ivar's mounted warriors.

To Edmund and his men, Ivar's army had made an immediate impact as they rode over the ridge, a mass of horsemen, their flags and pennants flying, power and colour advancing on the bridge. The sound of a mounted force was different from the usual army with its foot soldiers, a scattering of horses and, in its rear, wagons mostly drawn by oxen or camp followers. Before Ivar's army came into sight, it could be heard, raising expectations. With the unusual expected, it was the unusual that was seen. To the eye, the horses all looked the same, even though Ivar had been forced to accept what was to be found

280

and available in the large numbers he required. The warriors also varied in size and shape, but the eye focused on the equipment and the banners. The mind, considered the approaching sound, added the most impressive details, raising the lowest to the highest. To Edmund's men, they were being joined by a force of the strongest warriors, mounted on the finest horses.

As the two armies came together, Ivar, with his bodyguard, Einarr and Wulfmaer in company, continued riding to where he could see Edmund and his immediate supporters. The remainder of his army chose the ground to form their camp and set up lines for the horses. There was no mingling of the two armed groups because neither knew the other. With a Saxon army forming at a meeting place, as Edmund's force had formed on the previous day, the groups merged together as old friends sought each other out. Where the previous day had contained something of the fair, today, allies kept in their own groups in uncertainty, but with cautious respect rather than apprehension. Both groups blindly accepted that their alliance was wise because it had been agreed by their leaders.

As the leaders came together, it was the first time that Edmund had met with Ivar, although he recognised Einarr and Wulfmaer from some distance. He was surprised to see Gudhrun riding alongside Einarr, having assumed that, like his cousin, the Lady Gytha, Gudhrun would not accompany the army into battle, yet there she was, the weak sunlight glinting off her coat of mail and her weapons.

As they came close, all of the riders dismounted and Einarr walked towards Edmund, Ivar by his side and Gudhrun following with Wulfmaer.

"Your Majesty," Einarr greeted Edmund, "I am honoured to meet you again."

Stepping slightly to the right to bring his father into the centre of the meeting,

"May I present our leader the Lord Ivar", more in statement than request.

Edmund was again surprised. When he had first met Einarr, the young warrior was clearly a prince, dressed in clothing that would be beyond even a seasoned and successful warrior. As Ivar's party had approached, Einarr was again well dressed, but now with the finest mail and equipment. As the tallest, any observer would have taken him as the leader of the host, even if he wondered at his youth. Wulfmaer had the campaign clothing of a young warrior from a smaller village, not the poorest garb, but not the materials that a wealthy young man would wear. Gudhrun was dressed well, matching Einarr's outward signs of substance, a head or more taller than Wulfmaer. Had Edmund not already met her, when she was at Kett's Hall, he might not have realized that she was a young woman. Had she been wearing her helmet, he might have had difficulty in recognizing her. As the party had dismounted and walked towards him, he wondered where Ivar was. He had assumed that father and son would be of similar appearance, the differences being only in age and the richer dress of a King leading a powerful army. Yet here was a man he did not recognize who was noticeably shorter and lighter in build than Einarr, even more curiously, he was dressed modestly, even poorly. With his black hair and dark skin, it seemed impossible that Einaar was his son, or that he commanded the loyalty of a multitude of warriors.

As his surprise was fading, Edmund felt the presence that flowed from Ivar like a great force. He realized the power of the eyes. He appreciated the king's bearing, a man of great power, accustomed to having others do his bidding without question. For Edmund, it was a mixture of thoughts and emotions as he adjusted the image that he had built up in anticipation. Ivar simply was not what he expected, in any way. After what he could only accept as disappointment at first sight, he was now coming to understand how this man could have built up a great host, brought them with him as he crossed the sea, now at their head as they marched towards what could be a great battle, joining with allies they knew nothing of.

"Your Majesty," the two men almost chorused, each keen to extend the greatest courtesy to the other, as they stepped together and clasped arms.

Again Edmund was surprised. The voice was soft and quiet, almost caressing. Edmund found himself leaning in towards Ivar so as to catch every word. Again, it was not what he had expected.

Ivar was not disappointed in any way with Edmund because he had based any preconception on the accounts he had received from Einarr and Gudhrun, to a lesser extent from the accounts of Gytha and Wulfmaer. Even then, Ivar had not formed any hard expectations because he believed in making his own assessment, wherever possible, from direct meeting. As they exchanged the usual pleasantries and rituals of a first meeting of leaders, Ivar was making an assessment that he would have full confidence in and which would require major new information to modify. One of the attributes, that had placed Ivar where he then was, combined listening, observing and evaluating others and situations very quickly, making few mistakes in the process and having full confidence in his own abilities. This was almost the opposite of Edmund's capabilities in decision-making.

Ivar could see that his new ally reached decisions slowly after much agonizing. That was a serious weakness and explained why the rebellion had become established and was growing. A decisive King would have dealt with Esla long before he presented a serious threat. It also explained why the Saxon army was weaker than the expedition that Ivar had assembled to support Edmund. The King's reluctance to reach decisions transmitted anxiety and doubt to those who might otherwise have supported him fully. Ivar suspected that Edmund could count on less than one in every three of those earls and freemen who should rally to their King. The rebellion was probably no larger.

Those who actively supported neither camp would also equal the other two groups in numbers, therefore holding the balance.

This gave Ivar confidence because his force, which was less than a tenth of his total strength, was more decisive than the undecided Saxons and therefore carried Edmund towards victory. The only danger was that Esla had already been reinforced by Northumbrian warriors and had joined with all the other treacherous Anglians. Ivar doubted that the Northumbrians had already joined up with Esla and he could be confident that his remaining forces would deal effectively with the Northumbrians if they arrived. The probability was that the Northumbrians would arrive by the river, discover to their cost that the fort was already lost to an enemy, and be destroyed before they could combine with Esla. If they landed elsewhere, the stronger forces of Ivar would bring them to battle, or march towards Ivar, trapping the Northumbrians and beating them on the anvil formed by Ivar's force.

Ivar knew that the unexpected was always possible in war, almost a given, but his assessment of Edmund was, overall, favourable. Against the weakness of indecision, Ivar could see that Edmund did not lack courage, was well supported by his close circle, had the look of a competent warrior, leading an army that was more than equal to anything that Esla might assemble against them from his close supporters.

Forty One

While the new allies were becoming acquainted, considering their next actions, their adversary was trying to grapple with decisions of his own. Esla should have had some real advantages. The major advantage was that Edmund did not have a clear idea of how much local support Esla could rely on and no idea of what assistance the Northumbrians would provide. Esla doubted that Edmund was even aware of the support committed by the Northumbrians and promised by the Mercians. The weakness was that Esla did not have much idea either and was relying on very unreliable information.

Although Esla did not lack personal courage, he was accustomed to sending others out to do his bidding, while he sat in his hall and raged. Always a squat figure, Esla had become fat from lack of exercise. His arms were still strong but he was no longer able to move as a warrior must. It was difficult to see how he had become the focus for treachery against Edmund. Neither were the most decisive of leaders, but Edmund was young and fit. He was also as attractive as Esla was repulsive. He was good natured and generous, where Esla was forever imagining slights, holding grudges, with a notorious temper that was matched by his inherent greed. Perhaps there lay the real, if perverse, reasons.

Earls looked for a successful leader who could make decisions, who was not afraid to be unpopular. Edmund was not a natural decision maker and was too generous with others. That made his earls cautious, then treacherous. Their people followed where they led. With Esla they knew exactly where they stood and they saw the growing threat posed by the Northumbrians to Edmund's rule. They wanted to be on the winning side in the battle that must come.

The arrival of Ivar and his warriors changed the balance

completely but was not yet appreciated by those who would change allegiance again at the moment that Edmund was to be seen on the winning side. Esla did not understand this remaining advantage to Edmund, or the threat it posed to him should his allies learn of the new balance of power in the Three Kingdoms. This favoured Edmund strongly. Esla still believed that his men held the fort and that the first Northumbrians had arrived with a further cargo of weapons. He believed that the main force would arrive at any time and would give him an unbeatable advantage over Edmund.

Esla did have a time and a place for the meeting with his Northumbrian allies, but he believed his Saxon allies would be at the meeting place as agreed. It was less than a day's march from the site chosen by Edmund to meet with his Norse allies. It was also on the day agreed by Ivar to meet with Edmund. A set of coincidences that are the stuff of history. The difference between the plans of Esla and the plans of Edmund was that the King had exchanged messengers regularly with Ivar, but his treacherous earl had no recent contact with the Northumbrians and must trust that nothing had disrupted their agreed meeting.

Esla had little choice in the matter. Where Wulfmaer and his mother provided most of the messengers for Ivar and might raise only mild curiosity that there was so much communication with Edmund, the situation was very different for the Northumbrians. Sending messengers to Esla by land would have raised curiosity along their route. Once into Edmund's territories, they would have aroused great curiosity and news of their passing would soon have reached the King. Sending messengers by boat was little different because they would have been seen sailing up a river and Edmund would again have received knowledge of their voyage.

Messengers could have been sent with the shipment of arms and had been before Ivar took the fort. As the shipments were not at agreed dates, but varied according to completion of arms and sailing conditions, Esla had no firm knowledge of the shipment that had been taken by Ivar. From his cousin's seriously inaccurate report, Esla believed that the shipment had arrived safely and it would have been shortly before the Northumbrian warriors were due to arrive to march on to their meeting at Aelfnoth's Stone. There would have been little point in sending a messenger ahead when the Northumbrian army would arrive at almost the same time, and there was always the danger that a messenger would fall into the hands of the King.

As usual, Esla was torn by doubt and suspicion. He had agreed the same meeting place and date for those Anglians who had committed to join him in insurrection. Small groups would already be on the move towards the ancient meeting place. At dawn, Esla must lead his own people to the meeting. All he could do was to trust that nothing unseen had disrupted his plans, but even in good times Esla was not a trusting man. In the absence of practical methods of checking, all he could do was develop his black mood. The only certainty was that none of his people would willingly ride close to him, avoiding his anger.

When dawn broke there was little to improve Esla's humour. He immediately missed his closest subordinates. He may have mistreated Birdoswald, but he had still relied on him to do his bidding. As far as Esla was capable, he had held a fondness for his creature. The warriors collected together, waiting for him to lead them to the meeting, did not inspire any great confidence. There were only thirty four, of which only six were mounted. That would slow his journey to Aelfnoth's Stone. They were all well equipped, but some were beyond the age for battle, some were young and ill-trained and those that might be considered trained and of military age, several were clearly not at the peak of fitness. He could only hope that those converging on the Stone would be adequate in numbers and ability. He could not be certain of the support of the other earls and he might not know until some changed sides during the battle.

To maintain the mood of melancholy, the rain fell steadily from a leaden sky and dripped from the branches of trees as they made their way towards their destination. The wind was light and the air still mild, but the steady fall of rain was miserable, the early light poor. Esla could hope for improvement but experience inclined to a wet day and a wetter night ahead. It was not the best of campaigning weather and late in the season. The harvest had been gathered in but Esla realized that the battle was likely on his land and it would be his harvest stores at risk from the King's soldiers.

From a discouraging start, there was some improvement. The rain became lighter and then broken into short showers. The party remained together and no mishap befell them as they made their way towards Aelfnoth's Stone. Even better, a straggle of warriors joined his party as he advanced, swelling his numbers and encouraging optimism.

Forty Two

As the two armies moved to their meeting places and then prepared to move together into battle, Red Osten received the first reports of Northumbrian ships. He already knew of the storms further North along the coastline from those boats that continued to arrive with supplies and men ahead of the harshness and short days of full winter. He was therefore not surprised to learn that small numbers of Northumbrian boats were collecting off the coast, before following the path he had himself taken up the river towards the fort.

From the watchers reports, the vessels were warships of average size and condition. From those already to be seen, the Northumbrian army would not be as large as they had feared, but it might be too early to make a final count. All he could be certain of was that the first boats presented little threat to their own defences and it seemed unlikely that they would begin making their way inland until after first light on the morrow. They might even delay further if their fleet had been widely scattered by the storms. It was too early for Osten to consider recalling the roving patrols, because there was still a risk that the Northumbrians might plan on several landings along the coast but, from the first observations, there was every appearance that the Northumbrians were unaware that the fort was in new hands, that their ships were observed from the shore, that they intended making the same landfall that Ivar had made, making their way to the fort before marching off to meet Esla and the other rebel earls. The watchers would continue to observe and send in a stream of regular reports, but now was the time to bring the fort up to full readiness, prepare the force on the island, and move more of the boats away from the lake. Ivar had ordered them to remain in the rough harbour on the island until battle seemed likely and the place of attack was recognized. He had done this because the boats gave his forces at the fort mobility to attack any landing further along the coast, or multiple landings at several locations. Battles at sea were never as easy to control, but they divided the force less than sending out several large patrols, or small armies, to scattered locations, and they avoided the risk of missing those dispersed landings.

Now that the Northumbrians appeared to be preparing to sail into an unexpected battle at the lake, it was time to bring forward preparations for that event. Osten had considered leaving some of the captured Saxon boats in the harbour to reassure the Northumbrians, but also to provide a means of escape for the small force on the island. For that eventuality, he would leave the ferry rope in place, but prepare to cut the rope to frustrate any attempt by the enemy to benefit from it. Once he knew the full extent of the Northumbrian fleet, Osten could decide whether to send part of his force outside the fort, ready to attack the Northumbrians from behind, trapping them against the massive walls, where those inside the fort could harass them from above. Osten would have to use his judgement, but there was an attraction to having a force outside for a double surprise, with the option to be ready to ride off to reinforce Ivar once victory had been achieved over the Northumbrians. For now, Osten would walk the walls and check on the warriors, the stores and the readying of the artillery. This was the time to bring up the materials to rain fire down on attacking enemy boats. He would also take the ferry to the island to make sure that everything was prepared and orders fully understood by its defenders.

Ivar had been very clear in his instructions to Osten. Although he expected his lieutenants to make decisions from direct knowledge, the objective was fixed. No Northumbrian could be allowed to escape. Every boat must be accounted for and taken into their own fleet or broken up. If the Northumbrians were defeated here, they must not be able to send any messages back to their king. As long as he remained in ignorance of what had happened, he would still be unprepared for the battles that were to follow the ending of this coming winter. If he learned the truth before, the battles would be that much more difficult and uncertain. Osten therefore carried great responsibility on his young shoulders and would have to draw on every fragment of experience gained in past battles. Ivar knew that he could rely on Osten. He had considered leaving Einarr to command the fort and he had many battle-hardened commanders to choose from, but he had favoured Osten over the other senior captains, wanting Einarr to gain experience of a major battle on land, working with allies.

Red Osten was an ideal choice, popular with his comrades, a sound reputation, and a remarkable ability for one of his short years. Ivar was already picking the most prominent young warriors to serve Einaar in future years. They would serve him well and mentor those of the next generation that Einaar would select for leadership. Ivar knew that many of his long-trusted comrades would decide not to campaign after the battles that would come in the next year. There would be a strong sense of loss, but Ivar knew that those who had mentored him were soon to be beyond the age for campaigning. Some would remain because their contribution was knowledge and experience, not leadership in battle. Those, like Gisi, would serve as long as they had breath and could stand a voyage. Their knowledge of navigation and the seas was far beyond the younger sailing masters. Ashore, through the winters, they would pass on their knowledge, as they did when time permitted at sea.

Having cast about his command from the height of one of the fort's towers, Red Osten decided to collect about him his senior armourers, carpenters and masons, making his way to the island by the ferry. The capstans were still to be installed and the heavy rope was hauled into the captured Saxon warship. Two warriors in the stern fed the rope over the planking as the party in the bows hauled in more rope. Progress was steady and the journey out into the lake and the island harbour was easier and faster than it would have been by manning the boat's oars. The rope ahead broke free from the water and shook off a thick spray as each new exertion applied tension and brought yet more rope aboard. Very soon, the distance had closed and the boat was inside the palisade that broke out of the lake in protection of the rough harbour. As the boat had approached the two wooden towers that guarded the harbour entrance, the chain boom had been lowered to allow them passage, to be smartly raised as the stern came clear of the entrance.   As they had approached, the carpenters and armourershad been keenly inspecting the palisade, looking for any defects or opportunities to further strengthen the defences. By the time that the boat was inside the small harbour, all were satisfied with the work completed. On landing, Aggi pointed out some improvements that could be made to the gateway that led into the island's fort. Osten approved his suggestions and one of the party was sent away into the fort to locate its carpenters and carry out the improvements.

Red Osten would have preferred the rising ground to be broken up with obstacles, but there had not been time enough to attend to this. As it was, the gently rising slopes to the mound, on which sat the artillery, did at least provide a clean field of fire for the archers on top of the mound. Around the outer palisade, a firing step had been built on the inside face of the tree trunks, a narrow wooden walkway from which the defenders could throw stones and spears down into boats attempting to close with the wooden wall, and a place for archers to stand. Beneath the firing step, shelters had been built to accommodate the warriors. In parts, it was still provided by old sails stretched out from the firing step, pegged to the ground like tents. In other parts, Aggi had already put up wooden buildings that were warm and snug against rain, snow and biting winds that would soon be a daily feature.

Like a crown sitting on the head of the mount was an inner palisade, lower than the main walls but still more than the height of a warrior on its outer face and shoulder height on the inside. It provided a final stand to which warriors could fall back from the outer walls if necessary, under covering fire from archers already stationed to protect the artillery. The mount was just below the level of the top of the inner palisade. The artillery was a single large trebuchet on a turning platform that could be swung by a team of warriors, time had not allowed the building of a second war engine. Below the platform was kindling and oils to be ignited in an emergency, destroying the trebuchet before victorious attackers could turn it on the fortress across the lake. At the extreme of its range, the artillery posed only small threat to the fortress and the Northumbrians might not have the skill anyway to make use of it, but Ivar was not taking any chances. He had ordered Osten to make sure a most dependable warrior was to be standing by ready to fire the materials in the pit. Ivar would have liked a way to deny an enemy the well they had dug there for the garrison, but the intention was to make sure that the island fort could hold out until the enemy was defeated, or reinforcements sent across.

The armourers checked the artillery piece and its supply of ammunition, questioning the crew on their duties. The ammunition was made up of stones and balls of dry materials that would be soaked in oil and set on fire just before they were launched at attacking ships. The armourers reported to Osten that they were satisfied with the weapon and its crew. The carpenters had reported that they were content with the defences they had built. Osten decided that he would send over more men that day and leave only two longships in the harbour, joined together and ready for the garrison if withdrawal became necessary. He could have withdrawn both ships, as a final withdrawal would be difficult under attack from enemy boats, but he knew that the warriors on the island would fight better if they knew escape was an option, an option which honour would not allow them to use unless ordered.

The island's defences reviewed and strengthened, Osten's party was ferried back to the fortress and undertook the same review there. This was no less exhaustive but longer. There was so much more to review. True, the old walls and towers of the fortress were in perfect condition and the main gate was a massive structure, the gates reinforced by Aggi's carpenters to withstand a greater assault than any to be expected. Within the walls, there was abundant water from the wells, the store houses were stocked to see them through the coming winter, there was abundant shelter from the weather, and the armouries were stocked to arm additional warriors. Osten was not surprised to find that all of these capabilities were battle-ready. The same was true of the artillery mounted on the towers and of the ammunition stocked close to the great weapons, with more in easy reach. Any attacking fleet would face great metal bolts from the giant crossbows, amongst a mixture of stones and flaming balls, long before they came in range of spear and smaller weapons. Those that closed the great stone walls would be engulfed by Ivar's special weapon.

In battle there was always danger of a surprise, but Osten thought it unlikely that an attacking fleet would be able to fight a way into the fortress.

By the time that all of these inspections had been completed, night was falling, and extra sentries were placed on the walls against surprise attack.

Forty Three

Esla was feeling more optimistic, at least by his own standards. They had broken camp shortly after first light, the rain had stopped and he had ordered a fire lit. This had given his party their first hot food since leaving his village and everyone felt rather happier for it. It had been an uneventful march without anyone dropping by the wayside. There were some sore feet as the warriors suffered a lack of general preparation and fitness. The horses were little better, but all had managed to make the journey.

As they now came out of a wood they could see ahead of them the grazed slopes of the small hill, on top of which stood the rough shape of Aelfnoth's Stone. It had stood on this low hill since long before the Saxon's came to the islands. No one knew how long it had stood, but it was well-weathered and streaked with moss on one side. On its sides were strange markings that no one comprehended. It stood taller than two men and was six paces around its base. An object of mystery but long a rally point for armies gathering to defend the lands it overlooked. Esla was pleased to see it standing there as the marker of a peaceful journey. He was more pleased to see an army gathered around it, his army. There looked to be more than six hundred warriors there awaiting his arrival, few horses, but more men than he had hoped for. Looking across the valley below the hill he could see three more groups making their way to the Stone. It was still before the middle of the day, so there was time yet for even more to arrive.

Like Edmund's army, these warriors looked more impressive from a distance. Like his supporters, they came together as small groups and from villages that could not provide all the trained warriors they had promised. This did not dampen Esla's uncustomary enthusiasm because he expected this and mirrored their capabilities in his own group. If battle was joined with Edmund, the two armies would face each other in a line that contained few if any archers. The armies would move together and the battle depended on the determination to trade blows over hours. Both armies would weaken, the winner being the army that managed to stand longest, with fewer defections. It would be a brutal trial of strength and stamina, leaving little to great tactical skill, or the brilliance of one general.

Esla could not yet see any Northumbrians and this did begin to unsettle him. That absence was compensated by the presence of his local allies and with more men than he had expected them to raise. True, the quality left something to be desired but there were many skilled warriors, with good equipment, in apparent fitness for the campaign.

Esla comforted himself that their northern allies would arrive to swell his ranks, but with those already waiting for him he expected to more than match the size of Edmund's army. Some of those now arriving brought news of Edmund rallying his forces nearby at Berthold's Bridge. As they had passed before Ivar and his army had arrived, they were able to report that Edmund had fewer men.

Esla was encouraged not to delay seeking out Edmund and bringing him to battle. Those who owed him service had all arrived and they brought the numbers they owed. Here and there, Esla could see weaknesses, a few untrained men to make the numbers, some warriors not at their peak strength, and some deficiencies in weapons. Unlike Edmund, Esla had arrived without a baggage train carrying spare equipment and supplies. He could see that some of his fellow conspirators had brought a few wagons, but whatever they carried in food and weapons would soon be dissipated across the assembled force. The Northumbrians were due to arrive with a baggage train carrying the weapons and supplies they had shipped to the fort during the Summer. It would be wise to wait for these additional men and the supplies they would bring, but Esla could see an advantage in defeating the King without Northumbrian help. Had fewer of his people and those of his fellow traitors arrived at the meeting place, Esla might have considered delaying until the Northumbrians had joined them, but all the indications were that he had a superior force already and the King might even now be advancing towards him. Unlike Edmund, Esla could make decisions quickly although he made as many bad decisions as good.

Through the fringe of trees to the west, the ground sloped gently down to a small stream. This area had been farmed for generations and had been neglected only because plague and conflict had reduced the population. "Pity," thought Esla, "this had once been a wealthy area contributing to my treasury".

Just as the slopes of the hill, on which sat Aelfnoth's Stone, had been grazed for generations, the line of trees, it was not thick enough to justify calling it a wood, much less a forest, hid what might be on the pastures behind. If Esla moved his force into the trees, he could watch anyone coming from the West where Edmund would be. His force would look smaller against the tree line and Edmund might be tempted to cross the stream, beginning to march his warriors up the slope. Esla could then sweep down and trap Edmund against the stream. It looked to be a credible plan. The question he had to ask was whether Edmund would already be heading towards him. If he was at Berthold's Bridge, he could either wait for Esla to come to him, or he could decide to look for Esla and bring him to battle. If he did take the latter course, he would probably head to Aelfnoth's Stone, knowing it to be an ancient meeting place for armies. Esla concluded that Edmund would not come to him. He was convinced that the King's indecision would prevent him from taking a decisive step. This could enable Esla to first destroy any small forces sent out to locate him. What he did not know was that Edmund was no longer required to take the decisions, but could follow others.

In a confident mood, Esla formed up his forces and began to move towards the tree line. It would mean no more fires so his warriors would have to rely on cold food and hope that there was no return to heavy rain, or a clear sky with a sharp fall in temperature, but this was a small price to pay for a strong advantage in battle tomorrow or in the days following.

There was now a probability that Esla would bring Edmund to battle and defeat him before any Northumbrians had arrived. That would allow him to turn the Northumbrians back home and reduce the need to give way to whatever demands they intended. Esla might even be able to take the crown from Edmund and rule the three kingdoms in his place. That appealed to his natural greed, promising to give him all of the wealth of the three kingdoms. He might still have to face a Northumbrian attempt to invade, but he was already thinking of how he might enlist the help of the Mercians at no direct price. They had every reason to fear a Northumbrian invasion of their own lands and might see a greater need for Esla's support than they might perceive as a need for him. Everything seemed to be moving to Esla's favour and he was already thinking how he might exploit the possibilities to his own benefit. He might have to make some gifts to his local allies but then a King always needed to buy some favour, whilst wielding the club to instil fear. Esla had a great preference for the club but he felt himself more than a match for the other earls who had turned to him.

Esla now had to keep the morale of his own forces strong and convince them that there was no need to await the Northumbrians. That might not be too difficult because they would also see personal advantage in taking Edmund in battle without Northumbrian help. What would be critical would be the belief that they would triumph. There was still a risk that some might defect back to Edmund as the battle began. There was also a risk that some of his fellow earls would not engage the King's forces robustly, waiting to see who would triumph. Esla knew there were risks, but he had taken some hostages to stiffen the support of the earls he least trusted. He believed that it was fear and greed that bound most of his allies to him, feelings he knew, feelings he trusted.

Esla was further comforted by the thought that he held the King's cousin as a hostage, together with Wulfmaer and others taken during the months before. If battle went badly, he could still bargain with these prisoners.

Forty Four

Once more we come to the end of an enjoyable evening. Morag is understandably held in her thoughts for her dearest Robert. She knows that he stands into danger, but she also knows that our sanctuary is part illusion, that her husband has sailed early to be our vengeance if fortune goes against us here.

Now that we meet frequently to share an evening meal I feel my grief slipping away, yet I am closer now to my dearest Margaret. I gain so much joy from my grandchildren, and from their parents. In my mind the years have slipped away these last weeks. I can do nothing for my body but accept that it grows older.

Then even here I improve. We must accept that in the coming months a close escort will be necessary when we ride along the strand, but I will enjoy the exercise and relaxation of riding with my grandchildren. Maybe also I will take their mothers with us. Then there is the practice at arms, which does me as much good as it does them.

I realize now how low I had fallen after the death of my precious Margaret. Perhaps in grief everything is excluded beyond the pain and the loss. Now I feel stronger and I know again the breadth of interests that I once took for granted. This may not be a moment too soon. The storm clouds gather as ambitious Lords struggle to exploit the weakness of our Queen. I can see that only deepening as the months draw past. It brings danger for our family because one group will gain victory in the months, or years, ahead. I hope that we will be on the side that triumphs, but it is too early to know, too many twists and turns of fate, of error, of malice. I can only try to keep my wits about me, use every guide from our past, our expectations for the future. I know that I must build my strength to give my sons time, to use what experience has given me that they have yet to gain.

Tonight, I no longer feel the loss, the solitude when my grand children are shepherded to their beds by their mothers. I realize that these evenings have gained, each on the other. I know now that it has been as much the lack of stiffness that my grief once brought. I am now comfortable with all of my family and I see now more future for me than I could have believed bare weeks ago.

We have developed into what are now natural habits, a greater appreciation of each. The meal in the turret room begins our gathering. We can relax with good food and casual chatter. When we step down into the chamber, each has a favoured place and we can relax further. The Saga of Einarr unfolds each evening but it is no longer a monologue, a mere story telling. It has become a true education for all of us, transportation to another place, a place at once familiar, at once alien.

I now recount the tales with questions from my audience and discussion. The characters have developed their form and stand amongst us as much a part of the evening as we are. They are taking flesh and we can see that they are our family. We learn their fears and joys, seeing that they are familiar from our own existence.

It is a comfort to know that in past generations, our family has met challenges and triumphed, seized opportunity and prospered. The family saga was intended to guide future generations and it is as fresh now as when it began. Each generation has added a layer of experience to the stories before. We are the same as our forefathers. In each age there will be details that are new, but much remains unchanged.

As I gaze into the dying fire, I can see the faces of the past, of the present and of the future. Most of all I can see my dearest Margaret. I can hear her gentle voice, I can feel her presence, we can talk to each other, to say the things that we never said before when other matters distracted us or kept us apart. I have learned the value of our conversation and of the Saga. I can look at the matters of today from a different direction.

Matters, which are clouded, become clear. It is a god-like state where I can look down at the map of today and tomorrow, seeing what is hidden.

Tonight I rise from my chair with a fresh enthusiasm and a bolder hope. I seem to have shed the years. My bones no longer creak. As I rise, Kara uncurls herself and rises, waiting to accompany me to my sleeping chamber. The fire has now burned low. The rush lights are put out and with them the candles. There is a new lightness to my step as we walk across to the door to my sleeping chamber. I know that tonight I will sleep deeply, to dream, to wake refreshed, a new man, for a new dawn.

When I wake I will remember my father's sage advice, to greet the day as a grand day to die, to make the most of every minute, of every hour, to do that day all that I can as though it is my last day. There is so much to be done that is easy to put off the necessary actions, to think that it is impossible to select matters that urge action. As I fill each day, the demands become ever more possible.

Part Six: -

Hands of the Gods

Forty Five

The past weeks have seen a straggle of visitors. James Hepburn is safely in Norway and our ship has returned, but I know not when he plans to return. His enemies have gathered but our Queen has need of his services as High Admiral. I despair at her lack of skill in governing. James the Bastard continues to plot against her and hopes yet to replace her. Even his most enthusiastic supporters may hesitate at that. He cannot imprison her, or kill her. Even if he could, he has no fair claim to the throne. The best he can hope is that she marries, delivers a child, can be constrained, with James standing as Regent. If that is the course, I will be happy to appoint and pay the assassin of James the Bastard.

Elizabeth Tudor has offered one of her rejected suitors as husband. The Darnleys have some claim to the throne and demand the Crown Matrimonial as price of the marriage. I fear that it will end in sorrow. By all accounts, Darnley is little suited to marry our Queen, Elizabeth Tudor may have proposed him as mischief. His life is devoted to himself, to dancing, to playing the lute, to little else. Our Queen shares that with him, but needs a husband who can guide her, to lead her armies and fleet. To have a consort who is a shallower form of herself will not serve. It would aid the plans of James the Bastard to have a Queen and consort he can set aside, to control any child they may produce.

We canna oppose the marriage openly. All that is left as an option for us is to join with others, to encourage the Queen to think wider and with greater care. I fear that will not produce success. I wonder how our Queen can be so much less than her mother. The Dowager was a capable leader, a reliable Queen, even though she was French.

We are courted by many factions. Recent visitors have represented all those with the strength to make an effect, none of them likely to triumph while our Queen lives to rally their opponents. Their greatest ally is the Queen herself. In all her actions she is alien in conduct, language and likes. Much is not her blame because she was but a small child when she was sent to France to advance the House of Guise through marriage to the sickly Dauphin. She was discarded as the Dowager Queen of France to Scotland. That may have helped others to advance but it was little benefit to Scotland. Her half-brother assumed that her lack of ability would allow him to rule in all but name. He sulks now that he knows she will not give way.

For us it is almost of no matter. We hold our lands to the English border, we live by trade and war. It is not the Crown that most affects us, as those of our neighbours who would side with one faction or another. The sea is to our faces and not to our backs. Still, we must intrigue, as do the other families. We must decide what future we most want. For now, the power is in London with Elizabeth Tudor. She faces many battles of her own, but she has skill, courage, and advisors of substance, men who know their minds and will work for her cause.

Our natural allies are the corsairs on the French and English coasts. They are Protestant and that inclines us to support those Protestants in Scotland. That in time will place us against our own Queen.

For now I must keep us free from commitment to any cause, to let each faction believe we will favour them when the time for action arrives. That an attempt has already been made on my life makes little change to my strategy. It may have little in common with the fortunes of our Queen, but much in common with our history of dispute with some of our neighbours. It has long been the way that Border families hold first their alliances and foes within the Borders, but if an ally or enemy forms an interest beyond, that may determine grander alliance.

As visitors come and go, I still value the evening meals with my close family and grudge those nights that I must play the host in our Hall. Once was the time I enjoyed the game and the danger of intrigue, but no longer. I do only what I must for our family. With the weather continuing bitter cold, the snow deep across the valleys and the hills, our guests will scurry alone. Several have made but brief visits, cautious that they avoid those of other factions. Those who must travel the land face a cold and difficult journey. Those who can use the sea are better served with our own harbour within our walls.

Today we are free of intrusion. I much enjoyed a ride along the strand and have become accustomed to sharing my freedom with a close escort. We have developed a pattern that gives me space and peace, but allows my bodyguard to the comfort that they are a reliable shield. They ride in three groups, one group a little distance ahead, one group closer behind, one group closest on the landward side of me. To the other side, the risk is low. The sea provides no cover for an attacker. Today I have been accompanied by Mary, as is usual, but also by James, William and Gilbert. The twins each ride a small native pony, Mary has three ponies of choice, her favourite is Heather, a Norwegian fjord pony, little smaller than a Highland pony and with the same dark stripe along the length of her back. James now has a campaign horse to ride, the size and weight of my own horse. The twins and James are small against their mounts, Mary has almost outgrown Heather, only my mount, Hector, matches his rider. Against us, my escort and their mounts are well matched, campaigners, on campaign horses, their steel helmets bright in the winter sun, their long leather riding coats covering their steel breast and back plates, weapons hung from themselves and from their horses.

Following close behind are Janet and Morag, deep in conversation. They have never joined me before for a ride along the sand. I decided that they should join with us on most days when I could enjoy the outing. Over the weeks of early winter we have become close, enjoying our meals together. It is now natural for us to spend more time together, I to know them well, for them to learn what I still have to teach.

My opinion of Morag has never changed and I must admit that she is still my favourite, but my liking of Janet has developed steadily. I now know what lies behind her gestures and manner. Before I measured her against the superficial presentation. I can see now that she has been raised to stay in the background, where Morag has the familiar manner of a Galwegian, robust and straight forward, an equal amongst men and women. Janet has narrow features that do not lend themselves to a happy appearance, I must still admit that she can see slights where none are intended, I now have a fairer view of her and it pleases me. Perhaps she is also happier now that she is no longer judged unfairly.

After a long ride, we are all hungry. Our evening meal together has even greater relish. I enjoy eating in the turret room in any station of the year, in winter, lit by candles, the walls and windows covered by rich tapestries, in summer, lit by the sun, the views across the Firth magnificent. This evening, the heat has risen from the chamber, joining with a full hot meal to warm us after the cold ride. For much of our ride the cold went unnoticed in the beauty of a wide clear sky and a golden winter sun. As we made our way back to the castle, the sky had clouded and the cold was noticed by all. As we came in sight of the castle, it began to snow and the wind built up from the North. By the time we reached the shelter of the walls, we were all becoming very cold, a hot meal in a warm room was an inviting prospect.

As we completed eating, we were all bathed in the contented glow that comes from good food at a comfortable table. We stepped down into the chamber and its greater warmth. Jamie and his wife cleared away the remains of our meal as we settled into the chairs around the fire that Jamie had built up for us. Once again light from the candles and the rush lights danced in the armour and weapons on the wall above the fireplace. The tapestries glowed in the collected light, gold thread glittering in the rays.

When we were all ready, I began again the Saga of Einarr. The familiar figures joined me once more, the scenes unfolded and surrounded us.

Forty Six

Red Osten watched the approach of the Saxon warships through one of the loopholes cut through the massive walls of the fort. He could see thirty vessels already in the lake, with more entering from the river.

He was not surprised because messengers had been bringing a stream of reports from the watchers along the river to the sea. He knew that there should be fifty warships arriving at the lake. It was almost a relief to see most of the Saxon ships already within the range of his artillery.

It had been a nervous wait as the Saxons delayed entering the river. Had he commanded their fleet, Osten would have started to sail inland on the day that the first vessels had arrived, at least to reach as far as the first lake. The longer a fleet held off the coast, the greater the danger that a storm would spring up to disperse the ships. Seeing the reports that twenty vessels had arrived before dark on the previous day, Osten feared that the Saxons might land somewhere further down the coast. If they did, he would have to go out from the fort to meet them, in an attempt to prevent them from joining with Esla.

Osten remembered the wise advice given to him some years before. His mentor had taught him that an enemy could as easily be over-estimated, that errors came from assuming that the enemy had the same wisdom and experience. From there an experienced enemy could be under estimated but, just as dangerous, was to credit the enemy with wisdom and experience that was beyond him. It was possible that the Saxon commander expected more ships, but did not have the confidence that those ships could find the correct river unless they could find their comrades awaiting them at sea.

That was needed was an analysis of known facts and reliable deduction. Osten had no way of knowing how many enemy ships would arrive, how many warriors they would carry, or where they would make a landing. That they were still awaiting other ships suggested that no more than half the expected fleet had arrived, but a cautious commander might wait until all hope was lost of even one more ship.

That the commander was already waiting suggested that he would not attempt to enter the river until after dawn on the following day, but he might send one vessel ahead to land scouts and gain intelligence. Osten had to be patient, to continue to watch, to be ready to deal with the unexpected. To check and check again their preparations for the coming fight, and to make certain that the watchers were ready and vigilant.

Ivar had been wise to set up a watch system that could be maintained after an enemy had approached. Once the Saxons began to make their way up river, Osten needed continuing surveillance because other ships might follow later. Even if the enemy was awaiting a further twenty or thirty warships before heading up river, it was still possible for a second fleet of similar size to arrive even later. He simply did not know how many ships the Northumbrians owned, or whether they had other allies with more ships. Even so, fifty ships was a large fleet and it might be all that the Northumbrians could muster.

As the Saxons sailed into the lake, Osten could see for himself their strength and that it matched the reports that had been arriving from the chain of watchers. The largest Saxon warships were smaller than the largest ships in Ivar's fleet. They were also a small proportion of the fleet and he could see some that were only small trading vessels. To his eyes it looked like a collection of ships brought together with difficulty, some appearing to be poorly maintained. What did surprise him was that none of the ships' crews seemed ready for battle, most still in their sea clothes, few wearing mail coats, or standing ready with their weapons. It was curious. Osten would never make the mistake of approaching a fortification without his men ready for a bloody fight, however much he might expect it to be in the hands of friends.

The force was large in ships and men, suggesting that they were expecting to fight a major battle. It was difficult to be certain, but there must be a thousand warriors aboard the vessels, but that assumed the Saxons would fully crew their ships as Osten would have, had they been his. Assumptions were always dangerous.

Is the latest reports had arrived, watchers had made a count of the Saxons passing their hiding places. The account indicated a number of between nine hundred and twelve hundred Saxons. Even if that included sailors, who might not be expected to fight, or others, who were no more than passengers without fighting experience, the Saxon force had to number at least eight hundred warriors, but Osten was inclined to accept the largest estimate and find the force weaker than he had prepared for.

Against the enemy, Osten had a much larger, but divided, force, supported by a small number of friendly Saxons. The wisdom of Ivar's plans were now proving themselves. It was better that he had taken a relatively small portion of their warriors to meet with Edmund's forces, wise to take so many horses. That left Osten with six hundred warriors inside the fort, a further one hundred and fifty on the island in the lake and a further hundred aboard the ships rafted across the river inland from the lake. That gave him a rough parity of numbers with the lower estimate of the Saxons now approaching. He also had the watchers and the warriors dispersed inland along the river, and at the village of Depenham. More than half their total force was now housed in the growing fortifications at Depenham, with the roving patrols, ferries and small forts absorbing a further significant number. Then also there were the roving bands that Ivar had sent out to locate any surprise forces that might be sent against them at any location. Then there was the mobile reserve of mounted warriors held close by to the south of the fortress.

When all was counted Osten knew he could bring a far larger force to bear on the Northumbrian fleet and that the defensive positions gave him a very important advantage. To that he might be able to add the value of surprise because the

Northumbrians did not appear to realize that they were approaching an enemy. The final advantage in Osten's mind was that his comrades could out-fight any Saxon force of twice their numbers.

Against that, there had to be the allowance for the unexpected and Osten knew that he could not bring his additional forces to support the fort and island, except in grave emergency, because they might yet be needed to fight on another front or to defend against a second fleet. So he had to accept that the Northumbrians probably held the numerical advantage in the fight about to begin. To that, Osten had to decide when to trap the Northumbrian vessels.

It had been a quiet dry night but, before dawn, the wind had risen and heavy squalls of icy rain now lashed land and lake. Now, the wind had dropped but a steady downpour had begun. It dappled the waters of the lake and absorbed sounds not made by the rain. There was a cold greyness.

He had three places along the river where he could raise a boom. Each boom was made up of a heavy chain, with anchors on either bank. On the far bank, a thick post, cut from a tree trunk, had been hammered into the bank, screened by reeds from anyone sailing the river. The great chain secured to this post, being carried to the bottom of the river by its weight. On the opposite bank another massive post served as anchor, also being hidden from passing craft by the reeds that fringed both banks. What the booms lacked was a machine to tighten the chain, bringing it to the surface of the river. When the time came, a party of warriors at each boom must strain their muscles in raising the barrier. Raised and secured, the booms would prevent ships from passing in either direction.

Ivar has little chain available to him so that he could not build further booms. The first chain was pulled across the river at its first bend after the first lake. The third boom was built two ship lengths to seaward of the entrance into the second lake. The second chain had been located roughly midway between on the river between the two lakes. This would allow a single boom to be raised, or all booms to be used. The difficult decision would be in the timing. If the watchers were certain that no more ships would enter from the sea, the first boom could be raised as soon as the last enemy vessel passed out of sight from the boom. Given that the chain of watchers continued to the mouth of the river, there would be time to lower the boom if more vessels entered from the sea, allowing them to be let into the trap. The next boom could be raised once the ships had passed from sight. This would ensure that a retreating vessel would be halted before it could be seen by a late arrival and the two vessels would be unable to support each other. Red Osten could then send his mounted reserve to deal with any of the ship crews that might land in an attempt to break the boom. The most difficult decision would be for the raising of the boom where the river entered the second lake.

As Red Osten watched the ships entering the lake before him the second boom would have been raised, possibly followed quickly by the first boom. Messengers would bring confirmation of this, hoping to be able to reach and enter the fortress. The decision on the third boom was for Osten. He must allow all the Saxon ships to enter the lake before he ordered the boom raised. The decision was more difficult because the Northumbrians had yet to discover the ownership of the fortress. Raising the boom too quickly would alert them to the trap. The later they discovered that the fort was in enemy hands the greater the benefits of surprise.

The last Northumbrian ship was now inside the lake. All the vessels were passing the island and collecting together as the first vessels made for the quay. They still appeared to be unaware that an enemy awaited them. Red Osten saw the island's trebuchet slowly turning as Hunbogi prepared to fire on the last ships to enter the lake. Osten gave the signal to raise the boom, and the trap was closed on the Northumbrians.

Forty Seven

Esla had prepared his battle line. He could not yet see any of Edmund's warriors, but a scout had returned to confirm that the King was advancing in their direction. Esla shared Red Osten's expectation that the enemy was coming within range, unaware of his waiting warriors. The rebels would advance on foot as was common practice for a Saxon battle. Esla had few archers and must engage Edmund closely. He expected the King to cross the valley and ford the river.

Once all of Edmund's warriors had crossed the river, Esla could bring his men out of the trees, forming his battle line on the ground above Edmund. He expected to see the King respond by moving his line up the slope until he engaged the traitor's line. As Edmund advanced up the hill, Esla could bring his fresher forces down onto the King's line and force them back to the river and into the water. The ensuing confusion would disrupt the King's line and allow Esla to begin rolling it up, forcing the King's warriors into a rout, allowing his warriors to chase and destroy them. To Esla it seemed to be a simple plan that guaranteed success.

After a quiet, largely dry, night, the cloud had thickened and brought the first squalls at dawn. As the rain became increasingly heavy, the hillside was becoming slippery. This was not welcome for either side, but Esla would continue an advantage where it would be easier for his warriors to keep their feet, able to force the King's line back down the hill when the two armies came together.

Now he could see Edmund leading his forces down into the valley. He was surprised by the size of the force, it was certainly larger than he had been led to believe by his allies. Far from outnumbering the King's men, Esla's force was the smaller. He still hoped to see defections, before and during battle, but his earlier confidence was being shaken.

At least the King had only a few horses. Esla assumed that the loyal army had marched across the kingdom and would be more tired than his own force. As yet, Edmund was marching his warriors in a column, indicating that he had not expected to fight a battle. Esla ordered the first of his men to form up before the trees. He had divided his force into two groups, the second, larger, group still hidden from view amongst the trees.

Edmund saw warriors in line near the brow of the hill. He ordered his warriors to form a line of battle and advance down the slope to the river. His force came on in good order, their banners shaken out, shields held before them, spears and swords ready. The river was shallow, not much deeper than the knees of most warriors. The line advanced smoothly through the cold water and halted on the far bank, awaiting the order to march up the hill to engage the enemy.

Esla was not surprised that Edmund had halted his line on the riverbank. He expected the King to dither and delay before making a decision. So far, Edmund could only see the smaller part of Esla's force which the King's men comfortably outnumbered. The loyalists began to move again. They were advancing more slowly, but they continued to come on. Half way up the hill they halted. Here, the slope was less steep and the footing much improved.

Esla looked carefully at the opposing army. He gave the order to advance and his warriors began to come down the hill towards the King's men. Their comrades came out from the trees, thickening the line and expanding it to match the opposing battle line. In that order they came down onto Edmund's warriors as a roughly equal force but with the momentum of advancing down a slope.

The two lines crashed together. Edmund's men began to give way, slowly being forced backwards down the slope. Here and there a King's man lost his footing, to be trampled by the enemy as they remorselessly forced the King back down the hill. Shields crashed together, spears and swords stabbed, wounds were suffered on both sides. Esla stood behind and above his line, a feeling of satisfaction and anticipation. He could see that Edmund's line was wavering and steadily being forced down the slope towards the stream. Esla knew that once the King's men were forced into the water, warriors would fall and the line would disintegrate. His men would then be able to pick off the enemy almost at leisure. He felt that this was going to be a good day, his confidence rising once more.

Edmund and his loyal earls were in the front line of his warriors, urging their men on to greater effort and fighting with great bravery and determination, but they were at a disadvantage. There was much shouting and pushing as warriors recognized others in the opposing line. Shield blocked sword thrust, spear forced through between shields, shields were used as battering rams, but the warriors facing down the hill still held the advantage. It was a slow process but the end seemed inevitable.

Esla still wondered why Edmund had fallen for the challenge offered by an apparently smaller force uphill of him. He was not intending to argue with the advantage fate had presented, but he still wondered. Perhaps Edmund had not realized how steep the slope was. He would have been surprised to see Esla's line more than doubling as warriors joined it from the tree line along the hilltop, but then he might not be able to see clearly past the wall of Esla's shields. By then it was too late for Edmund to change tactics. If he had ordered his men back down the hill they would have turned to race down to the river, but Esla could then have sent his men running after them, faced by the undefended backs of Edmund's warriors. Edmund had little option but to stand and fight, hoping to blunt Esla's assault.

Just as Esla was enjoying what he believed would be his victory, horses pounded towards him. At first he thought the Northumbrians had arrived, but, as he turned towards the sound, he saw a large body of mounted warriors descending on his right flank, when he looked to his left, he saw another mass of horses riding towards his other flank. He was surprised that they should continue closing the distance on horseback, but then he had never seen a cavalry attack. In his experience, warriors used horses to carry them to the battlefield. Once there they would dismount and close the enemy on foot.

Ivar led the charge down and into the right flank of Esla's line. Einarr charged down on the left flank. As they rode into the Saxon line, they cut and stabbed with sword and spear, before riding clear, circling and riding in for a second strike. There was now confusion amongst Esla's men. They began to be pushed uphill by Edmund's line as his warriors took advantage of their opponents' loss of concentration.

The second strike by the Norse cavalry broke chunks out of Esla's line and some of Edmund's warriors had cut through their opponents. On seeing this, Einarr and his warriors dismounted and charged down the hill into the rebel ranks, while Ivar waited above them for the first signs of the rout, when he could charge into the fleeing rebels and cut them down. As Einarr's warriors crashed into the Saxons, Esla's line was fragmented by the force of impact. Some of his warriors formed groups that were surrounded by Norse and Saxon, unable to flee, but unable to withstand the attacking swords. Here and there individuals and small groups of Esla's men managed to break out and attempt to run from the battle. As they did, they found Ivar waiting for them. He sent groups of riders down after the fleeing rebels. It was no longer a battle but a simple killing of men who tried, but failed, to out-run the horsemen. Here and there a warrior turned and tried to put up a fight, but most were impaled on spears or hacked down as they ran. Those who stood to fight fared no better, the horsemen able to chose when to strike and when to turn away, their opponents had little choice but to attempt to counter the blows from swords and the thrusts from spears.

The hillside was soon strewn with the debris of bloody bodies. The debris fanned out from the line and became more scattered away from where the two Saxon armies had pushed and fought each other. Some parts of Esla's line still stood but each group became smaller as comrades fell and the inevitable end drew closer.

Esla had only managed to reach the tree line before a mounted warrior caught up with him and thrust a spear deep into his back. As he slumped against a tree trunk, his dimming eyes saw only the destruction of his ambition. His brain struggled to make sense of what was happening. Even as his head was separated from his thick neck, his lips were trying to form questions that would never be answered in that life. He felt no pain, only a spreading numbness, a dimming of his sight, a rushing sound in his ears. The man who had struck him down stood above him, he was already dead, part of the litter of war, his blood staining the grass, the body still slumped against the tree, the head beginning its roll down the slope, speeding as it rolled on its long journey towards the stream, only to be halted by bodies of those who had supported him in his treachery against the King.

Edmund was exhausted, too tired to order an end to the bloodshed. His warriors were now in a blood lust, a red mist across their vision. To have experienced anticipation of defeat forged their determination to wipe out all traces of those who had fought against them. The King was covered in blood but had only few minor wounds. Having been at the front of his battle line he had hacked and thrust along with his men. Blood had sprayed freely across the opposing lines as each line struggled to force the other away.

As Edmund held onto a discarded spear to support himself, every muscle ached, but none so much as those in his sword arm and in his back. Ceolwulf had made certain that Edmund had suffered no endangering wounds, before collecting together bodyguards to protect the King. He then collected together a group of warriors to range across the battlefield, bringing vengeance and death to any enemy still there.

Einarr and his warriors were as blood spattered as Edmund, but few had suffered any injury and none a disabling wound. He collected them together, to be joined by those leading the horses they had looked after when Einarr had dismounted to attack Esla from the rear. Ivar was still bringing his horsemen together. Some distant groups of riders could still be seen running down escapers.

Cries of the wounded were being extinguished. The King's men had been looking for wounded comrades, carrying them away from the carnage. Ceolwulf's band was making a great contribution by killing any wounded warriors who had fought for Esla. Torn cloth and banners fluttered in the freshening breeze that swept across the hillside. Men and women from the King's baggage train were rifling the bodies for anything of value, paying little attention to which side the bodies might have supported. As these human crows scavenged amongst the dead, they finished off any that had been missed by Ceolwulf's men. At the stream, warriors washed the blood from their clothes and armour, or cleaned their wounds. Monks who had followed the army to the battle were now providing more skilled attention to the wounded and comforting those who were beyond recovery.

Several loyal earls had sought out Edmund on the battlefield, relieved to find him little harmed. Warriors drifted towards this group, anxious to find friends separated during the confusion of battle. Edmund's army had suffered deaths and few were completely free of injury, but his losses were much lower than they might have been. He was very conscious of the debt he now owed to Ivar. It would never have occurred to him to employ cavalry, which had been able to work round behind Esla with its greater speed. Cavalry had also proved more effective in running down those of Esla's men who tried to flee the field. That the enemy was divided, the fleeter warriors trying to outrun the horsemen, Ceolwulf had been free to quarter the battlefield and finish off the wounded and the remaining small, scattered, groups that tried to fight on.

There was no quarter and the number of headless bodies continued to increase. In the long tradition of Saxon conflict, the victor usually exercised some restraint. There was no profit in killing neighbours and kin, reducing the labour force to tend the fields and defend against an invader. That tradition had been set aside. There would be villages with no men to return to them after this battle. Edmund would have to appoint new earls to take on parts of the land governed by Esla. Some villages would die out as surely as a plague swept through them.

Edmund was confused by the events. He had never intended such anger to run free against the defeated. It was against his nature and his sense of honour. Perhaps it was a mark of how little loved Esla had been within his lands and across the kingdom. Perhaps it was a reaction to having believed that they would be defeated by Esla, a rage born of unexpected relief.

For Ivar it was a very successful outcome. He had seen Edmund's debt to him grow. His own men were even more confident in their commander, and the Saxons were more impressed with his ability to win. This placed him in a very strong position to reach a bargain with Edmund.

Edmund was in a much less enviable position. True, he no longer had to fear Esla, but this day's battle did little to show the strength or weakness of Northumbria. That their ally had not just been defeated, but wiped out, did not mean that their ambitions had changed, or that they had suffered a defeat. Edmund could not know whether the Northumbrians had arrived and been defeated at the fortress, or were this day still wandering his lands. If they too had been brought to battle and been defeated, it was only one army and not one kingdom. They could be enraged by a defeat and determined to attack again with allies.

Whatever happened, Edmund knew he not only owed a great debt already to Ivar, but that he would continue to need his assistance until Aella was defeated and his kingdom humbled. The most comfort was the knowledge that all those who had joined him to fight Esla had stood firm, even when the fight seemed to be going against them. He could now identify all those he could trust. The least comforting lesson was that almost half of those who should have joined him had failed to arrive and, to their number, must be added the survivors amongst Esla's conspirators, and the kin of those who had been slaughtered. Giving quarter to the defeated Saxon enemy was not simple generosity, but wise leadership. For those killed, there would be sons and younger brothers who could become a new enemy. The women left widowed, or without fathers, could prove as dangerous. There could yet be a high price to pay for the carnage wrought by Ceolwulf and his killers. Must Edmund continue the slaughter to eliminate the families of all those killed this day in battle and in flight? If there had ever been any doubt, Edmund knew that Ceolwulf could be relied upon to show no mercy to the King's enemies. What was already beginning to trouble Edmund was whether he could control Ceolwulf when need must.

Einarr had enjoyed the battle. With Gudhrun at his side, he had cut into the enemy with great enthusiasm and effect. Both were covered in the blood of Esla's men. They had left a trail of bodies as they swept along the flank of Esla's battle line. As they progressed, the spray of blood had made it appear they must themselves be severely wounded, yet they had not suffered a scratch. Had they fought in the line they might not have been so fortunate. As opposing lines pushed and shoved each other, it was impossible to escape at least some minor wounds, the body covered in bruises from the fight would be common, even with the protection of mail coat and padded clothing beneath.

Eventually, they had run out of Saxons to fight. They leaned into each other to gather breath and strength, the continuous rain slowly washing the evidence of battle from their clothing, to mingle the blood washed from them with that already on the ground, leaving the grass red, becoming streaks and streams of red, washing down towards the river at the valley floor. Everywhere they looked there was the litter of battle. Scattered bodies, small mounds where groups of warriors had been cut down, tattered, blood-soaked banners hanging stiffly from poles or spears, fragments of clothing blowing across the slope, all combining with the moans and cries of the badly wounded, unable to crawl away from the carnage. Everywhere, the mutilation of the dead, the final insult to the enemies who had dared to challenge them.

Einarr looked about him, committing every sight to memory. Searching for lessons that would help him in the future. He had never before taken any part in a large battle, his experience being gained from raiding trips and skirmishes, or from the tales in the Winter Halls as old warriors recounted their stories of great deeds to those gathered with them around the fire. While Einarr looked to learn, Gudhrun was already thinking of food and drink. She was completely untouched by the sights around her. She had a mighty thirst and an insatiable hunger.

Forty Eight

With the trap sprung, Osten had now to deal with the Saxon fleet. As the great chain had been pulled across the river, no Saxon vessel could leave, or enter, the lake. Hunbogi had already selected the first targets for his trebuchet. Flaming balls arched across the sky from the island fort. The first striking the mast of a Saxon longship, cascading sparks and flaming fragments down onto the deck. The next two shots just missed their targets, sending up columns of smoke and steam, then the crew settled into a steady pattern of fire. They had many targets to choose from and were limited only by the time required to ready the trebuchet after each shot.

The other artillery on the fortress towers was no less active. They could range on targets across the lake. Their trebuchet fired flaming balls and stones at the oncoming ships. No one could deny the Northumbrian's courage and determination, but then they also had few options. Osten could see three of the smaller vessels on the western edge of the fleet detach and make for the river inland. He knew that they would be easily overcome by the warriors manning his vessels tied together across the river, but he would have to watch the situation closely. He might yet need to reinforce those longships. He might have to use them to enter the lake to attack the Northumbrians.

The steady rain might protect the enemy from fire spreading across ships and the trebuchets were running short of the flaming balls that had been so spectacular as the battle opened. The effects of the stones were less obvious until a vessel foundered. Everything was becoming confused. Vessels were still burning, but a growing volume of smoke was drifting and obscuring the view from the fortress and from the island. With the Northumbrian vessels still so close together and few of the warriors having their mail coats on, many were escaping the burning and sinking ships, to be rescued by neighbouring ships. Osten had to agree that the artillery had been well worth the effort expended in constructing it and training those who worked the engines, but the number of Northumbrian vessels meant that many would escape the bombardment as the artillery struggled to reload and fire again. The trebuchet was being loaded as fast as possible, but the giant crossbows were increasing their rate of fire, as their crews picked up a rhythm, their accuracy also improving.

Julius was running between weapons, urging on their crews and shouting at those bringing fresh ammunition to increase their efforts. He knew that the crews had received inadequate practice with the unfamiliar machines. That was a simple lack of time. Equally, time had not allowed enough ammunition to be prepared. All Julius could do was urge on the weapons crews and the people bringing up fresh supplies, there was no way of improving the situation until after the battle when they would practice and look to improve both the ammunition supplies and the methods of bringing ammunition up to the tops of the towers where they would be in easy reach of the gunners, but that only should they achieve victory. Julius blamed himself for not having done more before the battle began but he was being unfair to himself. What frightened him was that the Saxons might not defeat Osten's men in the fortress, but that they would not themselves be destroyed, when the great weapons should have been overwhelming.

With the exception of the first vessels to break away in an attempt to escape inland, the Northumbrians had kept together and continued to progress across the lake to the fortress. Sheer numbers dictated that the first vessels would be under the walls shortly. Part of their fleet was already turning to attack the island. Osten was little troubled by this. At worst he would lose the warriors on the island and those two boats still tied up in the island's small harbour. At best, many of the warriors would be able to ferry across to the fortress. Until that end was reached, the island would continue to divert some attention from the fortress and Hunbogi would continue to cause the Northumbrians casualties. The more pressing matter was to reinforce the crews of the longships moored together across the river inland. The warriors already there should have little difficulty dealing with the three small ships that were heading towards them, but the Northumbrians might attempt to outflank the fortress if the battle became too difficult for them in the lake. As the smoke drifted across the water, more ships could turn inland without their intentions being visible from the fortress. Osten considered it most likely that they would first attempt to escape towards the sea, to plan their next steps, but once they found the way barred by the chain boom, there was only the option of forcing a way inland, to put their warriors ashore and hope to try the fortress defences from another direction, or ignore it, striking inland to join forces with Esla. Osten was charged with preventing the latter course from being followed by the Northumbrians, at any cost.

The Saxon fleet was starting to fragment in an attempt to break free from the longships that were already on fire, or sinking after stones had taken out their bottoms. Most were trying to make for the fortress, a few were attempting to leave the lake to head inland, but most of the remaining vessels were making for the island. Hunbogi would be heavily outnumbered, his trebuchet now firing its last remaining stones at the advancing longships, his warriors manning the outer walls.

Osten was unable to send additional warriors to the island, but Hunbogi knew that he could expect no relief and was free to decide when to attempt to leave the island and make for the fortress. The first of the Northumbrian longships were already attempting to grapple the outer wooden palisade. Hunbogi concentrated on hurling his remaining stones into these ships. Finding the range was not easy because of the short distance from the trebuchet to the targets, but signals from those manning the walls indicated that the missiles were finding their targets.

Hunbogi had sent one of his most trusted comrades, Arne Ulvasson, to direct all available warriors to the part of the wall where the longships had managed to grapple the palisade. Arne selected a small group of warriors to stay with him as a mobile reserve, while the other warriors made for the part of the wall already under attack. His task would be to go to any other part of the outer wall that might come under attack, hoping to take some men from the main group, not having great expectations that this would prove possible.

He was being helped by the Northumbrians who were single mindedly attempting a breach of the palisade by sending more longships to join the first attackers. This was helpful because they had to scramble across the first boats to reach the palisade. Hunbogi and Arne would have been harder pressed if the Northumbrians had tried to attack on a wider front, stretching Hunbogi's men thinly. The Norse defenders equalled the numbers of Northumbrians who could reach the wall, the Norse still having the advantage of height, as they hurled spears and rocks down onto the vessels. Some Northumbrians were trying to knock defenders off the top of the palisade with oars and the defenders were rapidly exhausting the supplies of spears and rocks, with which to deluge the attackers. As more vessels joined the attackers, there was movement in the palisade, which was only a temporary structure. As soon as enough tree trunks became loose, a breach could be made.

Hunbogi called the warriors back to the inner palisade. Here they would have little advantage in height, the wooden walls being little more than the height of a man on the outside and less inside with the earth banked against them. Still, it proved a shield and its smaller perimeter would be fully manned, the now useless trebuchet standing in the middle of the area enclosed by the palisades. Below the trebuchet awaited the combustible materials that had been stocked as a precaution to allow Hunbogi to destroy the artillery piece and prevent its use against the fortress behind the island.

Hunbogi had decided to fight on to the last man if necessary. He knew that their lives could be sold dearly, but also that they could fight on longer, with fewer casualties, than if they had tried to use the ferry to reach the fortress, as the main body of the Saxon fleet now stood between them and their possible refuge. His tactic had one further advantage. As his warriors fell back to the inner walls, Northumbrians began climbing over the damaged outer walls. As they did so, stones and arrows from the artillery, mounted on the fortress walls, began to strike down the besieging Northumbrians. Osten was no longer constrained by the risk of striking his own comrades. In return for supporting Hunbogi's warriors, Osten was discouraging any additional Saxon longships from making for the island, at the expense of increasing the number making towards his own walls.

As the Saxon ships crowded together to make their landing, they had not noticed the oily flat waters between them and the quayside. Julius had been responsible for releasing the special flammable fluid down the leather tubes that carried it into the lake's waters. His earlier tests had been successful but today he faced the effects of steady rain and the unfavourable wind. Without these unwelcome conditions he could have expected the fluid to come to the surface and spread steadily towards the enemy. Today he must let the enemy draw closer before he released the fluid so that it was not dispersed by wind and rain.

The first longships were already into the contaminated shoreside water. Had they wanted to change their course, they would have been prevented by the press of vessels behind them. The captains of the other ships had already realized that the artillery, which had caused them so much damage in their approach, was now unable to reach down to them as they closed the massive stone walls. This gave them some respite before they came within the range of bowmen, spears and hand-thrown rock from atop the walls.

Julius watched carefully as the Saxons came closer. The discoloured water now reached almost half of the Northumbrian ships. At his signal, archers fired burning arrows down into the lake. Across the polluted surface, small flames flickered and leapt towards each other. Then, with a sinister whooshing sound, a great wall of flame sprang from the lake's surface, higher than the mastheads of the attacking longships. There was utter confusion amongst the Northumbrians. Those already in flames tried to move their ships away, only to tangle with those vessels coming on behind them. Flame leapt from one ship to another. The sound of screaming swelled as the flames died back from their first flowering. Those vessels at the front of the advance were now well alight and burning down towards their waterlines, their crews eaten by the fire. Those vessels furthest from the burning waters broke away and their crews searched for the best course open to them. As they moved away from the burning ships, they again came within the fire of the artillery on the fortress towers, but ammunition was almost exhausted. In scattering, they gained some relief as they divided the fire from the fortress. Some arrows from bowmen on the walls still reached them, but to little effect. Julius watched helplessly as the ammunition for the war machines was used up and they fell silent.

One group of Northumbrian vessels attempted to force their way out of the lake and back towards the sea. Others tried to force their way inland. The rest milled aimlessly in the lake beyond the island. Osten looked again at the island and saw that Hunbogi was still holding out and seemed to be gaining an advantage. He also appeared to have suffered few casualties. Osten could not see well enough to know how many warriors were still fighting, but wounded. All he could see were heads and a rough count suggested that Hunbogi still had seventy warriors who could fight on. There could be more because the trebuchet stood before those fighting on the far wall. So far, Hunbogi had not felt the need to fire kindling below the trebuchet to deny it to a victorious Northumbrian attack. If he could continue to hold out and gain the upper hand few repairs would be required to make the island fort fully effective once more, perhaps stronger. Osten could already afford to think of what was required after victory over the Northumbrians, but he was still some way from achieving a total victory.

With all of the confusion of battle it was difficult to know how much damage was already done to the raiders. The Northumbrians had lost at least half of their ships. Osten could also safely assume that they had lost a similar proportion of their fighting men. His own warriors had suffered few casualties. Even if Hunbogi had lost half his men, and that did nor appear to be the case, it would only be some sixty warriors. As yet there were no casualties in the great fortress because the Northumbrians had been unable to come within weapon range. Osten could not clearly see the struggle at his longships tied across the river inland. There was a vigorous fight continuing as more Northumbrian vessels tried to force their way inland and away from the weapons on the fortress walls. Osten had twice reinforced the crews there and ordered half of his mounted reserve to deploy along the riverbank, able to pick up any Northumbrians attempting to come ashore. He was not surprised at a lack of messengers as his men fought with the Northumbrians. Until they had fought off or destroyed the enemy, it would be difficult to spare any warrior to attempt to report their progress to Osten. Until they reached that point, he could only guess how well they were defending their boom of longships. He expected to lose at least half of the men fighting there.

Taken together, the scattered actions were deciding in Osten's favour, but the Northumbrians were yet to be beaten. The best assessment was that they were already so seriously wounded that their fleet no longer had any hope of achieving victory. Osten realized that this was not enough. He had to bring victory before nightfall. If he failed, the remaining Northumbrians might still be able to land in darkness. If he allowed that, his comrades would have to hunt down those who made it to the shore. They might be a single dangerous group, or many small groups that would require a great effort to track down and destroy. Any that reached Esla would be an unwelcome addition to his strength, perhaps proving a decisive addition. On this day, Osten had no idea how Ivar and Edmund were progressing in bringing Esla to battle and defeat.

Unless there was a surprise change, Hunbogi would be able to deal with the battle for the island. He was slowly gaining the upper hand, but now more Saxon ships were heading to reinforce their comrades. Where they had climbed over the outer palisade, there were no longer any of the enemy there. In the water, there were eleven Saxon ships, one of them still burning, three sunk onto the lake bottom with just their masts and prows above the water. The remaining seven longships were tied together and empty, their crews having made to attack the inner palisade, being closely engaged by Hunbogi's men.

Two longships had attempted to break out to the sea and were now under attack from a small party ashore who were depending on bowmen to fire on the ships' crews. Flaming arrows had been used and a fire was started, growing in one of the ships halted by the chain boom. The other ship was not yet ablaze, but many of the crew were already dead or wounded. Unable to return to the lake, or force a passage to the sea, the two boats were sitting targets for the bowmen and appeared to have no weapons to reach the Norse party ashore. Even if the second vessel was not set on fire by fresh arrows, the blaze would spread to it from the first unless the remaining crew could disentangle themselves and flee back into the lake. With a second party of Norse arrived on the other bank, the longships' crews had nowhere to swim to. Equally, the Norse could only reach the ships by swimming out to them and that would be a risky operation. That meant the small battle could continue on to darkness, unless Osten could send a ship to attack the Saxons afloat.

Across the lake, beyond the burnt longships and those unharmed, but still close to them, there was a press of Saxon vessels still attempting to force their way through the line of Norse ships tied together as a boom. This fight was proceeding equally. Defender and attacker were bow to bow. The warriors aboard were crowded into the confined fore decks where no more than six warriors in each vessel could reach six enemies. Where a warrior fell, or withdrew with heavy wounds, another could step forward in his place. It was a slow process where only the most fortunate would avoid a wound, but where few wounds were conclusive.

Waiting inland of the boom vessels, six of Osten's

remaining longships stood ready and fully crewed to deal with any enemy ship that forced a passage through the boom. Until that situation arose, there was nothing they could contribute to the fight. Osten had foreseen this possibility but there was no alternative. Had the ships been on the other side of the boom, they would have potentially faced the full force of the entire enemy fleet, rapidly overcome, without making any significant contribution to the battle. As it was, they were undamaged, able to tackle any break through, or later to sweep into the lake to deal with any remaining enemy ships that had survived the attacks on the island and on the fortress. For now, all they could do was cheer on their comrades at the boom.

Osten had managed to send archers to the banks on both ends of the boom vessels. They had been firing on the Northumbrian crewmen who were forced to wait and hope for their comrades in the bows to force their way onto the Norse ships. Some of the Saxon crew were archers and there had been limited return fire, which had not proved effective. However, the Norse archers were inflicting casualties on the ships closest to the shore. Where they fired high to strike the vessels furthest from shore, they could not see how successful their arrows had proven. Aboard ship there was little effective defence against arrows raining down. A warrior could only hold up a shield and hope that it would block the arrows falling on him. As with the battle involving the two ships on the seaward side of the lake, it was a slow battle of attrition. The archers ashore were the only means to inflict decisive injury but the conditions were different. To the landward sides, there was close contact afloat and Osten's men were taking casualties at the same rate as the Northumbrians. What the archers promised was a reduction of the Saxon reserves. On three Saxon longships the fight was tipping in favour of Osten's warriors. The Norse still had their full reserves, but their archers ashore had eliminated the Saxon reserves.

Birgvid, commanding Osten's men aboard the boom vessels, urged on his warriors facing the three weakened Northumbrian ships. As the Saxons gave way, Birgvid's warriors climbed onto the Saxon vessels, reinforced by their own reserves and by warriors from neighbouring ships. There was still much fighting to do, but Birgvid was starting to gain the upper hand. Once his warriors had defeated the crews aboard the three vessels, they could attack the flanks of the men aboard the next enemy ships, working towards the centre of the attacking vessels, but losing the advantage of their archers ashore, who could not safely fire.

Before the fortress there was something of a stalemate. The surviving Northumbrian vessels were just beyond the range of archers in the fortress. The artillery could still reach them but their ammunition was exhausted. As the remaining supplies were located and brought from the storehouses to the towers, the artillery fell silent for long periods. Loaded into carts, the ammunition was dragged to the base of the towers and then carried up to the waiting artillery. It had been fortunate that the artillery had been built and installed, but the production of ammunition had not started long before the attack, limiting the supplies available.

Osten now faced a number of decisions. He did not have the means to reinforce Hunbogi on the island, or to attack the Northumbrian vessels from a different direction. The situation on the island was now encouraging. Hunbogi had reduced his attackers to a number of small and uncoordinated groups, smaller in number than his own force. He could begin to take the fight to the enemy, sending a group of his warriors out of the central redoubt to attack isolated groups of Saxons one by one. As the other Northumbrians saw what was happening they tried to flee back to their boats, but Hunbogi was able to send his remaining warriors out from behind the palisade to chase after the enemy.

It was well past the middle of the day, but the island was now clear of Northumbrians. Hunbogi still had more than fifty warriors able to fight, with twenty more who were wounded but still able to fight from behind the protection of the redoubt's palisade. That was enough to crew a longship and still leave a small group on the island. These would be the wounded men who could still fight and set fire to the trebuchet if a fresh Northumbrian attack threatened to overwhelm them. There were still longships in the island's harbour but Hunbogi decided to take an empty, but undamaged, Northumbrian ship against the palisade. Those Northumbrian vessels on the lake would be unable to distinguish Hunbogi's men from their own comrades who had arrived in the vessel.

At the boom of boats, Birdvid's men were now making more rapid progress towards the centre of the Northumbrian ships. They were still taking casualties, but now at a much lower rate than an enemy that was reaching the extent of stamina. Osten had ordered more of his reserve force to join Birdvid, but the Northumbrians had no means to reinforce their crews. The end was now a matter of time, but that time was running out. As each Northumbrian ship was overrun, the surviving warriors were being driven back into the centre longship, where they impeded each other against Birdvid's warriors who were not impeded.

Birdvid invited the remaining Northumbrians to surrender and this they did. They had little to lose, now heavily outnumbered, few of them unwounded. If the Norse honoured their surrender they might eventually be set free. If not, they would die quickly and cleanly. In their surrender, Osten had won a number of undamaged longships that could be crewed and sent into the lake without opening the boom. He was now able to send more reinforcements to crew the most useful of the captured ships.

The cost of victory in this side battle was not small. Of the original crews and the reinforcements, thirty Norse were dead, a larger number wounded, some of these fatally, but the cost was acceptable and unavoidable. The enemy still had twenty vessels in the lake with little damage and with most of the crews uninjured. Some ships had gained additional warriors from those who had escaped the fire that engulfed their own ships.

Hunbogi had taken the captured ship from the island, making his way into the river after the two enemy ships that had attempted to escape to seaward. As he came up to them, their surviving crew thought he was reinforcing them, recognizing the ship he had taken. They only discovered their error as he came alongside, his crew swarming over into the first Northumbrian ship that had been undamaged by fire. The burning vessel was now burning slowly but would never be repaired. Hunbogi dispensed with the difficulties of taking prisoners and ordered all those wounded or surrendered to be killed and thrown into the smouldering vessel next to him. He could now bring his ship and his new prize to the riverbank and embark enough of his comrades ashore to fully man both vessels.

Osten had a clearer idea of how the battle was progressing. Messengers had arrived from both ends of the lake, their progress uninterrupted by the surviving Northumbrian fleet, which could see their movements, but had no weapon to reach them. He knew from their reports that the only Northumbrians that must still be dealt with were collected together closely in the lake between the island, the river inland and the fortress. Of the fifty ships that had arrived at the lake, only twenty were still manned and capable of fighting on. The chain boom was still barring escape to the sea. Hunbogi had two fully manned ships. Birdvid had taken eight more Northumbrian longships in the fight at the boom and the warriors to fully man them without removing the crews of vessels still rafted together across the river, blocking the route inland.

This was already a victory but not yet the required total victory. In their remaining boats, the Northumbrians might still have more than five hundred warriors. Without unrafting the boom of longships that guarded the river inland from the fortress, the available vessels were only half the number of the Northumbrian survivors. In daylight that was enough to surround the enemy but in darkness there was the risk that the Northumbrians could make a landing on the lakeshore somewhere, escaping to join forces with Esla. Osten had still not received news from Ivar.

The Northumbrian commander was not in a better position. The fleet's survivors were now commanded by Drefan, Ecgbruht having died in the blaze that destroyed his longship.

Drefan could see that the defences of the fortress would not be overcome with the means at his disposal. Fighting to force a passage up river was not a viable option. He had already tried that and suffered the eventual loss of ships and men. To make matters worse, the ships that had attacked the boom of longships were now in the hands of the enemy and he still did not know who that enemy was or what forces were at their command.

Esla had betrayed them. Either he had deliberately betrayed them, or he had failed to warn the Northumbrians that a major change in alliances had taken place that would frustrate the overthrow of King Edmund. Drefan would have been inclined to break out to the sea and return home to tell his King how they had been deceived by Esla, but that had also been tried. True, he had men and ships to attempt a breakout, almost half the original strength, but the width of the river limited the number of vessels at the head of the fleet, making the remaining ships almost an irrelevance. He did not know exactly what would face him as he attempted to leave the lake and head down river to the sea. He could not see as far into the river inland or to seaward as he needed to accurately assess whatever had blocked those ships already attempting escape. He could attack the island with his remaining ships but that offered no real advantage, promised more losses of men and ships, and could allow the enemy to besiege them.

Surrender was not an attractive choice, unless Drefan could negotiate free passage home. He doubted that was a likely outcome because the enemy was strong enough to destroy the rump of the fleet that forlornly clung together near the middle of the lake. If he faced King Edmund's men, he could hope that the most important warriors might be ransomed, even some of the poorer warriors might be fortunate. The remainder of his men would become slaves.

His real difficulty was that he was not certain of whom they faced. From all he had been told, King Edmund could not muster the numbers of warriors, ships and equipment that were ranged against him. If these opponents were allies of King

Edmund, there could still be some hope for ransom, but if they were another force with unknown origins and motives, Drefan had only a choice of how to die. There was no way in which he could identify what they faced. In his surviving ships, there was no one who had directly faced the enemy in close combat. The mighty weapons in the fortress were unknown to Drefan before he experienced their power, but that did not tell him anything useful. In all his experience against the Norse and the neighbouring Saxons, he had never seen their like before. Of the other ships and equipment there was nothing remarkable to identify where his enemy originated. He could only be sure when facing them across his shield and there seemed no prospect of achieving that without disaster.

As Drefan pondered the narrow choice of unattractive options, Osten also needed to make some urgent decisions. Until darkness fell, and the time for that was rapidly approaching, the risks were not great. The enemy ships were all visible from the fortress. If any of them made any attempt to move, they would be seen and preparations made to deal with them. Once darkness fell it could be a different matter. Even in the cloak of mist, or a moonless night, devoid even of starlight, Osten had sufficient men to ring the lake. Any movement of the enemy would be known, agreed signals bringing reinforcements to the point of greatest danger.

Then the situation seemed to change again. Four longships emerged from the broad river that snaked inland. Drefan could see that they were ships from his fleet. The leading longship appeared to be fully crewed. The other three emerging behind it seemed less fortunate but the surviving crew were managing to shake out their sails to benefit from a following breeze.

Osten could now also see the four ships. It was puzzling, because messengers had already told him that Birdvid had captured all of the Northumbrian vessels that had attempted to force his boom. From his vantage point atop the fortress walls, he could see the vessels, and the men crewing them, but he could not see them well enough to recognize them as Norse or

338

Northumbrian.

Drefan was also unable to recognize any of the crew, but the ships were familiar. He was unsure how a reinforcement of four vessels, three only partly crewed could help him decisively, but they would be a welcome addition and boost the morale of his other crews, taking them to almost half their original strength when they had sailed into the lake that morning with so much hope.

The lead ship was bearing off under oars, as the other ships emerged from behind her under sail. They were picking up speed but the light wind was insufficient for them to achieve a rapid advance towards their comrades. They were now in line abreast and Drefan assumed that they would soon drop their sails and drift the final paces to come alongside the outer ships of the fleet that still huddled together beyond the range of bowmen on the fortress walls.

A thin column of smoke began to drift from the middle longship. Then similar columns of smoke began to emerge from the other two longships sailing towards Drefan. He watched in horror as men jumped over the sides of the oncoming longships. Only the steersmen remained aboard. Then they abandoned their vessels as the columns of smoke strengthened and flames began to lick upwards to the sails.

The longship that had led the three burning ships into the lake had now turned behind them and was picking up those who had jumped into the water. That was detail that escaped Drefan, who was fixed on the burning ships that were almost upon him. He had little time to take any action. His own ships were too close together, some even tied together, to quickly put out their oars and attempt to row out of the line of attack that the fire ships continued to maintain. The situation was chaos as individual captains appreciated the danger and attempted to break away. Several longships became entangled, one or two began to open distance and would escape the fire ships. Drefan's own ship was beginning to break away.

The first fire ship crashed into two Northumbrian vessels.

Sparks flew up thickly into the air, Crewmen tried to jump into the lake to escape the fire which was now spreading to the two victims. The remaining fire ships followed their sister into the mass of Northumbrian longships. There were more victims. Smoke thickened and hid the extent of the conflagration, but bright windows of red and yellow glared through the thickening smoke.

Drefan and his crew had their attention drawn to the blazing horror that had been their comrades. They only realized their own danger as a longship came alongside them with some force. Grapples snaked across from it, holding it firmly to Drefan's ship and its shattered oars. Warriors leap across to his ship. At first it did not dawn on him that these were attackers in the shock of a sudden new factor in a very confused situation. Swords and axes were being wielded, his crew were being cut down. Then he understood and tried to marshal his men to the defence of their vessel.

The Northumbrians began to inflict casualties on their attackers, but their slowness to respond had cost them the initiative and they were being forced back, their numbers diminished under the fierce attack. Drefan made his last stand with his back to the mast, supported by a handful of survivors, but this was only slowing the final outcome. An axe cut deeply into Drefan's right shoulder and his sword dropped to the deck from nerveless fingers. A sword cut into his side and he began to slide down the mast to the deck. A comrade was cut down, falling across him. Finally the last Northumbrian was killed. There was no one able to draw satisfaction from the casualties they had inflicted on their attackers.

Birdvid ordered his men back aboard their longship and the grapples were cast off as his oarsmen fended their ship off what was now a funeral ship alongside them. Birdvid selected another Northumbrian vessel to attack. This was a smaller ship and even after the casualties suffered in attacking Drefan, Birdvid's warriors made short work of the second crew.

Across the blanket of smoke, Hunbogi had seen what was

happening. He swung his longship away from the island and came down on a Northumbrian ship that was breaking away from its burning comrades. The crew were desperately trying to bring their vessel under full control. They had yet to decide on a course of action, other than to escape the fire. They could still feel its heat and hear the cries of comrades unable to escape its deadly tentacles.

Hunbogi was able to run down the vessel as easily as Birdvid had closed in on Drefan. The enemy were only aware of the new danger as Hunbogi's longship crashed down their line of newly manned oars. At first they thought a friendly vessel had collided with them in its own attempt to escape the flames. As with Drefan's crew, they realized their mistake as grapples flew over them and the first attackers jumped the gap between the vessels, swords and axes already swinging to deadly effect. The fight was over almost as soon as it had started. Hunbogi suffered few casualties, none of them serious, as the shocked defenders struggled unsuccessfully to grab their own weapons to fight back.

Freed from their victim, Hunbogi's crew began to pull swimmers from the lake. All proved to be Northumbrians and were tied together around the mast. Hunbogi was reluctant to leave them to swim on, or to kill them in the water. He felt that they were warriors and deserved a more measured fate. He also knew that the work of fishing out bodies and swimmers would become necessary work if Osten was to satisfy himself of the totality of victory. The urgency to quickly kill the enemy was reducing as more captured longships were brought to attack the diminishing Northumbrian fleet. Hunbogi could now safely sail for the island's harbour and begin the work of repairing defences against any future attack.

Osten was able to look down in great satisfaction on what was becoming a total victory. He had watched Northumbrian vessels grappled and their crews defeated. He saw some crews had surrendered, and the fire still blazed fiercely amongst the tangle of ships that were unable to escape its burning embrace. Birdvid was now following Hunbogi's earlier example and fishing Northumbrian swimmers from the water. The light was fading fast, but there could be no significant escape of Northumbrians and their ability to present a threat had died.

The last Northumbrian longships were surrendering, or being overcome, a few deciding to fight to the death. Osten regretted that because it meant more casualties. For a battle of this magnitude, he had been very fortunate in low losses, but far from home they might yet need every man they could muster. There was still no news from Ivar. There remained the danger that Esla had survived, it seemed unlikely to Osten that Ivar had been defeated, and was withdrawing towards the fortress. He could not ignore the possibility that more Northumbrian ships could arrive, even a larger fleet than the one his warriors had just overcome.

Now was the time to start to clear the debris of the battle and to repair any damage to the fortifications and their own vessels. The first task was to send patrols along the shoreline to take any Northumbrians who had swum ashore. It was important to account for all the Northumbrian survivors. No one was to be allowed to escape and give warning of their defeat. Osten must continue these patrols for days, reinforcing them with patrols using their smaller ships, until the interrogation of prisoners and the detail of the searches could convince him that there was no escapee who could carry back news to Aella.

Much of the work would have to wait until the morrow's light. All Northumbrian ships that could be repaired would be added to their fleet or sailed to their homelands. Those beyond repair would be stripped of any useful materials, with the remaining parts being destroyed. That work could proceed at leisure, with repairs being carried out upriver at Depenham, or on the island. The next priority was to return all defences to their state before the battle and to collect ammunition for the great weapons. In this, Osten had decided that great stocks of supplies should be built up and the trebuchets and giant crossbows should have larger stocks of ammunition close to hand. If there was one lesson from the battle, it was that a lack of ammunition prevented an early defeat of the Northumbrians. Had their fleet been larger, the outcome might have been different. The fortress would always prove difficult for an enemy to defeat now that it was fully manned with alert sentries, the system of watchers and messengers, the immense strength of its walls. That Osten knew was not enough. Had the Northumbrians overwhelmed Hunbogi and occupied the island, they could have landed enough men to defeat the mounted reserve ashore and strike inland to join King Edmund's enemies. They could also have laid siege to the fortress, or roamed the countryside causing great damage, preventing any reinforcement of Ivar's forces from their homelands.

The natural urge to feast, to celebrate a great victory, must be suppressed. The battle was much narrower than its outcome suggested. There was much work to do, in preparation for any future attack, and Osten had yet to learn of the fortunes of Ivar and Edmund. He had sent a messenger to Ivar to tell him of the events and their outcome. Ivar might have already sent a messenger to Osten to call for reinforcements, or bring news of a victory, but the messengers might take several days to arrive at their respective destinations, days more to return with replies.

Forty Nine

Ivar and Edmund sat together with their captains by the trees that crowned the slope on which their victory had been won. The debris of battle still littered the slope below them. People were still searching for lost comrades, to take anything of value, and from curiosity, but no one seemed interested in clearing the tattered remains from the slope. Those warriors who had fought for Edmund and Ivar, suffering disabling wounds, had long been collected from the field of battle to be tended by the priests and monks. Many would surrender to their wounds. Those who survived their transportation back to their homes might be crippled, but a few would live to fight again. Esla's wounded had been killed where they lay.

But there was still the matter of the dead.

No one seemed to have the energy or interest in burial, or in removing the bodies for transport to their home villages. A group of priests had come to Edmund to urge that the dead be attended to, receiving less in response than they had expected. The best that Edmund offered was for the priests to make arrangements, using anyone from the baggage train who had no other duties to attend. With little light remaining, the priests attempted to separate the rebel dead from those of the King's followers who had not already been removed from the field. On the following dawn, they would bury the rebels in a common grave, before deciding how to treat the loyal dead.

Strangely, there was no sense of triumph, of celebration. Ivar had suffered very few casualties and, of those, most of the wounded would make full recovery. Edmund's warriors had suffered more heavily in the battle line. Those who had suffered no wounds were a rarity, either having the greatest luck, or having hung back from the first rank to let their comrades take the weight of Esla's men. The final count was yet to be made, but one in ten and more of Edmund's warriors had died. Had it not been for the Norse horsemen, Edmund would have been hard pressed to win, bloody defeat a more likely outcome. There was almost an air of depression over his supporters, at best a heartfelt relief, certainly no great feeling of victory.

This was the first great battle that Edmund had joined in, much less led. Then that was part of his personal depression, because he had not been the leader in any more than name. Ivar had devised the tactics for the battle, scouted the enemy position, decided how they would respond, how they would lure Esla into a trap that he believed was of his own devising. When victory had been assured, it was Edmund's long time friend and captain of his bodyguard, Ceolwulf, who had seen to the King's safety and then visited their vengeance on the remnants of Esla's forces. It was not what Edmund would have eventually decided. His natural fairness would have led him to treat his former enemies with generosity, far more than any deserved.

Edmund now had pressing matters to decide, but little inclination to reach a decision. Ceolwulf had already decided many matters by his ruthless pursuit of the rebels who were wounded, or attempting to escape back to their homes. Esla had drawn most of the available men from the villages across his lands. Those men would never return. The harvest had been brought in but, in the new year, every village would struggle to till the land, plant the seed and tend their cattle. There would be great opportunities for those who had honoured their debt to their King and joined him in this battle. Some would be given the honour of replacing earls and aldermen slaughtered on this field. Some would receive rich hides in the lands formerly governed by Esla and his supporters.

The opportunities for the King's men would be mirrored by the hatred of those who had lost brothers, husbands, fathers in the fight. Ceolwulf was not yet finished. He had decided to encourage Edmund to let him hunt down those who had been absent from the field as rebels or as Esla's supporters. He knew that Edmund would let him have his way, if only by failing to reach a clear decision. This promised continuing turmoil and increasing hatred that would be directed towards Edmund more than to his licensed executioner. In attempting to destroy every warrior, who had not fully supported Edmund, Ceolwulf was creating new enemies and sowing seeds of doubt and fear amongst the Anglians. He also diminished the King, which was not his intention. Had Edmund or his captain more experience and wisdom, they could have turned the victory into a new beginning for his subjects.

Ivar was in a more relaxed state. He recognized the advantages victory brought to him. The only concerns that kept him from a riotous celebration were his appreciation of the Saxons' melancholy and the lack of news from the fortress. He had no doubts of Osten's ability to lead their forces there and he was confident that any unexpected dangers would have been reported by messengers before attackers overcame Osten and his comrades. Even so, he did fret over the lack of information. He felt a caution because everything had gone so strongly in his favour and no General could expect to win every battle and suffer few losses. Ceolwulf's zeal in destroying every rebel had denied Ivar a source of information on how much contact had been maintained between Esla and the Northumbrians. The confusion in the rebel ranks, as they realized that the horsemen riding down on them were not friends, had not gone unnoticed by Ivar, or even by Einarr. It suggested that Esla was expecting large reinforcement and that could only come from the Northumbrians. The question that must go unanswered was whether Esla hoped for reinforcement, or had firm reason to expect it and know its origins.

There was some fragmented discussion between those leaders sitting together. There was a need to decide on the next step. Edmund was confident that Esla, and all the active rebels, had paid a high price for their disloyalty. There seemed nothing left for the army but for the Saxons to return home, the Norse to

347

retrace their footsteps to the fortress, and for life to resume across Edmund's kingdom. As night was falling no action was forced that day. Tomorrow in fresh light the decisions could be reached and a rested army could consider its line of march.

Edmund's baggage train was still across the stream, which had risen as the rain had swollen it. Many of his warriors would make their way across its quickened waters and make their camp beside their supplies. Ivar had decided to remain near the crest of the hill and urged Edmund to remain with him. It was more attractive to the Norse to remain on dry high ground, their horses fed and watered, to be tethered in lines, a screen of pickets surrounding the hill top with a view in all directions. In the remaining light, Ivar had instructed Einarr to take the horses in relays to the stream to water, then setting up the horse lines before the trees that crowned the hill. All their supplies for themselves and their horses were distributed across the mounts. They could see fires in the valley as Edmund's men looked to warm themselves and cook a hot meal, but Ivar's party would avoid fires that could be seen some distance away. They were used to a hardy life and were content to eat cold food from the packs, sleeping on the ground with just their cloaks for protection.

Edmund had decided to remain with Ivar and his men, but he also had Saxons for company, Ceolwulf remaining with his King and the bodyguard, Wulfmaer and his warriors also preferring to remain with their Norse friends, rather than descending and crossing the stream to the Saxon baggage train. If truth be admitted, Wulfmaer now felt more a part of Ivar's army than subject of King Edmund. He had built a strong friendship with Einarr and, during the weeks that followed their mission to Kett's Hall, all of the villagers at Depenham had merged with their new Norse neighbours and the practice had spread along the small communities beside the river. They were becoming a kingdom of their own and each individual was coming to think of a shared future.

One of Edmund's few decisions in the aftermath of battle had been to appoint Wulfmaer in Esla's place. He had yet to decide how rebel lands would be divided amongst his supporters, but it was understood that Wulfmaer would hold most of the land and villages that Esla had once taken as his fiefdom. There had been no discussion yet of what might pass to Ivar but, after this day, Edmund understood that what Ivar wanted would be his, with no man to challenge. The King might still hold his crown and head his kingdom, but he was no longer the power of the kingdom. Ivar was still at pains to treat Edmund as an equal and sovereign of the Anglians, but there was now no question that his was the power. So long as Ivar kept to the riverside and made no demands on a vassal Saxon King, Edmund could be comfortable with the situation. Even in giving Wulfmaer the lands and privileges that were once enjoyed by Esla, most of the Anglians would be untouched by the changed circumstances, but Ivar was now the shield against attack from the North. In many ways, Edmund welcomed the changes because they removed from his shoulders decisions that he would have agonized over for many weeks. For Ivar, the situation ensured that he faced no dispute with any Anglians, free to prepare for his march North in the New Year to bring vengeance down on Aella and his Northumbrians. That Aella had killed

Fifty

It had come again to a natural break in the telling of the saga. Once more I had an audience that was attentive, but it was time for sleep, to arise fresh in the morrow. It is no longer the saddest part of the evening for me. I know that we will share more evenings together, with the favour of the gods. It is now the time when I will again talk with my dearest Margaret, to share the events of another day, to seek her wisdom.

Once more at peace before the fire, I can see Margaret's face in the flames and the embers of the fire. Restored by good food and dear company, I can relax before the fire, my mug of Aqua Vita in my hand, its pale golden liquid familiar on my palate. There is nothing to distract me. The flames subdued rustle, the soft steady breathing of Kara as she lays curled up beside my outstretched feet. It is but a backcloth of sound.

I start with the easy matters, the day riding the strand with my sons' wives and their children. Perhaps it is an unnecessary tale because I felt Margaret with us as we rode, and someone else, but I know that she would smile fondly on us, pleased that they were my comfort and that I still had much to give them. Through all the years, I had been home but briefly and infrequently, my father in the place where I now am. First he was her mentor and guide, as she tended his household with her's, able to share the growing of my sons and compensate for the times when I was long absent. Then he was gone and Margaret took those decisions unaided. She made good choices, few mistakes.

I had been shocked when I had last returned to her. The illness was there in her face but she ignored it and carried on, finding each task more difficult and tiring. I was glad to be there with her for more time than we had ever shared before. At least my sons could attend all the matters that I must neglect, to spend the last days with my dearest Margaret. Her illness did not lay

351

between us, but lurked in the shadows, an unwelcome guest, unseen, but always there.

It had been hard to see her beyond her best, but now each evening I saw her as she had been when we first met, both of us free of the withering of age and ailment. I know that she will live with me now forever, that I shall never be alone, without aid or comfort. Each night I can share my hopes and fears, my joys and sorrows, always to a sympathetic ear that will never judge me harshly.

I have so many things still to consider, actions to take. When I awake, this night's conversation will have resolved important matters that demand attention. I will see more clearly than before. The Saga helps me much. I see the wisdom of the generations of heirs who have preserved the knowledge in its telling. They realized how little the matters of man change down the ages. I face the same decisions as did Ivar all those years ago. There are so many matters that bear the same stamp, with only minor differences. At home we face a changing mesh of alliances. We canna be certain who will favour, and who will honour, until the line of battle is drawn. Even many of our weapons are the same. Our fortress is dependent on the features that made Depenham such a happy alliance for Ivar. We lack a great stone fortress, but then cannon will make short work of mighty stone walls. Our peel is much stronger. From land the great marsh will keep a cannon beyond range of our wooden walls. From the sea, our own cannon would strike down on any captain foolish enough to approach us, his bombardment wouldnaye reach up above the cliff, but we could pour down fire on his deck.

If an enemy ever mastered our defences, we have men and ships beyond his reach. Our neighbours understand these things and would hesitate to directly attack our home. They know our vengeance would be terrible and swift. Within our homeland the real danger is from assassins, but even they would have difficulty now to find a way to us. The other danger is to strike some of us when we are away from our defences. For me to travel to neighbours, or to the Hollyrood, would be to invite attack but then

I have no need for such a journey. Others will travel to me and take the risks.

Where the voice of Margaret can guide me at home, the saga serves me well for all the other matters that must concern me, that and the experience that has grown with me down the years. We will build our holdings far beyond these shores, maintain our bonds with kin in the lands of ice, look into the new lands that hold mystery and great opportunity.

I thank those before me who had the wisdom to hold to truth in the Family Saga. When any history is handed down there is the strong temptation to modify the events that are recounted to make them easier listening, to bolster the reputations of our forefathers, to add excitement. The purpose of the Family Saga has always been to teach the next generation the lessons from the distant past and to show them who they are and where come they from, how to govern wisely and fight, with confidence and honour, in the interests of the family.

As sleep overcomes me, I can sink into its warm folds, my mind to think on through dreams, to order the events just past. To wake strong and refreshed and to continue preparing my grand children for the years ahead, that they may live the life they must.

Part Seven -

The Winter

Fifty One

We move slowly towards the Festival of Light in a long Winter that came early and gripped us in its icy chill. Snow has lain upon the ground since before the due end of Autumn. Any warmer days have been brief, failing to chase away the snow.

With each new period of heavy snow, the land has lost some of its features, the tracks and paths, through the hills to the North, filled with ice and snow, preventing some visitors from making their way to us. The only reliable route is by boat or ship along the Solway and even that is not assured. I prefer it that our guests arrive from the sea because their comings and goings are less evident to any watcher. Our boats and ships come and go, their voyages unremarkable, a passenger easily hidden from view, even with a retinue.

The relentless cold has made our ride along the strand a rare event, but has not given me the time I would spend with my family. Between the storms, visitors have come to us from the sea, staying longer than their business demands, as they wait for storm and tempest to quiet.

We have drawn into the castle some of those exposed homesteads, with their livestock, that they may shelter within our walls and draw food from our storehouses. In a less malevolent winter, each of the families would keep to their homes, their livestock drawn to them, the food and fodder in their own stores sufficient to see them through the winter. When winter strikes hard, as it does this year, the castle provides refuge and company. Much though I may dislike some of the visitors who come to intrigue, our own people are most welcome and it is a duty to ensure they survive the cold days ahead of us. Even those without blood connections, there are few of them in the Lordship, observe our customs and chose to be part of our community. Our values are their values. What we offer in respite is not a charity, but a return for the many services they provide in better times and times of conflict.

That has all conspired to make the Great Hall our meeting place and for all to take food before the hearth. Private dinners with my family have become less frequent at a time when I had hoped we would take every meal together in my quarters. When we have guests, it is my duty to eat with them and for us to entertain each other. When our people come into the shelter of the castle, the Great Hall becomes the communal place for food and association, the buildings abutting it providing sleeping quarters, with some family privacy. On these times, I can take an evening with my grand children and their mothers, but I also have a duty to share food with our people and for us to come closer together. Here, I am not a lord, but first amongst equals, as has long been our tradition.

Still, I have shared time with my grandchildren during the quieter days, to practice arms, and to add to their formal lessons. Their tutor has encouraged me to tell them of campaigns and voyages from my youth, helping them to learn of lands and seas beyond our walls, of why we seek out new lands and where each fits into its place on the Grande Globe. This device is new to me. I have been accustomed to seeing maps on paper and velum, sometimes in books and pilots, sometimes as single sheets that are rolled for storage. I was surprised how little the Great Globe reflected the world as I had found it. The lands of home, and of our neighbours, appeared much larger than they are, known distant lands are shown smaller and with little detail. Not even all the known lands are marked, much remains to be drawn onto the sphere.

I canna say that Master Urquart has fully won my trust, but he is an able tutor. As I have come to see more of him in the recent weeks, I have come to understand him better, but there is still something of his past that he hides. He has brought my grandchildren on and inspires them to fresh efforts in their learning. I now understand why he was keen to learn of navigation and the handling of ships. He hopes to fill the empty spaces on the Great Globe, to correct the errors of commission and omission.

It struck me that there is much still to discover, but also that navigators continue to hold their pilots and charts close to them as secrets of great value. Whoever created the Great Globe had little contact with sailors and soldiers, or of the making of accurate charts that a sailor can depend on in his pilotage. It has convinced me that we must share this knowledge by bringing our navigators to the schoolroom. The knowledge would continue to be held close, but the children of our lands would learn what was still denied to others. It will make us stronger, giving each child greater opportunity within our community.

Tonight we would again share a family dinner together in my quarters. I had been looking forward to this event with great eagerness for days now, as keenly anticipated as events of my childhood, those special treats that stay with us all of our lives.

I grudged the hospitality we must give our visitors. It would have been easier had our guests been people we might have freely invited to visit us for a valued company. Sadly they were not. These noble lords and their retainers are mean and careless. Their clothes may be of fine cloth, but they are filthy, often ill-patched. They seem unfamiliar with the benefits of washing themselves and their clothes. When they dine, they tear the food with their hands, ignoring the forks and spoons laid out for them. When they eat, they wipe their sleeves across their mouths and beards. Around them lie fragments of their meal, bones that they have torn the flesh from. I canna believe they live like this in Edinburgh, or Sterling, but then they must. At least our dogs eat well from the fragments so carelessly discarded.

I find their untidy ways unpleasant, as is their stench, but it is matched by their lack of intelligent discourse. When I dine with my family, we talk, and talk of many things with interest. Even my twin grandsons can hold a conversation with an adult. These guests are uncouth to the extreme. Their interests appear to divide between wenching, drinking, gambling, and fighting, their ideal being to combine all these interests in a single event. They contrast so with our neighbours, neighbours who do not all share our roots, but chose to develop interests in many things and to value cleanliness and a tidy appearance. I see little value in acquiring lands and wealth, without accepting the responsibilities that go with ownership, using the wealth to live well and to develop knowledge of all things.

Still, we must accept those allies that present themselves, accept their differences, attempt to play the generous host, without displaying more wealth and generosity than a good host must. Even so, it irks me that part of the duties of a host to these guests must include their separation when tempers flow as freely as the drink. They all seem so quick to take offence, where no offence was offered. I can well understand why they find so much difficulty in fielding an army and holding it together for a full campaign. That gives me little confidence in their support through the difficult times ahead of us. A careless word or a disputed wager is all that is required to see a lord leave the field with his men, even joining those he swore to fight against.

It was with more than relief that the recent storm abated, the tide stood full and we could offer our guests passage towards their homes. It would be a cold and lively passage along a snow-clad coast, the open galley providing little shelter for those more comfortable ashore. At least they should be well-washed as they journey home, huddled in the area close to the bow where a sailcloth awning provides some respite from the salt water that sprays above the timbers.

All of that falls behind me as we once more assemble in the turret room to take a meal together. My grandchildren are in good spirit, their mothers also in fine humour. Jamie is assisted by his two daughters in bringing to us the fine dishes. Tonight his wife is still unwell, which is not at all like her. She has always seemed immune to illness and I hope that this is not a sign of more serious ailment. Erin and Shona are already young women. When next Jamie appears,

"Jamie auld friend, please attend Annie and leave your Erin and Shona to look to our needs. Please tell Annie that I trust she improves and that I wish her well."

"My lord, my place is with you".

"And to obey? So go with my order to tend your wife."

Jamie did not put up further argument, which is unlike him. It makes me fear that this is not a simple winter illness. I will instruct our doctor to tend her on the morrow and to provide all that he can to aid her recovery. We are fortunate to have doctors and herbalists in our community. Edward is young, a success of my dearest Margaret's desire to see all of our people educated beyond what is commonly accepted in this kingdom. He lives here within the castle, but he also visits the villages and homesteads. His mother Elizabeth lives within our walls, one of our skilled herbalists. Together they provide all of the care that has been needed by my household.

We have made the most of our dinner together because I expect it to be the last for several days. Tomorrow I expect different visitors, Visitors I delight in entertaining. They are amongst our closest allies, but yet separated by distance and the bulk of England. I first met the Huguenots as a young man accompanying my father. They are an interesting people who occupy the western coast of the French, in regular dispute with their Papist neighbours. They had become close to their English neighbours across the Narrow Sea, with a shared distaste of the Papists, but even more for their shared trade as corsairs and smugglers. We soon found a natural affinity with these fine seamen, the start of the shared expeditions that roamed further westwards as the years have slipped by. The Black Hawk is drawn on the lines they and their English allies have developed, and she sails on papers from La Rochelle. The description of her class is from the Huguenot 'razored', ships where the great castles have been shaved to give a fast, manoeuvrable ship that could handle well with low placed guns, ships that can dance around the bulk of a ship of state. Ships that carry fewer, but more powerful, guns, intended to take on an enemy at great distance and to bring more guns to bear at any time.

Since the gun was taken to sea, ships of state have attempted to disable an enemy in a chase, to come alongside and board. For that, it is natural to place the most able guns in bow and stern where there is space for but a few. The many guns sprouting from the great castles are mostly small guns that can fire down into the centre part of the ship against boarders, or mutineers. With the new agile ships we can stand off beyond the range of the enemy and reduce his crew without risking our crew. The Black Hawk is one of the largest of the new ships, but soon she will be overtaken in size as we undertake longer voyages with the need for more food, water and ammunition.

This all seems so far removed from the days of Einarr, but it is not. The first goal of any voyage is still a successful trade and a search for new rich lands. The fight is only taken where friendly trade is denied, new settlements attacked. As I settle back in telling the saga of Einarr, it is the similarities that are most striking, providing lessons that my grandchildren must learn.

Fifty Two

Ivar had returned once more to the fortress. Since the defeat of Esla, he had made a special effort to visit Edmund as often as conditions permitted. He understood the tender feelings of the Anglian's King and he needed to prevent them from growing beyond control. Ivar was happy for Edmund to feel a mixture of fear and gratitude, but he must control those feelings to prevent Edmund becoming resentful, then rebellious. This required delicate handling.

Ivar had been careful not to invite Edmund to visit him at the fortress. This was not a lack of hospitality, but a practical caution. Ivar knew that the fortress would overwhelm Edmund with its massive walls, now fully garrisoned and equipped with equally massive weapons beyond the Anglian experience. For Edmund to arrive within the walls, he would feel every part the vassal king paying homage to his superior. Even meeting at Depenham would be unfortunate because it would demonstrate to Edmund what a powerful king could achieve. Lodin and his comrades had transformed a small village, on the borderline of subsistence, into a major fortification and a large trading centre with its own harbour and docks. There was no village or town in the Three Kingdoms of Anglia that approached its power, wealth and potential to grow further. Even Edmund's home at Rendlesham, or his favourite alternative at Kett's Hall, were pale shadows of the rebuilt and expanded Depenham.

Ivar did need a location to return Edmund's hospitality, but a place that would not remind Edmund of Ivar's power. It had been a happy consequence of the defeat of Esla that Wulfmaer had been raised an Earl and given many of the lands that were Esla's lordship under Edmund.

Ivar had been somewhat surprised at the ease with which Edmund decided to elevate Wulfmaer. In part, he was encouraged by the spirited fight Wulfmaer had demonstrated alongside his King, but the major persuasion had come from an alliance of Gytha, Einarr and Gudhrun. The King had an affection for his younger cousin and it was fortunate that she, with Einarr, Gudhrun and Wulfmaer had brought the news of Esla's treachery and then become an important part of the bringing together of Ivar and Edmund in an alliance that could defeat Esla and his allies.

That grant of possessions, as part of Wulfmaer's elevation, included Esla's Hall and its village. At Einarr's urging, Ivar had provided materials, labour and guidance to improve this village, which Esla had allowed to decline. Given the ambitions of Esla, it seemed strange that he had not tended his domain better, but then that was the reason. Esla had expended much of his resources in acquiring more and intriguing against the King, leaving him little capacity to maintain what he already held, driven by greed, not by wisdom.

Ivar had passed through the village on his way from Rendlesham to the fortress. He wanted to see how the work there had progressed. He had been well pleased with the changes Aggi had wrought. Wulfmaer had only a small band of warriors, expanded by a group of Ivar's warriors who could pass for Saxons. That provided only a modest company to defend the village, a company reduced by the need to mount patrols to range across Wulfmaer's new holdings.

Recognizing this limitation, Aggi had worked his magic once more. He had built a new earthwork, topped by a solid palisade, pierced by two gateways through which passed the only road through the village. Smeared with clay and mud, the palisade showed no obvious indication that it was recently constructed. It encompassed a larger area than that enclosed by Esla's less substantial fencing, which had been in sore need of maintenance. In building the new palisade, Aggi had diverted the village stream to flow around the village in the broad ditch that had provided earth to build the bank on which the palisade sat. The result was a set of defences that would keep out wild animals, any roving bandits, and even a small army, but was very modest in appearance. As it was some time since Edmund had last passed through Esla's village, there was little to suggest that much had changed since then, or that any work had been undertaken since Esla had been killed. It would suit Ivar's purposes well, and provide a comfortable and secure base for Wulfmaer. It would make an ideal place for Ivar to return Edmund's hospitality.

When he rode through the great gate at the fortress, Ivar was even more certain that what was now Wulfmaer's Hall would make a much more suitable place to entertain Edmund. In the short time since Ivar had ridden out to support Edmund's campaign against Esla, much more had changed than he had thought possible. Riding across the bridge to the main gate, not much appeared to have altered since the fortress had been under Esla's control. There were now sentries always watching the bridge from the gateway's twin towers, but that was not obvious because of the height of the towers and the breast wall that protected the sentry walk. The great gates had been well maintained before and the high walls stared impassively at anyone approaching.

Once through the doors it was all very different. The enormous space within the walls was now looking very busy and congested. The new buildings started close to the gateway. A broad road from the gateway led to the largest of the halls. In riding along that road, other roads led off towards the far wall, flanked by new buildings of differing sizes, some substantial store houses, some smaller halls, workshops, with pens between them holding cattle, pigs and sheep. Everywhere Ivar looked he could see people going about their business. The walls now enclosed a large village that offered more than many a town.

The most noticeable feature was war machines atop the towers along the waterside walls. Julius had worked hard since the battle on the lake. The fight had exposed the limitations of his necessarily hasty work to improve the defences before the battle. He had built weapons for the remaining towers which doubled the firepower should the Northumbrians attempt another attack. The most important changes were not the new weapons, but the improvements to the supply of ammunition for them to fire. Julius knew, even better than Osten, how close they had come to exhausting supplies early in the battle. Had the Northumbrians been more aggressive, they could have taken advantage of the slackening fire to either seize the island, or make a landing and march off to join Esla. That could have tipped the balance against Ivar and Edmund, turning their victory into bitter defeat. To ensure that this did not happen in the future, Julius had built cranes and storage spaces so that ammunition close by the weapons was greatly increased and new supplies could be brought up by the cranes to avoid the ready stocks being depleted. This was not just essential to providing missiles to fire, but kept up with the improvements in the operation of the devices. Since the battle, Julius and Osten had regularly exercised the crews, which increased the rate of fire and the need for more ammunition.

All the activity and the growth of the fortress community pleased Ivar, but it also convinced him that this was not a place to entertain Edmund. That Depenham was now greater than any other township in Edmund's realm was little compared with the power presented by the fortress and its occupants. The breaks in the winter weather were allowing more men and supplies to be brought in, swelling the populations of the fortress and of the new fortifications at Depenham. There had even been trading voyages as Depenham expanded, serving as a market place, trading wool and products for the goods brought in from across the sea. As the news spread, more merchants would seek this new market out. Ivar could now see the great advantage of developing Depenham. Lodin could attract traders, leaving the fortress to guard the route upriver to the town and avoiding the need to allow any stranger within the fortress.

Ivar was free to concentrate on preparing his army for the campaign that would follow the winter. He could send out small scouting groups as conditions allowed, increasing his knowledge of the Saxon lands. He could also send some of his smaller ships out along the coast to make maps of the coastline and the rivers that led inland. It would keep his warriors active and diverted from the inevitable boredom of winter quarters. Just as he could not afford to allow Edmund to become resentful, he also needed the Saxons around them to see friendly neighbours who presented no danger.

Then Ivar must acquire more horses. If he could mount all of the warriors he would take North after the winter, he would be able to move quickly and respond to any Northumbrian attempts to out manoeuvre him. The defeat of Esla had shown how horses could also be used as cavalry to attack an enemy's flanks and rear, then carrying his warriors to cut down any enemy fleeing the battlefield. Great though these advantages were, they presented two major challenges. The first challenge was in finding enough horses that were fit for the purpose intended. The second challenge would be in providing fodder through the winter and then to carry enough supplies on the march. Ivar would not be able to take supplies during the march until they were out of the Three Kingdoms of the Anglians. Even then, he could not loot Saxon villages without making enemies who would lie across his lines of communication as he marched his army North. Even should he plan to forage as the army marched North, the Spring would see the Saxon store houses depleted by Winter use, with the first produce of the new year being some time away from harvest.

For Ivar, the winter would be a trial and an opportunity. The trial would be enforced inactivity and suspension of communications with the homelands. Already, there were signs that this would be a long and deep winter. The days were rapidly shortening but there were still many days to the Winter Solstice and the Festival of Light. From what he had learned from the Saxons, the first part of Winter was usually warmer, with fewer storms. The worst of the weather would come after the Festival of Lights. With an early period of low temperatures and frequent storms, the second half of the Winter could prove very difficult, confining the warriors to the Winter Halls, a lack of activity to divert them from petty squabbles, an abundance of food and drink to increase tensions of warriors living close together in smoky darkness, tensions rising further if a long Winter began to exhaust the supplies for man and livestock.

One task that could maintain activity was the refitting of the remaining ships. In his original plan, Ivar had envisaged that most of their longships would return home, ready to carry the other two armies across at the end of Winter. Only a handful of longships would be retained and they of the smaller vessels. Any supply vessels that arrived through the Winter would return home as soon as weather and tide permitted. Events had changed those expectations. More ships had been retained and to those had been added two groups of captured Saxon ships. That resulted in a large fleet, some vessels requiring routine care, some suffering damage from the storms and others carrying the scars of battle. This gave Ivar fresh ideas that would keep his men active in even the coldest Winter and assist his march North when the weather improved.

As Ivar had already sent some of their smallest boats out along the coast to scout, he was collecting information on the fishing villages and any ports that lay along the Anglian coast and on to the coasts of the Northumbrians. He could now plan a raiding campaign along the coast. As he marched his army around the marshlands and North towards York, his ships could follow along the coast, meeting up with the army at points along their route, bringing fresh supplies, some being obtained by raiding along the coast. Through the Winter he would be able to refine the plans, bringing in additional warriors, for whom mounts could not be found, by ship, closer to the expected battlefield where he intended to defeat Aella.

Before all the plans were fixed, he expected news from his brothers about the landing of the Northern armies. Bjorn Ironsides would land on the Solway coast with one army. At the same time, Halfdan would land on the East Coast, North of the Northumbrian's northern border. Those armies would then sweep South to pin the Northumbrians between their armies and the Great Army that Ivar would be leading. That would require careful timing, a flow of messengers between the three forces, and reconnaissance to ensure that Aella was firmly trapped between the armies, separated from any allies who might attempt to come to his aid.

What troubled Ivar was his dealings with Edmund and the growing influence of Ceolwulf. With each meeting, Edmund seemed diminished and ever more reliant on Ceolwulf. Wulfmaer wanted to join Ivar's army with those Saxon warriors who were grouping around him. There were growing indications that Wulfmaer was acquiring more than Esla's lands, but also his position as a potential rebel against Edmund and Ceolwulf. Young warriors had been steadily joining Wulfmaer. He was a natural leader, known to hold strong relations with Einarr and Ivar, young and a rising star. To a young Saxon warrior he was a more attractive leader than Edmund, who was falling into the shadow of the increasingly disliked and feared Ceolwulf, who sought to kill anyone he considered a threat to Edmund.

This could present difficulties for Ivar in the new year. If Wulfmaer joined the march North, he would be a welcome addition to the army, but he would leave nothing to resist Edmund and Ceolwulf if that became necessary. Ivar would only have two points to defend his rear. The fortress could be defended successfully by a smaller force than Osten had had at his disposal, but there would still be need of patrols to detect any assault assembling against the fortress. Since Julius had strengthened the great weapons he had built, the fortress could deny any ships access to the river inland, but the remaining garrison would be too weak to take the offensive against any force, which could then attempt to go around them.

The situation would be little different at Depenham. Ivar had already decided to leave Lodin and a strong garrison to defend the village from attack, but not the numbers required to take offensive action against any would-be attackers. Ivar had arrived at the numbers of warriors he would leave behind by a count of his complete force and a calculation of the number he had expected to lose when they landed to establish their winter quarters. He had also received more reinforcements from home that he had not counted on arriving. The only weakness in his position was that any losses through the winter to illness or fighting would have to be replaced from the two planned garrisons.

Ivar could not be sure that the Northumbrians would not attempt a second invasion but that seemed increasingly unlikely as the weather deteriorated, the storms continued to roll across the land and Aella still had no firm news of what had happened to his first invasion, or to Esla.

By now Aella would know that his fleet had failed, but he was unlikely to know why, or the strength and nature of the victors. At the same time, Edmund was in no position to challenge Ivar, perhaps until the main army was on the march North. Ivar knew Edmund to be indecisive. Ceolwulf appeared to have no personal ambition other than to do whatever he considered necessary in what he thought were the best interests of Edmund. The greater danger there would come after the Northumbrians were defeated. Ivar knew that some of his men would decide to stay in these lands, bringing over their families and occupying land previously held by the Northumbrian casualties. Lodin would stay, having married Ælfwyn. Many of his friends would also settle in the area, bringing over their families, working with Wulfmaer to control the lands along the river to the coast. Unless something occurred that Ivar had not foreseen, the bulk of the Great Army and the two armies landing in the North would fade away, as groups of warriors returned home with their ships.

Ivar had no clear thoughts for these times beyond victory. He had no intention to stay on in these islands, after exacting revenge on the Northumbrians and their current King. He did want to maintain a trading position in conjunction with Wulfmaer, and his family, that now included Lodin. Even so he saw no permanent personal involvement, nothing more than the occasional visit when a trade was attractive.

He did have wider duties. When Ragnar was killed, Ivar was acclaimed as his successor, in the title of King of Denmark and Sweden. That did not mean that he was required to rule all of the people of Denmark and Sweden, making their laws and raising taxes from them. He would be regarded as the first amongst all the Kings and Carls of the People, and beyond the territories of Denmark and Sweden. Where he chose to go, many might choose to follow, but he would not order them, neither would his duties prevent him from undertaking great voyages for trade and exploration, or prevent those of his army who might wish to continue war against Saxons of any of the Saxon kingdoms of these islands.

For now, Ivar would concentrate his thoughts on maintaining the alliance with Edmund and preparing for the campaign he would undertake in the new year against Aella and his Northumbrians. He would continue to seek intelligence to aid that campaign. He would continue to strengthen his winter quarters. He would consider new threats, which might be presented by any alliances that Aella would seek to forge.

As Ivar was thinking of the current conditions and the next steps, Lodin and his new family would be thinking of how they could strengthen their position and of the opportunities that were presenting themselves. Lodin was grateful that Ivar had released him from his pledge to march on the Northumbrians, but he might yet join that great endeavour. At least he had the choice, he expected Wulfmaer to join the campaign, but then they could both support the campaign by remaining where they were. That was Ivar's reason for releasing Lodin from his pledge. By following his own interests, Lodin would provide a secure rear defence as the army marched North. By developing his new lands and looking to his followers and tenants, Wulfmaer was extending the depth of the rear defences and becoming a counter balance to Edmund, should that prove necessary.

When Ivar originally drew his plans for a campaign against the Northumbrians he could not count on any defence to his rear. He had to accept that the best conditions would provide him with winter quarters. When the new season followed winter, he would march away, through those Saxon lands before

Northumbria, hoping to avoid the distraction of any fight with those lands he must pass through. He would not rely or expect any further supplies from the homelands until after he had brought Aella to battle. He would rely on marching quickly on the Northumbrians, avoiding battle with Edmund's people, depending on rapid movement to keep his rear safe. If victory was not achieved, he would retire to the Northumbrian coast and meet ships from home that would carry his survivors away from their defeat.

Since those plans had been made, events had moved rapidly in his favour and changed his fortunes more than he could ever have expected. The winter storms would reduce the flow of ships from home, but it would not stop them and the numbers arriving would increase as the storms slackened. His communications with his brothers would be more frequent and dependable. He could time his march North much more carefully and co-ordinate more effectively with the armies his brothers would land in the North. He could also expect to meet with ships carrying more men and supplies at two, perhaps three, points on his line of march. Those considerations absorbed his thoughts. Plenty of time to think what next to do once Aella had been defeated.

There was one item that did require special thought, but did not urgently demand action. Whatever Edmund or Ivar might have thought, Gytha showed no desire to leave the fortress. Both had assumed that she would join Edmund's household once Esla was dealt with. By remaining in Ivar's base, he had gained a willing hostage should need arise, but Edmund might resent his cousin's lack of urgency in rejoining him. Gytha was comfortable where she was. Her friendship with Gudhrun had developed rapidly, even before Gytha had established her own household at the small Hall that Ivar had allocated for her use within the fortress. She had come to value both the freedom this gave her, the excitement of new experiences with new friends. Ivar had extended every courtesy so that she did not feel to be a prisoner. She had delighted in showing Gudhrun the ways of Saxon women, as Gudhrun had delighted in showing her a life under arms as she had come to lead it.

For Gytha, she would lose much by rejoining her Royal cousin. She would again become subordinate to Edmund's wishes and he would seek to find her a husband who was able to benefit Edmund and his kingdom. Gytha knew the possible choices within the court and favoured none of them. The thought of being married to a Saxon, beyond the three kingdoms, concerned and appalled her. Her new husband, whoever that might be, would rule her and all of her actions. She might retain her two maids but that did not guarantee how she lived. At least within the fortress, she was secure, comfortably fed and sheltered, with people she was coming to regard as her closest friends, who treated her as an equal.

Gytha had been surprised by the many similarities between the society she had been brought up in and the society from which Gudhrun came. Before, she had been brought up to think of them as barbarians, violent, uncouth, pagan. The Church had taught that the People were a plague, visited on the Saxons because they had failed to be pious, earning God's protection. Gytha now knew that this was false. Many of Ivar's people dressed more richly than any Saxon she had met. They were happy people who were generous with their friends. Far from being just the camp of a great army, some warriors had brought their families with them. Since the Peoples learned of Ivar's good fortune in establishing his winter camps, later boats had brought families of some warriors who had left them behind when the fleet had sailed. Children played within the fortress and wives and children accompanied warriors on the trips to Depenham, as the Saxons, in that now large village, travelled to the fortress.

At first she had thought that many were also Christian. They often crossed themselves on meeting. Then she understood that this was not a sincere belief, but a way of trading with Christians who were forbidden to trade with pagans. This new knowledge did not dismay her because, if truth be told, she shared the beliefs of many Saxons who were Christians in Church, but continued to follow many of the ancient beliefs of their fathers. In that, she greatly valued her distance from Caedmon and his fellow priests, their depressing manner hanging darkly over her joy of life, her love of freedom.

There, she could decide what to do each and every day. She attended feasts in the other Halls within the fortress. She could ride out with her maids in the company of Einarr and Gudhrun. She could visit Wulfmaer, as he could visit her. Then there was the treat she had not experienced before. She could join any ship travelling between the fortress and Depenham. She found a great enjoyment of travel on a ship, more comfortable than horseback, even in the most unpleasant weather. She was coming to see a voyage on the sea as a great and desirable adventure to look forward to. Gytha was also learning many new things. Old Gisi had taken a liking to her and was delighting in a new audience that did not know any of the tales that he told every winter round the hearth. As a young girl, Gytha had learned to read and to write, to learn other languages and dialects from the priests. Gisi could write the runes, speak many languages and draw charts, but his was a practical education. Gytha's attention to his stories was flattering, but she was also teaching him. The People had a rich oral tradition, the runes sometimes were clumsy, having difficulty in expressing thoughts. Gisi had long wanted to create a record of his knowledge that others could later use.

As he told Gytha tales of the voyages he had taken and the strange lands and people he had visited, she taught him to read and to write as a well-educated Saxon might. For both of them the time was flying by. It would be the shortest winter for them and, for Gytha, it filled time when Gudhrun was with Einarr and the weather confined her to the fortress.

She met many others. Even with the large population living within the fortress, Gytha was becoming recognized and liked by her neighbours. Einarr's aunt was one in whose company she delighted. Ulrika Ragnarsdottir was a handsome woman, not long widowed, who had arrived some weeks after the fortress was taken. Ivar had not been pleased to see his younger sister when she arrived, but soon found her a valuable addition to his camp. She assumed the position of his housekeeper and all enjoyed her sunny disposition. Ulrika was always happy and smiling. Nothing depressed her, even the many dark damp days that were common in the three kingdoms. She lifted the mood on a sombre day, her bright and decorated clothes bringing colour wherever she went. Gytha was enchanted. Having only previously come to know Gudhrun, and some of the other young women who had arrived with Ivar's fleet, Gytha had become used to women wearing the same clothes as the warriors and carrying weapons. Ulrika was completely different. Her clothes were made from many materials, with rich embroidery. They were a woman's clothes, a wealthy woman who could afford gold thread and beads, gold clasps and ornaments. Ulrika was tall, with long hair, the yellow of fine gold, deep blue eyes, a flawless skin and face that was perfection.

Living within the fortress, Gytha had come to understand that Gudhrun's people were very different from what she was taught by the priests. In many ways, they were much like the Saxons. There was no single mould from which they had emerged. If anything, they were a greater range of individuals than the Saxons she had grown up with. Most had a love for silver, gold and colours. They had a wider choice because they travelled far, trading in many places. Some of the ornaments and cloth were like nothing she had seen before. Where she had thought her family wealthy, she now saw displays of wealth that made her people very dull and poor. Once, her people might have been more like the Norse, but for hundreds of summers they had lived within these islands, raising their crops and cattle, using the materials available to them. They had also been constrained by their priests.

With all that Gytha was experiencing and enjoying, neither Ivar nor Edmund would easily persuade her to return to her cousin's court. Her new existence had awoken a part of her character that had always been suppressed. She had lived well before, now she realized that she had always been a prisoner, a caged bird, a bird in a gilded cage.

She could never expect to rule, but she was valuable trade goods. Her cousin was as much a prisoner, but with a very different future. He was but a boy when he became King, directed and manipulated by the Earls his father had favoured. He had been educated by the priests, trained to fight by warriors. His sense of duty developed by his mentors, to their advantage. He had become so accustomed to being manipulated that he found it difficult to make his own decisions. Just as he was beginning to master his own destiny, Esla and the Northumbrians had brought a crisis that he was ill-equipped to deal with. The necessary decisions had been taken by Ivar and Ceolwulf. Gytha knew that her only hope to retaining the freedom she was daily growing to accept lay with remaining far from her cousin's court.

Gytha was not only enjoying new freedom and new experience, she was developing all of the skills that a king would need. If her society had been different, she could have replaced her cousin to the profit of the Anglians. She was growing in confidence in her skills and she was surprised to find how well she could judge risks and advantages, encouraging others to support her. Ivar had recognised these developments and his liking for Gytha as a favoured daughter was growing. What he was not certain of was how he could best use this young Saxon woman to his advantage.

As her surroundings were changing Gytha, her friendship was changing Gudhrun. From her earliest memories, Gudhrun had shared her life with Einarr. This was never to anyone's plan. They had lived in the closeness that only twins would share. Becoming a warrior had been a natural, almost expected, consequence as Gudhrun eagerly embraced everything that was part of Einarr's life. Each could know what the other was thinking. When they were apart they knew what the other was doing, experiencing, risking. When they became old enough to voyage with Ivar, or with Einarr's uncles, they developed as brothers would. As they grew tall and strong and beautiful, they were apart from those who might otherwise be their friends and contemporaries. Others of their age were jealous of them, of their appearance, of their privilege, and also frightened of them. Gudhrun had grown more as a boy. As her friendship with Gytha grew, she was coming to understand things that other women of her age took for granted. As she looked in wonder at things any other woman would find natural, her bond with Einarr had not weakened, but it was deepening. She realised that this was a change that had started before she met Gytha. She recognized the changes but she did not understand them. She wondered if Einarr knew, but then in her soul she knew that nothing was hidden from him, as nothing of him was hidden from her.

Fifty Three

As the days continued to grow shorter, the storms became more frequent, the frequent rain had given way to snow. The rivers froze and the lake had become a sheet of ice, thick enough to walk across. The inhabitants of the fortress and the scattered defences upriver to Depenham ventured out as rarely as possible. There was food a plenty and the hearths burned through the days and into the nights. It was a time to enjoy the company of friends, to entertain the hearth companions. There were essential tasks but, if possible, they were completed quickly at the middle of the day. Arms and armour were cleaned more often than need be in the warmth and comfort of the Halls. Then, as the winter solstice approached it became warmer. The ice melted in the rivers and across the lake. The ground was muddy, slush lay on it, but the days were calm and the wide skies almost a summer blue.

Einarr decided take advantage of the winter respite, riding to meet with Wulfmaer. Gudhrun travelled with him, but Gytha decided to remain at the fortress. One of Aggi's carpenters was ordered to travel with them and stay to inspect work done in recent months as Wulfmaer continued to improve the village that was now his base. Three of the Saxons at the fortress also decided to join Wulfmaer.

The small party had ridden out at first light. They planned to camp at one of the hamlets on the road to Wulfmaer and complete their journey on the second day. Not knowing what food the hamlet might have to offer, each rider took a second mount, strapping food for themselves and the horses onto the remounts. They were well equipped for a change in the weather or poor supplies on their route.

Their ride went well and they approached the hamlet before nightfall. Gyrthingham was a very modest hamlet. A broad stream wound through the hamlet. The herres road followed along the eastern boundary of the village, with a street cutting across the hamlet and crossing the stream by a simple wooden bridge. The Hall was a small building, rectangular, timber framed, daub and wattle walls, roofed with thatch. A timber-clad building contained the mill that was the major justification for the hamlet. Five other small buildings completed the community. Two were round structures with conical thatched roofs, a small doorway, but no windows or other openings in their walls. The other three buildings were rectangular, long and low, each housing a family and their livestock through the short days of winter.

As Einarr looked around the village a stout old man appeared at the doorway to the Hall. This was Wifirth, headman of the hamlet, one-time warrior and now miller and lord of this very modest manor.

"My lord," he said with a strong and steady voice, addressing Einarr, "may I offer you rest and shelter in my humble home?"

"We would be most grateful gentle sir," responded Einarr, jumping down from his horse. "Will you permit us to contribute food for the table and for our mounts?"

Wifirth was eager to accept a contribution of food and fodder. His small community was not poor by local standards, but feeding six healthy young warriors and twelve horses would soon deplete the stocks they had stored to see them through the winter. A party of mounted warriors always raised fears. Wifirth had often been the reluctant host to Esla's patrols in all seasons of the year. Unlike these travellers, Esla's men had never offered to contribute to the hospitality, rather they would look around for anything they might carry away with them, including the women of the hamlet. There was no easy way. Until the travellers were within his roof, he could not know how reasonable they would be.

Wifirth's practiced eye took in his guests by turns. He

might now be an old man, but he still had his warrior's eye. He liked what he saw. He was surprised to find that one warrior was a woman, but all were equipped with good arms and armour, carried themselves as competent warriors and all had the look of relative wealth. He had heard rumours over the past weeks but he knew not how far to believe them. Now he had visitors who could tell him more and with assurance.

The horses had been quartered in a low barn behind the mill, fed and watered. The warriors were within the Hall, their baggage carried in by villagers, food prepared and laid out on the two long tables. It seemed that the population of the hamlet had filled the modest building. As feasts went, this matched the building that sheltered it. Einarr and his comrades had taken off their helmets and mail coats, the blazing hearth warming them after their cold ride.

Wifirth took the lead and introduced himself and his hamlet to his guests. Einarr followed and each of those at the tables followed on. This took some time and not every feaster was easy to hear, but when the last spoke, all felt that they knew something of the others and struck up conversations with their neighbours, Einarr's party being seated amongst those of the hamlet. It was a quietly convivial gathering. There was a gentle buzz of conversation, relaxed laughter and a dwindling supply of food and beer.

Wifirth was eager to learn of the world beyond his woods. Einarr was surprised by how little his host knew of the recent events. He knew there had been fighting but had no clear idea of who had fought, or where, or even the outcome. Even more surprisingly, Wifirth was unaware that a new Earl had been appointed by the King. He was pleased to learn that the new Earl was Wulfmaer, son of Ealdwulf. Although he had never met Wulfmaer, he had known Ealdwulf, counted him a comrade and friend. He was certain that Wulfmaer would be the fine son of a fine father, but the news of Ealdwulf's death was a surprise and sadness to him.

Einarr was learning the way of life that was common in

these lands but very different from his own experiences. For him, trade took the People across their own lands, around the coasts and through the wild seas. Information was essential to good trading, but Wifirth and his hamlet was isolated for much of the year. The local families brought their grain to the mill at each harvest. Wifirth also served as the local smith and neighbours came to him for repairs to tools, or for him to make them new equipment. Occasionally, travellers would stop at the hamlet, usually traders, and sometimes the unwelcome visits of Esla's men. This lack of frequent contact with others was the reason for a lack of awareness of what was changing around them. What contact they had with others was confined to the warm summer months, but the hamlet and the neighbouring scattered farmsteads were happy in the closed community.

Wifirth listened carefully to all that Einarr and his comrades had to say about the events of the past months. Those of the hamlet also listened with interest but they lacked Wifirth's greater awareness of the world beyond their boundaries. As a warrior he had travelled around the Three Kingdoms. Once he had been in a small army that had marched deep into Southumbrian lands. It had been some years distant, but he had seen so much more than his people. It was a long time since he had talked with strangers and it awoke a desire to travel again.

"My lord I have enjoyed so much the company of your band, but I would ask you one favour if you will permit," said Wifirth as Einarr completed the story of the battle and Wulfmaer's elevation to earl in place of the defeated Esla.

"If it is within my power to grant, I would be pleased to offer what I can to a generous host," Einarr responded.

"My Lord, would you permit me to join you on your journey to my old friend's son? I should like to meet him, to offer my loyal support and that of our hamlet"

"We would be honoured if you would ride with us," replied Einarr.

During the feasting, Gudhrun had happily consumed enough for at least two hungry warriors, but she had been quiet. She now understood that Saxon women had different expectations and duties. To them she was a novelty but also something to be wary of. For the men, it was a discomfort to talk with a woman, so different from their experiences, who was both a guest and a person of some obvious importance, treated by Einarr and those of his party as an equal and a comrade. Another might have taken this in discomfort but, for Gudhrun, the absence of diversion from the serious business of eating was to be welcomed.

By then, the number of people in the Hall had dwindled as neighbours returned to their own homes. Einarr's party settled down on the trodden earth around the hearth. They would take it in turns for one to stand guard, but each would enjoy an otherwise undisturbed sleep, to start the coming day refreshed.

The hamlet began to awake before first light. Einarr's party was given small beer and porridge to start the day. Wifirth joined them and, as soon as they had finished their meal, the party made its way to their horses. Packs were loaded and the riders mounted, Wifirth on a stocky horse that almost matched his stocky shape. Strapped behind his saddle was a long bundle and two sacks, one for his food and one for his horse.

It was another cold windy day with flurries of snow, but the riders travelled on in good humour and at a steady pace that would see them arrive at Wulfmaer's village before nightfall. Wifirth entertained his fellow riders with tales of his youth. The time went remarkably quickly and before they expected, the village came into sight.

Wifirth was amazed to see the changes. It had been some time since he had reluctantly visited Esla. Headmen were summoned whenever Esla was in need of new funds, making the visit a painful event, best avoided, but if Esla noticed an absence, he would send a party of warriors to collect what he needed, to

which was added their own greedy demands. Better to attend
Esla, hoping his mood was not at its darkest, and hope to escape
lightly. On these rare visits, Wifirth had found Esla's village in
need of repair, a tired fence surrounding a huddle of unkempt
buildings, its simple gates propped open during daylight.

Today, he and his fellow riders were approaching a
substantial palisade behind a boundary of flowing water, a new
wooden bridge leading to a gateway between two wooden towers.
Once through the gate, the riders were on a gravel roadway that
led through the village towards a gateway and sturdy bridge that
opened onto the road out of the village. It was some time since
Wifirth had last been there, but he saw new buildings and paving,
everything well-cared for and neat. Even though it was now
winter, there was activity and the people he saw appeared to be
young. He could not have imagined how much had changed. He
was also reassured because he had not entirely believed Einarr's
account of the recent events and he was half expecting to find
Esla alive and as disagreeable as ever. He knew now that the
accounts had been true. There was no possibility that this active
and well-attended village had any connection with Esla, other
than a past well-forgotten.

Einarr and Gudhrun had visited the village since it had
passed to Wulfmaer, but they were impressed by the many
improvements. Here and there they could see the hallmark of
Aggi's work. Where only weeks before, this had been a place of
despair and fear, it was now a place of hope and growing
prosperity. Even Esla's surviving kin had embraced the changes
cheerfully and accepted the young people who had come to join
Wulfmaer. As news had begun to spread, young men and women
had drifted towards the village, some from as far away as
Depenham. As they rode along the main roadway towards the
Hall that was now Wulfmaer's, Einarr recognised and greeted
Norse warriors who had been allocated to help Wulfmaer build an
effective defence. Wifirth would only be in the village to meet
Wulfmaer, before returning to his hamlet, but the Saxons in
Einarr's party would be making this their new home.

The riders reached the hall in the centre of the village to find Wulfmaer on the steps to greet them. He was very pleased to see Einarr and Gudhrun once more. They were more than friends of a similar age, more members of a family. He welcomed the Saxons who had come to join him. Einarr introduced Modolf, the carpenter sent by Aggi. Wulfmaer was grateful for this skilled man, not having an experienced carpenter in the village.

At that point, Wifirth stepped forward and bowed deeply. "My Lord Wulfmaer, I have not had the honour to meet you before, but I was a friend of Ealdwulf, your father. I am Wifirth the elder of the hamlet of Gyrthingham and miller. I come to pledge my allegiance to you."

"Gentle sir, I am honoured by your commitment and pleased to meet a friend of my late father. You are welcome in my Hall."

Before Wulfmaer could say more, Wifirth took down a sack from behind his horse's saddle and the long bundle that had been tied before the sack.

"My Lord, may I present you with this flour ground in our mill," offered Wifirth as he began to unwrap the long bundle. "My Lord, I would also wish to give you this. I have no son to follow me and I would that you accept the gift I would have passed to him. You may have its sister and perhaps you will pass this to your son"

With that, Wifirth laid the bundle across his arm, the opened end of the bundle displaying the jewelled hilt of a sword.

"When I was young and a comrade of your father, we did a service for a smith. He insisted on making two swords, one for your father and one for me. They were fine weapons that we carried with pride, and they served us well."

As he presented the hilt to Wulfmaer and folded back the

cloth, he displayed a handsome scabbard and a dirk that was in the same design as the sword. Wulfmaer was overcome. The sword was the exact likeness of his father's sword, taken from him when Esla had captured him. A sword now lost.

"You do me great honour with this gift. My father's sword was most treasured and sorely missed. To carry its sister will be joy to me. I am overcome."

With one hand Wulfmaer took the gift and placed the other on Wifirth's shoulder. Looking to Einarr and each of the riders in turn, "Come, I would share my hearth with you. We can tell of all that has happened since last we met."

As they entered the Hall, Wulfmaer's hand still on Wifirth's shoulder, the old man drew himself to his full height and the years seemed to fall away as he proudly walked beside the son of his old friend.

That evening was a great feast. Most of the company was young, but there were also older villagers and children. The food and drink was brought in through the evening. Even Gudhrun was sated, the evening progressing in boisterous good humour. Wifirth became the storyteller. He had been older than Ealdwulf, his mentor when their had both served the King's house, and he had a seemingly endless fund of tales, of his own experiences and of stories he had heard in his youth.

The days passed swiftly, but it would soon be time for Einarr and Gudhrun to make their way back to the fortress. Wifirth had stayed only two days and, when he prepared to leave, Wulfmaer insisted that he ride with a bodyguard from his warriors at the village. The old man would have refused, but he appreciated the kind gesture, it would have been discourteous to decline the escort and it would make the journey home safer and more pleasant. There had been more snow and there could be small bands of robbers roaming the land.

When Wulfmaer had seen Wifirth leave with his escort, he

could give his full attention to his friends. He had to admit to himself that he had neglected them, but Wifirth had been an absorbing surprise. He was eager to hear tales of his father as a young warrior and he was deeply touched still by the gift of the sword, which he had worn since Wifirth had handed it to him. Before he slept he had drawn the sword and watched the light from the rush brands dance and flow across the blue metal and flash fire in the jewel that completed the hilt. He marvelled at its fine craftsmanship and its exact duplication of the sword he had lost. Ivar had given him the best of the swords taken in the assault on the fortress that had freed Wulfmaer, but nothing could compare with this weapon and the link it renewed with his father.

Wulfmaer could now devote his time to his friends. They would go hunting and ride around his new lands. He would allow nothing to come between them. It was also a time for Einarr and Gudhrun to meet Frythegith.

On the day that Wifirth had departed for his home, another small party had arrived. There were two young women and six warriors. In the party were horses carrying heavy loads in bundles and in boxes. Leading these riders was Hunbeorht, a handsome young warrior, perhaps three summers older than Wulfmaer, one of the young women riding alongside him, the second woman riding close behind the leaders. The first woman was Frythegith, the younger sister of Hunbeorht. Her brother may have been handsome, but Frythegith was a great beauty. As the riders entered the village, her features were almost completely hidden by the fur-trimmed hood of her riding cloak. Even her eyes were in the shadow of the hood.

Wulfmaer was already standing on the steps to his Hall to greet them, conscious that this was a very important meeting. Wulfmaer's mother had chosen Frythegith to be his wife. They had met as small children but neither of the betrothed was sure what to expect. It had been so long ago, the meetings brief, but their parents already considered the two would wed, uniting the families. Now that Wulfmaer had become an earl, Frythegith's mother was anxious that the marriage be arranged without delay before someone else managed to force their daughter on Wulfmaer. From being the son of a minor, if respected, warrior, Wulfmaer had overnight come into riches and a powerful position. He would be sought by many families as a match for their daughters. Aebbe was a formidable and ambitious mother who had long been unhappy that her husband thought Wulfmaer to be good enough for their daughter. That was yesterday, but today made Wulfmaer the ideal son in law. Had he been a crookback of displeasing countenance, Aebbe would have only seen the importance and the promise of wealth that stemmed from his position.

Frythegith was two summers younger than Wulfmaer and did not know what she should expect. She had only a dim memory of a boy who had no interest in her. She had heard tales of his recent life as a warrior but that made him sound much older than he was. She was also unsure why her mother had suddenly warmed to the idea of marrying her to Wulfmaer, after years of complaining that he was unsuitable. She had not been looking forward to this meeting, the long cold ride doing nothing to ease her nerves.

Wulfmaer was no more prepared than his intended bride. He had no real memory of Frythegith from his childhood, or of her family. He was not thinking of having a wife and family of his own. The recent events had provided all too much excitement. He had never thought, never expected, to become an earl and certainly not at this point in his life. He had conflicting feelings. There was the fluttery sensation that was common before battle, there was a sense of unease, but there were many other sensations that he could not identify.

The riders dismounted and suddenly every thought was swept away as the young woman standing before him threw back her hood. His breath was swept away. He had never seen anyone more beautiful. She was perfect. Her startling blue eyes were set in a face that was smooth and perfectly symmetrical. Her hair was a rich golden yellow. For a moment Wulfmaer forgot the assurance he had developed as he learned to lead others. He struggled to find words. The object of his attention was no less affected. Here was a handsome young warrior who shared nothing with her vague memories of the young boy she had known before. There was determination, the stance of a warrior, but in his eyes there was a warm glow suggesting humour and humanity. For these young people there was nothing else around them, they saw only each other.

Wulfmaer became aware of sound, intruding on his concentration.

"Lord Wulfmaer, I am Hunbeorht. May I present my sister Frythegith. My father Daegbeorht was unable to travel. He has charged me with escorting my sister in his place and discussing with you the marriage of my sister to you, if it pleases my Lord."

"Hunbeorht I am pleased to welcome you and thank you for bringing your sister safely to my Hall," replied Wulfmaer, turning his head back to Frythegith, "and to see you again Gentle Lady, after all these years. When last we met we were but children. I look forward to knowing you, that we may both decide our future, but let me share my hearth, that you shake off the chill. I will have my steward see to your men and horses."

Frythegith was pleased by Wulfmaer's greeting, that he honoured her and had not taken her agreement for granted. Long past, their families had agreed the terms of the marriage, but Frythegith did not want to be bound to that without being happy in Wulfmaer's company and he in hers. She knew that the old agreement and his new power could bind her, if he was determined, against her desire. For him to suggest the need that both agree gave her the freedom of choice, not that her first judgement of him would suggest him unsuitable as her husband, rather she saw him as her image of the ideal.

She was glad that her father's health had prevented him escorting her, not that he was unwell, but because her mother would have travelled with them. Her brother could be bent to whatever she wanted, but her mother would have tried to negotiate a new bargain, had she seen Wulfmaer's wealth and position in his new rank. From what she had seen of Wulfmaer so far, he would have strongly resisted her mother, perhaps calling an end to the marriage talks, even with the original agreement the final settlement had yet to be agreed.

Once inside the Hall, Wulfmaer began his hospitality. Food and drink was already being brought to the tables. Wulfmaer's friends and close retainers were there. He began the introductions. Frythegith was surprised that most of those present were young. Those few survivors from the rule of Esla stood out as the lonely representatives of older generations. She was also surprised to find that half of those young warriors were not Saxon. Although they wore Saxon clothing, their names were not those she was familiar with. At the top table, sitting with her, her brother and Wulfmaer were Einarr and Gudhrun, unlike their comrades, who were helping Wulfmaer to establish his new lands, neither made any concession to Saxon dress and Gudhrun made no concession to female dress. Both wore their leather trousers and shirts, high leather boots, sword and dirk. Even in relaxation, they were protected by the tough leather and their weapons. Both towered over those present.

As the feast progressed, Frythegith and her brother Hunbeorht exchanged conversions with Wulfmaer, Einarr and Gudhrun. Frythegith was most interested to learn all that she could about Wulfmaer, but it soon became apparent that he had a close affinity with the two young Norse, and that he owed much to them. The conversation was lively and informing, but the background noise from all those in the Hall made it at times difficult. Frythegith was not troubled by this, knowing that they would share other meals together and quieter time together. She was also not troubled by the attention from the gathering. The rumours had rapidly circulated through the village. All those feasting this night knew that Frythegith was intended as the bride for Wulfmaer. In the times ahead, she would affect their lives through her influence on her husband. None present, save the young couple, Hunbeorht, and Wulfmaer's two Norse friends knew that there was any question about the union. Wulfmaer had confided in his two friends before Frythegith and her brother arrived.

Before he first met her as an adult, Wulfmaer had never set much by his betrothal. Since early childhood, he had seen very little of Frythegith or her family. He was aware of the conversations between his parents and that was all that provided a base for his knowledge. It had been clear that Frythegith's mother thought little for Wulfmaer and his family. She had never been enthusiastic about the betrothal and, as her ambitions soared, she hoped for a much better marriage for her daughter, one that would benefit the mother, if not the daughter. The result was that Wulfmaer had not felt any unswerving commitment to marriage even after considering the past friendship of his father with Daegbeorht. Had he known how desperately Aebbe now wanted to marry the young earl to her daughter, he would have lost any lingering interest in the match. That had all begun to change as he was struck by her beauty when they met again as adults, but it did not mean he would not consider the marriage agreement with great care. Both were conscious of how much had changed in so few days.

Now, days after that first feast, Frythegith and Wulfmaer were coming to the point where the marriage must be agreed, or set aside. Both were enthralled with each other. It seemed that an agreement was beyond question, and yet was something beyond and outside their feelings for each other. Frythegith had developed a friendship for Gudhrun who had become her chaperone for her visit. It was Gudhrun who was her companion in private moments, and Gudhrun who was always with Einarr when they joined Wulfmaer, Frythegith and Hunbeorht for their daily ride. It was a time to hunt and to see the lands that were now Wulfmaer's. There was no private moment between the young couple. After a day riding, the party returned to the Hall and it was time for what always seemed to be a feast, never a private meal.

Both Frythegith and Gudhrun were curious of the other.

Gudhrun had learned much from Gytha, but she could still not fully understand the life of a Saxon lady. That so much was alien was as much a matter of the warrior's life that Gudhrun led, as it was a difference between Saxons and Norse. In fact there was a great deal in common between the two peoples. It was different for Einarr because there was little difference between young warriors, that was after all their prime reason for life. For Frythegith, there was equal curiosity because Gudhrun was so very different, unlike those women of Frythegith's own society.

Gudhrun was much taller than Saxon women, her dress starkly different. She dressed like Einarr and their dress was harsher and tougher than the clothes worn by Saxon warriors, except in battle. Her own brother was typical of young Saxon men of the warrior class. His shirt, tunic, shorts, hose and shoes were soft materials and there was colour woven into them. Even the seaxe that he wore, more as an ornament of rank, was held across his waist in a decorated sheath, its hilt carved from bone.

Einarr and Gudhrun always wore clothes of leather and fur. Shades of brown, from yellow brown of their shirts, to the dark, almost black, of their leather trousers. The only concession to colour was the use of red leather for boots and sword sheath and the addition of silver for belt buckles and the tips of sheaths. Even the fur that trimmed their cloaks and made their jackets, was wolf or bear, the wolf fur streaked with darker hues amongst the silver. The cloaks were wool but dyed in dark greens and browns, or the heavier Winter cloaks of fur. Frythegith might have been even more surprised had she seen Gudhrun and Einarr dressed for battle. Where her brother and his comrades would have changed the soft brightness of the clothing for the dull cloaks and chain mail of war, Gudhrun and Einarr would pull on chain mail over their leather clothes, but helmets, shields and weapons provided colour. Their swords included gems as part of the balancing of their blades, and as a sign of wealth. The shields employed bold colour and Einarr proudly wore the helmet and carried the shield given to him by his uncle, to the displeasure of his father. These were flashing metal and gems with intricate designs, statements of wealth and power. Even the battle cloaks that both wore were dyed in a colour that was unknown to Frythegith's people, a deep purple cloth brought back in trade from the East.

The time had been rushing by Frythegith, so much to see, so much to learn and, for her, for her family, the highest of stakes. On this day she would know her future. It was a very cold day but with a bright yellow sun low in a pale blue sky. Wulfmaer had decided that they would ride East towards the sea, but an easy ride where they could rest at a hut in the woodland to eat. It had not been spoken of by any of them, but she knew that this was the day of decision. From there, her life would be changed forever. She was pleased that Gudhrun and Einarr would be with them, honest brokers if need be between her brother and her intended husband. She was also pleased that Wulfmaer's sister, Cyneberg would be with them.

Cyneberg had arrived only two days before, sent by her mother with a small escort and some supplies that Lodin and Ælfwyn had thought useful to Wulfmaer in his new home. Ælfwyn had sent a package of household tools and a selection of foods she knew that Wulfmaer was most fond of. Lodin had sent a similarly utilitarian package of axes and wood working tools. They had also sent two young women from the village to serve Wulfmaer in tending his household. Heiu and Cwenburg were a summer older than Cyneburg and cousins. Ælfwyn had decided that Cyneburg should travel with them and visit her brother, staying until the end of the winter. The three girls would provide companionship for Frythegith and Cyneberg's cousins would provide some balance in Wulfmaer's largely male household.

The riders had enjoyed the short distance to the hut in the forest. They had seen little game on their ride but the purpose was to meet away from the village and discuss the marriage contract. There were only two people in the discussion, Wulfmaer and Hunbeorht. By tradition, the discussion would have been between the two fathers with a scribe to record the details of the discussion. Under normal circumstances, the betrothal set the basis of the agreement and the future bride and groom were not essential attendees, rather they would not be encouraged to attend. The assumption of agreement would already be there, with the final agreement setting the place of the marriage and the terms of the dowry. For this meeting, Wulfmaer's father was dead and Frythegith's was unable to travel to Wulfmaer. In custom, Wulfmaer stood in the place of his father and Hunbeorht stood in the place of the sick Daegbeorht. That was not unheard of under the circumstances, but what was unusual was that Frythegith was present and the negotiators were supported by Cyneberg and two who shared no blood with either party.

Hunbeorht had brought with him a document that had been drawn under the influence of his mother. He was uncomfortable with this but he had a clear duty to represent the interests of his sister and of his family.

The hut was gloomy but a fire was soon established in the hearth and the party divided onto the two low benches on either side of the hearth. Once this had been home to a family, farming the land around it, but now it was a hunting lodge and a place where travellers could rest on their journey.

"Before we begin, would you be happy to marry me," asked Wulfmaer, facing Frythegith across the hearth. "I will not proceed to the agreement until I know what is your heart. Our families may have expectations, but only you and I will draw our lives on from this day. I now have power and position, but you would marry me and not what I have become."

Frythegith glanced towards her brother and then to Wulfmaer. "My Lord, you are a noble man and I enjoy your company. Any woman would be fortunate to serve as your wife. Our families betrothed us long ago, but I would know that you wanted me as your wife."

"Gentle Lady I would with all my heart take you to be my wife. If we are agreed that we both desire to be married, I will discuss the terms of agreement with your brother."

"Hunbeorht, as your sister wants to marry me as much as I want to marry her, a formal agreement is almost unnecessary. The draft you brought follows the betrothal, when everything today is very different from that time. Depenham is no longer my inheritance, but is subject to my earldom. In my Hall we are a band of warriors, young, without blood ties. If Frythegith is content, we will marry in two days from now, with you representing your father and your family. Cyneberg will represent my mother and our family. I expect no dowry to accompany Frythegith. What you offer on behalf of your family will be for her own benefit.   When the Winter ends, your family will come here to feast with us. If your father is still unwell, we will travel to him, but I will arrange the feast."

Hunbeorht was lost for words. This was not a marriage agreement, but a declaration by Wulfmaer, very different from the complicated agreement his mother Aebbe had expected Wulfmaer to accept without question. He knew that he should demand the agreement draft he had brought be accepted, but his sister was obviously happy with everything that Wulfmaer had said and done. More important was the power of an earl to make decisions and expect them to be loyally carried out.

When the betrothal had been agreed, his father was of an equal rank with Wulfmaer's father, they had served the King together as comrades. When Aebbe objected more strongly with each year to the betrothal, it was because she expected to achieve a better match for her daughter and to benefit from that herself. That she now expected to dictate the marriage terms was unwarranted. The most important consideration was that he adored his sister and she could bend him to her will. That she was happy to marry under any terms Wulfmaer decided, and with Aebbe a long way away, Hunbeorht felt that he could give way completely. He also recognised that Wulfmaer and his comrades were loyal friends, but dangerous enemies.

Then the final salve to his conscience was that he had seen

what Wulfmaer was building from his new position. He liked the thought of young people building afresh without the constraints of overbearing relatives and he wanted to be part of this new way.

Suddenly everyone relaxed from a tension they had not been aware of until it began to ease. Wulfmaer embraced Hunbeorht and then his bride to be. Einarr, Gudhrun and Cyneberg had sat quietly as the negotiations unfolded. Now they added their joyous congratulations. For Einarr and Gudhrun there was a further excuse to delay their departure. Intending to leave a few days after Wifirth had departed, they had remained to give Wulfmaer any support he might need in reaching or rejecting the marriage agreement. Now they would remain for the wedding, before taking the first good day to set out for the fortress.

Wulfmaer sent out a patrol of six warriors to serve as messengers. First they would ride to the fortress with a message to Ivar from Einarr, and then ride or sail on to Depenham with a message from Wulfmaer to his mother, before returning to Wulfmaer's Hall. Ælfwyn would then send a messenger on to Daegbeorht with details of the marriage agreement, the early wedding and the plans to feast after the end of Winter in celebration of the union. Aebbe could give way to anger but, by the time that the messenger arrived, Wulfmaer and Frythegith would already be man and wife. Anger from a distance would present no difficulties, save perhaps for the unfortunate Daegbeorht who might well become the focus of his wife's wrath.

Fifty Four

The wintry sun shone through the two high windows in the end wall of the stone building that served as church. The stone building had been constructed on the site of a Roman temple by St Felix, becoming his Minster, the first on the main island. Long since the Bishops, who had followed St Felix, had moved inland, away from the coast, away from the threat of raiders from the sea. The simple rectangular building was built from stone, taken from the Roman temple. Carved blocks with images of the Roman gods were used without regard in the outer face of the walls. On the roof were Roman tiles in place of the thatch that was a common roofing to the Saxons. The single entrance was a low doorway with a thick oak door, studded and banded in iron.

The wedding party had reached the church by crossing the broad moat on a wooden bridge that was lowered onto the wooden causeway. From this entrance the two visible walls showed no openings, other than the low doorway. In every respect, the church resembled a fort more than any Christian meeting place. The priest waited at the doorway to lead the party into his church, his worn, frayed, black robes brushing the ground.

Wulfmaer and Cyneberg followed the priest into the church. The two high, small windows in the South wall provided more light than was reasonable, illuminating the plain plastered walls that had been washed white, before an untutored artist had painted bright murals depicting scenes from the bible, or from his imagination. The single high walled room and vaulted roof was bare of furniture except for the simple low dark wood table, without carving, decorated only by two bronze candle holders, a plain bronze cross and some simple silver cups.

Einarr and Gudhrun had never before stood in a Christian

Church. They had heard tales of the raids on the great Christian buildings to the North where gold encrusted the buildings and fittings, that everywhere was evidence of great wealth, collected by the priests. This building was a disappointment. The meagre collection of metal articles on the simple, almost crude, wooden table displayed no idea of wealth.

Hunbeorht had followed in, escorting Frythegith, Einarr and Gudhrun behind them, and then the main party following. All of his new village had been welcomed by Wulfmaer as guests, but few had attended him. There were still the tasks of the day to be completed and the feast prepared for the returning wedding party. In all, twenty warriors and villagers accompanied six members of the principle wedding party. The church was not a great building, but it swallowed the party. They grouped before the wooden table and the priest, who had stopped and turned to face Wulfmaer. It seemed colder inside the church than it had been outside, and that a raw day. The only fire was provided by the two large candles at each end of the table. The light shone down on the wedding party from the two windows high in the wall and dust danced in the shafts of light. The rough stone flags stretched out to the plain plastered walls, the wedding party was a small dark island on a sea of stone.

The priest called forward Wulfmaer and Cyneberg. He had seen them out riding, but this was the first time that he had stood close to them. He looked around for someone else. Then Cyneberg stepped forward as Wulfmaer's supporter. The priest sniffed loudly at the thought of this noble lord being supported by a young girl. Cyneberg introduced her brother and testified to his honour, faith and chastity.

The priest then looked to his right and called forward Hunbeorht and Frythegith. Here he had nothing to question, Hunbeorht, evidently a high-born warrior, as supporter of the bride. Hunbeorht then introduced his sister and testified to her humility, faith and chastity. To this point, Einarr and Gudhrun could follow the ceremony, conducted in the local Saxon dialect, but the priest then broke into a strange and unfamiliar language.

Even the Saxons seemed uncertain, although it became clear that they were following a familiar ceremony even if they did not understand all of the words mumbled by the priest. Evidently there were prayers to the gods that the congregation were expected to agree with.

The priest then indicated to the two supporters to convey the hands of the young couple together. At that the priest wrapped a brightly decorated cloth around the joined right hands of the couple. This looked much like the wrapping of hands that Einarr and Gudhrun were familiar with. The priest then began to mumble again in his strange language and his monologue seemed to continue forever, certainly many more words than accompanied the Norse wrapping of hands. There was a shuffling of feet amongst the congregation as the wedding party stamped the cold from their legs.

Eventually, the priest fell silent and began to waive his hand across his chest as he looked at the couple, then to his right and left, to the congregation behind them. This done he addressed those present in Saxon, declaring the couple joined as man and wife, witnessed by those present. Suddenly the ceremony was complete and the newly married couple led the way to the door, followed by the priest, who was chanting something unintelligible and carrying the bronze cross, followed by the now thoroughly frozen congregation.

It was a relief to cross the bridge and causeway to where grooms held the horses. Einarr and Gudhrun felt the ceremony was less than they had expected. Wulfmaer and Frythegith were absorbed in each other, probably the only people present unaware of the bitter cold, the fitful wind sweeping up spirals of snow that danced away across the open ground. At least they could all now look forward to a short ride back to the village and the welcoming hearth at Wulfmaer's Hall.

As the wedding party entered the Hall and mingled with those who had remained behind in the village, their strangely subdued mood lifted immediately. There was laughter and singing, beer and food being passed around, the warmth of the hearth taking the intensity of the smith's forge after the chill outside. Villagers pressed to the bride and groom to wish them wealth and happiness. Minstrels entertained. A mountain of food rapidly shrank to nothing and the storytellers entertained the revelers with tales of daring and of love, of journeys to far lands and courage in battle.

The guests fell asleep where they sat, a few still awake talked quietly and they in turn began to slumber. No one noticed Wulfmaer and Frythegith slip away to spend their first hours alone together. Gudhrun and Einarr slumped together at the table. Hunbeorht was also fast asleep, slumped onto the table. Only Cyneberg was still awake, looking fondly at Frythegith's sleeping brother, her head propped on her left hand, her eyes struggling to remain open. The bodies sprawled about the smoky dim-lit Hall resembled the aftermath of a battle. In but a few hours they would be awake, stumbling through their chores, a few much regretting the quantities of beer they had consumed.

Fifty Five

Einarr and Gudhrun crested the ridge to the North East of Wulfmaer's Hall. They could no longer delay their return to the fortress and, with reluctance, they had loaded their four horses, said farewell to their friends and ridden out, heading towards the fort. With good fortune, they might complete their journey in a day, but that would require them to ride the final distance at night. If the weather turned yet again, they would have to find shelter and continue on the following day.

So far the prospects looked grand. The wide sky was a pale blue and the sun was rising from the East, chasing away the remaining shadows of the dusky twilight that preceded the dawn. In the short days of Winter, twilight could stretch at the dawn and again as the sun set. There was snow on the ground, but of little depth, the horses finding good footing as they stepped smartly on their way. The wind was strengthening and had settled firmly from the North East, the sun making little headway in raising the temperature.

Gudhrun rode alongside Einarr, but they exchanged few words in an easy companionable silence. Both glanced towards the East as the first ribbons of clouds streaked the blue sky, still white and of little substance, but clouds such as these were oft times the outriders of dense low cloud that carried great quantities of snow. They knew that it would soon be time to rest their mounts. They decided to put off the time for rest, dismounting and leading their horses. This provided little relief for their packhorses, save that the pace slowed.

After but a brief period of leading their horses, the cloud had thickened to produce the first snow and the wind began to strengthen, settling more firmly into an Easterly. As the cloud thinned and then built up again, the conditions were still acceptable but growing colder. Einarr knew that they must look for shelter unless the conditions improved. He was following a well-trodden track that Wulfmaer had recommended as a shorter route to the fortress. Having slowly risen to the crest of the ridge beyond Wulfmaer's Hall, the track had been descending for some distance as it snaked its way still to the North East into the teeth of the ever-stronger wind. The sun, when it broke through the clouds, was now close to its height and the descent had begun into darkness.

Einarr and Gudhrun had remounted and ridden steadily on towards the great forest that stretched ahead of them, reaching almost to the fortress. The bare trees looked stark against the darkened sky as they reached into the forest. Even without their leaves, the trees stood close enough to begin providing some relief from the wind and snow showers. The riders would soon be forced to halt and find what shelter they could. With the clouds growing heavier and darker, the light was fading early and there would be no help from moon and stars. It would become difficult to distinguish the track as the snow grew deeper and the light failed.

They were beginning to regret setting out as they had with no escort in company. They were on a strange track with no sure knowledge of any village or shelter ahead. Local knowledge would have been a great assistance.

Gudhrun was first to see the building ahead of them, slightly to the left of the track. She pointed it out to Einarr and urged her pair of horses forward. The horses seemed to understand that shelter was near to hand and they stepped out almost at the trot after the steady plodding with which they had been moving.

The building was a long low structure with a thick straw roof hanging out and down. As they closed in on the building it was larger than they first thought, but dark and forbidding. There was no sign of any light, not even the scent of wood smoke. Both checked their swords to make sure that they could quickly draw them. It paid to be cautious in this strange place. Einarr dismounted to force open the gate in the wattle fence. Almost equal to his height and twice that in width, it was held by the snow. He handed his reigns to Gudhrun and tried again. The gate gave sufficient for him to ease through, kick the snow away from behind the gate, forcing it wide enough for Gudhrun to ride through with their horses.

Einarr quickly decided to close the gate behind them. For a moment he considered leaving it open to provide an easy exit if the building offered danger in place of shelter. The thought passed briefly, the attraction of shelter greater and the confidence that he and Gudhrun could defeat any stronger threat than this building appeared to offer.

Gudhrun had already reached the building, holding their horses. Einarr caught up with her, seeing in the fast fading light that the building had a large door on the South-facing wall. There was only a thin covering of snow on the ground, the building sheltering that wall from the strong wind that was blowing snow in sheets and clouds. The door opened easily to reveal a gloomy interior. There was no light and no fire inside, but the temperature was already noticeably warmer than outside the door and much warmer than in the chill wind.

Einarr went to his horse and took his firebox and brand from the saddlebag. In the shelter of the doorway, he blew into the firebox, to be rewarded by a glow from which he managed to light the brand. The brand could not reach far into the long low building, but he found an iron stand hammered into the earth floor, a rush light fixed in its holder. The rush light spluttered into life as he held his brand to it.

He could now see down the building, perhaps to half its length. Facing the door were stalls for horses, or farm animals, but they were empty and had been cleaned since their previous use, whenever that had been.

"Gudhrun, bring in the horses and put them in the stalls," he called towards the doorway where she was standing, holding the horses.

She walked the horses inside the building and led them to the stalls, as Einarr walked down the building, still carrying the lighted brand, towards a wall of wattle that had been invisible in the background gloom from the doorway. To reach the wattle screen, Einarr had walked down the broad corridor that had the South wall to his left and the stalls to his right. A door of wattle was hinged from the wattle partition and swung inwards with ease. He could now smell sweet hay and straw that indicated the store had been restocked at the last harvest. Ahead of him was a space equal to the first space of the stalls, and he found two small fat lamps on the wall to his left. These he lit, their dim glow providing only sufficient light to make out the margins of the space to the wooden frame that held back the hay and straw. The wall to his left was pierced as the first space had been, the holes covered by wooden shutters.

At the end of this second space, was a second wattle partition. He had left open the first wattle door and he could hear that Gudhrun had closed the wide outer door, the noise of the storm outside no more than a faint undulating howl. He could hear her taking the packs off the horses, securing the stalls and talking quietly to the animals as she found their feedbags. With those comfortingly familiar sounds to his back, Einarr tried to open the wattle door ahead of him, to find that it opened towards him.

A third and final space opened before him. By the light of the brand he carried, he could make out an open space with a hearth at its centre, rough benches facing the hearth from both sides, simple wooden store cupboards along the wall to his right, and then bunks continuing to the end wall, following it round and then continuing back along the wall to his left, ending halfway towards the hearth. Heavy wooden shutters covered openings in the South wall to his left.

There were two more iron stands, holding rush lights and Einarr lit them from his brand, which was almost burned down. The hearth was a long trench, cleaned of ash from the fires that must have burned in it before. He saw a stack of logs mounded against the wall before the start of the bunks. There must be more logs stacked somewhere outside, but here was sufficient to make a welcoming fire and keep it burning through the night and into the next day.

Einarr stacked logs and kindling in the hearth and fired them with his dying brand. As the flame caught, the fire began to produce a strengthening light to augment the spluttering rush lights. As he worked, he had not heard Gudhrun come towards the hearth. She put down their saddlebags on one of the benches and came to stand beside Einarr. The heat thrown out by the fire hit them like a solid wall and they realized how cold they were.

When they rode out from Wulfmaer's Hall, they had been clothed for a long hard ride through uncertain territory. They had declined Wulfmaer's offer to send an escort with them, confident any threat that they might not be able to overcome could be out ridden. Over their leather trousers, they wore wolf fur leggings, below their chain mail coats they wore the wool padded coats and kirtles that they rarely wore for battle. Above the mail coats, they wore long wolf fur jerkin's, covered by thick riding cloaks, the generous hoods sheltering their faces from the cold and their swords strapped across their backs outside the cloaks. Even then the chill wind and snow had bitten deeply into them and they had been fortunate to come across this building before their horses failed, or they themselves gave in to the cold.

By now the combination of rush lights and the hearty fire had brightened the building and revealed all of its detail. It was a strange place, too large to be a farmstead, too small to be a Hall, perhaps a hunting lodge. There was no indication of recent occupation, but someone had cleaned the building and restocked the supply of fodder and the pile of logs for the hearth. Gudhrun had opened all of the rough cupboards and found only pots, a selection of beakers and a set of household tools. There was no food and nothing to drink. It was not important that there was no food or drink because they had their own supplies of food, beer and water that they had carried with them.

The storm was but a dull roar now. As a strong wind tore

over the roof's ridge, smoke from the fire was sucked out of the vent in the roof. It was everything, and more, that they needed to wait out the storm. They hung their cloaks over one bench and helped each other out of their mail coats and the padded undercoats which had to be drawn off over their heads. This clothing was soon steaming.

Gudhrun had returned to the far end of the building and brought back the packs that their remounts had carried. These packs contained food and clothing, a reserve should they be forced to shelter for several days. While Einarr added more logs to the fire, she walked along the line of bunks, looking behind the woollen blankets that hung across their fronts. The bunks were broad wooden platforms with a wattle partition at each end. With one exception, they were all clean and empty, just the bare planks. The last bunk, on the South wall nearest the hearth had a bed of moss and herbs, covered by sheep skins, but showing no sign of use since it had been cleaned.

As she came back past the packs, she pulled out two rough cloths and joined Einarr beside the hearth, handing him a cloth.

"Come my love, we must dry ourselves," invited Gudhrun, stripping off her soft leather shirt.

Einarr removed his shirt and they began to dry each other in the heat from the hearth, starting with their hair and faces. The rough cloth soaked up the moisture from snow and ice that had penetrated their outside clothes and its rough surface helped the blood circulate. Accustomed to snow and ice, they would have given priority to rubbing life back into frozen noses, but they had become used to the milder weather in these lands and had been surprised by the intense cold that had affected them on the last steps to shelter. As feeling returned to their faces and shoulders the heat from the fire began to help the restoration of bodily warmth. They had done this many times before, it was a natural part of the mutual care for two paired warriors, but they were overwhelmed by feelings they had never shared before. Lips

406

sought out lips, bodies pressed together with an urgency, in an embrace that was different from that of two warriors. They stripped each other of their remaining clothing and Einarr pulled Gudhrun down onto the sheepskins laid before the fire. Their bodies responded to each other without any deliberate thoughts. Sensation took them completely into a new realm. For Einarr there was some familiarity from the attentions of his slave girl Agata, but he had never experienced this depth of feeling. Gudhrun was not a comrade, not a woman, but a part of him and they were driven by forces of attraction that were more powerful than anything they understood.

Eventually the frenzy was exhausted but they had no sense of time or place. Their bodies lay together before the fire as did their souls. They had always enjoyed a special bond but now they had a full understanding of each other. They lay within a glow, a single being. They understood the past and the future. They lay together as the fire subsided. It mirrored them, the fierce flames exhausted, but still a hot core that would last beyond the start of the new day.

Gudhrun got to her feet and, holding Einarr's hand, led him the few paces to the bunk. She had a tenderness that neither had known before. They climbed into the bunk, the sheepskins soft, softened further by the herbs and grasses beneath the skins. They covered themselves with the sheepskins that Gudhrun had brought from before the fire. They lay in each other's arms in a gentle warmth, sleep stealthily overtaking them.

Gudhrun was first to wake. The building was once more gloomy. The fire was but a layer of embers and the rush lights had burnt themselves out. That much she could see by holding back a corner of the blanket that covered the front of the bunk. She gently released herself from Einarr's arms and slipped out of the bunk. The air was cold and she threw her now dry riding cloak around her shoulders. She was hungry, but first she placed more logs on the embers in the hearth and the fire began to come once more to life. The next step for Gudhrun would be to dig into their rations for something to eat and drink. She made two steps towards the packs and saddlebags, but something was pulling her in the other direction. Next she knew, she was standing beside the bunk, dropping her cloak to the floor and softly climbing back into Einarr's arms. As he began to wake, the frenzy again took them to another place. They rode the whirlwind, they lost all sense of time once more.

The passion subsided and they once more lay tenderly in each other's arms. Lips brushed faces, hands moved in slow caress. Like this they lay together oblivious of the passing time. With some reluctance, both rose and dressed, still not a word spoken, not a word required. There were tasks to attend, but little enthusiasm for them to part, even within the room.

There were some narrow shafts of light around the window spaces, some light from the fire, which Einarr again stirred into life. Together they walked along the corridor to tend the horses, new fodder, oats, and water. Then they realized that they needed to find more water. What remained in the water skins failed to completely fill the buckets for the horses, what was poured in rapidly disappeared.

Back at the fire, Einarr assembled the iron rods that supported two large metal pots above the fire. He then went to the distant end of the building and swung open the large door, through which they had entered the building the day before, intending to collect snow to melt in the pots. The brightness was startling. There was still dense cloud, but the newly fallen snow reflected every shaft of light that struggled through the cloud. Looking about him, he saw an extension of the roof at the far end of the building from where he stood. It had gone unnoticed in the failing light when they had arrived. There was very little snow on ground sheltered by the mass of the building and he quickly walked down the South-facing wall. The extended roof reached down to the height of his shoulder and he could see that it continued away as an addition to the building, its Southern face open to the sun on a clear day. Under this roof there was a large stack of logs, ready for the fire, and a well.

The well had a low wall around it and two leather buckets

were placed beside it, one being attached to a rope. He dropped the roped bucket over the wall, letting the rope run freely, to be rewarded by a distant splash. So the well had water without a crust of ice! This was a good piece of luck, he could carry water to the horses and there would be no need to melt snow. The storm seemed to have passed them but, with an ample supply of fodder and water for the horses, they could rest for a few days to make sure that the weather would hold for the final part of their journey back to the fortress. Einarr further comforted himself that the rest would be welcome for the horses and they would be able to complete the journey without becoming exhausted. Then there was the practicality of riding through deep fresh snow. A quick glance round the corner of the building revealed deep drifts and the bank of snow on the North Eastern side of the building reached almost to the roof's ridge.

There was a further consideration. Einarr was accustomed to making good decisions quickly, but he was struggling to decide how to relate to Gudhrun. Their old relationship could not be restored. They now shared new feelings and a new bond.

He was unsure of the reception he might receive from Ivar. It would be easy and natural for him to wrap hands with Gudhrun and they might be able to continue as a pair of warriors, but Ivar had always held deep reservations about his pairing with Gudhrun. What he did not understand was why. He was unsure that Ivar knew, but then his father was able to conceal his thoughts from others, so what was mystery to Einarr might not be mystery to Ivar.

Einarr had to admit to himself that he had no thoughts of a new relationship with Gudhrun before they took shelter from the storm. He had been frightened by the intensity they had felt and he was never frightened of anything. He felt the same confusion he had first felt as they made landfall, when Gudhrun had flooded his thoughts. He had known her as a sister, he had depended on her as a warrior, but now she was his world, yet he felt her somehow slipping away. For all of his life he had trained to become a warrior, then to become a stronger warrior, mirroring his father and his uncles. Gudhrun had fitted seamlessly into those expectations. She was the strongest, finest warrior that he could team with. They had learned to fight as one, each instinctively knowing what was needed by the other in a fight. Each knew that the other was entirely dependable, invincible. They were connected, that each knew exactly where the other was and what the next move would be.

Einarr was struggling to fit the past to the present. He hoped that what had been was now strengthened, better, not changed. Then in his heart he knew that much had changed. He was beginning to feel protective of Gudhrun, when before he knew that she needed no protection, she was as much his shield as he was her shield.

He tried to push the confusion and questions to the back of his mind as he brought water for the horses. The simple task failed to block the thoughts, rather it provided more space for them to develop and twist in his mind. He brought fodder and bedding for the animals. He gave them a short feed of oats. Still his mind churned. Then Gudhrun called to him and his mind cleared. He brought more water, this time for their use. As he opened the second wattle door, he saw her and warm feelings wrapped him in a gentle embrace.

While Einarr had been tending the horses and wrestling with his thoughts, Gudhrun had built the fire and laid out the contents of their packs and saddlebags. When Einarr entered the room, she was seated on a bench, carefully checking and oiling their mail coats. This was not a housewife mending clothing, but a warrior attending to the equipment on which their lives would depend. Einarr found this deeply comforting. It was a face of his old Gudhrun.

As he approached she made their greeting, "For ever my love",

and he responded, "My love for ever".

This time, the words carried greater meaning, a different meaning, a deeper meaning, followed by an embrace that was not their long familiar warrior's embrace, but two lovers meeting after a long separation. The embrace seemed to last for ever and was reluctantly broken. Gudhrun took one of the water buckets and poured water into both of the pots that now hung over the fire. Into one of the pots, she threw pieces of dried meat and measures of oats to produce a hot filling meal.

When the meat-laced porridge was ready, Gudhrun served it up in two shallow grey metal bowls. They sat together eating with crude wooden spoons. They had no wine or beer, but took boiled water from the second pot in pottery beakers. They had shared a meal together many times, just the two of them, but this meal was different, special, domestic. Not just a time to replenish energy, but companionable sharing of food in a home. It was as though they had long been man and wife in quiet domestic comfort. Einarr could have been a simple farmer home from the fields to his wife who had prepared, ready to welcome and feed him.

After a relaxed meal together, they shared the tasks of checking their mail and weapons. Once again they were back in familiar territory. Their mail coats were checked first, completing the work Gudhrun had begun earlier, and oiled with clarified grease. Dry sand was mixed with vinegar, then applied to their sword blades, polishing them to perfection. The same process was applied to their dirks. The shining oiled blades were then returned to the leather sheaths, their newly sharpened edges protected from anything that might dull them. Their two spears were checked and then the shields, their helmets and minor equipment. All of this work flowed automatically. Here, nothing had changed. They were still a warrior pair, filling time by caring for the equipment that would care for them. Their swords and dirks would be kept close to hand, even inside the relative safety of the building, but all of their other equipment, the saddles, bridles and related equipment, was carefully hung up by the line of cupboards, out of harms way but ready for immediate use.

Their daily chores attended, they sat before the hearth, enjoying the blast of heat that reached out to them. They talked of much and of nothing as they held hands and looked deep into each other's eyes. As they sat together, they felt the passion rising once more. They stood, embraced and kissed before moving the short distance to their bunk. Again they felt the intensity of feeling, becoming one.

Fifty Six

Four days passed swiftly since their arrival at the lodge. The wind had died to nothing, the snow had stopped falling, the clouds were swept from the sky. It was a dry cold, the snow crisp, the sun shedding some warmth across the brilliant, blinding, white landscape. Einarr and Gudhrun reluctantly agreed to break the enchantment of their refuge, saddle and load their horses, ready for the journey to the fortress. They made more porridge, eating it quietly together, neither wishing to break the enveloping silence of their meal. Together, they put their food, clothing and remaining possessions back into packs and saddlebags. Einarr quenched the fire in the hearth. They checked all of the shutters, and led their horses out of the building. Einarr made certain that the door and the gate in the fence were secured. They made their way out towards where they remembered the track had been. They and their mounts soon accustomed their eyes to the brightness that had been blinding after the darkness of the building. They must guess where the track cut through the forest. There was little sign that anything had moved since the end of the storm. Here and there were small tracks left by birds and the smaller creatures of the forest but, for the main, the white expanse was un-spoilt.

The sun reached as high as it was able, and the riders were grateful to have found the herres road that led down to the old Roman road. They knew that they would reach the fortress well before the light failed. Although the cold bit into them, the clear sky and the sun made this a more hopeful journey than the day they found the lodge. They could now ride side by side after a morning of one leading the other, at each brief halt, changing places and riding in silence. The horses were holding well and their last halt would be made as they joined the Roman road.

At this halt, they ate some of the remaining cheese and

bread, the meat already eaten before they restarted their journey. The horses foraged in the snow as though they knew stables and food were but a few steps further. The snow was not deep on the Roman road, but there were no tracks to spoil its purity. Einarr checked each horse and, satisfied that all were ready for the final short journey along the Roman road, he called Gudhrun to mount.

Gudhrun rode close alongside Einarr and they conversed as they rode. There was no need to force the pace and they enjoyed the steady progress. Einarr was surprised that no patrol had used the road since the snow storms but, with a network of small wooden forts in a line towards the coast, there was little need to send horsemen out, this being the first calm day without snow since Einarr had left Wulfmaer's Hall with Gudhrun. Behind them was a trail of hoof prints as the four horses had spread out and come together before spreading out once more.

Fifty Seven

When the fortress came into sight, the journey was almost complete. They could see tracks across the bridge, leading inland along the broad straight road. There were sentries on top of the walls and the two towers that flanked the main gates. As they rode across the bridge, the main gates swung open for them to enter. Inside the mighty walls, the roads between buildings had been swept clear of snow. Wood smoke rose from many of the buildings. It was a now familiar and comforting sight for the travellers.

Six days on a journey that should have been no more than two, a hoped for one day's ride, made the arrival, if not a relief, at least a grateful satisfaction. Yet it was uncertainty for Einarr and Gudhrun. They had discussed the future as they made the final stage along the Roman road. They agreed that they would wrap hands and set up their own household, but that required a discussion first with Ivar. Then there was a matter of where they would live out the winter. It was unlikely that they would find a building of any size to themselves.

Inside the fortress, they separated, Gudhrun to go to the Hall she shared with the Lady Gytha, Einarr to his father's Hall. Einarr had to report to his father on the progress that Wulfmaer was making with his new holdings, but he also had to tell him that he wanted to set up a household with Gudhrun. As he approached the Hall, Ivar already knew of his arrival.

Ivar welcomed his son back. He made no mention of the delays to the return. He had always been proud of Einarr's development as a young warrior, but the recent months had given him great confidence in the boy who was now a man, yet still young. He listened intently to Einarr's report on what he had seen at Wulfmaer's Hall and of Wulfmaer's marriage. He had been impressed by the young Saxon and seen his advancement as a great benefit to his own plans. He was pleased by what Einarr reported, confirming his own assessment of how Wulfmaer would expand into his new duties.

Although it was not the most populous portion of Edmund's kingdom, Ivar now had control and influence over almost a third of the realm. This had enabled him to spread his warriors without great risk. During the short days of winter they enjoyed better accommodation and avoided the friction that would have developed had they been confined to the fortress and their boats. As important was the space to set up workshops and training facilities to retain the edge that every warrior would need in the coming campaign. Wulfmaer and his family had been an important part of the good fortune.

When Einarr had finished his report, he then told his father of the journey back to the fortress and of his changed relationship with Gudhrun. As he spoke, Ivar's expression remained unchanged. There was no indication of disapproval.

"Einarr, you have always known that I have never seen Gudhrun as a wife to you, but you have never asked why. Have you never wondered why I did not approve of that possibility, but been content that you were paired warriors?"

"Faddi, I never asked of your disapproval because, before, I never thought of Gudhrun as my wife. I was happy that you agreed to us pairing as warriors."

"My son, I wanted you to grow to become a great leader, to continue my plans, and to make your own plans. I noticed long ago that you had an unusual connection to Gudhrun and she to you. I could not have chosen a better warrior for you to pair with. Her father is my oldest and closest friend. I could hope for nothing better than that our friendship be strengthened by the marriage of our children. What I saw in the bones was a great sadness in any future between the two of you. Any father would hope to protect his son, but you have a life to lead, be it short or

416

long. You have proven yourself this year as a warrior and as a leader, beyond all as a man, with the right to make his own choices. If your wish is to take Gudhrun as your wife, and she to take you as her mate, I wish you well and embrace her as daughter. That I will tell also to Peder. I know that he will be as pleased as I that our friendship now grows through the joining of our children"

Einarr was surprised by Ivar's response, but he was troubled by the prediction. Ivar and Peder were known as seers. He now saw his father's view of Gudhrun differently. He understood the reasons for Ivar's disapproval, not as disapproval of Gudhrun, but of what the prediction threatened. He shrugged his shoulders at fate. Now was not the time to question his relationship with Gudhrun. He knew that each day was a good day to die. Fate was no guarantor of the span of life. No prediction was ever completely assured. He would set that prediction aside, he would never share knowledge of it with Gudhrun, but set out to create his own fate with her at his side.

Ivar seemed equally determined to treat a situation that was, setting aside any doubts or fears. He could not change what fate might decree, but he could live each day for itself, to hope for the best future, to be prepared should the future not favour him and his kin. Einarr could expect now that Peder would share Ivar's acceptance, to wish well for his daughter and for his new son. He would use his dark skills to change the prediction. Gudhrun was his only child, a child he held very dear.

Having crested the summit of the meeting to receive Ivar's acceptance and blessing, Einarr descended to the mundane, as they discussed how he would form his own household. Ivar decided on a simple solution.

The Lady Gytha had been allocated a Hall for her household and the only available building had been far larger than she required. When that accommodation had been agreed, Gudhrun had been companion to ensure that the Saxon lady was protected and assisted during her stay. As with many of the Halls, the building was divided into several parts by simple partitions of hide or wattle, with the hearth in the middle part, a communal area, often fitted with bunks along one or both long walls. The parts at opposite ends of the long building provided space of an earl and his family and a space for private meetings. What could be easier than to allocate one part to Einarr and Gudhrun, one part to the Lady Gytha, the centre serving those of their households and for feasting.

Unbeknown to Einarr, his discussions with his father were mirrored by the meeting between Gudhrun and the Lady Gytha. Since they first met, Gytha and Gudhrun had become like sisters, enjoying each other's company and sharing secrets, fears, and joys. On parting from Einarr, for him to meet his father, Gudhrun had made straight for the Hall allocated to the Lady Gytha. They met with the emotion of sisters parted and reunited. Gytha was eager to learn of Gudhrun's travels, of Wulfmaer's progress, of the people they had met. As Einarr had begun his meeting with a report on what he had seen of Wulfmaer's Hall, Gudhrun began by describing their journey to Wulfmaer, of meeting Wifirth when they broke their journey, of reaching Wulfmaer's Hall.

Gytha listened with real interest, pleased of news beyond the fortress, which had become dull since Gudhrun had left and the weather confined most of its population within its walls. Gytha was specially interested in Gudhrun's description of how Wulfmaer was building his base and holdings. She had mixed feelings.

She still held obligations to her cousin the King, but she owed much to Wulfmaer for his support during their captivity. She understood that her cousin might in time see Wulfmaer as a threat and her divided loyalties would force her perhaps to choose sides. Then she had come to value her friendship with Gudhrun and Einarr. They had shared adventure. She had travelled to Depenham several times since she had chosen to live in the fortress. She had seen how Saxons and Norse had worked together to expand the village and erect defences that were formidable, to protect what was becoming a busy trading centre.

She could see that the time when she might have to choose sides was rapidly approaching, however much she hoped to also honour her family commitments to a cousin and duty to his kingship.

When Gudhrun reached the part of her story when Frythegith and her brother had arrived to discuss her betrothal to Wulfmaer, Gytha was taken completely by surprise. She had been aware that a messenger had stopped briefly at the fortress on his way to Depenham, but he had met with Ivar, the content of his message retained by Ivar, other than the news that Einarr and Gudhrun were delaying their return.

Gytha had been unaware that Wulfmaer was betrothed as a boy to the daughter of his parent's friends. It was not unusual for friendships to be marked in that way, but it was something that Wulfmaer had never mentioned in the conversations during their captivity. Gytha was even more surprised that Wulfmaer and Frythegith had married so quickly and in the absence of their families. A marriage between families of rank was an occasion of importance. A feasting might last for several days as the two families came to known each other better and to celebrate a union, which was both a happy family occasion, but also marked an important union between families of land and position. The importance of the new ties between families of rank was almost always marked by the attendance of the King.

Gytha was happy for Wulfmaer, although she had considered him as a potential husband for herself. Since Wulfmaer's elevation, he had become a more acceptable match and Gytha suspected that King Edmund might consider encouraging a marriage of his cousin to the new earl, helping to tie Wulfmaer more closely to the King. That was also reason for concern. Gytha was aware that Edmund's self-doubt might give way to resentment. His permission for Wulfmaer's marriage was not required because, by custom, the betrothal had been approved by his predecessor. Even so, he might resent that the marriage had excluded family and the opportunity for the King to attend as an honoured guest. He might become suspicious of Wulfmaer's intentions. Ceolwulf would certainly be suspicious that this indicated a great ambition and a threat to his King. He was already making attacks on other earls with far less to justify suspicion of their loyalties to the King.

Where news of Wulfmaer's marriage had given Gytha joy and fears, news of the new relationship between Gudhrun and Einarr gave only joy. Gytha knew nothing of Ivar's past discouragement of the union and she still did not completely understand all of the differences in Norse culture. She did know how Gudhrun and Einarr were in each other's presence and had never understood how their bond as warriors was not also a bond between man and woman. This was news that excited her and filled her with joy for a young woman she regarded as a sister. She hugged Gudhrun and insisted that she organize a feast for them. She also suggested they share her hall, unless they had already made other arrangements.

Fifty Eight

Gytha had set to, losing no time in organizing a feast for Einarr and Gudhrun, enlisting the help of Ulrika Ragnarsdottir. It was agreed that Einarr and Gudhrun would wrap hands before the feasting started. It seemed a logical arrangement to start the feast in this way and to start the sharing of the Hall.

Gudhrun had been delighted by the suggestion that gave a neighbour she and Einarr liked well. In the few short months they had known Gytha and Wulfmaer, they had become as siblings through their shared adventures as young people of similar ages. What could be better than to share the Hall. Beyond the feast, they had the Festival of Light to look forward to, speeding the nights towards the rebirth of Spring and Summer.

The only regret was that Wulfmaer and Frythegith might be unable to attend. Then Ulrika made such an obvious suggestion that Gytha was surprised that it had not occurred to her at the beginning. Wulfmaer's mother could travel to the fortress with ease, because ships were regularly travelling between fort and village. The return voyage to the fortress was often made with little aboard so that it would be unnecessary to send a ship specially. Within the fortress there was space for guests. The journey for Wulfmaer and Frythegith would be more taxing because they would have no alternative to riding but, with the weather stable, they could select an escort and ride to the fortress in a day, if they started at first light, took the shortest route, and rode to complete the journey quickly. Wulfmaer would be able to select warriors who knew the routes well.

With a fresh enthusiasm, Gytha and Ulrika doubled their efforts, determined to make this a feast above all others. Ivar sent out messengers to Wulfmaer and to Ælfwyn, inviting them to the fortress. All was prepared and ready, awaiting only the guests.

Ælfwyn and Lodin were the first to arrive, but they were only a day ahead of Wulfmaer and Frythegith. Wulfmaer was overjoyed to be reunited with his mother, brother and both his sisters, as they were happy to see him and meet their brother and new sister. Hunbeorht had decided to join Wulfmaer in riding to the fortress, as had Cyneberg. For them there was a further reason. After Gudrun and Einarr had left Wulfmaer's Hall, the attraction between Hunbeorht and Cyneberg had strengthened daily. Hunbeorht had asked Wulfmaer to approve their marriage.

Wulfmaer had closely observed Hunbeorht from his arrival. Initially it had been to judge how he should negotiate his own marriage to Frythegith, then to know his wife's brother better. He liked Hunbeorht although he was less certain of his ability as a warrior, or as a decision maker. Cyneberg was his favourite sibling. He was inclined to endorse the marriage but he understood that his mother would be a shrewder judge of the matter, with experience he lacked. He had been learning that a leader must recognize his strengths and his weaknesses, to know when another is better suited to guide him. Meeting together at the fortress would allow the family to hear Hunbeorht's request. If his mother agreed to the match, they might even arrange the marriage feast there, though it would be in the absence of Hunbeorht's mother and father.

The coming days would not be a single feast, but a series of feasts. No building within the fortress was of a size to hold more than a selection of the community. In this Winter, food was not short. There was ample supply to support feasting through the short dark cold days. The guests might have quickly filled the available space, but they would not reduce the food stores that it would be noticed.

The one matter that Ivar could not address was the invitation of King Edmund. It was an advantage that he did not see for himself the strength of Ivar and of the great fortress, but that might have been set off by the comradeship of feasting. The choice was made by nature and not by man. Edmund had already sent his apologies that the conditions did not allow him to travel to Wulfmaer's Hall. The fortress might be two or more days travel further. That gave Ivar an excuse should he feel the need for it.

The only choice left open was to hold fresh celebrations, that all could attend as the weather improved. There would be time before Ivar formed up his army to march North. It might prove a useful renewal of the agreement with Edmund, but that was in the future, now was the time to celebrate the joining of Gudhrun and Einarr, perhaps of others.

What the ceremony lacked in solemn ritual, it made up for in joy and feasting. It took place in Ivar's Hall, as the largest of the buildings, but one incapable of holding all who wished to join the feast. There was little space for the ceremony.

"We gather to witness the joining of my son to the daughter of my oldest friend," said Ivar in a strong clear voice that carried through the space of his Hall.

Many, who knew him well, were surprised because he spoke usually in a soft compelling voice that drew the listeners in towards him. To either side of him, and slightly in front, facing each other, stood Einarr and Gudhrun. Ivar held their hands and brought them together.

Einarr took the brightly coloured strip of cloth and looped it round their joined left hands.

"Before my kin and my comrades I declare that from this day Gudhrun Pedersdottir and I will be as one, for as long as we shall live," said Einarr in an equally strong clear voice.

He then drew Gudhrun to him in embrace and the roar of the witnesses threatened to lift the roof of Ivar's Hall.

That was all there was to the ceremony, but the feasting continued through the night. From amongst the guests, storytellers entertained the company, some with ribald tales, suited to the joining of man and woman, raising a family to increase the wealth and strength of the kin. Gisi told a memorable tale of improbable feats from his youth. Even Ivar became a storyteller, sharing the telling of his story with Gudhrun's father Peder. No one could remember a time when Ivar had been moved to entertain a feast in this way.

The tale was Ragnar Einarsson's courting of his first wife Thora. In this tale, Ragnar defeated the snake that had laid siege to Thora's dwelling. With Peder, Ivar spoke of the supernatural attempts to hold Thora in her prison and of how Ragnar had broken the spell to vanquish the mighty snake. Peder contributed to the telling and, between them, they held their audience in rapt attention, in total silence. The basic story was a well-known and popular Winter tale, but never before told in such a compelling way with the darkness that had attempted to imprison the King of Sweden's daughter. The tale concluded with the King Herraud giving his daughter to Ragnar. It had been a happy match until Thora died birthing their second son. It was a curious tale for Ivar, who was the son of Ragnar's second wife, and its bitter-sweet conclusion odd for such a happy occasion, but no one noticed these aspects as they followed the telling.

The feasting did not end in any formal way, rather, the feasters ate and drank their fill and more, falling asleep where they sat. As the new day broke, some stalwarts were still awake and others waking from a surfeit that would dog them through the new day, but few had any chores that could not wait until a new energy chased away the fog and pounding heads.

For Einarr and Gudhrun, the new day would mark the change of their relationship for all of their comrades and kin.

Fifty Nine

For what remained of Winter, the store houses were still well-stocked, there was a temporary end to fighting, a time to share stories around the hearth. Little thought was given to the coming campaign in the North. As the days drew out and the growing strength of the sun brought warmth, there would be time to think of battle again.

For Ivar it was a time to consider once more his plans, to make sure that his warriors did not grow soft in the Winter Halls. He felt strangely at peace in himself, his determination to avenge his father set aside for the moment. He was surprised by his pleasure that Einarr and Gudhrun had married. The prophesy was still a worry. To spit in the face of fate was not to be advised, but then a prophesy could be wrong, or be interpreted wrongly. He would remember to arrange a suitable sacrifice with Peder, to ask Odin to look kindly on their children.

The Lady Gytha would learn more from Gisi and help him to read and to write. They had already progressed well, together beginning to write down his experiences of the seas he had sailed and the people he had met. It was all so different from the teachings of the priests, but Gytha was inclined to believe Gisi. He had no reason to claim what was not, but the priests had an interest in teaching only what supported their version of history, this world and the world to come. She was already coming to understand the fundamental difference between the old religion and the Christian teachings. The old religions celebrated life and the inter-relationship of all worldly things. An assumption that life was to be lived without blame, that life beyond death was a part of the natural cycle. The priests of Christ would have their followers believe that life in this world was a painful and transitory state, where all attention must be put to the task of ensuring a good death and ascension into Heaven where the real life would begin. That attention meant buying a way into Heaven and that buying would involve giving money and goods generously to the priests.

She hoped that in time she could travel and see for herself what was true and right. When the opportunity presented itself to travel by ship, she would take it, even though it was the now familiar journey between the fortress and Depenham, and back to the fortress. Winter was tightening its grip, but that did not slow the river sailings, rather it increased the number of longships making the journey because they were not affected as strongly as a horseman by the snow and ice.

Gytha had become a familiar face to those living within the fortress. She was well-liked by those who met her, Ivar coming to regard her warmly as a daughter. When he learned of her meetings with Gisi, he had encouraged her in her growing interests in the sea and of ships. For now, he forbad her passage on those ships that still put out to map the coast, but only because he knew the dangers at that time of year. He promised that she could sail along the coast when the Winter gave way to Spring. He also promised that she could join Ulrika when she returned to Heddeby after they had settled matters with the Northumbrians. Promises that excited Gytha, something to look forward to beyond the growing warmth of early Summer.

On those days when duties permitted, Gudhrun had begun to teach Gytha the art of arms. Progress had been variable in the first days. Gytha discovered that she had speed and agility, but lacked the strength in her arms, something to work on and develop. Gudhrun had to adapt to her weaker opponent. With Einarr she had no call to hold back. She could attack him with her full strength and fury. He always had the advantage of reach, although not much advantage, and he had a greater strength to absorb her strongest strokes. They had practiced together so long that they were almost equal. With Gytha there was at first a great difference, Gudhrun forced to hold back, or risk discouraging her pupil. As the days passed, Gytha became stronger, more skilled and more of an opponent for Gudhrun, but Gudhrun would always have the advantage of reach and the knowledge to use her weight and strength.

Einarr was amused when he saw them first at arms. Then he appreciated that Gytha was serious in wanting to learn to use the sword. Now, when they were free of other duties, he would join them, to fight both together, or call advice from the sidelines. He soon found himself under pressure in fighting them both. The near equality with Gudhrun, the growing skill of Gytha, was beginning to remove any advantage he held from his greater reach and weight.

As they filled the short Winter days, they knew that much could change as they went off to battle, that this great host would become smaller, that comrades would not survive the conflict. For Gytha there was a growing excitement that she would learn of so many things. For Einarr and Gudhrun, they were adjusting to their new life, which was really two lives. They were still paired warriors and that much had not changed, but when they were together in their quarters, they had a different life with a tenderness they had not known before and a depth of feeling that embraced them.

Sixty

As this night's story telling came to an end, I felt deep kinship with Einarr and Ivar. In a few short months, I had come to know my grand children, developing a new thirst for life. When my dearest Margaret died, I could see nothing before me, beyond my grief. I could see no point to my existence. My sons were capable of steering our family into the future. With the discovery of my grand children and the rediscovery of the saga of Einarr, I had seen everything through fresh eyes.

I rejoiced in the wisdom of those before me who had the sense to preserve the lessons of history as they discovered them. In these shared evenings, we had experienced the comradeship and kinship of the past. In the cold nights of Winter, we had enjoyed the warmth of the hearth, of good food, of dear company. I could picture Einarr, his friends, his family around the Winter Hearth, the sharing of stories, just as we have joined in wonderful evenings that have brought us together.

Now, as then, great challenges and dangers stood ahead. There would be joys and sorrows, grieving for loved ones lost to battle, but that was almost a lifetime ahead, far beyond the comfort of the Winter Hearth. We had the Festival of Light to look forward to, the quickening, the rebirth in a new year. As Einarr had, all those years before, we had come through adventure and sorrow to joy, but the great adventures ahead would soon beckon us. When Fate grins at us, we will laugh back. I will look to the protection of my people, I will enjoy continuing the Sagas of Einarr for my grand children, and I hope to live, to tell all of the Sagas, before the times of Einarr, and with the sagas that continue beyond the time of Einarr. I wonder that I have been gifted the joy of a new zest for life.

Where Einarr stood poised on the next great adventure of his life, my anticipation is more measured and obscured. We will

429

not set out on a march to a great battle, neither will we join others on such an expedition. We will protect our own against any attack by others. That attack is less likely because those who would do us harm know that we would strike back with considerable force.

And yet our influence will be no less than the influence of Ivar and Einarr in the fate of nations. Without sending armies into battle, we will play an important part in the future of our Queen. I would that we could save her, but I know that we must save her heir, accepting that her foolishness, her lack of determination, may cost her life before it is due. I believe that what we will do in the coming months or years will resonate far beyond our lands and far beyond our times.

My path ahead is to act as the channel through which Elizabeth Tudor will talk to those hot heads who would risk all to imprison, or kill, their Queen. I must strive to find some way to the advantage of our kingdom, without serious harm to our Queen, but I know that she is a greater enemy to herself than to any other.

As I have told the saga of Einarr, I have been reminded that our strength is in our kin, that the sea is our highway to the future. In time, we may have little left in this place as distant lands draw us to them, but then that is also our past. We are a restless people, children of the seas. When we farm, or make the things we need, it is but an interlude. Always the sea calls us and nourishes us. It gives us choice and freedom, but it demands always our respect.

So it will be the time of the Festival of Light, we, our family, will come together. My sons will return, we will see the days begin to grow longer, the sun to regain strength. Each year we follow in the small the promise of Fimbulvetr, cleansing the past in ancient decay, to give way to Ragnarök in a joyous rebirth. Just as my crest, the Phoenix, turns to ash in the flames, only to spring afresh, more beautiful than before. There will be the new hope of rebirth, but there will also be a dangerous path that I must guide us along.

Ahead is a time of great change. It will not burst sudden

upon us. Our Queen will birth a child that will join two kingdoms, to forge one people, to shake the world, beyond any storm that can be conjured, beyond any expectations for a small group of islands, a small population, but that again is the past when our peoples came together and shook their world, tumbling mighty kings and changing history.

This night I shall sit before the fire, to see my Margaret once more in the flames, to talk of all that we would have said in life and all that lies ahead. I shall fall into sleep,   but not yet. We have so much to share, so much to ponder. I would that Margaret was with me still in life but I know that destiny calls for great efforts, even if that leads to sacrifice. We will be together again, to share an existence that this life has denied us. Yet there has been something else beckoning me that I do not understand, just feel, deep inside.

I feel the quickening, the awakening. It is familiar and yet distant. I know that, in some manner, I have passed this way before to triumph. There is an understanding that has not begun to take full shape, but I feel no foreboding and that comforts me. I know now that whatever stands against us will be overcome, whatever the cost shall be. My confidence will grow and aid me in the work to hand, that our family will be stronger for it. I was named for Einaar and I will honour that name in deeds.

Author's Note

This story was inspired by family sagas that, in many parts, did not follow established views of history. Although accepted history is changing towards them through archaelogical finds..

There were two types of saga. The popular sagas were tales and poems recited around the hearth during the long cold winters, handed down through the generations. Their intention was to entertain. There were many of these sagas but of them the only one to have survived the centuries and prospered is the Saxon poem Beowulf, a powerful tale that honours the warriors of the Northern lands, be they Saxon or Norse.

The family saga was different because it was handed down through generations as a private account of the generations that had lived before. The intention was to produce a guide, or manual, for the new leaders of the family. In the telling over generations, some errors may have crept into the family sagas but they were not intended to stroke anyone's ego, or intimidate outsiders. They may therefore prove to be a rare and pure record of historic events and activities.

The Galwegian families of South West Scotland, on the border with England, carried their sagas back into the Viking heritage of these families. Sir Walter Scot was inspired by the sagas in his writing and was an avid collector of such stories.

Over the years, the views of history have come to accept from the sagas what they once denied. There is a conceit that just because an account of history is written down, it must be correct, ignoring that much of history was originally written down many years after events, from oral history! The scribe was not only far removed from the events, but also following a political, or religious, agenda, deliberately distorting what fragments of original information remained, to fit that agenda.

When the Roman Republic and the Empire expanded out from Rome, in a period of significant global warming, there was a migration further North by the people of Europe. In their new Northern lands, these people flourished and multiplied. There is a lack of information on which to consider whether the Roman Empire began its rapid contraction because it had outgrown its ability to administer such an enormous and diverse area, or because global cooling had begun. Perhaps it was a combination of a changing climate and a decadence that had begun a social, military, and political decay. What we do know is that the reducing temperatures led to the people of the North expanding to the South, making considerable voyages in large open ships.

The very great gaps in knowledge of the past encourages us to artificially take a few events and cultures out of context. In recent years it has become popular to create a new doomsday scenario of catastrophic global warming, claimed to be caused exclusively by human activity, and to ignore all of the patterns of climate change over the millennia.

If we set that fashionable and extreme belief to one side and look at what is known of the past, the last great Ice Age drove the human population South to the Mediterranean. As temperatures rose, and the ice receded, people moved further North once more. We know virtually nothing of what societies preceded the Ice Age because the glaciers changed the landscape and the weight of ice forced down the land to an extent where, even today, the land along the North Baltic coast of Sweden is still rising, no longer being depressed by the weight of glaciers.

Since that Ice Age, the temperatures have risen and fallen in a series of cycles, which are poorly recorded. What we now know is that the global cooling at the end of the Roman Empire continued until the Medieval period, when a new spell of global warming was begun and continued until the start of a mini-ice age from the middle years of the Sixteenth Century. That new period of global cooling continued on into the Nineteenth Century. Since then temperatures have been once more recovering, but are still lower than in the Middle Ages and the Roman period.

Einarr's Saga began in the second half of a period of global cooling and this book has covered the period of his life when he developed into manhood. The narrator of the Saga lived at the start of a further period of global cooling and the start of a new pattern of migration, as seamen ranged out once more to rediscover lands discovered by those of Einarr's age. What we do not know with any certainty is how many cycles of similar human migration preceded Einarr.

In writing this book, I have researched the periods covered, to place into perspective the family sagas that inspired the start of this project. As I dug deeper, I came to realize that recorded history is much more fragile than we generally accept. The Saxon Chronicles, much lauded as a written history, were developed by scribes in various parts of the Saxon-controlled regions of the British Isles. They were Christian monks or priests who represented most of the literate population of the time. Their writings were not contemporary accounts of events, but based on recollections, oral accounts passed on over many years. When a chronicler confidently states the size of an army, or even the locations of a battlefield, he is really saying that the number of warriors was a large number and the battle may have been fought in a particular area, familiar to the chronicler. In many cases, he is fitting his account of history to integrate with established Christian teaching, or the views and ambitions of his patrons, who may have been his superiors in the Church, or secular leaders, nobles and Kings.

Even in modern times, we are partial in our recording of history. Some accepted accounts of events after 1939, in an age where millions of photographs and many thousands of miles of film have recorded events, literacy standards in Europe were high, with thousands of individuals' recording events in diaries and letters home, we still see new assertions published that overturn accepted accounts and prove to be correct.

Einarr's Saga has been written to entertain. I have attempted to avoid taking an historical setting that is wildly different from accepted views of history, but this is not a history book. There was a character Einarr Ivarsson, and other members of his family, who existed in history. Archaeological discoveries have validated some events and activities of the family saga that were previously dismissed by historians.

For Centuries, the Vikings were regarded as a plague of violent savages, having no merit as a people. We now know that this is very far from the reality. They did have a form of writing but they preferred to live on in an oral tradition. They were an inventive people, with a rich art and technologies. They were supreme seamen and ranged across oceans in sophisticated ships, employing navigation aids that have been lost in history.

We know relatively little of the longship beyond those preserved examples in Oslo. As these were funeral vessels, we do not know how representative they were of other contemporary vessels. Drawings and tapestries that have survived provide indications of variations in design and in the detail of construction. We do understand how Viking sailors used the sun wheel but we understand more widely the magnetic compass, which they also used. The other important navigation tool was the sun stone, but we have absolutely no idea what the sun stone was, or how it functioned. From the sagas, the sun stone was a stone or crystal that could see the sun through the thickest of cloud. It takes on a mystical form but it must have had a physical reality. We also have no idea what maps and charts they used, or how they recorded their tracks. Their sailing masters built up a huge knowledge of the appearance of the seas, but it is unlikely that they depended on memory alone.

The Viking impact on the development of Europe and the expansion to the Americas was significant. In England, the Vikings directly influenced national development and, then indirectly, through the Normans who were strongly of Viking stock. We now know that Vikings did sail to North America and build settlements, proven by archaeologists. That they sailed further, as sagas maintain, has yet to be proven by the discovery of the remains of settlements in far lands. However, we know that they sailed South down through the rivers of Central and Eastern Europe into the Black Sea, served as mercenaries in the Guard of the Emperor in the Eastern (Byzantine) Empire of Rome, and traded around the Mediterranean. There is also evidence that Vikings sailed along the Northern coast of what is now Russia and travelled by land far to the East, to areas that are now in China.

Most famous for their longships and seamanship, they were also skilled horsemen, making equally lengthy expeditions on land. Some expeditions involved starting by ship, hauling the ships across land, and also moving on land to other waters to build new ships to continue their expeditions.

Those people of the British Isles who followed and descended from the Vikings were to copy the process of long voyages in search of trade, giving the world a common business language. As with the Vikings, these later adventurers placed trade first and fought only when trade was denied, or when they were attacked. Galwegians, together with Border and Lowland Scots, were a remarkably high proportion of these adventurers. They sailed with Huguenot and English corsairs to prey on the Spanish gold and silver ships that carried this wealth back to Spain. They founded colonies and they made a significant contribution to the growth and dominance of the Royal Navy.

As with the Vikings, modern Britons face out to the seas and their future is through trade across the world. In time there will be new migrations beyond the boundaries of the Earth and its atmosphere. There will be new sagas told, or written, but in many ways they will be a grander retelling of the adventures of the past.

www.ingramcontent.com/pod-product-compliance
Lightning Source LLC
Chambersburg PA
CBHW030913050726
47498CB00003BA/712